I0667576

STONES
OF
DESTINY

Stephanie Welch

© 2021 Stephanie Welch

All rights reserved. No part of this publication may be reproduced, distributed, or transmitted in any form or by any means, including photocopying, recording, or other electronic or mechanical methods, without the prior written permission of the publisher, except in the case of brief quotations embodied in critical reviews and certain other noncommercial uses permitted by copyright law.

This is a work of fiction. Names, characters, businesses, places, events and incidents are either the products of the author's imagination or used in a fictitious manner. Any resemblance to actual persons, living or dead, or actual events is purely coincidental.

Printed in the United States of America

Published March 2021

Published by:
Southern Willow Publishing, LLC
1114 Highway 96,
Suite C-1, #340
Kathleen, Georgia 31047

Cover Art by Victoria Hawkins

ISBN: 978-1-7347354-6-8

"Life's challenges are not supposed to paralyze you, they're supposed to help you discover who you are."
–Bernice Reagon

My first book is dedicated to my parents. Without them, my love of the written word would not be as everlasting as it has become. To my husband who loves my fire; for that I am thankful. To my daughters, never lose your own fire.

CHAPTER ONE

"Amelia!" a strong voice called out, but I couldn't see who was calling me.

I headed deeper and deeper into the cave. Water dripped from stalactites above my head which echoed the song of loneliness all around me. Something was waiting for me at the back of the cave and I wanted to know what it was. It had been calling to me for a while now, telling me to come closer to see.

"Amelia!" the voice called again, but it was further away now. I must keep going; I had to find out what was back there.

"Lux," I whispered, and a ball of light appeared above my head to help me see as I walked on.

As I walked further, I suddenly heard the sound of breathing, low and methodical, as if someone was breathing in their sleep.

"Hello?" I called out. I reached to steady myself, skipping over a large rock before me.

"Who's there?" I called out again.

The musky scent of earth and rot greeted my nose, so I took a few more steps.

There was no vocal response to my question, but I could feel a presence. Something large and powerful was waiting for me. A sudden flutter of leathery wings from above momentarily spooked me. I inhaled sharply and gripped tightly to a rock for support. I closed my eyes and breathed in the smell of the earth which helped to calm my racing heart. Refocused and determined, I opened my eyes and continued on. For some reason, I kept getting pulled towards the back end of the cave.

"What do you want?" I asked.

I was aching for some sort of verbal response, but I was only answered by a low and ancient moan. I quickened my pace thinking that maybe someone was hurt. I knew I could heal them if I could touch them. Someone needed me!

I shouted, "Where are you? I can help!"

The moan grew louder and was much closer than I expected. I adjusted my vision once last time and finally found what I had been looking for. There, on the ground in a bed of moss and forest flowers, was a figure. I couldn't quite make out the form, but whatever it was seemed to be laying down.

"I'm here! What's wrong?" I called out.

My globe of light extended to where I could see the figure more clearly and I raced to its location, my knees stinging as I hit the ground to kneel beside the figure. I reached out to touch and assess the damage. When it moved, I stopped and waited to see what it would do or say next.

"Home" a guttural whisper echoed throughout the entire cavern and I stopped breathing.

"What?" I asked and leaned forward, listening even closer.

My dark brown hair fell to the side, blocking out what little light I had left from my orb and cast a shadow on the figure. I tried to quickly tuck my hair behind my ear, but as I moved, so did it.

With a tremendous roar, the figure rose, as if floating instead of standing, to tower above me. I screamed in fright and scrambled backwards. The heels of my palms scraped at the floor, but I could barely feel it as I raced away from the beast.

"Come home!" the figure shouted.

My orb went out and my emotions raced too quickly to steady myself. I heard another voice somewhere in the darkness calling out to me.

"Amelia!" the man's voice shouted again, getting closer. "Amelia!"

My gaze was fixated on the black mass before me. It kept changing shape, but was clearly becoming male in height and proportion. With a whisper upon the wind, a voice slid by my ear.

"There you are!"

My spine shivered at the venom laced within those simple words. Something inside my chest curled up and beat against my ribs, demanding to be let out.

"Amelia!" the voice calling me was changing, becoming more and more feminine. I turned to see who was coming, but was stopped by the hammering on my ribs over and over of something trying to escape. I flung my hands out, and a shadow skittered along my fingertips and took flight towards the object, straight for where its face would be. The beast screamed in agony and curled back within itself.

"Amelia!"

This time the voice was less urgent and more comforting. It was my mother's voice. I forced myself to look back at the mouth of the cave and there she was, Clarisse Wardman, walking towards me calmly. Her golden-brown hair, comforting brown eyes, and small stature were as a flame of joyful light in this dark abyss of sorrow. Her arms were wide open, and I scrambled to find my footing so I could run to her. As I took off I her direction, the beast stopped screaming and the shadow returned to somewhere within my chest, waiting and warm.

"Amelia, it's time to wake up darling. It's going to be a great day," my mother cooed, as I flung myself into her waiting arms and found myself falling.

With a start, I sat up in my bed, panting heavily. Sheets were thrown everywhere and I was covered in sweat.

"You are silly! What are you still doing asleep at is hour?"

I blinked heavily through the sleep in my eyes to see my mother, reaching to turn on my light. I squinted against the brightness and flung myself back in the bed.

"Did you have a nightmare, Princess?"

My mother's brow furrowed and she looked worried. I took one deep relaxing breath and felt myself calm down. It was a dream, only a dream. Nothing was after me and there was no cave.

I nodded in answer to my mother and she came to sit by my bedside.

"Oh dear, it has been a long time since you've had one of those. Are you okay? Do you need me to make you a tea?" she asked.

I sat back up slowly and shook my head.

"No, thanks mom. I'm okay. It wasn't near as bad as they used to be. At least is time, I wasn't riding on the back of some water beast who kept dragging me under water," I shrugged.

I stood up and felt the floor beneath me. I took another big breath in, steadying my nerves and my balance.

"Still, I don't like that you've suddenly had a nightmare after all these years. Maybe I should give you something to sleep better tonight before bed. Just a good relaxing tonic, nothing big," she interrupted.

I met my mother's gaze and instantly relaxed. There was something soothing in those deep dark orbs that no one else had ever been able to give me. I nodded lightly, agreeing with her. That seemed to cheer my mother up greatly. She always enjoyed being able to help people, whatever their ailment. It's why being an Earth witch came in so handy for her.

People were always asking for some herb, tea, or ointment to help with all different types of problems they came across. Whether it be emotional, physical, or mental, my mother was always willing to try and assist anyone she could. With a light tap on my knee, my mother popped back onto her feet with a smile.

"Good, now that that is settled, get dressed. I need you to help me at the market today. I've got a lot of supplies to pick up with the Summer Solstice approaching, and I'm going to need help carrying everything," she smiled.

I secretly rolled my eyes and groaned as I got off the bed. I winced as my palms touched the sheets, and looked down to see how red they were. I furrowed my brow and noticed small scrapes along them as well. My mother, who had her back to me still, kept chattering.

"It was nice to have you home for a bit. Your father was not as good at picking out herbs as you are, and I've been struggling for the past four years to get him to see that not all the same plants are going to give off the same effect," she rambled.

Mom began rummaging through my closet.

"If you asked him, he'd say it all came down to the soil the plant was grown in. What else could matter? But you and I both know it also has to do with the care the gardener put into those plants. I couldn't possibly put a rosemary in a tea for someone struggling with loneliness that was just grown on a windowsill all alone. It has to be from a large garden, where its friends grew, too, and they were all taken care of with a loving hand," she smiled.

I joined my mother at my closet and stopped her wandering hand with my steady one.

"I'll help you mom. Though, you know that I'm only good for carrying supplies. I don't even see what you and dad see. I just see the plants, smell them, and pack them in a bag. Nothing of what you say makes any sense to me, and it never will," I said quietly.

I felt my mother pause before she turned to me and placed a small hand on my shoulder.

"It's okay Amelia, your help was more than enough. Stop worrying and wondering about not having magic so much. It's been years and look at all you have accomplished," she reminded me.

I pulled out a short sleeve t-shirt along with a pair of jeans hung up in the closet. I still didn't look at her. Not having magic had always been a sore subject with me. At a young age I had tried and tried again to cast the simple spells, enchantments, and charms my parents did so naturally, but nothing had ever worked. Once when I was thirteen, I almost set our entire house on fire trying to cast a simple flame on a candle. That's really when I had stopped attempting magic altogether. Mom had tried to coach me, telling me to feel the magic within me, but I only felt emptiness there. Nothing ever came of me. Finally, after years of on again off again tutoring, I turned my attention to more mortal pursuits where I could be useful.

That was truly my drive. I wanted to be helpful like my parents were to so many people. My mother was sought after for her healing potions and teas and my people came to my dad, Daryl, for assistance in crop growth, land placement, and clearing rituals. No one ever came to me for anything. That was, until I started helping in the hospitals.

Around age sixteen, I took a job as a candy striper at a local hospital doing simple tasks like delivering flowers, helping move patients, and assisting in giving tours of the campus. That was where I shined. Patients were always asking for me when it came time to move them, or when they just wanted someone to talk to. One older lady, Gladys, always told me there was something calming about my presence and my touch.

I had taken my newfound talent as a sign from the Mother Goddess that I was meant to go into medicine, so I did. Immediately following high school, I found my way into a local four-year college that had a highly regarded nursing program, and I excelled. I did so well, that eventually other students came to me for tutoring, assistance, and guidance. I enjoyed finally being helpful and finding my place. A part of me, however, still mourned my inability to perform even the simplest of magic.

So many times, I had found myself wishing I could take away someone's pain as they were dying or in distress. I wanted to place my hands on them and ease it, if only for a moment. It was like I could see where the pain was, whether it be an infection, a tumor, or something worse, but for some reason I couldn't reach out and do anything about it.

When I finally achieved my goal and graduated the nursing program, I took the dreaded National Council Licensure Examination, or NLCEX for short, to complete my license. One or two of my classmates had already received their scores. I was so happy for them when they passed, but my results still hadn't come in and I was getting more nervous about finding out.

"I don't know if I'm up to going out mom. I really need to be here in case my scores come in," I sighed.

Mom watched me cautiously and then nodded. "I understand that, but this will take your mind off it for a while. We won't be gone long. I just need a few supplies. We will be home before lunch."

I breathed in deeply, knowing she was right, but I could feel the worry gather in me again.

"Okay, but not for too long," I responded with a small smile.

I knew it would make her happy to see me out and about. Mom was just that way, a little bit of a worrier. She liked to see my happy and, in a way, it would make me happy to get out.

"Perfect! I'll go get my stuff. Just meet me in the car and we'll head out. Say hello to your father, too, before we go. He's been hard at work trying to understand what's been going on with Mr. Hunter's soil sample from last week. I think he's gotten too deep in his head again," she sighed.

I nodded in agreement and heard her walk out of my room. I finished dressing myself and took one last look in the mirror as I ran my brush through the thick brown hair I had inherited from her. I marveled at the dark tan I got my from my father, along with his straight nose and my mother's high cheek bones. I leaned in and studied the one featured that had always baffled me: my eyes. Both of my parents had dark brown sultry eyes, but mine weren't the same shade. From a distance, they looked brown, but when studied closer, there was an amber film underneath.

The one time I had mentioned it to my father, he looked me over curiously and then shook his head. "Trick of the light, Princess. Nothing more. Yellow eyes aren't possible," he shrugged.

At fifteen years old, I was slightly disheartened. Now at twenty-two, I still saw what they refused to see.

"Princess! Let's go! I don't want to miss out on the morning sun," Mom called from the landing below, and I hurried after her voice.

The morning sun had always been something my mother and I experienced together when I was growing up, especially when I was upset. We would leave the house early, around six in the morning or so, and walk the neighborhood, go market shopping, or even tend the garden while the sun rose. I would resist some of the time, after a bad test, an argument with a friend, or just one of my bad dreams, but in the end, the sun rising over the horizon and spilling over my face as I performed some type of activity always made me forget the bad times.

I'm not sure when this ritual started, but it seemed as though mom figured out at an early age that the sun made me feel better. There were many times she drug me out of bed by my feet, even if it was to just sit on the lawn and wait for the sun, but she made sure it happened when I was down.

I stopped to give my dad a kiss on his white-blonde, fluffy hair.

"Don't work too hard dad," I muttered.

He leaned his head toward mine, allowing me to give him a kiss on his stubbly cheek.

"Not near as hard as you Princess," he smiled, and continued pulling samples and placing them in beakers. Before I turned, I watched him work for a moment. With a flick of his fingers and another mumble under his breath, the liquid turned a deep blue and he groaned again.

"It's like this man's farm has been cursed. I can't quite figure out why his levels are so off," he sighed. Dad narrowed his eyes closer to the now blue liquid and took it in, before turning back to a book before him riddled with a mixture of symbols and instructions.

"You'll get it dad," I smiled. I patted his back and started to turn away before a thought hit me.

"Oh! Hey! Keep my laptop near you today and refresh it every now and then. I've got the testing website up, but if a button comes up saying "View Scores," call me. Don't look at them, just call me," I instructed.

I placed the silver sleek computer next to him on his desk and he nodded.

"Thanks dad! We'll be back soon!" I called, and ran out the door after my mother.

"Goodness, we're going to miss the sun if you keep dawdling, Princess," Mom said as we both settled in and cranked the eco-friendly little car.

"We're fine. Let's get going and get back. I don't want to miss if my scores come in today," I repeated for the thousandth time. My nerves were beginning to get to me and the anxiety in my chest was becoming palpable. I felt my mother's warm hand resting on my own.

"I know dear, but this market run will be just the thing for you. Mother will provide, don't worry. She knows how hard you've worked and she won't let you fail," my mom smiled. I relaxed at my mom's form of comfort. She always had so much faith in the Mother Goddess, which was something I wish I felt more within myself. I had never felt that close to our religion.

The Mother Goddess was the entity that watched over all witches, protected them, and guided them in their trials. We weren't the most expressive of our beliefs. Mom and dad mostly observed holidays, such as the Solstice coming up, and prayed when they felt like the needed help deciding.

I had come to her once or twice in my life, but viewed my lack of magic as her telling me that the witch life wasn't meant for me. If she wanted me as a part of her community, she would have blessed me as every other witch was blessed.

The market was just opening as we pulled into the parking space. The first glimpses of the morning light were beginning to peek out beyond the trees. The rays of light cast a rainbow of hues amongst the fog that had settled overnight, but was beginning to burn off.

"Clarisse!" a woman from a bright pink tent shouted and waved us over. "I have got just the thing you were looking for last month. I know you were looking for violets to plant in your garden, but I found a wonderfully grown stash all natural just last week and knew I had to bring them for you!"

My mother squealed in delight and skipped forward, leaving me behind to peruse the rest of the stall. Violets were essential during the Summer Solstice, as Solstice was the best time for mom to infuse her oils and potions for the rest of the year. The sun at its highest peak always brought out the most potent of magic in her earthen type spells.

As my mother haggled over a good price with the woman, I ran my fingers over a plant box of rich moss and instantly breathed in the smell. As I did, I felt a heat at the back of my neck, and I turned to see the sun was rising over the treetops to greet the world. I turned fully, my hand still firmly rooted in the moss, and closed my eyes. I waited for the familiar peace that I felt when I greeted the sun in this way.

The daughter of two earth witches would naturally want to find herself surrounded by greenery when she recharged, relaxed, and centered herself. The minutes ticked by and the heat rose from my neck to my chin and then up my face. As my eyelids got lighter from the sun shining down on them, I smiled. Something deep within my chest fluttered and came to life, as it always did at is time of day.

The sounds around me disappeared and I felt the warmth and acceptance the sun always gave me. My heart and chest swelled, and I stood there taking it in. I could feel the little bit of magic within me in those small moments. It did little flips, twists and turns, and seemed to enjoy basking in the sun as well. I smiled to myself and placed my free hand over my heart.

"One day," I whispered to what I always dreamed was my magic. "One day I will find a way to open you up, and then we can be together, just like the Mother intended."

The little piece gave one last wiggle and then went silent. I felt my mother's hand gently loop through my arm. "Feel better, Princess?" she asked cautiously.

I nodded, "Immensely. Do you have everything you need?" I asked, looking at her wicker basket full of greens and colors.

She shook her head, "Not yet. I want to speak to the goat soap lady one last time. I think I can help her with some of her recipes, but I don't want to spook her too much."

I rolled my eyes. "Well, you might want to stop opening every line by telling her you're a witch."

Mom giggled. "You would think after all these years living in is town, some people would just get over that, but no. Some still hold on to those old hates and fears. Oh well, I'm going to give it one last shot at nudging her towards a better recipe for that one calming lotion she tries on people. Frankly, when I tried it, the thing gave me a rash."

Mother shook her head in disgust and then led me off across the parking lot towards the maroon tent top, where the young woman audibly groaned at seeing us approach. Twenty minutes, and a lot of sweet words later, mom had the woman writing down her helpful suggestions, and even offered to try them for her to make sure they worked right.

"I don't know how you do it, but even people who aren't that open end up listening to you," I smiled and reached for my mother's basket. I waited as she looked over one last stall of potted plants. Without even looking around her, she reached down and waved her hand over the tops of some particularly sad looking daffodils. As in taking in a deep breath, they rose collecting radiant color from the magic my mother shared with them and stood at attention.

"Mom! Are you trying to catch someone's attention?" I whispered, but she waved me off.

"Sue me for using a sprig of magic to spruce them up," she shrugged. She reached down to lovingly stroke the newly created blossoms.

"Who owns this booth anyway? These poor lovies haven't seen attention in months. Bless the mother, they think no one loves them," she crooned to the plant and I rolled my eyes. Without waiting for her to give the booth owner a piece of her mind, I snatched my mother's jacket arm and dragged her away.

I placed the basket of goods and another bag of soaps away in the trunk and sat down in the seat next to her.

"It's my helpful spirit dear. They see it in me, just like people see it in you. It's why we are both so good at what we do," she continued our conversation from before the daffodils. Mom grinned to herself and I giggled just rolled my eyes.

We pulled up to the house minutes later. When I got out of the car, dad came rushing outside, his phone in his hand. "Princess! I was just about to call you. I think the button came up on the screen for you to see how you did!"

"You didn't look, did you?" I asked nervously.

I worried, but he shook his bouncing curls and moved aside as I ran in the door. All the dread that I had seemed to let go off less than an hour before suddenly came crashing back on me. I raced to the dining room that was littered with dad's work equipment and saw my laptop sitting dead center on the kitchen island. I stopped moving, too afraid to go closer.

This was it: I was going to find out if all my hard work had paid off the past four years. The degree hanging on my bedroom wall would mean nothing if I failed this test. I gulped and grabbed at edge of my light jacket, tugging slightly at the zipper.

"Go on, Princess. We know what the worst can say. Get it over with," Dad nudged me gently. I heard mom place her groceries on the kitchen table behind me and hurry over.

I walked forward and sat down on the hard barstool, still warm from my father sitting there only a moment earlier. I swiveled the mousepad and the screen lit up. It was the testing center page, and sure enough, next to my name and the word NCLEX was a bright blue button to view my score. There were only two options at this point: o scores, no averages, just two words. Pass or Fail. I could only hope that all my hard work had given me enough to make the page say that I had passed.

I took a quick breath and stared the screen down, my eyes scanning for the only line that mattered.

Wardman, Amelia V.: NCLEX-RN: PASSED

I covered my hand with my mouth, unable to catch my breath. I had done it. I was officially a registered nurse. Everything I had worked for was finally coming to fruition. My heart stopped for a moment before I heard my mother's squeal from behind me and her arms came crashing down into a huge hug.

"You did it! You did it, Princess! You passed! Oh, I'm so proud of you," she cried.

I let out a huge bark of a laugh and stood up to embrace her. Dad bent down and looked the screen over once for himself and then came up smiling and clapped me on the back.

"I know you could do it, Mia! You're too smart to not do it," he cheered.

He came from behind me and wrapped me in a hug. The three of us stood there laughing and cheering at my success. I felt a tear of relief curl up at the corner of my eye and I choked out on last laugh.

"No tears, Princess! This is amazing news," mom smiled. She leaned back and wiped the tear away for me.

"I know, I'm just so overwhelmed with relief. I can't believe it's over finally," I whispered. I looked back at the computer and marveled over that simple little word. PASSED. Suddenly, my phone rang and a friend from nursing school's name popped up.

"Oh! That's Rebekah from school. Maybe she's calling to tell me she's passed, too," I said. I lunged for my phone to share my good news with everyone who would listen. My parents gave each other a happy hug as I walked out of the kitchen to the back patio and answered the call.

"I passed!" I heard the scream from the other end before the phone even reached my ear. I smiled genuinely at the sound of her joy.

"Me too!" I screeched back.

For a few minutes, we both laughed and lightly sobbed through our joy. Rebekah had been my closest friend through all of this. We had met sophomore year, around the time we both were applying for the nursing program and we stuck together. We studied, prepped, and worried over every step together, along with some other friends who had come and gone, but Rebekah had been the one I had always leaned on. She was bubbly and much more vivacious than I was. I fed off her happy energy when I felt down, and she came to me when she was struggling with being low.

We continued talking about how relieved we were and went over some questions that we had found troubling and difficult. Then we moved into the conversation of finding work.

"I was thinking of going back to the hospital I worked at when I was fifteen. They're always looking for night nurses, and I would love to stay home for a while and save up money," I admitted to Rebekah. I kept my voice low, mostly because I hadn't mentioned to my parents about wanting to stick around for a bit longer.

"Oh, that would be nice. I don't get that choice. My parents practically told me that I've got one month to find work and an apartment, or they're giving me a bus ticket. Being back at home after all those years at school isn't going well," she sighed.

I could hear the seriousness in her voice.

"I can imagine. Don't you still have that last sibling living there? Didn't he just graduate high school or something?" I asked.

Jacob had always been a sore topic with Rebekah. Throughout our friendship, she was constantly fielding phone calls between her parents and her youngest sibling about their most current argument over one thing or another. At one point, she had even left school for a few days to see to him in the hospital after a horrible car accident that had unfortunately involved alcohol almost killed him. I had always wanted siblings growing up but seeing the heartache and trouble her youngest one had caused Rebekah; my only child status seemed a blessing from the Mother.

"Yes," she sighed heavily. "But he keeps talking about this very European thing called a gap year like it's some excuse for his laziness. When my parents threatened to kick him out, he rounded on me of all people, and they had to lay the hammer down on me too to leave in a timely manner."

My brow furrowed at the harshness of the sentence Rebekah clearly didn't deserve.

"Wow, that's a little much wasn't it?" I replied.

I was worried for Rebekah back in her childhood home. Maybe I should offer that she move in here with us for a while, or even offer for us to get a place together. However, I knew this wasn't going to go over well. Rebekah wasn't from my little town and she had always spoken of moving to a large city with a huge hospital. She eventually wanted to move on and get her master's degree in midwifery and a small little hospital like the one I wanted to work in wouldn't cut it.

"I guess so, but it really wasn't my place to stay longer than absolutely necessary. And it's not their place to support me any longer. I'm an adult with a degree and a license to work now. I'm already running through hospital job openings in Atlanta as we speak," she said.

I could hear the mouse of her computer furiously clicking away.

"Atlanta? That's far away," I responded.

I tried to think of exactly where in Georgia the city was but having grown up all my life in different small towns in the Midwest, I only knew it was somewhere in the northern part of the state.

"All the better to live my life. They have a fantastic birthing center there that's up and coming, and I want to get in on the ground floor as soon as I have the years under my belt," she said.

I shook my head. Rebekah had always been the planner in our pairing. She was always looking at what was next, planning, and taking charge of the situation. I was good at planning out things, too, but I guess being the oldest of four kids had made her a natural leader. I felt the same drive and passion she did, but sometimes my nervousness quelled my fire.

I learned at an early age that I was never going to be able to do the one thing that came naturally to my parents. That lesson inspired a fear of failure deep within me. Mom and dad never intentionally made me feel that way growing up, but I knew there was an undercurrent of disappointment in my lack of magic. So, I had clung to Rebekah's spark, letting it ignite my own when it came to my drive to do well, accomplish more, and even speak up when things weren't right.

"I'm glad you are already figuring it out. If you need somewhere to crash for a little while, just let me know. My parents wouldn't mind having someone else in the house for a while. You know they love you!" I reminded her.

"Oh, I love them, too, but this is my responsibility now. I've got this," she sighed.

"I wish I had your confidence, girl," I said.

Rebekah let out a huge snort and laughed. "What are you talking about? Of course, you have it! How many times did I come to your door upset that I wasn't getting something right?"

I remembered the weeping blonde-haired Rebekah knocking on my dorm door at two in the morning because she couldn't figure out how to stick the needle in the orange.

"How many times were you there when my brother called to complain about something my mother said and you were the one to snatch the phone away and rip him a new one?" she laughed.

I cracked a smile, but that hadn't been funny at the time. Jacob had been unnecessarily nasty to his sister and I was sick of watching her wilt under some seventeen-year old's ridiculousness. I usually let other people handle those issues and then help pick up the pieces afterwards, but that had been one of the few times in my life where my anger had boiled over and I let Jacob have it.

"You've got the confidence, Amelia. You're a lot more patient than I am. You'll see. I bet you will be Head Nurse within two years of getting the job and everyone will see how awesome you are," she said.

"Thanks, Rebekah. Hey, listen, I've got to run. I didn't really get to celebrate too much with my parents before you called, and they will probably want to do something," I laughed.

I could practically hear my mother banging around in the kitchen whipping up some sort of cake or something.

"Yeah girl, for sure. Call me later and let me know when you apply. I want to see you before I leave for Georgia," she said.

I rolled my eyes. Her confidence was sometimes was sometimes too much to handle. We both said goodbye and I clicked the screen off. I rose from the wicker chair and looked out onto the lawn where the sun was fully up, and the heat was starting to settle for the day. The flowers were swaying in a gentle breeze and a single hummingbird darted by, heading for the feeder mom set out by her honeysuckles.

"Are you done talking to Rebekah?" I heard her call from the kitchen. I turned and plodded my way back in where they both waited on me.

"Surprise!" they both shouted in unison, my mother much louder than dad. Mom was holding a pretty yellow cake with a nurse's uniform drawn on the top. I smiled brightly. I knew she had been up to something in the kitchen, but only magic could have made a cake that fast.

"You guys didn't have to do this," I laughed. I scooted back on the barstool and shoved my phone away as mom cut me a slice.

"Nonsense! It only took a moment and you've earned it. We're also going to go out to dinner tonight to celebrate you. Wherever you want, just name it and it's yours. Then, when we get back, your father and I have a gift that we've been waiting to give you," she smiled.

My astonishment must have shown in my face. Being an only child, I was used to getting the full brunt of all their love and attention at every little thing I did, but this was a lot in one day.

"We don't have to do all of this. I don't even have a job yet. Maybe we should wait until I find employment before really celebrating," I offered. I stabbed at the piece of cake before me and shoved it in my mouth. The buttercream felt heavenly on my tongue and I savored the wonderful first bite.

My father shook his head vigorously. "Unacceptable. You have done something great academically, mentally, and emotionally. You have put all your hard work into something and achieved it. As your parents, it's our job to shower you with praise. Besides, it's not like I'm getting anywhere with my work lately, so I need a distraction from my failures. Your accomplishment is wonderful."

He gave a side eye glance at the same beaker with blue liquid from this morning and huffed.

I laughed and patted his shoulder, "You'll get it dad, you always do. But fine, I get it. Let's go get sushi tonight. And I want to sit at the grill and pretend to be wowed by the tricks."

Dad winked at me with a smile on his face. "You got it, Princess."

Later that afternoon, while I was kneeled working on some flowers for my mother, I felt a cool breeze whisper past my hair. The breeze was colder than I was expecting, and it caused me to look up at the tree line behind our two-story home. The forest that laid beyond had remained untouched from the development of the town and still held an aura of mystery about it. I had never much paid it a lot of attention, having moved here to this town in high school. My years of playing in the woods and exploring the flora and fauna all around me had long passed once we got settled into this neighborhood.

Something at the edge of the forest caught my attention and interrupted my thoughts. I squinted to see through the sun. I could have sworn I saw movement, but upon closer inspection, nothing rustled in the trees or bushes below them. I dabbed at the sweat forming on my brow and shook my head. Must be a trick of the light playing with me. The sun was already beginning its slow descent and

I needed to hurry and finish the task so we could get the flowers boiled before we left for dinner. As I turned to go back inside, I took one last glance at the tree line, trying to see if I saw whatever it was that had caught my attention again. Still, nothing moved, and I shrugged my shoulders. The birds were still warbling, and the bugs still zipped around.

"Mia! Bring those clippings in and throw them in the pot. Your father went ahead to shower, so you're next up," my mother called out to me from the back door.

I obediently turned to follow her voice inside, but something still nagged at the back of my mind that I had seen something in the forest.

An hour later, we arrived at the restaurant. I was not surprised to find that it was not very crowded, and we ended up getting our seats right away. I knew that being a Tuesday, many diners were not out and about.

My mother glanced over the sushi menu and I could practically hear her salivating. "Oh, I really am feeling the yellow fish tonight, dear," she said.

I picked out the two different rolls I wanted for myself and handed the menu to my father who sat on the other side of me. He shook his head and laughed, "Steak hibachi for me and that's it. You girls devour all the nasty ocean dwellers you want. I'll take my land meat as the Mother intended."

Mom scoffed and leaned over to snatch the sheet of paper for herself. "Spoil sport. The Mother gave us all types of meat to eat, not just cow and pig. Fish is better for you, as you know."

"And full of mercury, as you know Clarisse. I deal with that horrible stuff enough in my work that I wouldn't dare touch it in my food, too," he playfully chided her.

I shook my head at their silly marital banter. For such low-key peacemakers, they sure could pick at each other enough.

"Goodness you two, you act like an old married couple or something," I muttered and reached for my water glass, taking a huge gulp. I hadn't had time between working in the garden, my shower, and getting ready for dinner to grab a glass of water. Dad was a stickler for eating early. He didn't like the throngs of people that usually filled up a restaurant once most people got off work, so he made sure we were always seated by five o'clock.

I glanced down at my blouse. I had tugged at my loose material multiple times on the way to the restaurant because the warm leather car seat stuck to it easily. The simple yellow fabric was easy to dry and thankfully I had worn tan shorts to keep me cool as well.

Mom was in one of her typical bohemian all wool floor length dresses that had spaghetti straps. Thankfully, she worse the sleeveless version, because if not, she would probably die from heat exhaustion. She, however, had chosen strappy beaded sandals while dad and I kept our sneakers on. Balance had never been my strong suit, so wearing heels or shoes without a lot of support hadn't been much of a good choice for me over the years.

After a few more minutes of playful bickering, the chef finally arrived. We pretended to be astounded by his tricks of tossing food around, lighting it on fire, and the forever crowd pleaser of making the onions look like a train. A child and his parents at the table joined in our fun, clapping, and cheering at every new excitement. When the chef threw a piece of chicken and it landed in the woman's drink, the little boy grew extremely distressed at the thought of her drinking it, so the waitress quickly replaced it. After that minor inconvenience, the whole table then gave a final round of applause and the chef bowed at his exit.

Mom and I split her plate of chicken hibachi and immediately began tucking into our sushi while dad happily ate his steak.

"We do need to talk for just a moment though, Amelia," my father announced about halfway through the meal.

I suddenly paused. I never liked it when he used my full name. Having been nicknamed Princess at the age of four, Amelia just sounded wrong coming from his lips.

"Sure," I said slowly, placing my fork down. My stomach began to flutter with nerves. What could this possibly be about?

"Your mother and I wanted to make clear what your plans for living arrangements were now that you've passed your exam. I would expect you will be looking for a job soon?" he asked.

I nodded, glancing between him and my mother, who was fiddling with her fork and looking at my father. Mom doesn't like confrontation of any kind and always lets my father have the first word.

"I am going to apply for the local hospital in the morning. I know they have a night position open almost immediately," I explained.

Dad gave a nod and then continued.

"That's good. So, you should, but we were more concerned with where you were going to live," he said.

I swallowed hard. This was it. They were going to kick me out. Maybe all that talk Rebekah had said was going to be true for me, too. Maybe they wanted me to get out and make it on my own. I was willing to, of course. I didn't want to be a burden on my parents in anyway, not after everything they had done for me over the years, but I didn't think they would make me move out so soon.

"Oh, stop it Daryl! You're scaring her," my mother hissed. My mother jumped in and grabbed my hand, which was shaking slightly.

"Look at me, Mia. Stop worrying, we're not kicking you out. In fact, we want to make sure that you will stay with us for a while longer," she explained.

My heart stopped for a fraction of a second and then kickstarted back. With a huge sigh of relief, I slumped in my chair.

"Oh, thank Mother," I breathed. "It's not that I want to stay with you guys forever, but I wanted to stick around and save up some money first. I've got those student loans to pay back and I wanted to get my schedule at work figured out before I committed to an apartment first."

Both of my parents relaxed immediately.

"Oh good. We didn't want you to start out on the wrong foot either. And don't worry about those pesky student loans either. Your father has already handled that on his own," she smiled.

I turned blinking in amazement to my father, whose face lit up.

"Surprise!" he threw both his hands out. "This is the surprise your mother was talking about earlier. We saved up the money over the past few years and just a week ago went ahead and paid it all off for you. No loans, no debt! You have a truly clean slate to start your life, Princess," he smiled.

My jaw dropped. Those loans were no small chunk of change. I had always known my parents were by no means poor, but I had insisted on taking out those loans to build my own credit when I was eighteen and was planning on spending years paying them off. It had seemed like the adult thing to do.

"You didn't have to do that!" I squealed.

I was shocked. My parents were really into huge gestures like is, but I really hadn't expected is. When they had said surprise, I had thought maybe a stethoscope, or some pricey nursing shoes, not my entire life set up for me.

"You're our only child, sweetheart. If we can't do is for you, then what kind of parents would we be?" Mom reached up and tucked my hair behind my ears. "We are so looking forward to watching you get out in the world by yourself, but we want to make sure it's the safest and easiest way possible. We didn't have parents who helped us get started when we were your age, so we are determined to give it to you."

I nodded my head, thinking of the grandparents I never had. Growing up, when I had asked why no one ever came to grandparent's day at school, both my parents grew sad and told me a story of how they had grown up in foster care together out on the West coast and didn't have any parents around. They had met in high school and both had no friends until dad caught mom helping some flowers grow behind the foster house. Mom had been terrified he would tell on her and she would be thrown out, but he revealed he was an earth witch too by making some rocks form into her name on the ground. They instantly formed a bond of friendship and eventually love. Once they were both of age, they packed up their bags, got married at city hall, and drove off for somewhere better. They both worked while my dad was going to college for a degree in geology and my mother flourished in her business of teas, herbs, and all things holistic. I arrived not long after they got settled and we had all been together ever since.

"We just want to make sure you don't have to start at the bottom like we did. I can't promise we will always be able to do is for you, this may be the last time we can, but you will allow us is one last gift before heading off on your own," my mother said.

A tear welled up at the corner of my eye for the second time today and I vigorously wiped it away.

"You guys are the best. I promise I won't stay long. Just enough to get my feet under me and a little savings. I won't be moving far even when I do move out. I plan to stay at is hospital for a long time if they will have me," I explained.

I hugged them both tightly.

"Oh, they'll have you. Darla and I stayed in touch all these years. You know your old candy striper coordinator. She was so excited and ready to see you working there as a nurse and has already told everyone you're coming," mom smiled.

I pulled my parents in closer for one last hug. "Thank you, guys. You two really are the best parents a girl could ask for."

Mom squeezed my hand one last time and dad clapped my shoulder. "Enough wallowing, lets order dessert and get on home before the crowd gets too much."

Dad glanced around his shoulder just as three cars pulled in the parking lot. I rolled my eyes and signaled to the waiter that we were ready to order dessert.

The drive home was full of smiles and laughter as mom commented on the clouds moving in and predicting rainfall that night. She always mentioned there must be a water witch in her lineage to be able to sense those kinds of things, but dad always theorized that the earth knew when it was going to rain and told her. Whatever the reason, she was always right, which came in very handy on school days when the sky looked clear at first, but by the time school was out, it was pouring and I was the only one with an umbrella.

"Daryl, you left the light in the kitchen on again dear," Mom mentioned as we pulled up to the house.

I unbuckled my seat and leaned forward. "No, he didn't," I corrected her. The kitchen was completely black. Mom stopped unbuckling and looked around herself. She furrowed her brown heavily and looked taken aback.

"I could have sworn," she muttered to herself, but dad was already out of the car and headed to the front door.

"Let's get in before the sky opens up," dad called and rushed to find the right key.

I looked at mom once more, but she was still staring at the kitchen window that was facing the road.

"You're just getting old mom. It's okay," I teased and took off behind my dad. As I stepped up on the front porch landing, I heard my mother's door slam shut and she began her way slowly up the path.

"I think it's a great night for one of your mother's bedtime teas and a good murder documentary," Dad winked at me and I chuckled to myself. He hated those kinds of shows, but he knew I loved them. I loved figuring the case out and solving the crime. I loved that stuff. Dad on the other hand saw it as a waste of time and preferred changing the channel to some nature documentary.

The key turned effortlessly in the lock and dad and I both spilled into the front entryway. Casually, I reached to flip on the light. It took me a moment after the satisfying click to realize nothing happened. It was still dark in the hall. I cocked my head to the side and clicked it a few more times before calling out to my dad. Mom was walking into the house uneasily, hand still on the door frame.

"Dad! The powers out," I mentioned, and he stopped walking down the hallway to the kitchen and tried a switch further down. Again, nothing happened.

"Strange. I didn't see any lightning on our way home. Exactly how bad is this storm that's coming Clarisse?" he asked.

My mother shook her head and slowly closed the door behind her. She took a cautious step and investigated the laundry room that connected to the side door we had entered from.

"Not really anything to worry about. I'm not sure why it's out either. Maybe I left something on and it flipped a breaker. Or a someone hit a power pole right before we got home," she said quietly.

Dad ruffled his white hair and then motioned to me. "Let's go check out the breaker, Princess. Your mother can go ahead and light the stove for tea while we turn the house back on."

I nodded obediently and slipped my sneakers back on from where I had dumped the by the door. Dad led the way, and as he did, lit a light orb above our head to see better. I suddenly felt a chill in my spine, remembering my dream from this morning. I eyed the orb, but still followed him into the one car garage that we used as storage.

We gingerly picked our way across the mess of boxes and junk we never used anymore and found ourselves standing in front of the grey breaker. Dad flipped it open and read the number's map on the side, bringing the orb closer to his face so her could read the names. I checked the second breaker but didn't see any sitting in the center indicating they had been flipped.

"Hallway," he muttered and then reached for one numbered five. With a quick flick of his wrist, he turned it off and back on. "Try it now Clarisse!" he shouted. We waited for a moment, but we heard no sound from inside.

"Clarisse!" dad called again, but my mom was silent. "Maybe she can't hear me from the kitchen. Can you go flip it, Princess? I'm not sure exactly what's going on here."

Dad kindly split his orb and enchanted the second one to follow me, so I didn't trip. I was beginning to feel a little helpless again in the dark. I nodded and turned to make my way back to the house when I large pot fell in the kitchen beyond.

"Mom!" I shouted and took one more hurried step before my stomach sank. A shuffling of multiple feet arose from inside and something heavy was shoved.

"Clarisse!" my dad caught sound of the commotion and he ran to me. Just as he made it to me, a sound that will never leave my mind reached us.

"MIRROR!"

The scream echoed throughout the house, the corridors, and our hearts. I moved to lunge for the door, but my father instantly grabbed me and pulled me back behind him.

"No!" he hissed, but I felt his hand shaking on my arm.

"Mom!" I cried, but my father flew into action, as if he had prepared for this moment his whole life. Without another thought he ran to the back corner of the garage and pulled at an old dusty sheet. I tried again to get to the door, but he yanked me closer to him and finished pulling the sheet off. It was the old mirror that had followed us around our whole life. It was a nasty wrought iron monstrosity that looked as though it belonged in a dark Disney film. As the sheet came free of the decoration, the steps I had heard inside quickened and became louder as they made their way to the garage.

My father placed me between himself and the mirror and grabbed me firmly.

"Whatever you hear, whatever you see, don't speak. Just listen. I'm going to open a portal and send you through it!" he whispered.

I opened my mouth to interject, but he clamped a hand down on it.

"We don't have time for arguing, Amelia Vida Wardman. No nonsense. Now, when it opens just jump through. Don't look back, don't think, and don't worry about us. Your mother and I will be fine!"

The rest of his instructions were cut off, but I heard a low chuckle form the doorway.

"Daryl!"

The large figure filled out the doorway and my stomach rolled. Images flashed through my mind of where I had seen this before and it hit me, in my dream! It was the dark mass I had seen in my dream this morning. My mind whirled again, and I gasped. I had also seen it this afternoon in the trees. This was the figure I could have sworn I saw moving around just beyond the tree line.

"Bonum est te videre."

The figure droned and walked towards us. My mouth fell open. Latin? Why was this man speaking Latin? Growing up, my parents had tutored me in the basics, and I could read some, write a little, and speak even less. It certainly had come in handy while studying medicine, but never had I heard someone use it as a primary language. It was supposed to be dead.

"Etenim hos annos," the man paused in speaking and looked me over.

My father took a step back and grabbed my hand.

"Communicare," he whispered, and I felt a tingle of magic jolt up my arm and into my ears and on my tongue.

"I see you've been hiding a really big secret."

Suddenly the man was speaking English and I blinked, looking down at my hand. My father glanced at me, to make sure I was understanding, and then turned back. He must have cast a language enchantment to assist me in listening.

"You were always a pathetic little boy, Michelo Unda. Looking to please anyone stronger than you!" my father hissed at the strange man. There was a venom I didn't recognize laced in his voice.

"Give her to me, Daryl. Or I'll have to take her by force. Heretia is growing impatient," the man hissed.

I sucked in a breath and felt the cold glass of the mirror stop me from moving further back.

"You must have me mistaken for some coward that finds you intimidating," my father laughed. He hid his casting hand behind his back. I tried not to look at it as it began to glow dark green. He was casting a spell in his mind and attempting to keep it from this guy.

"No, I knew you weren't a coward. Ignorant, simple, but not a coward. I figured you might have something up your sleeve, that's

24

why I know you're over there trying to open a portal," he chuckled, and took a step into the garage, hands out as if in surrender.

Through the setting sun in the distance, I caught a glimpse of the man's face. It was hard, with a scar running from his right temple to his lip. His eyes were a light blue; so blue that they might as well have been white. I took a mental note of all of this for when the police arrived if we made it out alive.

My father's hand grew a little brighter and the mirror behind me grew warm. I tried not to jump, but it startled me just enough that I sucked in a loud breath. His eyes darted toward mine and his grin grew into a wicked and feral thing.

"So, this is the one we've all been looking for all these years," he growled. His voice was low and sinister. It made my skin crawl like ants marching up and down my arms over and over.

"Princess, find the Earth Prince. Your heart will know him, as his will know yours. Find him, and then find us. Don't hold back, and don't let fear stop you," my father whispered, hoping only I could hear him. He never turned his head from the man who advanced slowly on us.

The mirror behind me grew warmer and I sank a little back into it. Its solidity was evaporating and turning into something else, a watery material. I heard the song of a bird echo from it, and the heat of a second setting sun. A gentle breeze tickled the backs of my legs and it caused me to jump.

"Stop trying, Daryl. She's coming with me!" Michelo warned one last time.

Finally, a flash went up and the entire mirror gave off a glow. I turned in that instant with a start and saw not my reflection, but a hillside. Fluffy white clouds moved lazily overhead and the warm breeze grew stronger and smelled of fresh grass.

I didn't have time to really look because Michelo suddenly began shouting. I whipped my head back to see my father widening his stance, readying for a fight. My father, the man who had never even swatted a fly and wouldn't even eat fish, was getting ready to go to blows with this giant demon before us.

As in on cue, a dark glow rose from Michelo's chest and his feet came off the ground.

"Now!" my father shouted, and with one final shove, he sent me flying into the mirror. I fell backwards, never stopping, as I hit what was supposed to be the mirror glass. There was no crashing sound, no thud. I just kept falling through the air. Eventually I felt the bright sun hit my face as I entered through the portal. Before me, I saw Michelo rise and fly towards my father, his feet not on the ground. I instinctively screamed and threw my hands out, but I caught nothing. I kept falling for what felt like minutes, when suddenly my backside hit the ground and I cried out in pain.

My tailbone barked in protest and my arms flung out to steady myself before my skull joined my butt.

"Go!" I heard my father shout one last time before he sealed the portal with a wave. The last thing I saw was my precious father turning around and casting a shard of green light at the flying intruder, but the light didn't stop him. I heard my father shout in anger and then there was nothing.

That was the only glimpse I got before the portal slammed shut. I panted heavily for a moment before the feeling of loneliness sunk in. I looked around and knew that my mother and father were gone, and so was the portal. For the first time in my life, I was utterly, hopelessly, and soundly alone.

CHAPTER TWO

The sound of birds surrounded me from my seat on the ground. For a split second, my mind went blank as I sat there and looked to find the source of the chirping. Suddenly, everything hit me at once. My heart began pounding in my chest. My breathing picked up and I scrambled to get my feet under me.

"Oh Mother, oh Mother! Not good, not good, definitely not good!" I said aloud as I pawed at the ground.

I felt nothing but leaves and grass beneath my fingers. I frantically crawled to the spot where the portal had just disappeared and reached out into the air grasping at nothing. Cool crisp air met my fingertips and there was not a whisper of magic to be felt. No tingling, no static electricity, nothing. My parents, my home, and my whole world was gone. I was left here in Mother only knows where with nothing to protect me, no idea where I was, and no direction to head in.

Panic began to set in. I looked around in every direction to try and see if maybe I recognized where I was. Surely my father would not put me somewhere I didn't know how to get to help. The sun was setting in front of me, so that had to be the west. I tried to remember the times my parents had taken me camping and the survival skills they had tried to instill.

I searched from my place on top of a tall and barren hill, but I didn't see anything I recognized. There was no town, city, road, or even a waterway that would give me any indication on where I was.

"Wha-? What do I do?" I asked out loud.

I sat back down and curled into myself trying to think clearly for a moment. I looked above me and all around. I could see one sun overhead beginning to set, one large hill with nothing on it, and miles and miles of nothing but trees in all directions.

"Where am I?" I asked the birds still singing sweetly overhead, but they gave no response. The sun was setting, and night was coming. I needed to find help and fast: the clock was ticking for my parents.

"Breathe, just breathe," I whispered to myself.

Suddenly, an idea came to mind. A Find Me spell! Any witch within a certain radius would be able to sense it and hopefully would come. I hadn't really encountered a lot of other witches at home, since my parents only kept a few friends throughout my life. Maybe they sent me somewhere near one of them and they would help me. I wasn't very skilled at this spell. I wasn't skilled at many for that matter, but it was simple enough and was usually the first spell children are taught at a young age in case they get lost.

Summoning my breath back to me, I stood up and tried to remember the wording and motions. I placed my right hand over my solar plexus and my left over my abdomen, closed my eyes, and recited the words that I thought I had forgotten.

"Mother Goddess, here my plea. Help a friend come find me," I said quietly under my breath, as if someone were around to hear me speaking what they might see as nonsense.

I stood waiting, unsure of what exactly I was waiting for. Usually, if I successfully completed a spell, I would feel it. It was like a tingling energy from my hands or from the middle of my chest, but I felt nothing. Absolutely nothing.

I looked around and took another cleansing breath. "Mother Goddess, here my plea! Help a friend come find me." I spoke these words louder, convinced the birds were laughing at me as they continued to sing and chirp. Still nothing.

I could feel the panic start to rise again. Of all the times to be completely inept at magic, right now was not it. Finally, fed up, I stomped my foot.

"Mother Goddess! Here my plea! Make someone come find me!" I shouted and looked up at the sky. It wasn't until the words came out of my mouth that I realized I had said it wrong, but what was the point? It wasn't like it was working anyway. I let a sob slip through my throat and crumpled back to the ground, tears welling up and spilling over. I allowed myself a few moments of wallowing, but I knew in my heart that I was going to have to pick a direction and just start moving. It was as I kneeled there, alone on top of that Mother forsaken hill, that I heard it.

A gentle whisper caressed the hair next to my ear, feeling like breath gently wafting over my skin. I looked up, certain it was a person, but the breath had been a cool one, not hot like from a human. There was nothing there, but as I scanned around me, I felt it again at the same ear.

"Amelia."

I gasped, startled. The sound wasn't being spoken, more placed in my mind.

"Welcome home."

I stood up straighter.

"Who's there?" I shouted, attempting to figure out which way that cold wind had blown.

"Who's out there?" I asked again, starting to rise. I still couldn't see anything as the sun began to set and a pinkish glow coated the hillside.

"We've been waiting for you." I heard the whisper again.

"Who ARE you?" I shouted. The mention of the word home brought the dream from this morning back to the forefront of my thoughts. What was it with me today? Had I suddenly had a vision? Should I have paid more attention to the dream? In frustration I stomped my foot and grabbed at my head.

Nothing. I got no response and it felt as though the breeze died down as I spun in place, desperate to find the location of that whisper. I had to get off this hill. I had to start moving. I had to get back to my parents and help them. Suddenly, a crack of branches and a flurry of birds took off to the sky. I gasped, startled at the suddenness of the motion. Next, everything went dead still. What little I knew about wildlife, mostly from documentaries and not personal experience, I knew that everything going silent was never a good sign.

Not good at all.

Nothing seemed to move, nothing seemed to even whisper a breath until the low growl came from the edge of the woods right below me to the West. Right into the setting sun. It was a horrid sound and very animalistic. I took a light step backwards toward the East and began thinking of ways to hide. Whatever it was that just made the noise was certainly nothing I wanted to find alone out here with no way to protect myself.

I apparently couldn't even rely on simple magic such as a protection ward or a *Never mind Me* spell. I held my breath when I thought I saw a distinct movement in the trees coming from the direction the growl had just emitted from. I picked up my pace and turned to start running away. That's when chaos erupted.

A thunderous roar broke the setting sun and every animal within a mile radius scattered. I decided to do likewise and bolted in the opposite direction as fast as my feet could carry me. The earth shook with the feeling of four heavy feet pounding its way towards me.

"Oh Mother!" I shouted to myself. This was it. This was how I was going to die: some horrific bear or mountain lion was going to hunt me down and tear me apart. I wanted to cry, but my body wouldn't let me. I just kept running, crashing more like it, into the other side of the forest. I jumped and swerved and kept heading straight. I stumbled slightly when my shoulder ran into a large tree, but somehow, I kept upright.

Branches whipped in my face when my hands weren't fast enough to move them, leaving my cheeks stinging. Sweat broke out on my forehead just as another roar overtook the purple and pink lighted landscape, this one much closer. In only moments I could hear the beast panting and grunting as it made its way over the hill and headed for me. I didn't even dare a glance, but it already seemed to know where I was.

I took a huge chance and screamed for help. Maybe someone was around. Maybe a hunter or a hiker or a small cottage was nearby that would hear me and come shoot this thing or let me inside their car or house.

"Help me!" I shouted a second time.

The grunting was getting closer and so was the crashing of trees and branches as it continued barreling towards me. I still didn't dare look. I kept running until a huge stump came up out of nowhere and jabbed straight into my foot. I summersaulted over it, landing soundly on my back with my face staring up at the sky as the beast that had been chasing me vaulted with a loud grunt and crashed down at my feet. Skidding to a halt it turned to face me. I looked up at it and everything fell out of my stomach.

"Mother fucking Goddess," I muttered to myself.

It was the largest and sickliest bear I had ever laid eyes on, which wasn't many as I'd only ever seen them at the zoo when I was younger. It was about twice the size in height as a normal bear, but about half the size in girth. Its limbs and body were unnaturally gaunt, and I could have sworn there were extra bones to create an even ganglier monstrosity. Then, to my utter astonishment, the beast rose on its back hindlegs and walked towards me.

There was only a singular black pit in the middle of its face staring at me. I held back the vomit that was trying to make its way up my throat. The beast roared. Saliva whipped my face and forearm as I tried to cover myself. I couldn't help it; I took one last deep

31

breath and, summoning all my courage to scream, slammed my hands into the earth with such force it went numb for a second.

"HELP!"

Finally, as if waking up for the first time, a massive surge of electricity shot through my arms, down my hands, and all the way to where I was sitting on the ground trying to scramble backwards. It went into the ground and radiated out, like a beacon call to whatever could hear it. The pulse of magic was powerful enough to knock the bear-beast back into a tree. With a thunderous crack it busted the large tree into splinters and its head whiplashed with a snap. I shivered at the sound of bone hitting so hard. I hoped it was dead from that impact. I was so wrong.

The bear-beast shook its head, as if clearing its mind, and roared again. This time, it crouched down to put forth even more power into its killing cry. I took one last breath and closed my eyes, preparing myself for the first and only blow I would receive before I left this world on the wings of Death.

Suddenly, I heard a whizzing sound from straight over my head, followed by a muted thud, then another and another.

Whump. Whump. Whump.

Three thuds in direct succession, followed by a scream of fury. I heard a gigantic crash and I dared to look.

There, not five yards from my feet, was the bear-beast with three arrows sticking out of its chest. It was pawing at them with one hand and staggering back on the other three away from me. I didn't wait. As swiftly as I could, I hauled myself up and started running in the direction the arrows had come from.

The bear-beast roared in anger again and two more arrows flew by me. It sounded as if they hit their target twice more. I kept running without stopping, but I could not see the source of the arrows that were quickly becoming my saving grace. I stayed straight and prayed to the Mother that whoever the blessed archer was didn't hit me on accident because I blindly ran into its path.

"Breathe," I reminded myself when the edges of my vision began to grow black. I kept sprinting away from the hell-like noises now summoning its energy behind me.

I started to turn and look, when at that moment, a male voice called out. "Don't look! Keep running!"

I didn't even question the order, but did as told. I tucked my head down and kept dashing and jumping through the trees. As I passed by a particularly large oak, I whipped my head to the left just in time to see a black mass descend at a free fall to the earth and begin walking towards the bear-beast's direction.

The screaming from the bear persisted, but it wasn't moving. I decided to stop and look. I ducked behind the oak, and panting heavily, turned to see what was happening. The last two arrows that had been fired seem to have been attached to anchors that were planted firmly in the ground. I could feel the enchantments running up and down the line holding the bear in place. I shook my head in confusion. There was no way someone would openly be using weapons like this laced with magic.

The dark looming figure that I had just passed was stalking towards the beast. Two hands went up, and with a swift movement, removed two large broadswords that had been tucked into what seemed to be backstraps underneath an exceptionally large black cloak.

"What the hell?" I whispered out loud. I stared incredulously as the figure approached the bear and circled it once.

"So, Nandina? Decided to come on out and play a little with us today, or were you getting sick of our friends in Maravette constantly beating up on you?" he asked.

The Bear-beast let out a hideous low grumble. "Theodeus."

I caught my breath. What was that noise? I looked up and around, just as three more figures dropped silently to the ground from the treetops. They made their way to the gathering as well, encircling the beast laying prone on the forest floor.

"I see you bring the entire Elite Guard to just whip me back into place for a few more years."

If my stomach did not drop out completely before, it certainly did now. The struggling bear just spoke without even moving its lips! I quelled a massive gasp, biting down on my hand.

"Nandina, you know very well you aren't supposed to be over here in Suravia, but then you go and kill three of the High King's Hunters. What did you think was going to happen?" hissed the first warrior, a man by the sound of his voice.

The bear-beast grunted an uncaring noise.

"If those were High King's Hunters, then I pray to the Mother Goddess for you in the coming years!"

The voice went cold as the figure whipped off the hood to his cloak and pointed both broadswords at the beast's neck.

"What it that supposed to mean?" he shouted.

I caught a glimpse of dark brown hair and lightly tanned skin.

"Cool it Theo, you know he's just talking trash to get you mad. Let's send him back behind his protection wards in Maravette and be done with this," another voice said.

The largest of the warriors who brandished a single sword stepped forward and with a touch, persuaded Theodeus to lower one blade.

"It means that you need to think about how I got out in the first place, runt. You need to consider that I am not the only of the Wild Beasts to be set free in the recent months and I will not be the last. Something is coming to change the balance and you, and your kind have no one to stop us this time!"

Nandina's voice grew with power as it spoke, resentment trickling from its meaning like the blood spilling from its side. Without warning, Nandina began to haul itself up with a vengeful and wicked laugh.

Theodeus, gave a loud shout and with a single swing of both of his blades, removed the head of Nandina cleanly. Hot, wet blood poured from the stump in a shower of red before the now lifeless body crashed back down to the earth. The strings, alive with magic laced across its body, went quiet and the entire forest remained still for a heartbeat.

"Well, that was piss poor management. See what happens when you decide to let Theo take the lead on something for once, Will?" uttered a small female voice. Long white locks tumbled down her back as she walked forward to examine the creature's now severed head.

"This is his Kingdom, Wynnie, and he grew up in these woods. It wasn't the worst idea in the world to go ahead and dispose of the beast," a voice replied. A blast of shocking red erupted into the space as the largest warrior pulled back his own hood, speaking to the tiny woman at his feet.

"What do you think it meant? I had heard something was loose around Lotho, but not that there had been any more Wild Beasts released recently," Theo asked aloud, in a more subdued voice. He seemed to be disturbed more by what the Nandina had said than what he had done.

They all went silent and looked on as the small woman reached out and picked up the head. To my horror, she ran a finger along the bloody stump and immediately licked that same finger. I gagged, bile filling the back of my throat. Everything halted and I clapped my hand over my mouth, ducking behind the tree.

"You can come out now, girl. Seems we owe you a debt of thanks for sending out that beacon and dragging us right to the Nandina," the man they called Will bellowed.

I peered out warily. "I-I'm so sorry if I caused any trouble. I just needed some help and I was lost, and that thing was chasing me and I just panicked," I mumbled, wringing my hands together attempting to calm their tremor. My voice was shaky from all the physical exertion of the past half hour, but wary of these strangers who clearly had no regard for personal safety.

"That's okay. We wanted to take it more by surprise and put it back where it's meant to be, but I guess ridding the Kingdoms of this

Ancient Beast once and for all will have to do," grinned the large man who shrugged his shoulders.

I took a small step out.

"Kingdoms?" I asked. "What kingdoms?"

The group of four looked between each other confused. "These kingdoms, the ones we all live in. What other kingdoms would be talking about?" The woman they had called Wynnie asked and turned to fully face me, my breath caught.

She was gorgeous. She was a tiny little woman with the face of an angel. Her skin was the color of alabaster and her eyes shone like two blue diamonds in the night sky. She was an ethereal fairy meant to be gracing the home of the Mother Goddess, not digesting dead bear blood in a forest. I quickly recovered, cleared my throat, and looked back to the red head.

"Okay, umm, well, let me put it another way. Where am I?" I tried again.

All four figures started walking towards me briskly. Instinctively, I backed up into the tree for support.

"You're in the forest district of Suravia on the Earth Island," a voice explained. The last member of the group finally spoke, his hood still in place. He was the archer that had saved me, as evident by the bow slung across his chest.

"E-Excuse me?" I stammered.

I guess the strangers finally decided to look me over and saw something quite different from what they were expecting. As if my jean shorts in contrast to their cloaks and riding boots, my shock, and my clear confusion to what was going on was not enough of a hint that I was clearly foreign.

"Who are you?" Theodeus narrowed his eyes at me, as if taking me in for the first time.

"M-My name is Amelia Wardman, I don't think I'm from here. You see, my parents were attacked, and they sent me through a portal and told me to run. I'm supposed to find someone, apparently I will know him when I see him." I explained.

Will, who seemed to be in charge from the way the other three kept looking back to him for conversational direction, narrowed his bushy eyebrows. Thankfully, however, he didn't step forward again, I couldn't get any further into the bark of this tree if I tried.

"Who are you parents?" he asked slowly.

"Clarisse and Daryl Wardman." I answered, hoping that would mean something to one of them, but I wasn't holding out much hope at this point.

"Who attacked you?" Wynnie asked, coming around the other side of Will. I noticed she was positioning herself in the only open hole I had to dart away to my left. A slight feeling of indignation swelled up within me. What did she think I was going to do? I had nowhere else to go, obviously.

"A man named Michelo. He was speaking Latin but my father cast a spell so I could understand him. They were after me, but both of my parents were kidnapped, possibly hurt, trying to get me away." The group shifted uncomfortably and looked towards the still hooded archer.

"Michelo, you say?" he asked me, and I nodded.

The archer removed his hood and a large head of ashy brown curls sprang forth. It looked as though at some point, he had tried to keep it controlled in a bun on the top of his head, but the strength of his curls was not to be tamed.

"How do you know who Michelo is?" Theo asked this time. It's like they were taking turns, trying to distract me from concentrating on a single point. This was a method nurses used with small children they were trying to stick a needle in without them noticing.

"I-I don't know, my dad called him that. They seemed to know each other, but I have no idea how. I couldn't tell what he said at first but after I could hear the Latin, he was wanting me to go with him, something about Heretia growing impatient." As the last bit fell from my lips, I felt a sharp tug at my shoulder, and someone yanked me sideways.

I cried out, but immediately quieted, sucking in a breath as cold steel pressed against my neck. My eyes darted back and forth, realizing Wynnie was missing from the group. I knew they had been trying to distract me.

"Now, I'm really getting tired of these lies, little girl. Why are you here?" A helpless whimper accidentally escaped my lips. I wasn't usually this much of a coward, but everything was happening so fast and I wasn't given anytime to process this big mess I found myself in.

"Please!" I cried, the panic welling up in my throat and threatening the loss of all my senses.

"Please, I need help. I'm not lying. I'm just as confused as you are, and I'm lost, and my parents are probably hurt. Please, they're all I have. They're all I've got in this world and I need to help them. That's all I'm trying to do, I swear." This was it, my last attempt before these people ended me here. I wasn't sure why they didn't trust me, but my story sounded crazy even to me.

"Leave her alone, Wynnie." Came a vicious warning. Wynnie paused and looked towards Theo who was taking slow steps towards me and reaching out. Wynnie relaxed her grip and allowed Theo to snatch me away from her.

"Why suddenly so soft, Theo? Like what you see?" Wynnie snickered sardonically. I gasped a huge breath of relief and gathered my wits about me again. Barring soiling myself just now, that was about as pathetic as I had ever been, and I didn't like it. I felt the warmth of Theo's hand leak into my skin and begin creeping my arm. I looked down at the point where our skin contacted and marveled. That wasn't a very normal feeling. Theo must have felt the odd sensation as well and quickly removed his hand from my person. I looked up at him, hoping to see an answer to that odd encounter but he was already ignoring me and looking to Will for direction again.

Will was studying him closely, as if he wondered why Theo had spoken up for me as well, but eventually just shook his head.

"We need to get to the capital and fast. I suggest we not go straight for the High Stronghold, but one of the Safehouses close by," he ordered. Will turned towards his group of merry men and one woman.

I shook my head in disbelief. "Are you not listening to me? My parents are in danger and I need to find whoever it is they sent me for. I've wasted enough time as it is with that bear thing over there, and then this interrogation!"

"Nandina," the interruption came from Theo and everyone went silent.

"Its name was Nandina and it was an Ancient Beast that roamed this world and once commanded respect and honor. It was not a bear thing as you so ungraciously put it."

His voice was low and cruel as he stared me down with his two dark green eyes. His mood was as turbulent as the emerald sea that raged within them. I stared him down for a moment, incredulous at his constantly changing mood within mere moments. One second, he's protecting me, the next second he's berating me over something I couldn't possibly know about. I wondered what was going on in this man's head.

I sucked in my breath and glowered back at him. I felt that little snap inside of me go off, the one that broke loose when I tore into Rebekah's brother for being so unfair. That little piece that snapped in third grade when Johnny wouldn't leave Christina alone and kept lifting her skirt up and laughing. I had taken a rubber ball and, calling his name for attention, lobbed it at his private parts as hard as I could. If he was going to be that crude and disrespectful, I made sure he was going to feel that pain. I might be a little more passive than most, but I didn't accept being spoken to as an idiot or watching those around me who couldn't protect themselves get hurt. So, I gave him a little dose of that mood change he was giving me.

"I don't exactly give a flying shit what its name was now that you mention it. What I do care about, however, is finding this man my parents told me to, finding them, and then getting the hell back home where we belong. I didn't ask to be here, I didn't ask to be chased by the *bear beast*," I made sure to exaggerate my title for the Nandina,

"And I sure as hell don't care if you want to sit here and give me those nasty little brooding glares you seem to think work so well on people. I want to go home, and I want to get there as quickly as possible. No stalling, no Safehouses, just the man my father called "The Prince," and I'll be on my way." I made sure to emphasize my point by shoving into his personal space like the four of them had been doing to me this whole time.

Mad Mia was out, and she wasn't a very pretty person.

Theos' three companions all turned and looked at him with amusement.

Wynnie whistled, "Wow, someone that isn't afraid of you, Theo. She really must not know who you, or we, are for that matter."

She smirked wickedly and gave him a jab to his shoulder. The playfulness fell dead on Theo as he gave her a melting glare.

I looked between them slowly and demanded, "Why don't you enlighten me on the way to meet whoever it is I need to see."

The gruff red head shook his head in answer. "Can't do that, girl. Not without getting to the bottom of this on our own. Now, I do not recognize your name or your parents' names for that matter. Where exactly are you from?"

I narrowed my eyes at him, but at least someone was starting to try to help me get to the bottom of this. I took a deep calming breath to answer him logically.

"I'm from Missouri in the United States."

All four gave me a blank look. Slowly, they turned their heads to Will, waiting for his response. His face instantly fell, and his mouth formed in a hard line.

"No, no dear. That is certainly not this world," he said distantly with a tired sigh.

"Then, where am I?" I asked for the thousandth time.

"My girl, that is a long tale that is best given somewhere safe. Preferably somewhere with a fire, whiskey, and many comfortable chairs." He suddenly looked up and squinted over the horizon, as if just now noticing the sun was almost completely set. I shivered against the chill of the night. Will snapped back into leader mode.

"Wynnie, you go ahead first and make sure the house is secure."

The small woman waved her left hand quickly in front of her face and in a blink, she was gone. I gasped, startled by her sudden disappearance. My parents had never just vanished like that in front of me ever, and seeing blatant use of magic was making me jumpy.

"For someone who performed a pretty strong Finding Spell, you seem to be pretty shocked at simple magic," the archer scoffed. I turned to look at him, blinking in shock. I had almost forgot he was there in the last few minutes. He truly was the quiet type that would kill you without even breathing a sigh of relief.

My cheeks flushed slightly in embarrassment.

"I, I was never very good at magic, so I stopped learning after a while," I explained, not that I felt as it was any of their business.

Theo rolled his eyes with an exasperated sigh and looked to Will, "Can we go now? I'm starving."

Will smiled, "Sure, and how about since you decided to lob off the Nandina's head and cause a huge mess, you get to help Transport Amelia here." A bark of laughter escaped from the archer who I still hadn't caught a name for. Not like anyone had bothered to do introductions around here, so I was playing a nasty game of catch-up. I inwardly rolled my eyes, just like a bunch of men to forget their manners.

"Shut up, Tim, or I'll reconsider since it was your grand idea to even save the girl," Will warned. Tim winked mischievously at Theo and with a ruffle of ashy brown wild curls, he was gone as well.

"Aw, come one Will! She admitted herself she is bad at magic. What if she gets lost? I'm not a teacher, I'm a warrior and this girl is just going to get herself hurt if I do it," Theo argued.

Will shook his head, unfolding his tree trunk like arms. "Too bad, maybe if you had not lost your temper with the Nandina, I would have let you slide."

With a boom of laughter, he clapped a large hand on Theo's shoulder and was gone. I gulped heavily, stones falling into my stomach. There was silence for a moment while Theo stared after the spot his friends had just been before turning to me. Something in my chest fluttered as our eyes met. Heat rose from my feet, but I mentally tamped it down. No time to get all doe-eyed over a guy that clearly wanted me gone and found me a burden, which I was.

"Good Mother, why do I keep getting stuck doing these things?" Theo muttered to himself and then turned to me. A moment of silence later, he held his hand out, "Come on."

I vehemently shook my head, "No you really don't understand. I am terrible at magic. I can barely even light a damn candle by myself. I will literally get us both killed if I attempt something like this. I have never even seen this kind of magic." I wrapped my arms around myself and shivered. It was really starting to get cold out here and the dead body was starting to smell.

"Fine, then stay out here and rot. There's literally no one for a good hundred miles, and if you think the Nandina is scary, you should face a pack of She-Wolves running out here," he paused for dramatic, and frankly unnecessary, effect. "And it's mating season."

Panic gripped my stomach. "No wait! I'm sorry, just," I blew a worried breath, "Tell me what to do and I'll try."

After a moment of contemplation, Theo gave a massive sigh and rubbed his face vigorously. "Here's what you need to do. I'll direct your *Transport* since you clearly have no idea where to go, but the actual act has to be on you."

I nodded and summoning my courage, planted my feet firmly on the ground.

"Have you ever moved an object?" he asked. I cast my eyes down and shook my head.

"Seriously? It's like the first thing babies do without even thinking about it." The exasperation in his voice was evident.

"No! I am telling you; I am horrible at magic and know nothing. Please do not mock me right now, just tell me what I need to do to get out of here. I'm cold, I'm lost, and if you leave me, I will be alone again." I could not stop the whine from edging into my voice.

"Please, just tell me what to do," I begged again when he did not respond. I held my hands out to him as if he would need to take them. Theo sighed heavily with resignation.

"Think about disappearing, think about creating a hole in space where the other end leads you to where you want to go. Since you have never been to the capital, don't worry about visualizing the end, just imagine the hole."

I closed my eyes and conjured up a hole in front of me.

"Focus on it hard, and on the count of three, take your left hand and move it from one side to the other of the hole," he instructed. I nodded, trying to get a better grasp on this concept of a hole.

"Ready? Breathe a deep cleansing breath and let us hope you don't get ripped in two cause you're not concentrating enough."

"Not helpful!" I cut him off.

"Sorry, but it's true. Now one, two," I felt his hand clamp down on my shoulder and suddenly a picture of a street lined with lamps and a small two-story townhome came into my view.

"Reach out, and three!"

With all my might, I swiped across the vision before me from right to left.

Chapter Three

It was like being smacked in the face with a bolt of electricity and for the first time in my life, I felt magic like never before. Power welled inside me and I was suddenly glad Theo was holding me, and me not holding him, because I may have let go from the shock. From the top of my head, all the way to my toes, magic tickled its way over me, even trying to run up the hand of my unwilling guide. Mere moments whizzed by, when suddenly a "pop" noise sounded in my ear and my feet touched hard ground once again. For a moment, nothing moved. I waited, breathless, eyes closed and just hoping I hadn't messed up.

My ears were still numb from the sensation of Transporting and the new feelings it invoked. Was this what I had been missing all this time? Was that what mom and dad felt when they helped a plant grow or asked questions of the scrying glass?

"Are you coming?" It was Theos' voice that finally broke the fog, like from a dream.

I shivered trying to catch my breath and opened my eyes. Streetlights illuminated the road in front of me. Rows upon rows of identical houses flanked either side of the perfectly laid cobblestone street. Dark had already settled over most of the sky and I looked up to see not only real fire streetlamps, but an endless starry night. While it wasn't quiet, the noise of this place was much different. Footsteps and light chatter interspersed with laughter instead of cars and radios filled the space around me.

People milled around, barely glancing in our direction, nonplussed in the least that two people had just appeared out of thin air in front of them. All dressed in basic fabrics that looked handsewn or crafted. No nylon or tight-fitting garments, definitely no jeans. Wool, cotton, loose flowing blouses tucked into comfy skirts and fluffy sweaters. It looked like a mix of early Tudor England, with a touch of bohemian influence. My mother would love it. But where was I?

"Did I do it? Are we here? I really did it?" I asked.

A huge smile cracked my face as I took in the sights around me. The joy of what I had done began to set in and I grew giddy with myself. Twenty-two years of never knowing what I was missing out on and suddenly, I wanted more.

"Yes, yes you did it. Congratulations, you're not a puddle of witch goo in the street. Now get inside before someone realizes how absolutely insane you look," he rolled his eyes. Theo reached back and grabbed my elbow, yanking me forward.

I practically tripped over my sneakers, but even that could not keep me grounded. My entire body was quaking from excitement. I had really done it! I had really done magic without hurting myself or anyone around me. Theo rushed us into the first house on the right, dragging me along the steps and into the house and turning back only to slam the door shut firmly.

Theo made two quick movements of his hands and the door glowed briefly before fading. I recognized it as a protection enchantment. My parents did it all the time back home, but I never seemed to get the hang of it. The second time I had ever attempted it, I burned a hole in my apartment door and dad had to come Clear it for me.

"I can't believe I actually did it," I whispered to myself. I stared amazed at the door, not even noticing my surroundings.

"Wonderful, you can officially do what every teenager does without thinking when they are pissed at their parents for not letting them out of the house." The gruff mumble was supposed to be a huge insult, but I didn't even take notice. My entire aura was floating, and I could not have been more pleased with myself. Theo stalked off into a door to the right and I followed with a huge smile on my face.

Everyone was in the room, sitting around in lounge chairs. Wynnie had a wine glass in her hand and was idly sipping away. Will seemed to be still shucking all his weapons off and Tim was looking at the window warily, as if checking to make sure we weren't followed.

"By the way, I'm not buying the act anymore."

My attention snapped to Theo has he walked stiffly to his group of friends.

"What I just felt coming off you is far from weak magic. You are not some pathetic excuse for a witch like you told us. Whoever or whatever you are, you're lying," he sneered.

Theo slumped into a chair with venom in his eyes. I blinked multiple times in confusion, shaking my head a little to clear my ears out. I had to have heard that wrong, my ears still must be muffled. I found a seat closest to me and perched myself on its edge.

"What power? I don't have any magic. I couldn't even close that window curtain if you held a knife to my throat," I explained, pointing to where Tim was still keeping watch as I followed Theo into the room.

Theo leaned forward, "Oh really? Then explain to me why your whole body begins to electrify when you focus on magic. It's like your skin even comes alive. And why was I able to connect so easily to you? If it was that hard for you, it would have been like wading through mud to show you where to go," he seethed. The twit then turned to face the group. "Will, something is not right with this and I don't like it. I say we call the High Guard and have them take her. She's probably a spy for Heretia!"

47

A cacophony of banter instantly rose up as Theo, Wynnie, and Tim began arguing over the best course of action. The noise was almost deafening as they each vied for dominance in the conversation. Only Will kept silent as the debate of who I really was waged on. The panic must have been evident in my eye and he noticed it.

Without a word, Will lifted his hand and the three quieted. "I think something else is much more pressing than determining if she's a spy for Heretia. If you three babbling buffoons hadn't noticed yet, Amelia isn't exactly from here."

I sat up straighter. Relief flooded over me. Finally, someone was taking me seriously.

Wynnie gave a small scoff, "It could be an act, Will."

A touch of anger sparked in my throat. I was thinking of saying something in my defense, but Will pointed to me.

"You think we have that kind of material here in all of Medeis? Heretia wouldn't dream up something that hideous, let alone useless," he noted.

I pulled my bare legs closer to myself, my shorts weren't hideous. Wynnie nodded her head in agreement and I huffed.

"If you're done making fun of my clothes, would someone mind telling me where I am," I asked. I grabbed a knitted throw blanket laying across the back of the wingback chair I had found myself in and laid it across my lap.

"I gather I'm not in the United States, for certain. But I'm not sure where Medeis or Suravia is. I've studied maps a long time and those aren't on any I've seen."

Will nodded in encouragement.

"Well, that's because, Amelia," I held up my hand to stop him suddenly.

"Mia, please call me Mia," I instructed him.

I wasn't a very formal type of person naturally but something about the atmosphere of this place, made me want something a little less stiff. I was hoping that by people calling me Mia instead, I would feel a little more relaxed with the environment. Something was giving me this feeling of formality, as if a Duchess were sitting right behind me and judging everything I did. Like when you suddenly go to a very old aunts home and you, miraculously, are okay with drinking tea out of very fine china.

"Mia, then," Will inclined his head towards me, not helping in the undertone of decorum that was bugging me. "That's because you're not even on Earth." His alien pronunciation of the word Earth was almost missed in my sudden sweep of shock.

Will graciously gave me a moment to recover while he fielded questions from his colleagues.

"You mean you think she's from," Tim began quietly and then floundered off, unable to remember something suddenly.

"Yes, I think she's from the Original World. The world all humankind started," Will finished for Tim.

"Thousands of years ago," Will began, turning back to me. "All humans, witch and mortal alike, lived on Earth. Mostly in harmony. Our practices and our magic were used for the betterment of everyone, and we witches were sought after for help, guidance, and leadership in many situations. It wasn't until around your year 300 A.D. that everything changed. The Emperor Constantine had a mother, Helena, who was a fanatic of a new religion, Christianity, that was rising from all powerful Rome. She was relentless in her pursuit of items she thought related to it. She even went as far as hiring witches to assist her in locating a few objects. Once these hapless witches did, however, she turned around and had them persecuted for their magic."

I sucked in a breath, it was a great fear instilled within all witches throughout my known history, being found out and hunted for it.

"The entire magical world grew fearful and prayed to the Mother Goddess for help and she listened. She sent us a Druid, Augustina. The first of her kind, and through her, the Mother created a separate world for the witches who followed her to Medeis to escape death. They came to cross over through the portals Augustina set up in the thousands, most followed by witch hunters the entire time. Some made it, others did not. Augustina eventually had to make the hard choice to seal them off, only leaving a few pieces behind in the Original World for anyone who wished to use later."

I thought back to the ugly old mirror that had sent me here, was it really that old? I shook myself out of the thought and turned my attention back to Will.

"The witches came here, and guided by Augustina, set up a new world in our own way. For hundreds of years, we lived in peace without another word from the Original World, save for a brief influx around the printing of a certain book in 1486."

I knew what he was talking about instantly, every witch did.

"The Malleus Mallificarum," I whispered.

The feeling of a heart stopping in utter dread is not a pleasant one. It's like the wind being knocked out of you at the same time your skin goes clammy and sweat breaks out. The Malleus Mallificarum, written by Heinrich Kramer and Jacob Sprenger in 1486, was the most damning piece of work on how to detect, hunt, question, and kill a witch. It brought the world such techniques as "Swimming the Witch," a barbaric practice where the questioner would tie a suspected witch to a chair or heavy board and then drown them in a stream or lake. If the suspected witch floated, you burned her because she was a witch, if she drowned, she wasn't a witch after all, but she died, nevertheless.

Countless lives were lost over hundreds of years, both magical and mortal, because of this book and its instructions. It spouted off extremely false accusations and demonized the magical world. Witches still lived in its shadow even today, and learned at a young age to stay hidden to some degree if not completely. My mother had always been lucky in her work that no one held these sentiments of hate and distrust.

"Apparently it caused such a stir in the Original World, that witches began looking for the portals again to escape. We took them in here and they brought with them their new science and technology, giving Medeis a boost it hadn't had since its founding."

The feeling of being thrown back in time finally clicked with me. This world hadn't had any new influence since the 15th century. That's why the clothes looked so odd and why there was real fire in the streetlights instead of bulbs. This was a world stuck in the past, or so it looked.

"It looks as though, however, that Michelo has created a portal from Medeis to the Original World to find you. However, now we have come to the moment where we have to ask why." Will shifted forward in his seat, placing his elbows on his knees and steepling his fingers in front of his face.

It took me a moment to understand that he was waiting for me to speak now.

"I, I don't know. I couldn't catch much of the first part of what he was saying because it was in Latin, and I don't know that much. My parents only got me so far as conjugations of verbs," I explained. I held my hands out in front of me to show I was hiding nothing.

"Wait, but you're speaking Latin now. You obviously know enough." Wynnie interjected and I raised an eyebrow.

"No, I'm not. I'm speaking English." Wynnie looked to Will for answers, yet again.

"Must be the spell your father cast. A permanent language spell so that you could understand and speak it for while you were here. See, most of the witches who came to Medeis, were from the Roman Empire or one of its holdings. Everyone spoke Latin. When the Second Wave came later, those witches just decided to learn the language as it is already the language of magic. I don't know what English is, but you are speaking fluent Latin right now, but you must not know it."

I leaned back in my chair and my mind whirled, this was a lot to take in. I felt confusion, lost as to where I was or why this was happening to me. I felt hurt, that my parents had never told me about any of this. They obviously knew, or they wouldn't have sent me here. I felt alone without them. I was worried for them. And as I sat there, beginning to listen in on the continuing conversation between the Guard over whether I was a spy or not, I felt angry.

I was angry at my situation, angry at my parents for lying to me about a safer world, angry that I wasn't felt heard, and angry at Michelo for ruining the life I had worked so carefully for. Anger, anger, anger. As I sat there, stewing to myself, something inside of me latched on to that anger and the feeling kept growing. It seeped into all my thoughts, it clouded my vision, it burned my throat and my adrenaline climbed higher and higher. For the first time in my life, I felt the need to punch something.

Attempting to redirect my attention to anything else, I turned back to the conversation in front of me.

"I still think she's lying. How could Michelo possibly create a portal to the Original World? Only the Mother or a Druid can do that. We need to get her to a truth enchanted room and question her. Give me ten minutes and I can have her singing all of Heretia's secrets like a bird." Wynnie's smile was sadistic and while I usually would cower from a comment like that, as I abhorred violence, that piece of me that was still latching on to my anger snapped.

"No! No!" I shouted above them all, standing from my seat to try and get their attention. "I am not a spy! I don't even know who you're talking about. I just want to go home!"

Will flung his hand in my direction, and just like that, my words were taken from me. I touched my face in horror. If I could have spluttered in defiance, I would have. Will had cast a Silence spell on me, sealing my lips together.

My mother had always taught me that using a spell like that on a person was highly disrespectful and only used to belittle someone. Even toddlers were given more respect during one of their tantrums.

One last even more potent feeling creeped through me as my breathing picked up its pace, fear. I was scared out of my mind and no one was listening. My parents were Mother knows where, with Mother knows who doing Mother only knows what and no one was listening! I felt all the rage and fear flow into my mouth fighting the Silence spell. It felt like tape being peeled away as my emotions tore and scraped at my lips to get it off. Fighting to surface, I finally gave in, let the rage flow and the power it held tore the spell asunder. Finally, I felt the invisible tape fall away and, with a vengeance, I blew my shit.

"Don't EVER do that to me again!" I screamed.

I exploded into the room. I felt it. In that moment, I felt my magic snap like a twig inside my head and pour like a flood into the room beyond me. The fire in the hearth blew up two sizes, causing Wynnie to jump away and shatter her glass of wine in the process. The now empty chair nearest me was thrown against the wall and the windows near Tim groaned and fluttered. I gasped and backed up a step. Had I done all that? Was Theo right? Was my magic stronger than I had ever thought?

Next thing I knew, I was being pinned down by two exceptionally large and very rough hands.

"Control yourself woman!" Will shouted. I blinked twice, feeling the emotions suddenly ebb away into nothing, leaving me an empty shell. Everyone in the room was silent as the fire died back down and the house quit rattling.

"Did no one ever teach you to handle your emotions? You could have killed everyone in this house and possibly in a near vicinity if you'd kept shouting."

I could see the veins on his forehead bulging. However, his eyes were wide with fear as well, an emotion I hated to mirror back to him.

"Then listen to me and stop trying to say I'm some spy or liar. I am not, I just want to go home and you four are being unnecessarily paranoid," I fired back, but all the heat was gone from me everything having been spent on my single outburst. Tears were starting to well up on the edges of my eyes and my voice cracked.

Will waited a few more breaths before letting me go. He continued to crouch over me however while I sat up.

"You don't get to Silence me, and you don't get to boss me around. I am a grown woman, not some stubborn child. I'd thank you to treat me as such." I knew my current state of teary-eyed burgeoning hysteria was not exactly making my case for being a grown woman, but I'd had a very rough day. I looked around and stared each of them down. Silence fell and I could see the gears between their ears whirring as they analyzed the tension in the room.

"We're not being unnecessarily paranoid, you know." It was Tim still by the window who spoke first. I scoffed in annoyance.

"Yeah right! I mean, what do you think I am going to do? I am not even from this world. I'm bad at magic, and frankly, I have no interest in staying longer than I must. You four are sitting around talking about torturing me for information I don't have! What is there to be paranoid about?" I threw my arms out in irritation.

The blonde cleared her throat and jerked her thumb in the direction of the fireplace that I noticed she had deftly removed herself far away from.

"Other than being paranoid for my eyebrows?"

Theo snorted, "You mean that single eyebrow you never get plucked, Wynnie?"

Wynnie, with two clearly distinct and well-groomed eyebrows, scowled heavily. Tim suddenly jerked Theo's chair back a little, spilling a few drops of his own wine onto his sleeve.

"Sorry," Tim muttered, though he looked anything but.

"No, we're not talking about you as a person, per se. But what you might be. How do we know that you are not from the Ancient Kingdom, a spy for Heretia?" Tim explained, taking his place up by the window.

Will held out his hand to help me up to my feet.

"I really have no idea who you're talking about, and frankly, I don't have the time to sit here and explain how little an idea I have. Will you please just take me to the Prince like my dad asked me to so I can get back to them?" My pleading fell on practically deaf ears. I did notice a subtle change in the air of the room. Wynnie shifted closer to Theo, who leaned forward slightly.

"Who is this 'Prince', your father told you to find?" he asked slowly.

I shook my head, "I have no idea. All he said is my heart would know him, and his mine. I guess maybe he knew my parents so he's got the be in his mid-forties or older. Is there anyone who goes by that name that falls under that age range?" I finally felt like I was getting somewhere, the right questions were getting asked.

Tim shook his head but seemed to not be looking at anyone in the room.

Will also confirmed his answer. "Only people that age around here are the High Kings and Queens."

My shoulders sagged. What was I going to do now? Wynnie stood up from her chair to pour herself a small splash of what looked like brandy and knocked it back.

"Well, I still don't trust her and after that outburst we just saw, I say she's a danger on magical grounds alone, not to mention nefarious ones. Even if she is who she says she is, she needs to be tested and then Bound so she can't hurt anyone till she returns to wherever she came from."

"You guys do know that I'm standing right here," I complained, this was getting old. Do they treat all newcomers this way, or was I just special?

Will smiled. "Then go sit in that chair you so ungraciously knocked over."

His three companions snickered, but I obliged since I was so exhausted.

"What is being tested, and will it take long? I really want this over so I can just find my parents and go home," I muttered.

"It's nothing really, just a type of Rite of Passage adolescents goes through to determine the origin and level of their magic. It is simple really and any Priestess can do it. We will go tomorrow and have it done. I will warn you, this test reveals your inner truths to everyone, so if you are hiding anything from us, you need to confess now. If we find out you really are a spy, we will kill you without a single hesitation." Will explained evenly, never once breaking eye contact.

I gulped. "Well, as I said before, I'm not lying, so that shouldn't be a problem."

Will nodded his head firmly once.

"Well, that settles it then. Let's eat and go to bed. First thing in the morning, Theo and I will take her down to a Priestess and see what there is to see."

Wynnie sat up straight and grinned, her hand playing with a dagger she had produced from what seemed like nowhere. "Or we can force her to tell us now with a Truth Enchantment." She gave a very playful smile to Will, the grin wicked and bone chilling.

I recoiled in my seat.

"No," Theo said darkly. "No, that's illegal without actual reasonable cause for forcing an enchantment on someone. The High Rulers would not be happy if they ever found out that we were taking those kinds of matters into our own hands."

There was a silence for a horribly tense moment, and I felt myself grateful to Theo in that silence, even though it sounded as if he was just really following the law. I did notice however, that was now the second time he had taken up for me above the almost zero everyone else had.

"So, food?" Wynnie suggested, bouncing out of her chair, and crossing to another door, throwing it wide open. It was if she hadn't just happily threatened my life moments before. She was an odd little psychopath. Immediately, my unease melted just a little as my senses were inundated from all angles.

Smell upon smell of delicious meats and sweet fruits attracted my nose and made my mouth water. Theo and Tim quickly sprung from their posts and found seats around the table, seemingly close to whatever was their favorite dish. Wynnie was already devouring what looked like a duck, and in the back corner I could see a small maid waiting to bring more wine or add more food at a moment's notice.

"Allow me," Will offered his arm with a gracious smile and I gingerly took it, wishing decorum allowed me to descend upon that table with as much familiarity and gusto as those three had.

Will seemed to suddenly change demeanor as well and took up his post as more of a host of the house. Instead of the leader of this crazy hodgepodge of characters whose emotions were rollercoasters I was only too happy to be rid of.

"While they are happily stuffing their pie holes with pie, let me formally introduce you to everyone. I think that's safe enough. It's not like everyone in the Five Kingdoms doesn't already know who we are."

Theo grunted and eyed me warily. Will had decided to seat me on Theo's left while he himself took up the head of the table to my own left. Wynnie sat across from me and Tim sat across from Theo.

"I am Wilhelm Corso, a fire sorcerer from Elevetia and Captain of the Elite Guard. We are a for hire military squad that is open to four of the five kingdoms. Mostly our missions are used by the High Rulers of those kingdoms to keep an eye on more delicate matters such as capturing the Nandina you met today."

I nodded in understanding.

They were basically mercenaries, but where did they draw the line? In mortal history, there had been talk of these kinds of groups, but they were usually nefarious.

Will continued around the table, not having noticed my troubling thoughts. "This here is Wyndetta Lily, hailing from Maravette, our current country's neighbor. She is a practically skilled Air Sorcerer and slightly crazy. Don't mind her earlier comments too much, we certainly don't."

Wynnie wiggled her pinky at me from where it was holding a vicious looking, but different from just moments before, knife.

"That is Timothy Unda next to her and his home Kingdom is Lotho. He is a Water Sorcerer, naturally, from that kingdom and an excellent archer."

Tim nodded his head silently and then returned to his own plate. I nodded in return, but frowned, trying to remember where I had heard that name before.

"Finally, we have the illustrious Theodeus Varillian, Earth Sorcerer, from this fair kingdom of Suravia where he is," Theo cut Will off with a sharp clearing of his throat.

"That's enough Will, she doesn't need to know our personal histories. She barely even needs to know our names," he interrupted.

Theo glared Will down with such an evil eye that I shuddered. Both Wynnie and Tim suddenly became interested in their plates of food.

"Okay then. Apparently, manners are something Theo was never taught," Will said slowly as if he was not sure why Theo was acting like an uncouth baboon, which apparently was not his normal demeanor.

"I'm really sorry if I'm such a huge inconvenience. Really, you do not need to go to any trouble to be nice to me. I just want to find my parents and go home," I explained, trying desperately to find an avenue from escape from this group. I wasn't sure these were the right kind of people I needed to help me. I needed a Prince, not mercenaries.

All ignored me, but I got the feeling it wasn't about me anymore, but some other tension in the group that was like an undulating river beneath the surface of the desert. The silence was stifling as we all ate without another word. Wynnie and Tim were carefully watching Theo. Theo was badly hiding that he was watching my every move as if I was going to stab him with my soup spoon, and Will was tactfully acting as if nothing was going on at all.

At some point, my stomach was full enough that I decided I could escape this torture without starving through the night. I wiped my face and looked at Will.

"I'd like to go to bed now. Do I need to sleep on the front room couch?" I asked.

Will shot me an incredulous glance and slowed his chewing before he threw his head back and barked the most ostentatious laugh I had ever heard. Blinking, I looked over at Wynnie and Tim for confirmation that I was not crazy. They were both smiling wryly to themselves.

"Good Mother no! This is a carefully designed house for the Elite Guard. Rooms are magically created to accommodate however many bodies are filling it. All you have to do is go up the stairs and pick one of the doors. Just write your name on the chalkboard outside, and the room will create itself to be whatever you need."

My jaw dropped. Where had that kind of magic been all my life?

"Whatever I need?" I parroted.

Will, who had calmed down, nodded. For the first time all day I noticed there was a bright twinkle to his chocolate brown eyes.

"Yes, a bathing room, a bed the right size, clothes that will fit you perfectly, and there will even be necessities personally designed for you. Everyone's room will be different, but just remember to write your name on the board. One, that is so everyone knows it's a taken room and won't just walk in on you accidentally, but two so the magic works. Go ahead, go give it a try."

"Yes but," I started to say, but Will interrupted me with a wave.

"No fear, it's not based off your own magic, but the magic of the creator who I can promise you was a wise and powerful Sorcerer many years ago."

I nodded at the reassurance. The maid stepped forward, looking as if she wanted to assist me, but a loud clatter of silverware, plates, and a chair being thrown back halted her.

"I'll take her upstairs," Theo was looming over me. I looked up at him and almost squeaked. His green eyes were darker than before, like storm clouds swirling in their centers.

"I was going upstairs anyway, and I think it was best if no one lose sight of her till we can lock her in a room," he continued.

My face fell into a pout. How many times was this going to keep coming up?

"I don't need watching, I'm not doing anything wrong. I can show myself up, thank you," I sneered.

With a stomp, I moved my chair back and began towards the door.

"Oh no you don't! I'm making sure you actually get to that room and that you stay in it!" he countered.

Theo grabbed my elbow and I yanked it back. I felt the jolt again when he touched me, and I was determined to eventually find out what it was, but not locked in a room with him.

"And how exactly do you plan on doing that, Theo?" Wynnie asked with a smirk. I saw her wink at Tim who just bowed his head in utter annoyance of the display.

I suddenly went pale at her insinuation.

"I'm going to stay in the room with her," he replied.

My stomach twisted. The mere thought of someone so gorgeous…

"You most certainly are not!" I shouted as heat began to flame up my neck. Theo ignored me and turned to Will.

"Say I'm not right that someone doesn't need to stay with her and make sure she doesn't try anything funny." Will stroked his beard, deep in thought.

"You are not seriously considering making me stay in a room alone with someone I don't even know who clearly would like nothing more than to see me thrown in a dungeon and turned on the rack?" I rounded on Will's other side away from Theo's grasp and stared him down.

"Oh, I think he might want to see something else. I'm not talking about torture, but it certainly might contain a dungeon of sorts," Wynnie cackled viciously.

"Shut up Wyndetta, no one is asking you," Theo roared.

Wynnie shot up, "She'll stay with me then, prick."

But Theo only stiffened and quickly ran around Will's chair, attempting to snatch at my arm again.

"As if, she'd wake up gutted from nose to navel and all her appendages stacked into a pile next to her after you finished toying with those knives of yours!"

I took a large step away from both of them, yanking my elbow back. Again, a strange feeling had started creeping up my arm and it was really starting to freak me out.

"Stop it! Both of you. I'm not staying the night with anyone at all and that's final!" I yelled.

Theo reached for me, but I slapped his hand.

"And if you touch me again, so help me Mother, I will neuter you right here and now," I snapped.

Everyone's brow furrowed "What's neuter?" Theo asked.

"Ah," I paused and stumbled for a moment, blushing furiously. "It's where I make sure you can't have kids."

Every man in the room either took a step back or jerked a leg across their lap.

"That is what I thought. Now, if you would, please move aside and leave me alone. I'd like to get some sleep," I was finished with this argument.

Will held his hand up for silence. "Hold on. Even though I don't agree with Theo's suddenly tactless manner, he does have a point. I'm sorry, but until we know more about you, someone does need to stay with you, and unfortunately, Theo is the best choice."

"WHAT?!" Wynnie and I asked at the same time.

"Wynnie, it's your night to report to the Council, and I more than likely need to accompany you since Theo here decided to slay the Nandina. Lots of questions will be asked and they will be asking about Amelia. Tim over here, well, sorry Tim, but you snore like an absolute dragon with a head cold, so I would never put my worst enemy in a room with you, let alone a woman who might really just need some rest," Will chuckled.

Tim silently threw his napkin at the red head and went back to eating something that looked like a custard.

"So, it's settled then," Theo announced, and moved like he was about to grab my elbow again.

I raised my fist and moved my legs ready to kick him in the groin when he suddenly thought better of it.

"Nothing has been decided by me," I seethed.

Will rose to his full height and I was suddenly reminded why he was the leader of this group of warriors. His hulking presence instantly took up the entire room and when he crossed his arms, every muscle rippled against the strain of his shirt. Not only did he seem wise and a good people manager, but he was a powerhouse to boot and you really didn't get to say no to someone who could snap you in half.

"You will either share a room with Theo for one night only, or we will kill you right here and now. You can't be trusted inside the city in case you are not who you say you are. This is your option, and if I were you, I would just get used to Theo's sudden bad attitude toward women and put up with it," he glared.

I gulped and nodded meekly.

"We will see you in the morning. Tim will be just across the hall and Wynnie and I will not be back until extremely late, but we will be back eventually if you need anything. I do trust Theo," Will snapped his head towards the brooding figure in the corner, "will find his decorum and manners and help you with anything you need."

Theo just scoffed and looked to the wall to break the menacing glare from his Captain.

"Now, it's settled. Good Evening Amelia and may the Mother bless your dreams," he finished.

It was most definitely a dismissal. I nodded and mumbled blessings in return like a chastised child, moving to leave the dining room. I scurried past Theo without looking at him and quickly walked up the steps. I came to the first door off the landing and reached for the handle.

"Don't do that!" Theo reached and I instinctively moved my hand away. "Don't touch it until you write your name. If the room does not know who to appear for, then it will be a black hole into an abyss that you could easily fall into. Always, always write your name, or any name for that matter," he instructed.

I looked up at him and stared. Now that I was finally alone with this man, I was able to get a good look at him. He had dark brown hair that was short, well-groomed, and brushed to the side. His skin was very similarly toned to my own, rich with color. Those eyes, like two exquisitely crafted emeralds shining from a fine piece of jewelry. His well-shaped mouth and straight Greek nose finished off his beautiful face.

Not in defiance, but out of curiosity, I held his gaze. Theo cleared his throat awkwardly, grabbed the chalk, and wrote his name on the board. When he reached for the handle, it was my turn to grab for his hand.

"Well hang on, I don't want to sleep in a room that's isn't comfortable and won't have any clothes for me," I snapped up the chalk and wrote my name beside his.

For a moment, Theo stared at our names written on the board together and then nodded, reached for the handle, and opened the door.

Chapter Four

When Theo opened the door, the smell was the first thing that hit me. Mixtures of sandalwood, frankincense, and rose floated around me and I closed my eyes to breathe it all in. It relaxed me and almost instantly I felt comfortable, probably the magic purposefully picking smells that would set me more at ease. This room was less of a bedroom and more of a haven. I really needed to figure out how this magic worked and take it back with me. Having a peaceful place to go after a stressful day at the hospital would be just what I needed.

"Oh, that's heavenly," I muttered. Theo didn't budge from his place in the doorway. He seemed to be waiting for me to make a move into the room first.

"Well, are we just going to stand here or are we going to get some rest?" he grumbled.

I motioned my hand to allow him to pass first, but he shook his head.

"No, I don't want you slamming the door behind me and running off."

I rolled my eyes as I walked in. "Like I would even make it past the front hall," I mumbled under my breath.

The room was not overly large, but it was certainly bigger than any dorm or bedroom I had ever occupied in my life. A vast four poster bed with sheer curtains took up most of the space. A wingback chair and a small round table sat by the double window that overlooked a garden. A large armoire with two oak doors stood on the wall that shared the door, and to the right of the bed, was another door next to a fireplace.

My best guess was that the door led to a bathroom, given that was where all the amazing smells emanated from. I could distinctly detect smells familiar, such as honeysuckle and roses, and some that I could not place at all. The ones that I could not quite place were all dark, musky, and frankly erotic to my feminine nose. I breathed in deeply letting those sensual smells envelop me for a brief calm moment. Something about them seemed to ease some of my tension.

Reopening my eyes to continue investigating the room, Theo shut the door behind him. I continued along the wall with the window, glancing casually out onto a pretty garden that, from what I could tell, needed some tending to. It was then that I noticed a small sitting couch on the other side of the armoire that could not be seen from the door. There were two plump pillows that sported an emblem of sorts, a simple circle divided into four sections by a cross. I racked my brain for why I recognized it. I had seen this symbol before and had pointed it out in my father's books. He had smiled, pulled me onto his lap, and showed me the page I was curious about.

"This is the alchemy symbol for Earth, Princess," he had explained and pointed to the circle with the cross in the middle. "You will only really see this in potions recipes." He smiled, just as my mother had wafted in from outside, smelling of mint and lavender.

"Well, there and back home," my mother commented over her shoulder. My father had tensed his arm around me, and my mother had even paused for a second at the sink. As a small child, the comment had meant nothing to me, but now as I remembered the entire scene in my mind, I guess I should have asked questions. Never again did I remember my mother talking about back home and that must have been her one and only slip.

Snapping back to the present, I reached out for the pillow and picked it up, running my fingers over the symbol. My parents had been Earth witches, both of them. Did they come from Medeis? Had this kingdom of earth witches been their home? Why had they gone to the Original World?

"I'm not taking any chances with you," Theo was turning away from the door and he halted, swallowing hard. His face lost all color as he looked to the pillow I was holding. I looked up, noticing his strange behavior.

"What's wrong?" I asked and looked him once over. He shook his head, a single hair never falling out of place. The sudden moment of panic was gone and was instantly replaced with his cool, collected, and hard demeanor.

"Nothing, I just wasn't expecting to see that here of all places. It's been a while since I've been back in Suravia so, it just caught me off guard." He crossed his arms over his chest, and I had a hard time getting my mind to not wander off at the sight of his pectorals bulging in the white tunic shirt he was wearing. I guess I had missed him chucking the leather jacket he had worn earlier when we entered the house. The shirt was of a very thin material, and it wasn't hard to begin imagining what he had going on under there.

"Why would this symbol catch you off guard? Aren't we in the Earth Kingdom?" I asked.

"This isn't the symbol of Kingdom. This is the Royal Crest of the High Kings and Queens of Suravia and their families," he turned and stalked towards the bathroom.

I furrowed my brow, something about him still seemed off and I wasn't feeling like this needed to be the end of my questioning. A little nagging feeling fired off in my brain again. As a nurse when I think a patient isn't giving me the whole story, I prod a little deeper. I ask questions that beat around the bush, or I change tactics altogether. This was one of those moments I felt like I wasn't getting the whole story.

I tossed the pillow back on to the couch and moved to follow Theo. I wasn't ready to bust in on a closed bathroom door to get my answers, but I was trying to keep him in the main room long enough to tell me everything.

"So why did it startle you? Are you afraid of the High Kings and Queens for some reason?" I asked.

Theo gave a loud bark of laughter at my question that startled me.

"Afraid of them?" he repeated and then faced me. He flung out his arms.

"What's there to be afraid of? They can't touch me anymore; they can't get to me and they certainly can't control my life." His voice grew louder, and he seemed to not be speaking to me anymore. I took a wary step back. Theo huffed and his arms dropped down with a smack to his thighs.

"I might as well tell you, Will tried to downstairs. You're going to find out one way or another." I smiled to myself in satisfaction, there it was. The thing he was hiding and didn't want to tell me. I knew there had been something held back. Even the rest of the guard had seen it and commented multiple times on how strange he was acting. I finally got him pinned down and now I was going to learn the truth. Theo stalked over to the offending pillow and picked it up, never touching the symbol hand stitched on its fabric.

"This damn symbol has haunted my life for as long as I can remember. It is engraved in the cradle, clothing, weapon and very life of every member born to a reigning High King or Queen of Suravia. It is something we can never escape, even if we never end up becoming High King or Queen ourselves."

I blinked, "We?"

Theo closed his eyes, "Yes, we. I am Theodeus Varillian, son of Ogden Varillian and Vanessa Varillian, two of the five High Kings and Queens of Suravia. My entire life and destiny are wrapped up into this symbol, and it follows me everywhere like a bad luck charm." He chucked the pillow back onto the couch with a sneer.

"It's here because my name is on that door and even the oldest magic can sense royalty, no matter how far I run from it."

My mouth fell to the floor in shock. Magical royalty? I did not even know what to say to this revelation. The only thing that seemed to come to mind was, "Oh, is that all?"

Theo looked stunned. "That's not usually the reaction I get when people realize who I am for the first time." A small smile cracked on his face.

I instantly recovered my composure at that smile. It sent a flutter through my heart and my back straightened even tighter. 'Get it together Mia.' I chastised myself.

"Well, excuse me for not knowing exactly what to say. It's not every day a girl is dropped into an alternate world finds out she's sharing a room with a...." I fell silent, as a brick of realization slammed down over me. My heart stopped and I felt my jaw go slack, my eyes widened. Slowly, very slowly as if unsure he would still be there when I looked back, I raised my eyes to Theo's. I saw it then, I saw that he knew what was hitting me square in my mind. He knew I knew.

"With a prince." I finished in a whisper.

We both stood there in silence for what seemed like forever as the words sunk in. He was a prince, was he the prince my father had sent me to look for? The prince that was supposed to help me, that my heart would know. I didn't feel like I knew him, nothing about him was familiar. Then another thought crowded its way into my consciousness. Every time he touched me, my skin felt weird. My magic responded to him, but I wasn't completely sure what that meant. I wasn't used to wielding magic at all so this was new to me, so maybe that meant nothing.

"I didn't want Will to say anything because you had mentioned your father instructed you to look for a prince, I didn't want you thinking that was me for any reason," Theo admitted.

My heart gave a double beat.

"But you are one, you are a prince. You could have told me that. You lied to me earlier, in the woods when you said you didn't know anyone like that." Theo began to shake his head.

"No, no you asked if there was someone way older who was a prince. I'm only twenty-five, and I walked away from being a prince eight years ago on my eighteenth birthday. I'm not the man you're looking for. I have no idea who your parents are and they wouldn't have known me," he clarified, but that wasn't what I was wanted to hear.

Again, that unnecessary anger grew. Starting in my gut and welling up inside. I backed away from Theo and stared down at my hands. I began to panic; I didn't want to do something stupid again like I had with the fireplace. I closed my eyes and tied to breathe deeply, but the feeling grew.

Suddenly, I felt something fly past my head. The rush of air threw my hair in my face to where I couldn't catch a glimpse of what it was. I ducked out of instinct, but the object was not coming for me. It whizzed through the air past me and straight for Theo.

A loud whack was followed immediately by, "Shit! What the hell was that for?"

I untucked my head from my arms to see a book on the floor in front of a crouching Theo who was holding his nose. Blood was trickling down his fingers and his eyes were closed shut. I was horrified, had I done that? Guilt seeped in and I crawled on the ground over to check his nose. Theo backed away from me, but I had to make sure he was okay.

"Oh! I am so sorry!" I reached for his nose but he swatted me away.

"Don't touch it!" he snapped and turned his back to me. I snatched his hand into mine, ignoring the feeling it created when we touched, and I looked him over.

"Oh, come here. I'm a nurse. I just want to make sure it isn't really broken," I instructed.

Theo gave me a wary look. "What's a...nurse?"

I blinked twice and then smiled, "It's like a healer, but without magic. Now let me see it." I guided him to the edge of the bed and pulled his hand away. I gingerly touched the bridge of it, making him wince. "Sorry, just give me a moment. I don't think it's broken. Should be nothing more than swelling, some discomfort, and a nasty bruise by morning."

Theo winced.

"You will need some ice though. Where is the kitchen and I'll grab a bag?" I wheeled to the door and reached out to grab the handle.

"NO! DON'T!"

That was all I heard before my hand grazed the door handle and a gigantic boom of energy blasted me from my feet. I was violently thrown across the room and I landed on the floor in front of the wingback chair. My head slammed into the leg and my vision went black for a moment from the force of the crack. My eyes swam with tears and I slumped, too stunned and in pain to move. I felt the floorboards creak as Theo raced across the room and hovered over me.

Moments later, the door swung open with a crash and Tim came storming in. "Mother of All, what is going on in here? I expected some shouting, but are you seriously trying to kill each other?"

I moaned lightly as the pain intensified. I could not summon the energy to move.

I felt two strong arms cradle me gently "She tried to touch the door after I enchanted it and it threw her into the chair."

"Do I need to call a healer? And one for you, too?" Tim asked. I guess he saw the damaged to Theo's face as well.

"I'm fine, she was leaving to get me ice after she hit me with a book. Go get Esmerelda from next door. She's the only one I trust to keep quiet," Theo ordered.

I heard Tim walk quickly to the door before chuckling to himself. "A book? She's got some arm, that one."

"Just go!" Theo roared and I winced at the level of his voice. My head was on fire.

"I've got you," Theo said soothingly. He stood up slowly, still cradling me, and laid me down on the bed. In my brain fog, I did not realize what was happening and I nuzzled my face up to his chest, trying to find something comforting to latch on to. Theo sucked in a breath at the touch and went very still.

"I'm really sorry," he whispered, keeping his voice down.

I moaned something unrecognizable and finally was able to lift my hand to my aching head. "My head," I stuttered, the words feeling like cotton in my mouth. I heard footsteps coming quickly up the stairs.

"Don't move, wait on Tim to get back with Esmerelda. Don't say anything. I'll do all the talking," Theo whispered in my ear.

The whisper felt good. His warm breath slid down my face onto my neck. I moaned again and leaned into his face.

"When you're done trying to make out with my patient, I'd like to look at her," a booming female voice interrupted.

I tried to crack my eyes open, but even the light that was coming from the fireplace was too bright and I shut them tightly.

"I was just trying to get her to relax," Theo defended himself to the newcomer.

"Sure, okay." I could practically here the eyeroll in the voice.

"Let's see what we've got here. What happened?"

I felt two cold, but soft hands grab both sides of my face.

"There was an accident and she fell back against the chair leg. She hit her head pretty hard," Theo explained.

"The same accident that caused your black eye?" the voice snorted but continued to move my head around.

I frowned at the movements.

"Does this hurt?" she asked, as she pushed my head up.

"No," I managed to moan.

"Well, at least she's coherent and vocal. That is a good sign." I felt someone hover over me and I cracked my eyes to see who it was.

"My name is Esmerelda, you can call me Ez. I just want to look at the back of your head quickly. You don't move, Theo will do the lifting." Her hazel eyes looked over my shoulder where Theo still stood guard.

"Help me roll her over and let me look at the back of her head," she instructed.

Theo's strong arms wrapped around me and he pulled me close while she pushed at my shoulder to get me to roll.

"I think it's okay, she's just really stunned and will have a major headache for a few hours. I will leave some swelling reducers for a tea she can drink in about fifteen minutes when she really comes back around to help with the pain. Now you, let me look at the nose," Ez instructed.

Theo rolled me back to a lying position, I was starting to clear from the daze and opened my eyes further.

"Amelia already looked at it and decided nothing was wrong, but I could probably use a swelling reducer as well just in case," he smiled. His smile was warped from the swelling his nose was starting to accrue.

"Amelia?" Esmerelda asked.

I still could not turn my head to see the healer very well, but her voice was still noticeably clear.

"She's Amelia," Theo nodded to me realizing that I was trying to open my eyes.

"She can introduce herself now that's she's fully awake." He leaned over to help me up, but I waved him away.

"I don't want to sit up yet. I'll get dizzy. I'll be fine in a moment or two," I whispered. Suddenly, Theo was shoved out of my line of vision and Ez came back into view. Her voluptuous figure, pale skin and those hazel eyes greeted me with a radiating warmth that made me feel at ease.

"Well, good evening broken head! You that rough in bed that you knock out yourself and the lover in one fell swoop?" Ez chuckled to herself, but I felt my eyes fly wide open.

"What the hell Ez! That's not even close to what's happening here!" Theo yelled in our defense.

I finally heard Tim bust out laughing from the doorway where he had apparently taken up unnecessary guard duty. Ez's eyes glittered with mischief and she winked at me.

"Come on dear, let's get you sat up and drinking some herbal tea before your head hurts even worse," she encouraged. Two gentle arms wrapped themselves under my armpits and hauled me up to a seated position where I finally got a good look at the healer as she swished away to put my tea together.

"Timothy be a dear and heat up some water for us. Quickly please before Amelia here gets the worst hangover of her life," she laughed again.

Tim nodded and walked into the bathroom, taking the empty cup from Ez as he passed, still shaking with quiet laughter.

Ez was beautiful; so tall, curvaceous, and stunning. Her mere presence took up the whole room and it was brighter and merrier for it. I felt safer knowing she was there, like nothing would hurt me and she could take care of anything that happened, medically or physically. She had the most luscious black hair that fell past her backside. Light from the fireplace bounced off her curls beautifully. Her enchanting eyes sparkled with merriment and wisdom.

Despite her buxom shape, which I completely envied, she floated like a butterfly through the room. This woman was a swan hidden in a person's body. I caught myself staring at her in absolute amazement and shook my head, immediately regretting that from the sharp pain that shot through it.

"Oh, don't do any sudden movements till a few minutes after you finish this tea," Ez cautioned, handing me the cup Tim had returned with. The tendrils of steam swam around the edges, but when I took a sip it was the perfect temperature.

"I've made one for you, too, Theo, but I need to speak with you in the hall first," she said.

Taking hold of another cup, Ez walked into the hallway waiting for Theo to follow. Theo sighed and slid off the bed. Tim shot me a raised eyebrow when the door closed behind her.

"Wanna know what they're talking about?" he asked with a wicked grin on his face.

This was not the Tim from earlier that I had met that was all broody and sullen. He had been paranoid then. He seemed to be much more relaxed, mischievous even. He even had a constant joking grin on his lips.

"Don't you think that's a little rude?" I mumbled into my teacup, eyeing the door warily.

He flopped down next to me on the bed and without asking, placed his left hand around the back of my head and over my left ear. I looked to see his right hand over his own right ear. "Yeah, but what's life without a little fun right?"

He closed his eyes and I could suddenly hear the two voices inside my head arguing. They were still out in the hall, but I could hear them clear as day with this magic.

"Do you think I'm a complete idiot Theodeus? Do you not think I see she is not wearing normal clothes? Do you think I do not notice the evidence of an enchanted lock or that you're banged up, too? Why is that girl locked in a room with you? Why did she attack you and where the hell is she from?" Ez was demanding.

I heard Theo take a slurp of his tea.

"I don't know if I can tell you all that. You'll need to ask Will to see what he wants to tell you, but he won't be back until after his and Wynnie's meeting with the High Rulers."

Ez scoffed. "You are playing the dutiful member of the Elite Guard under Captain's orders and it's a load of crap, Theo. What is going on here? Who is she?"

"I really can't say anything Ez, I'm sorry," he answered again.

I heard Ez smack his shoulder.

"I call bullshit! You tell me now or I am going to see my mother this instant. Something isn't right here, and I don't like it."

Theo grunted, "Your mother is as likely to listen to you as mine is to me. Just drop it! All you need to know is her name is Amelia and up until just recently we believed her to be dangerous, so I was on guard to watch her overnight. That's it." Theo slurped down the rest of his tea.

"Dangerous? What danger? She's a slip of a thing and why recently?" Ez was still pushing the issue.

Theo moaned in exasperation.

"Okay, fine! Just shut up and do not make a big deal about this. We thought she was dangerous because she just showed up, okay? I mean, out of nowhere, portaled in from the Original World claiming that Michelo had attacked her parents and they sent her here to find help. I am not sure who her parents are, but they sent her to seek help so whoever they are, it must be something. Ez, you need to stay out of this, for Mother's sake the last thing we need is your loudmouth trying to butt in everywhere."

It was a plea, but also a warning. Who was Ez to Theo? They were close and he felt comfortable letting her in on this.

I could hear Ez tapping her foot. I looked over at Tim whose face was unreadable as he too listened intently.

"Well, you didn't answer me on why you recently think she's not a threat," Esmerelda urged him on.

"Because she has no idea about anything. She has no idea how anything works here, who I am, who the Guard is, nothing. She doesn't even know about herself. She's got something powerful deep down inside of her, but she has no clue. She claims to have almost no magical talent, but every time I go near her, I just feel this deep well of magic inside of her. I've never felt that off anyone in my life, but she is different than the rest of us, I can just sense it. Will and I are taking her to get Rited tomorrow to see what she's got and to determine what level her threat is before we take her to the High Rulers," Theo explained.

There was a silence for a moment before Ez spoke again.

"This better be good if I'm going to shut my mouth. I'm supposed to see my mother tomorrow and I have half a mind to say something. If this girl was sent here to get help, then you should let her at least speak to them first. They might have all the answers and you guys are just yanking the chains around stalling."

I nodded to myself. I really was beginning to think Ez and I were going to get along.

"I mean, have you explained how the Rite works to her? Does she even know what to do? It's not trivial magic she'll be subjected to," Ez warned.

I heard the door handle twist and Tim snatched his hand away from my ear, leaping to the wingback chair and settled down in one swift movement acting as if nothing was the matter. I put my teacup to my lips and downed it, trying to sit up straighter.

Tim started laughing loudly, slapping his knee just as Theo walked back in the room. "You are really a treasure Mia! Who knew you were so funny?"

I gave him a slightly quizzical look and then, realizing what he was doing, put a large smile on my own face.

"And that's not even the funniest thing that happened that day. You should hear the time I had to insert a feeding tube into a man who had the gag reflex of an owl," I laughed.

Tim continued to laugh as though he had the faintest idea what I was talking about. I looked over to see a stunned Theo wavering in the doorframe.

"Oh, hey guys! You were out there forever, so Tim and I decided to tell occupational hazard stories that were funny later," I smiled.

Tim nodded and looked to Ez, "You've got some good ones I'm sure, Ez."

Ez winked wickedly and stuck her tongue in her teeth, "You know it and they usually involve you, Timothy."

Tim's neck blushed and he started chuckling. "Yeah. Good times."

Theo was still silent as he moved next to the bed, placing himself between Tim and myself. "You feel any better? Sorry again about the door."

"Forget it," I reassured him. "Things like this happen to me all the time. It's partly why I became a nurse, to fix my own wounds."

"What's a nurse?" Ez blaringly pried.

"It's what you do. I am a healer of sorts. Well, the doctor is really the healer and I'm more of the one who takes care of all the other stuff. Makes sure the patient gets their medications, take vitals, and assist the doctors in any procedures they might need help with," I informed her.

"Oh? And where do you do that?" she urged.

Theo cleared his throat and raised an eyebrow. Ez threw him an innocent green doe-eyed look.

"What?! I'm not allowed to ask basic questions to get to know my patient?"

I waved him off, "It's fine. I do this back at home, in my world. I am not exactly from around here, but I am a witch. Well, my parents are the real witches."

I finished the last sip of my now cold tea and handed Ez the cup. "I'm looking to get back to them. I'm not really sure how to do that, but they sent me to find help."

Explaining this in a calm manner sounded a lot more rational than how I did it earlier in the forest.

"Oh, that's horrible. Well, luckily you ran into these guys. They can take you directly to the High Rulers in the morning. Say, I'm heading up there myself, why don't you tag along. I can get you right in," she sang sweetly.

Tim almost choked, holding back his giggles from his seat by the window.

"No," Theo replied darkly.

"Will wants her Rited and that's what we're going to do first. Captain's orders. She can go see them after."

Ez just shook her head and scowled at him. "Theo," she started to warn, but he cut her off.

"You can leave any other herbs you want Mia to take and we will see you later, Ez. That will be enough," he whispered. It was a final warning.

"Theo, Esmerelda is just trying to help," Tim stood up, his focus starting to get a little intimidating.

"Why don't you go with her, Tim," Theo ordered.

I shivered at the coldness that settled in the room.

"I was just leaving anyway. Ez, let's go. I'll take you home," Tim said. He came around the bed slowly and took Ez by the hand, stroking it with his thumb gently.

"Come on, it's getting a little crowded in here and I'd rather hang out at your place till it settles down."

Esmerelda nodded, but I could distinctly make out a twinkle in her mischievous eyes. With one last glare in Theo's direction, they both left and shut the door behind them.

"That was a little rude. She was just trying to help, more than what you guys have done for me in the past few hours," I huffed. I started to move off the bed.

"Don't you start in on me, too! I am just following orders, for Mother's sake! Will said no and that means no. I will not disobey my commanding officer for anyone, let alone some stranger who Ez seems to have found a soft spot for," Theo thundered.

I stood up in that moment and stared him down.

"Shout at me again and I'll give you another black eye to match the one you've already got." I walked straight for the bathroom door and slammed it behind me.

With my back against the door, I slid down and cried from exhaustion.

CHAPTER FIVE

The bath was the exact thing I needed, after a good cry of course. I was overwhelmed from the day's events and a long hot soak in a tub with all my favorite smells helped calm me down. After washing my entire body of sweat and muck, I ducked my head underneath the water and held my breath for a good long while trying to find peace with the sound of the water in my ears.

When I finally could feel my lungs screaming, I came up and took a breath of fresh air, letting it fill my lungs with only positive energy. I did this one more time, attempting to banish any negativity for a while and make myself relax. As I got out, I looked around for something to wear to bed and realized I had not brought any fresh clothes in with me.

"Great!" I muttered. I grabbed a towel and opened the bathroom door.

Theo was stretched out across the bed, still in his regular clothes, staring up at the canopy. He jumped up when I opened the door.

"You said these rooms had clothes in them, right?" I asked and crossed the room, opening the doors to the armoire.

"Yes, but it won't be clothing you're used to, so if you need help with anything let me know," he replied.

I scoffed. "A night gown is a night gown. I am fairly sure I'm old enough to know how to put that on. Or am I not allowed to wear anything but what I was so unceremoniously dumped on your doorstep in, Your Highness?"

Theo winced at those words and I knew I hit home.

"Listen, I'm sorry for earlier today. I'm sorry for dinner and I'm sorry for just now. I've just completely lost my mind over all this because I'm trying really hard to prove myself to everyone," he admitted. I turned to face him and scowled.

"You don't seem like you have anything to prove to anyone here, especially me. So why the act?" I turned back to open a drawer lined with what looked like lingerie and barely-there slips. I quickly slammed the drawer shut and kept searching for less revealing items of clothing.

"I'm not really supposed to be in the Elite Guard and a lot of people think I'm only doing it because I'm no good at anything else. I follow Will's orders because if I don't, people will just think I'm playing around and not being serious about my job."

I stopped searching and sighed. "Well, if you're trying to prove yourself as the serious tough guy, you are going about it the worst way possible. Stop being a jerk every time I speak. Stop acting like I'm some demon meant to be burned at the stake and stop trying to dominate everyone in the room. I'm not saying go against orders, but you don't have to be so overbearing and mean to everyone in the process."

I finally found a drawer with a light silk gown that reached to my knees and held up by two single straps. "Besides," I continued, "I'm not the bad guy here and neither are you. I really don't even know who the bad guy is. I just want to go home. The faster you help me, the faster I'm out of your hair, out of your life, and back to my own."

Theo looked out the window and sighed. "You're right. I'm sorry. I am going to go wash up while you get dressed and I'll sleep on the couch. In the morning, I'll wake you up and we will go to the Rite and then to the Stronghold. I will help you get home, Amelia. I promise."

I nodded an acceptance of his apology and watched him close the door.

I was already in the bed facing the window watching the moon rise in the distance when the door reopened. Theo stepped out with a towel around his waist. I remained still and breathed slowly, pretending to be asleep, attempting to avoid any conversation he might want to have with me. I heard him lightly pad over to the armoire and pull out some clothes. The towel hit the floor and I squeezed my eyes shut. He could have at least gone back in the bathroom to get dressed. I kept my eyes shut while he slipped clothing on and creaked onto the couch.

He turned to face me. His wet hair fell over his beautiful, tanned face and covered his thick, long, black eyelashes. His full lips parted slightly, and I noticed his arm under the pillow was rippled with muscles. His chest was a sight to behold with its masculine definition, leading down into a waist that was just as chiseled as I expected, given the rest of him was practically god-like.

He was probably the most gorgeous man I had ever laid eyes on. I caught my breath and turned away, feeling the heat rise in me for no reason at all. I had to get away from this place as quickly as I could before my hormones made me do stupid things. Get yourself together Mia; you're acting like some teenager with uncontrollable hormones. I slammed my eyes shut one last time and recited a simple sleeping incantation in my head forcing my mind to close off and fall into a deep slumber.

What felt like only moments later, I was startled awake by the memory of eyes staring at me through a gap between the two worlds. I struggled to catch my breath and sat up, trying to remember where I was.

The moon was leaving the night sky and I could see a faint tint of the sun peeking out on the Eastern horizon. Without much thought, I rose from the bed and rubbed my shoulders, banishing away any chill from the morning air. Trying not to wake Theo, I slowly opened the door and looked around. Every door had a name on it, meaning everyone was back in the house and sleeping soundly. I looked down the stairs into the dark entry hallway below and then looked to the other end. I saw a set of stairs leading up to a door at the top of the house. A roof access!

I didn't want to break anyone's trust by leaving for a morning walk, but I also didn't want to wake anyone unnecessarily to accompany me on a tedious morning ritual. I decided the roof was a great place to catch some peace and breathe in the morning. Without grabbing a jacket, I walked to the access door and quietly stepped out onto a third-floor patio.

There was a small table and two chairs, flowerpots, and some open space that would be perfect for meditation. I was not going to try any bending or stretching in bare feet and with only this skimpy nightgown on, but I could at least stand and greet the morning head on.

I walked to the edge and placed my hands over my solar plexus and breathed in deeply. Crisp air filled my lungs and lifted me up onto my toes. I felt my arms instinctively raise above my head and come together, my leg coming up to rest on my other legs knee and balance itself.

I held the pose and found myself breathing deeper. My energy centered itself along my spine. It was comforting to find this moment of peace. I released the position and opened my eyes to see the sun finally coming up over the other houses and greeting me in return. I smiled. It was as if the sun and I just had the most wonderful conversation.

A throat cleared behind me and I turned to face the intruder on my tranquility. It was Will, wearing a loose, cotton tunic-like shirt with what I could only assume was breeches covering his legs underneath.

"I didn't know there were witches who still communed with nature every morning," he said.

I smiled and shook my head. "It was just a little morning peace. My mother called it 'Greeting the Sun' and we did it when we felt stressed or upset. I don't get to do it often, but it's nice when I can find a moment."

Will nodded and joined me by the rails, placing his hands solidly on them and steadying himself. He looked down at me and I blushed, realizing I was out here practically in my underwear around an exceptionally large and lumber sexually attractive man.

"I should go back inside," I mumbled and began to turn, but he caught my hand.

"Amelia, Tim told me what happened last night with Theo."

I didn't look at him, but I did nod to let him know I had heard him.

"You have to know that Theo isn't fighting with you specifically. It's his upbringing that he fights with. There's a lot of people out there who think that Theo is being childish running around with us, fighting Wild Beasts. When he should be up at the Suravian Stronghold getting ready to be High King."

I pulled my hand away and turned back.

"Well, why is he? I mean, it is not an invalid question. Why wouldn't you want to be in a position where you can make things better or do things your own way?"

Will looked out over the rooftops, sighing heavily.

"It's not simple. Just because you are born to a High King or Queen doesn't mean you will be one. Every child of any High King or Queen can ascend to one of the five thrones when a vacancy occurs. The only requirements are that they are a relative of a High Ruler and that they wield the Element of the kingdom. There's others with claim to his throne if he didn't want it," Will explained.

I didn't really understand anything he was saying, but it wasn't my world. "It just seems like maybe he's trying to prove himself too hard," I mentioned.

Will and I both were looking out over the city, taking it in. I could see townhomes for miles, all similar to what we were in now. Something about it struck me as very Elizabethan London with chimneys smoking up into the morning sky, the sound of movement in the streets, and vast cobblestone roadways and sidewalks crisscrossing the city.

"What is the name of this city?" I asked quietly.

"Moravan. It's the capital of Suravia and behind us is the High Stronghold where the High Kings and Queens live," Will explained.

"Why is there more than one ruler?" I asked.

Will scratched his head. "That's how we do it. One ruler is too powerful and we've always believed in the Elements of magic, so it made sense that for five elements there should be five rulers. Plus, five heads are better than one in making decisions. Every one of the five kingdoms have five rulers, except the Ancient Kingdom. It only has one."

I nodded my head. It made a little sense, but I was still confused. "Five elements? There is only four: Earth, Air, Fire, and Water."

Will nodded, "Yes, but there is a fifth one. Life. See, life is its own creation and entity. Those with the element of Life as their guiding power are rare because of the danger they pose. Basic level Life wielders usually become healers or midwives, but Life Sorcerers are even more rare, and are very volatile because of what they represent."

I curiously asked, "What's that?"

The large man looked incredibly sad at this question and bowed his head.

"They hold the power of resurrection and, sometimes, death. There is only one living Life Sorcerer and she is not someone you want to ever meet or piss off. She is the sole ruler of the Ancient Kingdom and she is only that because she killed all the others and their families. No one dares to challenge her rule or authority as sole ruler of the Ancient Kingdom because of her power."

I blinked hard. "Wow. I never knew. My parents never told me about any of this. They never told me about Medeis, actually," I admitted.

Will grunted, "Maybe it was for a good reason."

I let that revelation sink in. A throat cleared from behind us and we both turned. It was Theo and Wynnie standing at the door. We hadn't even heard them approach.

"Breakfast is ready, and we need to get moving if we want to find someone to do the Rite today," Theo said. He seemed a little shy, refusing to look me in the eye. I smiled at him and he looked away quickly, retreating down the steps back into the house.

Wynnie watched him go and huffed, "Men," she muttered something else and shook her head. She had her white-blonde hair tied back up off her face and the braid wrapped into a tight bun at the top. "I'll help you get dressed. This is actually a big deal and the Priestess won't preform the Rite unless you're dressed properly."

I nodded and followed behind her. Will placed his hand on my shoulder and gave me a warm, reassuring smile. "You're going to be fine. Once it's over, we will head straight for the High Stronghold and get you the help you need."

I thanked him and quickly followed Wynnie down back to my room. Theo's masculine, earthy smell still lingered and my heart picked up a pace. Wynnie was already rummaging through my armoire.

"It'll have to be simple. No jewelry, no makeup, your hair down, but frankly I always thought that was a little ridiculous. For most people this is a grand affair. Everyone usually has a feast and party afterwards where people bring gifts that attribute to the Element the person wields. I remember mine!" Wynnie was rambling. I could tell she felt the awkwardness in the room and was attempting to cover it with girl talk. Something I didn't know she could do. Last night had been a rollercoaster, but even that didn't compare to how odd Wynnie had struck me. She was so ready to jump to violence, or something gruesome but here she was now flicking through soft satins and cottons.

Did everyone here have some horrible history there were trying to cover? Did she think something happened between me and Theo? Was she possibly even jealous? I went to sit on the bed and waited.

"I was so excited. I had mine back home in Maravette, the Air Kingdom. No one was surprised when I came back with an Air stone. My mother was absolutely thrilled because her mother had been an Air wielder and I was named after her. Dad really didn't care. He was already lining up hundreds of suitors to marry me off to. He spent a lot of money that night on a grand ball. It was funny though, that was the same night I ran away for the Elite Guard and never went back." A sudden air sadness crossed her blue eyes but, like a flowing river, the sadness passed by and suddenly disappeared.

"What were your parents?" she asked me, attempting to change the subject she had chosen.

"Earth witches. Mom stuck to plants and herbs. My dad was all about rocks and the ground," I explained.

Wynnie nodded, "That's sounds about right. Well, then it's probably a good chance you will be an Earth witch, so be ready for that."

I nodded. "How exactly does this Rite work?"

Wynnie pulled out three simple dresses that she approved of and began laying them out on the bed. "You walk up to the Priestess and ask to perform the Rite of Understanding. She will take you into a room with five stones and recite an incantation. You will kind of go into a trance of sorts as the spell is meant to reveal what is inside your heart and soul and not so much your head. When I did it, the white stone that represents Air started singing to me. I still remember that little tune because I had never heard it before and have never heard it since."

She paused for a moment and attempted to hum. "No, that's still not right. I can hear it in my head, but I can never get it to come out of my mouth. Anyway, when you come to yourself, you will be standing before the stone of your Element and the Priestess will ask you to take it. If you can hold the stone in your hand without it shattering, that is your Element. If your family is waiting for you, she will come out of the temple and make a huge announcement. If not, she will say a few sweet prayers to the Mother in your honor and send you home."

That didn't seem that hard. I wasn't sure why Ez was making a big deal about it.

"Is there anything that could make it dangerous for someone?" I asked.

Wynnie stood up straight and stared me in the eye.

"Well, yes actually. It can be hard for some people, mostly because they don't fully understand themselves. A few stubborn idiots attempt to reject their Element and unfortunately that's not really allowed. It tears up their mind and rips their soul. I've only seen one boy go through it. Allegedly, he had already determined he wanted to be a Fire wielder, but when his element came up Water, he rejected it and refused to approach the stone. The incantation tried to force him to accept the Water stone and when he attempted to grab the Fire stone, it destroyed him. From what I understand, he physically recovered but mentally, well…"

She got another faraway look in her eye. "Mentally he was never really right again. See, when you reject who you are, the magic strips you of what you were given. It's as if it feels you are ungrateful and takes it back in a very savage way. No one understands why it's done this way or why the magic is so vindictive, but we are always taught that you are given your Element for a reason, so don't question it."

I sat there, stunned into silence as I thought about what she was saying. Wynnie snapped back into the present and grinned, a wicked thing it was.

"Don't worry about that though. If you're going home, it doesn't matter what your Element is. You just need to do it and get it over with. Just remember to breathe and listen to what calls to you the most," she explained.

I nodded my understanding slowly and turned my attention to the dresses she had laid it for me. "Which one do you want to wear? All of these are plain enough to please the Priestess, so take your pick," she motioned for me to come forward.

I ran my hand over the soft fabrics looking over the rainbow of hues presented before me. "Yellow, it's my favorite color," I answered.

Wynnie gave a stifled squeal, "This will look amazing, good choice! I'll find some matching slippers and we'll go down to breakfast. Go ahead and clean up in the bathroom. Remember, no make-up, no jewelry and hair must be brushed and loose."

I acknowledged my orders and took the dress into the bathroom with me. The dress was pretty. It was a simple yellow shift. The neckline hung in a sensible U-shape that reached down to cover my cleavage without revealing anything. The bodice was very form-fitting but hung at a more comfortable shape beginning at my hips in an A-line style. There was a simple dark yellow cord that served as a type of belt, tightening my waistline.

No adornments, no lavish jewelry. Just how I liked it. I brushed through my hair and let it fall all the way down, reaching the middle of my back.

Wynnie was waiting on me with some simple yellow ballet type slippers. "My, if someone isn't a daffodil personified!"

I gave her a shy smile and accepted the shoes.

"Ready to eat? The guys are all ready to leave and you haven't even had some bread to put in your stomach. You're going to need your energy. Sometimes the Rite can take a little longer than excepted and the incantation is a little taxing on a person," Wynnie explained. This sudden turn in helpfulness was a little worrisome, but maybe she too was coming around to trusting me. We weren't friends by any means but it was a start to at least be friendly.

I looped my arm through the elbow that she had waiting for me and together we descended the stairs. Three chairs pushed back as we came around the corner to enter the dining room and all three men turned to watch me walk in. Tim and Will both grinned and Will came around the table to pull out a seat for us. Wynnie bowed her head in thanks and ushered me to the table.

"Well, gentlemen, how does our little wayward witch look for her Rite?" Wynnie asked, bouncing in her seat gaily.

Will let out a hearty "Hear, hear." Tim lifted a glass in my direction in a toast. I blushed slightly and sat down at the table.

"Theo? Nothing to say?" Wynnie eyed him shrewdly.

"What? Oh, you look fine," he said offhandedly.

I turned to look at Theo who was staring at his plate as though the bacon was the most interesting piece of bacon in the world. My heart fell a half an inch, but I shrugged it off.

A brief silence filled the room but was instantly cut off by Theo leaning back and looking to Will.

"So, what did the great and powerful Rulers have to say last night to Wynnie's report?" His change of subject was enough to give a person whiplash. Will, whose drink glass was covering most of his face, shook his head in an annoyance at the young man who was obviously avoiding something about me.

"Nothing that wasn't expected. They weren't thrilled the Nandina was killed and I'm sure your father is going to be calling on you soon. Your mother was slightly interested in Mia here, but I told them it was ongoing, and we would inform them more after we had finished our investigation of the situation," Will replied.

I set my fork down, "Did they say they would help?"

Will's eyes grew a little sad. "I didn't tell them anything more than we had found a lost stranger in the woods up north and that you might have some important information for us. I didn't feel like involving everyone just now was the right thing to do. Best not get in over our heads if nothing can be done just yet."

Hope drained from me. This was getting really depressing.

"Hey, cheer up. You'll more than likely find yourself being interrogated by Queen Felicity within a few hours and then you'll be begging us to bring you back here," Tim flashed me a reassuring grin.

I attempted to give him a smile in return, but it fell too quickly, and I went back to picking at my food.

"I'm not really hungry, can we just go and get this done?" I finally announced.

Will looked to Wynnie and she gave an approving nod. He paused for a moment, drumming his fingers on the table. "Sure, let's get going. We'll all go with you, and then we will head for the High Stronghold afterwards, if you're up for it."

Everyone stood and started making for the door.

"Hold on, let me get my stuff," Wynnie announced and rushed upstairs to her room.

"What stuff?" I asked Tim who was slipping a knife into his belt and another one in his boot.

"Oh, probably just her travel stuff. A few knives, some blow darts, a vial or two of poison, and then more than likely her lock pick kit," he said nonchalantly.

I blinked incredulously. "Poison?" I repeated absolutely flabbergasted.

"Yeah, Wynnie always like to be prepared." Tim winked at me and then turned to shove another knife into another boot. I stood there in shock as Will strapped a sword on his belt, and Theo grabbed one of his own to a sheath on his back. There was more steel in this front hall than I had seen in my entire life, and I was not completely comfortable with it. Eventually, Wynnie rejoined us, but I couldn't find a single weapon on her. Brown leather riding boots that fight tightly against her calf held the bottom half of a tucked in tight pair of pants. Her shirt was also tight to the skin, short sleeved and cut into a sharp V at the neck. If she had anything on her I couldn't see it. Where was she hiding it all?

"Ready?" she asked as we stepped up to the doorframe, not seeming to notice my stares.

"Ready," I replied and warily took her offered arm.

CHAPTER SIX

The Temple was not exactly how I pictured it in my mind. The five of us walked a few streets over before turning into the gated courtyard of a particularly large mansion home that looked no different in design from the townhomes that lined both sides of it.

"Are we here already?" I asked, shocked that this standard looking home was a temple.

"Yep!" Wynnie said excitedly and stopped at the bottom of the stairs leading up to the front door.

The courtyard somehow was incredibly quiet compared to the noise and bustle from the street we had just come from. My guess was magic made it tranquil here. Will smiled and walked up the steps. I went to follow, but Wynnie held me back.

"Once she comes out and Will introduces you, that's when you walk up the steps and say 'I have come to preform my Right of Understanding. Will you help me discover my soul's true destiny?' She will then lead you in and show you to the room. We will be in the waiting room up front when you are done. Most importantly, you must wait until she recites a Closing spell to seal off the initial incantation. If you don't allow her to do this before leaving, your soul will remain open until someone else does it," Wynnie explained.

I nodded and looked up at the door. Theo was standing at my other elbow and I shivered lightly at his proximity.

"Don't be nervous, this is exciting," Tim whispered in my ear from behind.

A tall stately woman emerged from the door and after a few brief words from Will, she nodded in my direction and looked me over once with a judgmental eye. I took a step forward and felt a hand grab at my elbow, pulling me lightly. I paused and turned to see Theo holding me back.

"Mia," he sounded nervous but he was trying to keep an air of uncaring about him, "Please be careful."

I set my foot back down on the ground and held his stare. He seemed genuinely concerned as well as scared. I marveled at this man's ability to hide his emotions, but I still saw right through them. He needed reassurance and I felt obliged to give him that.

"I will, I promise," I said.

Theo nodded and released me. With a cleansing breath, I squared my shoulders and marched up the steps towards the statuesque woman awaiting me. I came upon the last step and made myself look the Priestess in the eye.

"I have come to preform my Rite of Understanding. Will you help me discover my soul's true destiny?" I recited exactly as Wynnie had instructed me.

The Priestess gave a small, comforting smile, and bowed her head in my direction. "Come in, my child and let's hear what the Mother has decided for you." She opened the large oaken door and ushered me inside. I walked forward a few steps and stopped, not sure what to do next.

"Follow me, your friends will be waiting for you in the front. Do you understand what is about to happen?" she asked.

I nodded in affirmation.

"Good, this way then. I can already tell you're going to be an interesting one," she smiled. She led me down a darkened hall to a small wooden door.

I barely noticed the inside of the home; my nervousness gave me laser focus on only one thing: that door. I could tell the house was coated in darker colors of all hues and variation. Curtains and tapestries lined the walls, but I couldn't understand what they depicted or what the art woven into them meant. Probably nothing that would make any sense or difference to me. The Priestess stopped at the door and turned the handle, walking in first.

I followed behind her. This room even darker than the hallway.

"Please stand here and face this wall. Now, take deep breaths while I ready the incantation and prepare myself to guide you through the Rite," she instructed.

I nodded and closed my eyes, centering myself and listening as she bustled around the room lighting certain candles and burning different types of incense. Finally, she settled behind me and put both hands on my shoulders.

"Oh, you're good at that. Barely a waver in your spirit. Now, don't really listen to what I'm saying. Just focus on my voice in general and when you start to fall into the incantation's trance, don't fight it. Remember, this is a process to understand the soul the Mother has given you. There are no lies in here, and if there is anything you are hiding, your spirit will present it to me. Also, do not reject what the Mother shows you, it won't end well. If you are unhappy with what She reveals, that is for you to come to terms with after the Rite."

I nodded my understanding at her instruction.

"Here we go." Her low, melodic voice began chanting an incantation I did not recognize.

Trying to do as told, I focused not on the words, but on the sounds she was making. Within moments I could feel the room begin to spin and my feet became light. I felt myself stumble to the side, but her hands held me in place steadily. I took another breath and relaxed.

Fall into it, relax, and go with it. I reminded myself. I felt the stumble again, but instead of trying to stop it, I fell. I fell into a whirling vortex in my mind devoid of noise, only the feeling of weightlessness. I continued to keep my eyes closed and fought the urge to throw my hands out to catch my fall. I fell for a good while before finally I had a sense of being upright and I heard a voice say, "Open your eyes to your destiny."

I immediately opened my eyes as commanded and before me stood five pedestals, each with their own crystal ranging in different colors.

"Listen and obey!" came another command, but I couldn't tell the direction from which it had come.

I looked over the five crystals, but nothing was calling out to me. I waited for a moment and when nothing changed, I decided I needed to be closer. I was weak at magic, so maybe they couldn't feel my presence enough from this far away. Slowly, I walked to my left and stood in front of a blue stone. As if on cue, four of the five stones all began a low glow from deep within them. White, Blue, Green, and Red: Air, Water, Earth, and Fire. They were all easily recognizable to anyone who lived in a witch's home.

A low hum began and grew louder as I stepped closer and closer. I reached out to touch the green stone, but it shook slightly on its pedestal, so I jerked back and waited. I didn't want anything to happen to me like it had to the boy Wynnie had mentioned earlier. The hum grew slightly louder. I waited for a few moments, and then as suddenly as it began, the humming stopped. All four stones went dark. I stared blankly and wondered what do I do now?

Without warning, the last stone, the yellow stone, sparked to life. An iridescent beam of light pierced its way through the darkness. I smiled and covered my eyes. Of course, it would be the yellow one that lit up for me.

Yellow had always been my favorite color and it now it called to me. There was no song like Wynnie had said she heard, but instead it hummed like electricity. Power emitted from its very core. I reached out and touched the stone. It was warm and it felt good in my hand.

"Amelia," a whisper sounded in my mind.

I whipped my head around. It was the whisper that I had heard on top of the hill when I first arrived. The one that I couldn't find out where it was coming from and had died away so quickly.

"Amelia," it whispered again.

It beckoned me closer and I reached out with both hands. The stone became brighter as I brought it closer to my face. Tendrils of darkness began to creep in on the edges of my mind's eye. I wasn't scared. In fact, they seemed to be guiding my hands to the yellow stone.

"Welcome home," the low voice said in my ear. Suddenly everything exploded.

All at once, the four other stones shattered like glass. I shouted in alarm and fell back dropping the yellow stone to the floor. It didn't shatter as it fell to the ground; it continued to emit bright beams of light. The shards of yellow light took on a life of their own and began twisting their way towards me. They attached themselves to my hands and began crawling up my arms.

It was still warm and even though a part of me was freaking out, I couldn't stop them. I didn't want to. The light snaked up my head, tickled my forehead, and began caressing the entire length of my body. I almost giggled when it touched a certain rib on my right side.

Eventually my whole body was ensconced in the warm light. I gazed in wonder at the bright colors and dancing entity as it twisted and stroked my fingers and arms. It was like a huge hug and I smiled longingly. Enthralled, I never even noticed the figure of the Priestess as she came in front of me and placed her hands around my throat.

The pressure was gentle at first, almost unrecognizable, but as the light began to recede from my body, I felt the pressure grow greater. Finally, as if my brain turned back on, I could feel the throttle of her hands completely around my neck, attempting to squeeze the air from my throat. My lungs were already screaming, and my body suddenly began to thrash around in response.

"No!" she shouted, and I kicked out, knocking over two of the pedestals beside me.

I gasped and clawed at her hands.

"It cannot be!" she shouted at my face, terror filling her eyes. Panic welled up inside of me as every instinct took over to live. I flung out my arms scratching her cheek weakly with my nails. The whole room was beginning to go dark as I struggled against her. A loud crash sounded behind us.

"What in the Mother's name is going on in here?" I heard a voice shout overhead.

The Priestess wouldn't let me go. I could feel that I was nearing the edge of unconsciousness. All at once I heard another loud commotion and air rushed into my lungs again and I fell to the ground coughing and gasping loudly.

"Seal her soul!" I heard Wynnie shout. I could tell the Priestess was sobbing as she performed the Closing enchantment. Two strong and warm arms lifted me carefully and before I could open my eyes to see what was going on, they carried me away.

"It's okay. You're safe now, Mia. I've got you," his steady voice said.

It was Theo's whispering in my ear as he ran out of the temple and onto the street. I moaned in response and curled up into his strong chest. I could hear his heartbeat racing as he hurried me back to the Safehouse.

"You're safe now. I've got you." His words were the only ones I heard, and I melted into them. My body was exhausted, between the Rite enchantments and then nearly being strangled, I could barely keep my eyes open.

"Tim! Get Ez!" Theo thundered. He kicked the front door in with a crash and I grabbed onto his shirt tightly with both hands, shutting my eyes even tighter.

I barely bounced in his embrace as he leapt up the stairs with as much grace as he could muster. I guess our door was already open because the next thing I felt was him laying me down on the bed. I started to open my eyes and look at him.

"She," I started to mumble, but the fire on my damaged throat prevented more from coming out without a racking cough.

"Shh, don't speak. Let Ez see you before you try to use your voice," he whispered. He knelt onto the bed and pulled me up into his lap. I snuggled close into him and breathed deeply. Another cough shook me.

"I'll kill her for trying to hurt you," he promised to me quietly. I didn't even know how to respond to that, so I just remained silent and tried to catch my breath.

Footsteps pounded up the stairs and Ez shouted from the hallway.

"I need water boiled immediately and I need someone to light the fire in her room so I can see better," she barked her orders to everyone in the house that would listen. I peeked my eyes open to see her come flying in. She was a vision of emeralds in the beautiful gown she was wearing.

"Lay her down flat. Don't let her move her neck too much. What the hell happened to her?" Ez demanded as she set her bag down and pulled Theo away from me.

He refused to budge and made Ez move herself to the other side of the bed to examine me. I reluctantly let Theo go and allowed myself to be laid down flat with no pillow under my head.

"The Priestess was trying to choke her to death. Mia was in the middle of the Rite when we heard a crash. Will and I ran in to find the Priestess standing over her with her hands around her neck. Mia wasn't fighting very much, so the Priestess had to have attacked her while still in the middle of the Rite," Theo informed her.

Ez's hand moved away from my throat to my hands.

"Oh, she fought alright. Look at the blood underneath her fingernails. Mia here got that Priestess good from the looks of it!" I could hear the grin in Ez's voice.

There was more footsteps and Tim entered the room with a blazing tea kettle, followed by Will and Wynnie.

"Will, light that fire for me so I can see her better."

Will flicked a hand in the direction of the fireplace and a blazing fire roared to life.

"Not that hot! You don't want her to sweat to death," she snapped. The fire suddenly burned lower and Wynnie cracked the window. Cool restorative air flowed into the room and filled my lungs, it dried the clamminess that had settled over my skin when my heart rate had dropped from the suffocation.

"Okay Mia, I'm going to place my hands on your neck and touch it very lightly. Let me know if it hurts and where," Ez instructed.

Two cool, strong hands delicately stroked parts of my throat and I winced at the tenderness around my trachea. Ez continued to the back of my neck where some muscles were seizing up.

"I think she's going to be okay. Nothing looks like it's in the wrong direction. Her breathing is even, and it's not twisted like anything is cracked or punctured. She is going to be sore and her voice will be a little damaged for a day or two, but overall, I think she fought hard enough to make it out," Ez smiled.

A huge breath of relief was heard throughout the entire room.

"I'm going to leave some pain remedies and a few tea bags to relax her neck, so the pain doesn't get worse, and a few for swelling. Make sure she takes them as needed and don't be a hero, Mia," she warned, giving me a raised eyebrow.

"No need to be in pain or discomfort. If these aren't doing it for you, send someone for stronger stuff and I may even do a Pain Free Charm to get you through the night."

I gave her a single small nod to let her know I understood.

"Go ahead and sit her up but keep a pillow behind her head. Don't move her around too much. No talking for the rest of the day and tonight. You can try out your voice in the morning, but I swear to the Mother if I hear you attempting to warble a tune in the bath, I'll come finish the job myself," she laughed.

Theo gave her a dark glare, "That's not funny, Ez."

Ez brushed him off. "It will be in a few days. I'm just ahead of my time." With a wink, she exited the room in the same flowing fashion she had entered. Theo leaned over me and came into my line of vision.

"I'm going to lift you up now and get your teas ready."

Will came around my other side and each one grabbed a half of me. Like a ragdoll, I was sat up in the bed. Wynnie stuffed a plethora of blankets and pillows around me to make sure I was comfortable. Tim handed me a steaming cup of tea with the teabags Ez left for me. The warmth felt good on my fingers and I took a single sip, instantly coughing from the heat on my sore throat.

"So, now that we know she's going to live, does someone want to tell me what in the name of the Mother just happened?" Theo rounded on everyone in the room and a dark cloud swept over the group.

Will stepped forward blocking Tim and Wynnie.

"Theo, calm down. No one here did anything wrong and we are just as furious as you. Wynnie has the Priestess locked up in a chamber in the temple under guard. We were going to head back to interrogate her the instant we knew Mia was going to make it. We will get answers and she will be handled."

Theo backed down and took in a breath. "Sorry, sorry," he muttered. Will gave him an understanding look and placed a hand on his shoulder.

"Relax, Theo. The maid will look after Amelia for a minute and get her whatever she needs. We three are going to see the Priestess now."

Theo's head shot up. "No! I want to be there. I want to hear this excuse for attacking a helpless witch!"

Wynnie shook her head. "I'm going to agree with Will on this one. The moment we know anything, I will send Tim with information to give you answers. Every question will be asked." A shadow fell across the beautiful woman's eyes before she continued. "And every question WILL be answered to my satisfaction."

I shivered at the threat. I could only imagine the ways in which sweet, innocent looking Wynnie could get her answers.

Theo nodded, "There better be some good ones for this."

Everyone stood in agreeing silence and then, with a gesture from Will, they were gone with Wynnie in the lead. I watched them leave, the tea cooling in my hands. Theo didn't even wait for them to leave the room before he rounded on me and started fussing like a mother hen.

"Are you okay? Do you need anything? What can I get you?" He hovered over me, looking over my entire frame, at the suffocating concoction of fluffiness that was pillows. I shook my head slowly.

"Are you comfortable?"

Again, I shook my head and began to move a pillow away from me.

"Here, let me get that," Theo was flustered but he removed the pillow for me and I leaned back much more comfortable .

He reached over me carefully and started removing some of the blankets tucked up under my legs. I shifted around, attempting to help him, when he placed a hand on my chest and gently pushed me back. "Don't move, let me do it."

I stopped and allowed for this pressure of his hand on me to lay me back against the headboard. Why did this sudden, gentle touch make my heart flutter?

"Why?" I choked out suddenly, unable to control my curiosity any longer.

"I don't know why she attacked you, but Wynnie will get you answers. Don't worry about that, she's good at her job." Theo didn't look at me as he answered but I shook my head.

"Why are you worried about me?" I asked very slowly. I took it one word at a time. Theo waited patiently for me to finish.

He stiffened, "I," he stuttered and then looked at me honestly.

"I don't know," Theo sighed heavily and sat down on the bed, dropping his head to his hands.

"I felt it," Theo finally whispered after a moments tense silence.

"I felt her hurting you. I felt your fear. I felt your pain. I felt all of it." My eyes widened in surprise. This wasn't what I was expecting to hear from him.

"And when I did, I felt this overwhelming urge, this absolute desire to make it stop. To fix it, to rescue you. I mean, I naturally like helping others. Righting wrongs, and defending people, but not like this. The entire sprint down the hallway to get to you felt like I was being torn up inside. I just had to get to you, to get you out of there." I remained absolutely still.

"I've been scared in my life. Scared I wouldn't amount to much, scared of my father. I've been worried I've made the right choice, worried that people will talk about me if what I do isn't exactly right. But for the first time in my life today," he lifted his head and met my eyes, his green swimming with emotion. "I felt terrified. And then I saw you fighting her, I saw you limp on the floor and this overwhelming agony just jumped and I grabbed you and ran. I'm sure I'll pay for snapping at Will later, but right now, I just have to make sure you are okay."

I slowly nodded, acting as if I understood.

With a quick slap to his leg and a jump Theo sprung to his feet and held out his hand.

"I'll help you get into the bath and have a maid bring in more hot water for another tea," he said gently.

It took me a moment to realize what he was suggesting. Was he trying to help me bathe? I vehemently shook my head and began swinging my now free legs around to get off the bed. He moved to set me back down, but I smacked his hands away and gave him a warning glare. I don't care what kind of crazy emotions he had going on concerning me, but that was not happening.

"Okay then. What do you want me to do?" he asked.

I firmly pointed to the door and then at his stomach just as it let out a large rumble of hunger that I'm positive Ez could hear if she had her window open next door. Theo chuckled to himself and lazily scratched the back of his head.

"I guess I didn't eat that much this morning, but neither did you. I'll go get us something while you bathe and get dressed." I nodded in agreement and Theo turned to leave the room, shutting the door for privacy behind him.

I took a quick bath. I didn't want Theo to panic that I was taking too long and barge in on me naked and wet. In his exhaustive state of emotions, I wasn't exactly sure what he deemed as the demarcation line of appropriateness. I also wasn't willing to test its limits either.

As I patted my hair dry, I sat down at the wingback chair beneath the window and looked out. It was only midday and the streets below were teeming with merchants, buyers, and passersby. No one seemed to even realize what was going on in the world around them. Everyone had a purpose here in this world and they looked happy.

I realized I had not seen even one homeless beggar, a child in scant clothes, or even anyone who looked remotely angry. It was if they were blissfully living an existence that was unfamiliar with the sadness of life. I would miss this world when I went back to mine, but I did miss my life there.

I started thinking about our house, would anyone have reported us missing yet? I thought about Rebekah, she would have at least tried calling me by now. Her curiosity probably wouldn't peak for at least one more day, it wasn't even twenty-four hours since I'd been gone yet.

Hopefully, now that this whole Rite ordeal was over, Will would take me to the High Rulers and we could get my parents back and I could head home. My eyes welled up at the thought of my parents. Were they okay? Where were they? Would I see them again?

Sorrow gripped my heart as the tears fell silently to my lap. I suddenly didn't want to be alone. When I heard footsteps making their way up the wooden staircase I didn't wipe away my tears. Without words, I looked at Theo and his face fell as he saw the tears that etched a river down my face.

"Are you in pain?" he asked quickly, and I shook my head.

Theo walked across the room and knelt in front of me, grabbed my hands, and looked deep into my eyes.

"My parents," I croaked out and bowed my head, trying to stem the new flow of tears.

"Oh," he muttered and began stroking the back of my hand with his thumb. "You miss them?"

I nodded vigorously and made a shuddering gasp to catch my breath.

"You're worried about them?"

Again, I nodded.

Without thinking, Theo scooped me up in his arms and sat down in the chair I had occupied.

"We will find them, Mia. I promise." He tucked my head under his chin and held me close as I continued to cry into his shirt, clutching at the fabric. We sat there for a moment, him stroking my hair and me sobbing like an idiot.

We stayed like this for a while, until my tears stopped flowing and I sat up wiping them away. This change in Theo was sudden, but I was grateful for it. I liked the compassionate and understanding man that held me close way more than a hard-hearted suspicious warrior from last night.

"You get dressed, I forgot to make you more tea. I'll be back up in a moment, go ahead and start eating too."

I took a deep breath and searched through the armoire for something to wear. I heard his footsteps quietly leave. The room must have figured out my favorite colors, because now only blues and yellows remained.

I selected a dark blue dress that was light to the touch. Two straps held the heart shaped bodice up that led into a loose but comfortable skirt. As I checked the fit in a mirror, I heard voices below and went to the top of the stairs to see who was talking.

"Wynnie is a little upset she didn't get to even start before the Priestess confessed everything," Tim's' voice floated from the front door.

I hurried down the steps and found them in the front room. Tim was removing his cloak and Theo was shutting the door behind him. I knocked on the door and both men turned to see me waiting for them to let me in.

"Mia, Tim just got back, and he says he's got some news about the Priestess' interrogation," Theo explained.

I nodded and took a seat next to Tim. Theo pulled one of the cups from the tray and handed it to me.

"You're looking much better. I was just telling Theo that Wynnie is beside herself. She didn't get to exact revenge for you in the end," Tim began.

I blinked twice, floored that Wynnie was so bent out of shape at not getting to torture someone.

"Tell us everything," Theo prompted.

Tim nodded and shook his shaggy head. "There really isn't that much to tell. The Priestess was waiting for us in the room we had locked her in, pretty calmly if you ask me, but that didn't last long. Wynnie is kind of known throughout all five kingdoms as something of a sadist, so when she realized that's who would be questioning her, she crumbled. Her story is that she did it to save you."

Theo and I blinked in disbelief.

"Save her? How could killing someone save them?" Theo shouted.

"That's what Wynnie asked and the answer was simple. You see, Mia, what she saw during your Rite scared her senseless. It seems as though your Element is Life," Tim said.

I blinked again, clearly lost in the novelty of the statement.

"But not just any Life wielder. You're a Sorcerer," Tim explained.

The conversation with Will that morning on the roof came flooding back. I remembered his every word: "There's only one living Life Sorcerer and she is not someone you want to ever meet or piss off. She is the sole ruler of the Ancient Kingdom and she's only that because she killed all the others and their families. No one dares to challenge her rule or authority because of her power."

"That's not possible," Theo began, then shot me a nervous glance. "I'm not saying she's helpless, but she is no Sorcerer."

"That's what the Priestess saw," Tim disagreed, "Apparently, the Life stone reacted so strongly to Mia's presence that it actually began consuming her and trying to mold itself into her magic."

They both looked at me and I had to reluctantly nod my head.

"The Priestess was terrified of not just having another Life Sorcerer alive and one that powerful, but of what Heretia would do to her if she ever found out. She concluded that Heretia would discover the truth and start asking questions, probably coming to the Priestess herself. You know how that usually goes." Tim pulled a thumb across his neck. "She claims that she was doing it not only to protect herself, but Mia, too, from what would happen to her if Heretia every got ahold of her. Allegedly, it's to protect the kingdoms from a war that Heretia would wage to eliminate the Life Sorcerer."

Theo slumped back in his chair and gripped his knees tightly with both hands. Sensing his struggle to not haul off and go kill the Priestess himself, I placed one gentle hand upon his knee to calm him. Without looking at me, he covered my hand with his and squeezed. The action did not go unnoticed by Tim, who raised an eyebrow.

"So, what does Mia do now? What is Will going to do about it?" Theo asked.

I had a few more things to say about that, but they could wait for now. I returned my attention to Tim who was still going on about the conversation between them and the errant Priestess.

"Will is sending the Priestess away to Maravette. She begged him for mercy and asked to be cast out quietly. She doesn't want Heretia finding her now that Amelia lived. I think Will is inclined to do so and quickly. He will go before the High Rulers tonight and present his case, asking for their cooperation in not only getting rid of the Priestess, but quickly helping Mia to find her parents and get out of Medeis before all hell breaks loose. I think it's safe to say that they will be keen on doing just that if what the Priestess claims is true. I have no reason to not believe her at this point. It makes sense really," Tim explained.

I gave him a quizzical look.

"I mean, look at the facts. No one has seen or heard of a Life Sorcerer in over twenty years. It's practically gone extinct. Before that, they weren't everywhere, but they weren't unheard of either. People could go to the Life Sorcerer if they needed to question a dead person briefly. They could summon spirits that had departed for information and gain wisdom from ancient rulers. They were also the keepers of knowledge as they wrote almost everything down. Creating volumes of accurate history because they had spoken to those who had been there. They had the ability to be impervious to magic that could control the mind or a whole person, so they were excellent at going into situations where one might be in danger of manipulation by magic," Tim continued.

I wasn't quite sure what that meant but decided not to worry about it.

"Life Sorcerers were also Proctor's of clinics and amazing healers," he went on. "Ez can take herbs and spells and help people with them through a little determination, but Life Sorcerers could just lay their hands-on people and they were healed of just about anything. Then suddenly, after Heretia took power in the Ancient Kingdom, they just stopped appearing. The ones that were alive either disappeared or they dwindled away."

Theo reached over and handed me a bowl of stew that had cooled down enough to not rip my throat to shreds.

"That's all well and good, but that still doesn't justify what that woman did to Mia. I want to see some punishment and I will have it," Theo said defiantly.

Tim raised an eyebrow again, clearly wondering about Theo's sudden change in disposition towards me. "That's not for us to decide. It's for the High Rulers to decide after they take Will's recommendation and he's going to say to send here away quickly and quietly."

Theo stood and paced the room, running his olive-skinned hand through his chocolate brown hair. His green eyes glinted with anger and frustration.

"Then I'm going, too. My father will hear me out," Theo announced.

Tim turned in his chair and shook his head. "What is your father going to care about your opinion on what's to be done? He never has before."

It sounded like Tim was purposefully prodding Theo at this point.

"Well, he's going to listen to me now if I have to lock him a room and make him hear me out," Theo thundered back.

"There will be no Varillian confrontation tonight." Will's booming voice interjected and the three of us jumped, not having noticed Will come in.

"Where's Wynnie?" Tim looked around his Captain for her.

Will went silent as his eyes darkened. "Wynnie is, well, taking it hard," he replied and turned away from the conversation. I was puzzled at this, but it wasn't my place, nor was I in any position to speak up about it.

"I've sent word to the High Rulers about what's happened and I'm going to meet with them tonight. I would think this would be the thing to get them to see you, Mia. So, let's all just rest up for the reminder of the day. It's barely even lunch and a lot has happened. I actually have errands to run in town, blacksmith and such, so if anyone wants to go with me you can. I thought about hitting the barber too on my way back in." Will scratched at his bushy beard that seemed to be bothering him.

Tim jumped up and so did I. I felt like getting out of here. My voice may not work very well, but my legs did, and they needed stretching.

Theo grabbed my hand and spun me towards him. "Where do you think you're going? Ez said to rest."

I pulled away from him gently, seeing the worry cross over his face. I pointed to the sun and then to my throat. All three men blinked at me confused. I rolled my eyes in annoyance. I needed the sun to feel better, it always did and I figured it could only do me good now.

Tim cleared his throat. The noise made everyone turn to look at him. "You are a Life Sorcerer, Mia. You don't have to keep quiet anymore." I stared blinkingly at him, not understanding what he was hinting at.

"You can heal yourself," he continued. I jumped at the realization of this ability that I should have now. I looked down at my hands and marveled. Could I really do it? But how? As I stood there, worrying over how I could ever manage this I watched Theo's strong tanned hands cover mine. They gently squeezed my own and I looked up at him. Instantly, my fear settled, and I relaxed into his grip.

"We can't help you with this, we don't know anything about it. There will be no one to teach you so you're going to have to go with your gut on this one. Just touch your throat and see what you can do." I nodded and removed one hand, touching my throat. Taking a breath and closing my eyes, I waited. The medical part of me envisioned the muscles of my throat and the damage that was done to them by the Priestess. I saw the bruising that would be there, the muscles contracting and becoming stressed.

As I thought about all that might be wrong inside my throat, I felt my hand warm up. The feeling escalated and began seeping into my skin. The warmth felt good and I thought about what that warmth could do. It could reduce the swelling, remove the bruises, relax the muscles. I physically could feel my throat listening to my wishes and my throat loosened, the pain went away and my whole body relaxed.

As I breathed a sigh of relief, pride swelled up inside of me and I opened my eyes.

"Did it work?" Will asked, suddenly extremely interested. He had come closer and was looking me over carefully. Theo quickly took his other hand from mine and the loss of his warmth was heavy on my heart. I smiled, however and opened my mouth.

"I don't know. You tell me." I asked with a clear and steady voice. Tim's smile cracked wide open and he gave a hearty laugh.

"Look at you!" he clapped his hands together and came to give me a congratulatory slap on the shoulder.

"I guess we do have a Life Sorcerer on our hands after all. This will certainly help your case with the High Rulers." Will leaned back up and crossed his arms, but his eyes were twinkling with excitement.

"Well, now that Mia's all better, let's go. I need to get a new string for my bow, and I think Franklin's working today. I don't like his son touching my stuff." Tim moved to grab his weapon that was resting by the front door. Will snorted, "Give the kid a break. He's still learning." Tim didn't even look back as he slung the bow across his chest.

"I get that, but it doesn't mean I want him touching my second most prized possession." I furrowed my brow and Tim winked at me. Instantly I caught his meaning and rolled my eyes.

"I gave you a chance, didn't I?" Will called after him as we all walked out the front door.

"But I was a natural! Franklin's kid is a little lacking. He's been apprenticing for four years and I still find fault in his work. If I was still struggling to hit my target after four years you would have kicked me out of the Guard and sent me home, begging my nephew for help." I watched as the two of them walked ahead of the now silent Theo.

I could tell his public display of softness had not gone unnoticed by the other two and he was probably struggling with that internally. He seemed to care a lot about the image people had of him and that no one ever questioned it. How would his sudden turn regarding me look? The anxiety came off of him in waves, so I decided to take his mind of it.

"So, umm, how did the Elite Guard get started?" I asked casually as we headed down the street behind the two bickering Guardsmen.

"Will's father started it. He had been a son of a general and Will's grandfather had directed him to create a small Elite reconnaissance team his home country of Elevetia could use in emergencies. It really stuck and other kingdoms would call to use them for certain problems that required finesse. Thefts, transport guards, fact finding missions, kidnapping recoveries. Situations where expertise was needed but in small, quiet numbers. Will grew up watching them leave for missions and wanting to go. Finally, when he was sixteen his dad let him. After a few years, his father retired and one by one, so did the original Elite Guard. He picked each one of us up as needed and now here we are." Theo seemed to relax as telling the history of the Guard took his mind off his own ego for a moment.

"How old are each of you? I know you said you were twenty-five," I remembered. I kept going, this seemed to be helping his mood greatly.

"Will is thirty-two, Tim is twenty-four and joined at the same time as me. Wynnie, however, is twenty. She only came to us two years ago and it shows. She still has a lot to learn, but her predecessor wasn't even as good as she is at the job, so Will let a lot of her behavior slip at first. Now, it's like reigning in a wet cat to get her to behave sometimes. However, all you have to do it point to a building and she can get you in there, no questions," Theo shrugged his shoulders.

"So how did he find all of you? Put out an advertisement? Head hunting?"

Theo shook his head and glanced at Will who was way ahead of us but had stopped to look over a booth full of leather material.

"We each found him, actually. Tim needed to get out of Lotho. When his much older sister, one of the High Queens, died Tim's nephew took the throne." I nodded.

"They don't get along?" I asked but Theo shot that down with a shake of his head.

"No, Tim and Tom get along great. In fact, they are more like friends than uncle and nephew. Tom is only a year younger than Tim. It was a whole mess apparently when his sister turned up pregnant at sixteen and Tom was sent away as a baby until she came to the throne and demanded him back. They were best friends growing up. But when she died, a lot of people thought that since Tom was illegitimate, that Tim should take it. Tim never wanted it, and so, to make it easier on his friend, he heard about the Elite Guard and left."

"What about Wynnie? She was talking about her family earlier before the Rite, but it seemed like an unhappy situation," Theo huffed.

"Wynnie is tough. Not just physically and mentally, but her history is as well. I know you don't know anything about them, but she comes from the Lily family. They are the most powerful, non-Royal family in Maravette. They own mines and business all around their country and practically half the land. Wynnie was born the third of three children, one boy and two girls. Each child was expected to grow up and perform for the family. Her brother was to take over the business and the two girls were to marry well, possibly even royally, to keep the family powerful. They got their wish with her sister who married into the Royal Family there when Wynnie was seventeen, not even six months before Rite ceremony. When it came time for her to be Rited, she was already feeling the pressure."

Theo's eyes darkened as he relayed the next part of Wynnie's story. We had come to the booth both Tim and Will were at. Will seemed to be in a heavy bidding war for some piece of leather with another customer and no one was paying us any attention.

"She came home and instead of being happy she was a Sorcerer, not just a wielder like her sister, her father literally turned around and announced the asking price for her hand had doubled due to her power status." My heart fell, poor Wynnie. For her own father to treat her like some cattle for sell to the highest bidder must have been a huge betrayal.

"She had wrestled with who she was for so long. She had always been compared to her perfect sister and always found lacking. Apparently, fighting was the only thing she was better at and instead of garnering their love and attention, it just made them see dollar signs. I guess she snapped that night and in the early hours of the morning she snuck off. It took her a day to get to the border with the horse she had stolen and then another to find us," Theo suddenly smiled to himself.

"I still remember her riding up. She was so tiny, so dirty but dressed in this jeweled gown and all her pockets and bags lined to the stitching with jewels and gold. She offered to pay to get into the Elite Guard. Of course, Will sent her away at first but she kept coming back. Over and over, she showed up. Day after day. Each day with new clothes and a new weapon she had bought with the gold. Finally, Will let her try an obstacle course. He did need someone her size. She passed with flying colors and Will let her in. Will then made her take all the money and put it away, never to touch it again until she decided to retire."

I joined in his smile. I liked to hear the story of Wynnie's tenacity. I wish I were as brave as her, but I had planned to move back in with my parents the moment I could. Being on my own had terrified me, but Wynnie. She had run away at barely eighteen and never gone back.

We were finally moving on from the stalls and heading to an actual building with smoke and dust billowing from the large open double doored entryway. This must be the blacksmith they had wanted to see. Tim waved to us and took off across the street to another store front, pulling his bow off as he did.

"I guess you're going to ask about me, next?" Theo asked and leaned against the doorframe of the blacksmith's, crossing his arms.

I shook my head, "Not really, I figured if you wanted to tell me you would." I looked in the building and decided staying on the street was best. It was dark inside and filled to the brim with burning hot fireplaces and loud crashing metal banging into each other.

Theo smirked, "You think you're sneaky, but I see through it. You're about as sneaky as a cow on a cobblestone street." My face fell, I wasn't expecting to hear that phrase. Theo straightened up from his place at the door.

"What?" he looked around quickly. "What's wrong?" the alarm rose in his voice.

"That phrase, my mother used to say it all the time to me when I came downstairs in the morning." I answered him. Theo's shoulders relaxed.

"Yeah, so? I wasn't trying to be mean."

"No, it's just…mortals don't say that because they don't have cobblestone streets anymore. My mother was the only one who ever said it to me."

My shoulders sagged. "You're just confirming my suspicions that my parents actually came from here, and not just Medeis, but Suravia itself. I just wish they had told me instead of lying all these years." I turned away from Theo and went to go sit down on a simple wood bench set up outside the noisy shop.

"I'm sure they had their reasons. A lot of parents do. We can ask them when we find them," Theo attempted to reassure me.

"But when will that be? Here I am, walking around in the sun when they could be held up in some dank dungeon being tortured." I fought the fear and anxiety back. Pulling strength from the noonday sun as it beat down on my head.

"Hey." Theo grabbed my hand again. I felt the shock of our skin touching once more but didn't pull away this time. I waited as I felt it move slowly up my arm.

"We're going to find them. My father will listen now. You're a Life Sorcerer you are definitely a commodity to him now. Don't worry."

This did make me pull away from him.

"A commodity? I'm not an item, Theo. I'm a person and so are my parents." I stood in defiance and stared down at him.

"I know that, you know that. Everyone knows that, but my father doesn't. He's sees people as expendable. If they are useful to him, he keeps them around and safe, the moment you aren't useful, he ignores you. Trust me, I know." Theo stood with me and turned me to face him.

"You ready to hear my story? Well, here it is. I'm a prince, only son to two of the thrones. I have no choice. I have to take a throne when one of my parents die. There's only one of me, so my choice was made for me when my twin sisters died hours after birth," he explained.

I winced at this, no one liked to hear of babies dying, and me especially. Having studied with Rebekah, who longed to be a midwife, I had heard nothing but the wonders of babies. Pictures of happy smiling chubby cheeks had lined our dorm room walls.

"My mother died emotionally that day as well, and all but abandoned me to the whims of my father who had always seen me as weak and less than. He took my care for people, my passion for helping, and he used it against me. He punished me for being soft on people, he took my things away for not always being in time, being perfect or doing what he thought was the right thing. I grew up always in fear of not being perfect, of not getting it right," he admitted.

My heart bled for him, that was not a way for a kid to grow up.

"As much as he hated me, he had to see me as useful to him. It made me hate everything about the High Stronghold, the only thing that held me together was Ez. Her mother is one of the other Queens and she was in the exact opposite problem to me. There was only one throne and three sisters to compete with. Ez happily removed herself from the equation, and when she left, so did I. I couldn't take it without the only person who I could talk to. She was like the sister I never got to have, so I left out and went to go find Will. He was in Lotho at that time, so I went there and begged for a spot. Luckily, the only thing that I was glad my father did was train me to fight." Theo straightened his back and looked out over my head.

"A good King is also a good Soldier. So, he forced me onto the training grounds when I was only eight. I trained with the best from every kingdom. I had even met Will a few years before I was eighteen, and had dreamed of being in the Elite Guard since then. I was so happy when Will said I was the best he had ever seen, and I've been with him since." Theo hung his head again and I took a step back.

"So yes, I get why you're mad at being told you're a commodity. Because I was one for eighteen years. And I will be one again one day, and I hate it. But that's all we are, Mia. Commodities. We might as well be the best one to them while we have to be."

CHAPTER SEVEN

It was hours later before we all finally got back to the Safehouse, goods in tow. Tim was still gushing over his new bow string, stroking it lovingly.

"If that's how you treat your second favorite most prized possession, I wonder how you ever get anything done at all." I joked out loud as we poured in the door. Will and Theo burst into a hearty round of laughter and fell over on the couch in the front room.

"No seriously guys, look at this craftmanship. I knew, Phillip was going to be something one day. He puts his dad to shame!" Tim flaunted the bow again and Will kept chuckling.

"I thought you were never going to let him touch your stuff again and it always had flaws?" he prodded in good fun. Tim pouted and turned his back on us.

"Well, I can't always be right, now can I? Even a blind horse can find its way to water at least once if it keeps going straight." Tim stormed up the stairs in an attempt to escape our raucous laughter. Finally, after we all calmed down, the maid came in to let us know that dinner was ready. Will and Theo both took off for the dining room, leaving me to stop the maid and ask after Wynnie.

"Mistress Lily has not returned as far as I know, and even she cannot get past the Safehouse wards so I would have been alerted to her coming in." I nodded my head and released the maid to begin serving the meal.

Dinner was a much more relaxed affair than the previous night. All of the disbelief and mistrust was gone after today's events and everyone ate and talked as friends. Will and Tim took to asking me about my life growing up in the Original World and everything new there.

"These car things sound great. Wish we could get some, horses can be slow at times and when we're on a mission finding somewhere to change them out can be a hassle." Will commented.

"I like the sound of the guns. However, they probably would put me out of a job." Tim brought up between chewing his roasted chicken. I nodded they most certainly would and I bet Wynnie would love them too. I tried not to worry after where Wynnie had gotten off to, since no one else seemed to be the least bit concerned.

Eventually, we finished up and Will headed up to the Stronghold to fill the High Rulers in and push for a meeting with me.

"I'll do my best, but I'm sure it won't take much convincing. I'll let you know in the morning." I nodded and watched Will leave the house, hoping whatever he planned to say worked. After a time, Tim wandered off to bed and Theo announced he was tired to.

"I'll take the couch again, but if you don't mind, I'd like to bathe first. Wait a bit before coming up." I nodded and found a book on one of the shelves and settled in for a bit. The book was a pretty basic read, a story of a young man fighting for the woman he loves, but it filled the time and eventually I fell asleep on the couch.

Suddenly, I was in a run-down stone temple. The walls were hung with vines and pieces of the building were littering the ground at my feet. I carefully stepped over them and headed for the altar taking up the front of the sanctified space. The only noise was that of dripping water and my footsteps. One single glass window took up the entire wall behind the alter and I wanted to get a better look at it. It was clearly of three people in an offset single row, one on top of the other. At the top was a depiction of the Mother Goddess, a halo of light around her top half and her eyes closed head tilted to the side looking down on the other two. The middle figure slightly to the Goddess' right was a man in full fighting armor, shocking auburn red hair and decked out in weapons. His own head was also tilted down to look wide eyed at the third and final figure that was directly below the Goddess.

It was another warrior, but a woman with a crown on her head. Corn yellow, blonde hair floated around her person and she wielded a single sword pointing down in both of her hands in front of her. She was staring out at the viewer with a penetrating gaze, daring you to come forward.

"Listen." A whisper hissed past my ear as I looked upon the woman's gaze. Her eyes were bright, shining and...yellow? My brow furrowed as I reached out to touch the glass.

"Listen and learn." This time the whisper was accompanied by a loud whoosh of air and I jumped, straight out of my dream and onto the floor of the front room.

Startled, I sat up in a panic and looked around the still empty living space. The fire had died very low and the book I had been reading was now under the couch I had fallen off of in my panic. Making sure that no one but me had caused this, I rubbed my elbow gently where it had made heavy contact with the floor. Instantly, my hand warmed and the pain ebbed away.

"Cool." I muttered out loud to myself. If my magic stayed with me when I went back to the Original World, I really was going to use this newfound Life magic. As I began to haul myself up off the floor, the doorknob twisted and I paused, waiting to see who it was. Maybe Will was back and I could ask him how the meeting went. I took a few steps to the door and watched as a drunk Wynnie fell through the doorway and stumbled straight into me.

"Whoa!' I shouted and grabbed her by the waist.

"Lemme go," she drawled and attempted to push me away but only fell on me harder.

"Wynnie, stop moving and come over here." My nurse side kicked in and I had to get her sitting before she hurt herself. Wynnie let me drag her to the couch and she plopped down like a dead fish. I ran to the dining room where a hot carafe of tea still burned and poured her a cup.

"Here." I shoved it in her hands and moved it to her lips.

"I don't want that shit!" she yelled and shoved it away, flinging it across the room and onto the carpet.

"Wynnie!" I chastised and went to grab it.

"Who cares? It's just a rug, it's nothing important. Just like I'm nothing important." She slurred her words together groggily. I stopped my fussing and knew instantly what this might be about.

"Wynnie, you can't say that about yourself. You are too important." I came to sit next to her as she hauled herself ungracefully into a sitting/half leaning position across the arm of the couch.

"Says who? Not my own mother apparently. According to her letter which came in last night, the only thing I and every other woman in Medeis is good for is marrying for money and locking it down with babies." I shook my head; this wasn't healthy thinking.

"No? Didn't you hear? I'm an aunt to twin boys! The second High King of Maravette is now father to two amazing boys and my sister is the pride of the kingdom. My brother is also getting married to a wealthy merchant from Lotho's only daughter. The business is going global." Wynnie made a whirling congratulatory spin of her finger and then slumped over.

"Well, that's great for them Wynnie, but that has no bearing on your worth and you shouldn't let it." I touched her shoulder; she jerked and sat all the way back up but had a hard time keeping her balance.

"No? You don't think so? Because my mother certainly does, and she really let me know that I was worthless. 'When you finally learn to grow up, then you can come home and live up to what you were meant to do with your life.'" She recited with a drunken imperious tone.

I sighed, my heart going out to her struggle. I had never had to deal with my parents not supporting my decisions, but I had dealt with feeling inferior in my life just as Wynnie was.

"Listen, just because you're not what they think you should be doesn't mean you aren't being who you were meant to be. I can see where not having your family accept it can be hard, but it shouldn't stop you from seeing the family you've created for yourself. Take the Guard for example, they love and accept you for who you are. Will, Tim, and Theo let you be who you are and accept it for what it is. They don't ask anything from you other than hard work and being true to yourself. They just want you to be the best you can be, and I don't think drinking is what they want for you."

I reached out to take her hand in mine, forcing her to give me her attention.

"It's not what I want for you." A tear welled up in the corner of Wynnie's perfect blue eye.

"You are better, stronger, and so much more capable than this. I see it in you, and I've only known you two days. You are brave, you are strong, and you are much more caring than you let people see. You are a fighter and a protector. So, what if you're not living the life you thought you would live? You're living this one, and its suits you much more. The Elite Guard gives you a purpose, and it gives you a family. Don't throw it away or ruin it wallowing over a life that would have made you unhappy." Wynnie slumped her head on my shoulder.

"But what if I do still want some of that life? What if I do want to be married? I may come off as hard and unfeeling, but I still want that kind of love, too," she sniffled and I wrapped one warm arm around her and pulled her close.

"You're still figuring yourself out a little more, dear. Give it time. Learn to be happy on your own, for who you are, before you ask someone else to come in and join you in this life. The Mother knows when you are ready and when you get there, she will throw that person in your path with such force it will knock the wind out of you. Because whoever is meant to put up with you, is going to have to be a very special kind of personality indeed." I gave her shoulder a little squeeze and Wynnie looked up, nodding.

It was like consoling a small child whose favorite toy had broken, and it some ways it was. Who knows what kind of isolation and upbringing Wynnie had endured? Maybe no one had ever spoken to her this way before. She seemed to crave this type of affection and understanding.

"I think I'm ready for bed now. My head is already starting to hurt and Will is going to murder me if he sees me this drunk again." I nodded in agreement.

"I'll help you up there and bring you a tea to drink, just don't throw it away this time." I smiled and took her hand again to lift her up.

I quickly ran and grabbed another steaming cup and then led her up the wooden steps to her room. After quickly waiting for her to change, I handed her the cup, made sure she drank it, and tucked her in.

"Mia?" I heard Wynnie call from the bed. I turned back, waiting to see if she needed anything more.

"I'm sorry for being so skeptical of you yesterday. You're a better person than I deserve," she muttered from under the sheets.

"No, I'm not. I'm exactly what you deserve dear. And your skepticism is what makes you good at your job, never lose it." I snuffed out the candle and shut the door behind me with a final, "Good night."

As the door snicked shut I turned to head to my own room when I jumped, startled at seeing another figure standing in the darkened hallway.

"Thank you," Tim said quietly as he watched me leave Wynnie's room.

"It's no problem. Everyone has a night like this occasionally." I waved it away, but Tim shook his head.

"No, thank you for listening to her. Will is a fantastic captain, but he's a soldier first and foremost and those deep issues that get in the way of work sometimes go over his head. Wynnie is always trying to prove herself to us so much that she never opens up like that, but even if she did, I'm sure none of us would have been as gentle as you were with her now. So, thank you for giving her that."

I stood there stunned for a moment.

"I will always be there for someone who needs me. In whatever form is asked of me. It's my life's calling and my purpose." I moved to enter my own bedroom, planning to not wake Theo from his own slumber.

"I'm starting to think your purpose is greater than you believe." Was Tim's only reply. I turned to ask him what he meant, but his bedroom door was already closing. With a sigh I opened my own door very slowly so as not to create any noise and creeped inside.

Theo was fast asleep on the little couch, the infamous pillow tucked up under his head. A small blanket hung limp around his waist, but he wore nothing for a shirt. I couldn't help myself. I stood there, looming over him, and looked down upon the body that stirred something within me like nothing else ever had.

I know Theo had mentioned feeling this need to protect me, to be near me, to make sure I was safe, but I realized that there was something more there. I felt a need, a need to see him, to reach out and brush the one single lock of brown hair away from his forehead. It took me everything to stop myself, no need to make myself seem like a creeper in the middle of the night. The well-defined chest rose and fell in the moonlight, breathing deep and even.

There was something about this man that made my magic stir within me, it reached for him. I hadn't asked him about it in depth yet but maybe the way he wanted to protect me was the same reason I felt heat when we touched.

Mother only knew, I concluded and stepped quietly to the bed, relaxing into the sheets, and closing my eyes for a good heavy slumber.

I was awoken to obnoxiously loud banging on the door all too soon.

"What the-?" I heard Theo bark from his place at the couch and I opened my eyes just in time to see him yank his pathetic excuse for a blanket away and storm to the door. With a hard yank he threw it open to stare down the sun rise offender.

"Do you have any idea what time it is?" Theo loudly whispered. I hadn't sat up yet from my fog of sleep, so I still had no clue who had been beating our door down. I looked to the window to realize the sun was barely even peeping out over the rooftops. With a groan I rolled back over and covered my face with the extra pillow.

"You see that? You woke Mia!" Theo huffed and turned to walk back into the room, allowing the intruder to follow in.

"I have a clear idea of what time it is, actually. Unlike some of you, I went to bed on time and rose early to come check on my patient." Ez's voice floated into the room like a dove in the early morning cooing its prettiest song. I instantly sat up and smiled.

"You seem to be chipper." Ez grinned at me, holding a tray of cups and vials.

"And healed too." I said out loud. Ez's face fell and so did the tray of mixtures.

"What in the Mother!" she exclaimed and rushed to my side.

"How-? I mean, what did you…" her voice trailed off unable to comprehend my miraculous recovery.

"Turns out, Mia here is a Life Sorcerer, it's the reason the Priestess attacked her. She healed herself, Ez," Theo reported. Ez's eyes ping ponged between Theo and me, mouth still wide open.

"A Life Sorcerer? A real one? After all these years and one literally just drops in from out of the sky right next door to me?" Ez's hands began to shake. I quickly crawled over, took her hands, and pulled her down on to the bed to sit next to me

"Yes, Ez. A real Life Sorcerer. See?" I touched my throat that was clear of bruising and marks.

"All better. Awesome right?" I smiled and Ez leaned in to check, hands still shaking. As she leaned back away from me I heard her breath catch and tears began pouring from her eyes.

"Hey!" I consoled her and scooted even closer. "What's with the tears?" Ez just shook her head.

"We've just...we've been waiting so long Mia. So long! Life wielders have been attempting to recreate the magic that Life Sorcerer's could do to save lives and we've failed horribly over the last two decades. Over and over, we have searched for the ones who went missing and now..." she looked at up me, watery eyes meeting mine.

"And now here you are..." she choked up again and fell back into my shoulder.

"This is the greatest blessing to healing the Mother has given us in such a long time. The whole world is going to be thrilled to learn you're finally here." I patted her back, but I also smiled. My magic felt her relief release into the room. I thought about all the people that the wielders had been unable to heal. Knowing there was magic out there that could save them and not being able to get to it. The frustration must have been intense, so her sudden torrent of emotion was only understandable.

"No one is to know," Theo interjected, dampening the mood in the room.

"What?" we both asked together.

"No one can know about Mia. Her life is in danger because of her magic." Ez shot up off the bed, ready for a fight with her best friend.

"You're kidding me, right? Theo, we need her! This world has needed a Life Sorcerer for so long. Think of all those we have lost because of not having people like her anymore. Think of the sick, the dying, the young. Think of your sisters!" Ez shouted the last devastating blow. Theo's face went incomprehensibly dark. His green eyes turned almost black in his anger, and his face went red with rage.

I felt it then, that same pull Theo had mentioned he felt with me. I felt his anger, I felt his pain, his fear, his uncontrollable desire to throw Ez from the nearest window for bringing up his infant sisters. It hit him like a truck and so it hit me as well, but Ez had been right and Theo knew it.

"Theo…I'm so sorry. I didn't mean to say that." Ez immediately back tracked and took a step away.

"Timothy!" I shouted at the top of my lungs. I heard three quick footsteps down the hallway and Tim came into view, hair wet and damp from a morning shower. Without a word, I grabbed Ez's hand and dragged her to the door.

"Get her out of here." I commanded and shoved Ez into his arms.

"What's going-?" But we had no time, Theo was storming after Ez with hate and death in his eyes.

"Just go!" I screamed and moved to shut the door, Ez turned back as it closed.

"I'm so sorry!" I heard her throw one last plea as I slammed it closed and turned to face down Theo.

"Stop!" I threw out one hand and he halted instantly, my hand coming to rest in the center of his still bare chest.

"Theo, stop." I repeated, gentler this time. I had to get his attention, I had to calm him down. I wanted to help him, but he had to listen first.

"Listen to me, what Ez just said was wrong, so wrong on so many levels. But it was a mistake and she knows it." Theo turned away and started pacing the room, his breathing becoming uneven.

"Just calm down and think for a moment. Don't let it eat at you. What happened all those years ago was no one fault, least of all yours. I wasn't there but I do know birth, and sometimes not even magic can fix what's happening."

"It's the single worst event that ever happened in my life, Mia! And she just threw it in my face as a guilt trip to get what she wanted," he shouted, I didn't even flinch. This anger didn't scare me, it prodded me further into action.

"Yes, she did use it. But not for what she wanted, but for what Medeis needs. Theo, I am a Life Sorcerer, I am also a nurse. She's right, if people need me I will go help whether I use magic or not. People are going to find out, and no matter how much danger that puts me in, I'm going to go where I'm needed. I'm also going to use this magic to find my parents and help them too." I reasoned.

"What about after?" Theo snapped at me, I blinked a few times and shook my head.

"What do you mean?" I asked.

"After you find your parents, aren't you planning on leaving with them? What good does it do this world knowing about a Life Sorcerer only for her to leave us again and go missing." My heart fell. He was right. I wasn't planning on staying. My heart broke remembering how relieved Ez had been at finding out a Life Sorcerer existed. There I was sitting here, planning on disappearing just like the rest once I got what I wanted out of them.

"Maybe I could stay a while or go back and forth." I wasn't sure how that would work with any job I took, but I could find a way to help both worlds. It was amazing to me how attached I already felt to Medeis, there was just something about this place. I felt at ease here and I didn't want to leave forever, but I wanted to continue my life back on Earth, in the Original World. Wasn't that what I was meant to do?

"I don't think it's going to work like that Mia." Theo seemed to have control over himself finally. "I think you're going to have to make a really big decision here soon. One that doesn't affect just you or your parents. Maybe the Mother has a plan for you, and you need to just open your eyes and see it." Now Theo was counselling me, I shook my head.

"But what if I'm not ready to make that choice? What if I make the wrong one?" I questioned out loud. Theo passed by me, his emotions ebbing away slowly from my heart. I felt my magic tug to be near him, but I held back.

"We never are Mia. The Mother doesn't wait until we're ready. Maybe, instead of spending your time focused on going home, you should see what Medeis could offer you. Just…think about it." And with that, Theo shut the door to the bathroom, leaving me feeling terribly alone.

Theo didn't speak much the rest of the early morning, Tim took Ez home in tears and I met him in the front room to explain.

"Wow, I mean I knew Ez could stick her foot in it sometimes but Mother. That's a doozy even for her." Tim blew out a huge breath and leaned back.

"I've got Theo calmed down, but he brought up a really good point. We really can't tell anyone about this. First off, Heretia might come looking for me. And Second, Tim I'm not planning on staying here once I get my parents back…I don't think." I reluctantly admitted the last part.

"Well, that might be something you need to figure out and quick. Word about you is going to get out and I'll be honest. All the kingdoms are going to go crazy trying to get your help." I nodded in agreement.

"I just don't know what to think anymore. I do appreciate what this world can offer me, but I have a life back in the Original World."

"A job?" Time asked, eyeing my carefully.

"Not yet, but I had just found out that I could start applying."

"Friends?"

"One really good friend, Rebekah. She was applying for her own job across the country." Tim leaned forward.

"We're you going to go with her?" I shook my head.

"Well, no, I was going to stay home for a little while longer and then get an apartment."

"Romantic interest keeping you back?" I blushed deeply.

"No, nothing like that."

"So, tell me again why it's imperative you go back?"

My mouth fell open, stunned into silence. Tim shrugged his shoulders and I watched him leave to grab breakfast that had been set up for us in the dining room.

I didn't get time to think over what Tim had just made me realize when Will came clomping down that stairs, a smile on his face.

"Well, they came to the agreement last night. The High Rulers want to see you today right after we eat. The Priestess has been fully removed to a safe location in Maravette and is no longer an issue either. Whenever you finish eating and get dressed, we will head out."

The news was supposed to excite me, I was one step closer to getting my parents back but after Tim's comment, it just let like I was one step closer to an end I wasn't ready to face.

"What's wrong?" Will asked, seeing me continue to sit rooted to my spot.

"I'm coming to realize that things maybe happening that may take choices in my life away from me. I mean, how do you handle being one of a kind in a world that isn't your own? How do you make a decision of what step to take next if you're not sure where it will lead you?" This was not what Will was expecting and he shifted uncomfortably in his spot.

"Uh…well, I guess the only thing you can do is just keep going and keep doing what feels right until the decision just comes to you."

The silence fell heavy in the room as I continued to stare into the empty fireplace, thoughts whirring through my mind. Thankfully, Theo and Wynnie saved Will from trying to salvage the conversation on his own.

"Ready to eat? I'm starving." Wynnie slapped her flat stomach comically and gave it a vigorous rub. Theo looked over to me and his face fell, seeing my distress.

"Mia, you okay?" he checked with me. Hearing his concern snapped me out of my personal reverie and I nodded my head, plastering a smile and standing to join everyone in dining room. I decided to just push aside all the worry, all the anxiety and just focus on what was more important than myself, rescuing my parents from Michelo.

The High Stronghold wasn't as large as the name suggested, but it still loomed over the city atop a giant hill acting as an imposing stone guardian to the people of the town. I was, however, in awe of the architecture of the vastly overkept landscape surrounding it. Garden upon garden rose around us as we made our way up the hill path towards the looming gate at the entrance. One solitary guard unit stood at the door at the top of the stone steps, adorned in green livery with the symbol for Earth emblazoned on their chest.

The walking trek to the Stronghold had been mostly silent, and I had enjoyed getting to see more of the city for myself. The further we had gotten into the center the less shops we came across and the more high-end living quarters. The clothes seemed to get more refined and instead of walking, carriages began to pass us on the street. More than once, Theo had to pull me out of the way of an open top carriage carrying an occupant that didn't even notice our presence.

"Is it going to be weird entering the Stronghold for the first time since you left?" I turned to Theo, trying to settle my racing nerves over meeting with the High Kings and Queens.

"Yes and no. No, because I have come here once or twice since leaving and it's always been for work. Just like this time. But yes, because seeing my father is always weird," he answered.

"I'm sorry I'm making you face him again. If it weren't for me, you wouldn't be coming up here." I wrung my hands together, the nervous energy starting to well up.

"Hey, don't worry about me. This isn't about me in any way. This is about getting your parents back." He gave me a small reassuring smile and I felt my shoulders relax.

Will walked ahead of us, back straight and sword strapped to his waist. Two guards met us at the massive front wooden doors.

"I am Wilhelm Corso, Captain of the Elite Guard. My men and I are escorting a special guest of their Majesties and we are expected."

One of the guards looked down the group. To Tim, wearing his bow and arrow, his eyes lingering over Wynnie's petite frame a little too long, to me and finally to Theo beside me. With a startled jump he snapped to attention and bowed. The second guard followed his companions gaze and instantly matched his reaction.

"Welcome back, Your Highness. Your mother, Queen Vanessa, has asked that you meet with her urgently." Theo rolled his eyes and shouldered his way forward but still stayed behind Will.

"Always a golden ticket, Theo." Will snarked from over his shoulder and then led us through the front door. Theo continued his brooding silence as we quickly ushered ourselves in and waited for the doors to shut behind us. As we stepped across the threshold, I held my breath. There was clearly an immense amount of magic involved here because the interior was much larger than the exterior. We were standing in a vaulted ceiling reception area with two large hallways lined with paintings on each side and a massive marble staircase leading up to another floor of even more hallways and doors.

Another set of large wooden doors sat underneath the staircase directly in front of us. The Alchemic symbol for Earth was etched into the wood and I could hear the magic humming. Every color imaginable was either woven or painted on the tapestries and art in this place. Plush chairs lined the walls and priceless vases sat upon antique tables in every corner. Everything was gilded in either marble or gold, including the statues around the top of the circular ceiling.

It was like something out of Buckingham palace during Queen Victoria's glorious reign of showmanship and glamour. I was in a trance of awe as a footman of sorts approached us. He too gave a quick head nod to Theo and directed his attention to him only.

"You and your fellow Guardsmen are instructed to wait patiently. An unfortunate occurrence has held up one of the Majesties with making it to the meeting on time, so it will be an hour later than expected. I will show you to the Morning Room where we have some drinks waiting for you."

Theo huffed, "Which Majesty?" he asked, clearly annoyed at the delay.

"Queen Felicity. It seems her daughter arrived about an hour ago for a private audience."

Theo gritted his teeth, "Esmerelda," he hissed.

I grabbed his hand quickly, as he made a move to stalk off.

"Why don't you give me a tour while we wait, Theo." I steered him away, leading him down a random hallway away from everyone else. The three other Guardsmen stared after us blankly.

"Is something going on here?" Wynnie whispered loud enough for me to hear.

"Just don't ask," Tim whispered back, but we were getting too far away to hear anymore. Theo shook me off and turned to head down another corridor.

"Theo, wait! Just leave it alone. Ez is doing what she feels is right, none of us can say any different." I pleaded and followed him blindly. The need to reach out to him struck me in my gut again.

"Please, Theo. We'll meet with them all in just a bit. I doubt anything she has to say to her own mother changes anything. Just, let it be and when we see them all together everything will work out." Theo stopped in his tracks and hung his head.

"It's just," he began and then faltered.

"Just what?" I prodded. This anger that flared up inside him was unhealthy and I got the feeling he had nowhere to release it his entire life, so he had just bottled it up.

"Tell me what the problem with Ez talking to her mother is." I circled around him and bent down to catch his eye.

"It feels like she ran off to get her way. It's something her sisters would do, but not Ez. Never Ez. I always trusted her growing up, but now with a Life Sorcerer in the picture I guess things have changed for her." I nodded.

"Then trust her now. Don't let your emotions cloud who you know her to be. As you said, you two grew up together. She was the only one you could be honest around, trust that. Trust that she is a grown woman and is going to make the right choice. I don't see Ez being the person to be so selfish all of the sudden." I felt Theo's heart slow down, his breathing even out and his anxiety dissipate as he listened to me.

"You're right, Mia. Mother, you're always right. Why are you so good at this? It really is starting to get annoying." Theo gave me a fake annoyed look and then smiled.

"Must be a Life Sorcerer thing. It's like when someone is emotionally hurting, I just feel the need to help make it better. I don't know, but I'm starting to feel nosey about it. Like I can see things that I'm not meant to see. I've got to find a way to turn it off or people are going to stop talking to me in general." I attempted to joke, but Theo cupped my chin in his hand and made me look at him.

"Never stop caring, Mia. It's who you are, and I promise the world would be a much worse place if you did."

I had no words for a response of any kind. I just felt the warmth of his hand on my face and the leap of my heart as we just stared at each other in silence. Theo's eyes darkened ever so slightly and just as I could have sworn he was about to lean in to kiss me, light and quick footsteps echoed down the hall. Theo jerked away as fast as lightning and I was left feeling empty and slightly stupid.

"Her Majesty Queen Vanessa is waiting for you in the library." Came the footman's instruction from behind. Theo looked past me and acknowledged the man with a curt nod.

"Well, I'll take you to the Morning Room and then go meet with her before we get this meeting started." Theo offered his arm and I took it. The footman cleared his throat to get our attention.

"Her Majesty requests that Miss Wardman join you."

Theo raised his perfectly manicured eyebrow and nodded his dismissal.

"Well, well," he mused, "Seems dear mother has taken a particular interest in you." He gave me a wicked grin and led me down a side hall to a set of doors.

"Do I look okay?" Fussing over hair and clothes had never been my forte, but meeting a Queen seemed different.

"You look great, Mother isn't the scary one…he comes later." I swallowed the lump of fear in my throat and waited as Theo threw open the doors.

The library was stunning. At least three stories of shelves lined the massive cathedral like room. Ladders, desks, and lamps littered the sides of the space for quiet study while the entrance held couches, large tables, and chairs of all kinds. A large stained-glass mosaic of the map of Medeis adorned the window high above and glittered as the morning light filtered through it.

"Oh my!" I exclaimed and placed my hand on my chest to still my beating heart. I took a deep breath and let in the intoxicating smell of papers, leather, and ink. A place after my own heart. I could spend days just wandering around and collecting volumes that interested me for later study.

"Wonderful isn't it? I didn't know where a good place to meet quietly would be, but since no one ever seems to darken this door, I figured the library was as good as any to say hello to my son in private." A strong clear voice rang out and I jumped slightly. I hadn't noticed the blonde woman sitting silently in a wingback chair facing the doorway, the light from the window behind had her in shadow and she was eerily still.

"Mother." Theo walked forward and kissed her cheek dutifully.

"Theodeus, my dear. It's good to see you. However, I'm slightly disturbed as to the reason we're all here today."

Theo took a step back and motioned me forward.

"This is Amelia Wardman, mother. The Life Sorcerer we found in the Northern Forest two days ago. The same woman the Priestess attacked yesterday." Queen Vanessa nodded her regal head, her neck impossibly thin. If I could have ever been an artist, which I most certainly was not, I would have drawn her and called it 'Ice Queen'. Almost white, blonde hair was pinned back sharply from her face in a bun, her imperious gaze missed nothing. Her brown eyes, while handsome and comforting on Theo, were dark and penetrating on her. It's as if she saw right through me and I struggled to move, let alone greet her.

"Usually, people bow when they meet me, or any royalty for that matter," she hinted, an arched brow picking up sharply, a look I had just seen mirrored on her own son's face.

"I'm so sorry, I'm not really sure what to do." I hurriedly stumbled through a curtsy and then stood there, desperately trying not to wring my hands.

"Wardman, I know that name. Tell me, it had slipped Captain Corso's mind when I had asked the first time. What was your mother's name, child?" Vanessa asked me coolly. She never rose from her seat.

"Clarisse." I answered hesitantly. "Did you know her?" I finally squeaked out. Vanessa waited a moment, smirking to herself before finally speaking.

"Know her? Why my dear girl, she is the only sibling and heir to the fifth High Throne of Suravia."

My knees fell out from under me. Thankfully, Theo saw my distress. In an instant he had me sitting on a couch.

"Th-That's not possible. She never told me anything about that," I whispered. The words were stumbling over my tongue.

"Oh no dear, it's very possible. Not only that, but I think quite probable from the looks of you. King Michael is sitting on his throne only because your mother decided to step down and marry a man who wanted no part of royal life," she frowned.

"If you knew my mother, then why did Theo not recognize her name when I told him? If she was supposed to be the High Queen, why had he never heard of her?"

Queen Vanessa Varillian closed her eyes and took a tired shaky breath. "Clarisse's' mother had her written out of the books and all Five Rulers agreed to never speak her name again. She was an outcast and was banished. Not that she cared. Your mother was never one to dwell on those things, and frankly, she loved your father more than anyone ever guessed. I always suspected they were Paired, but I had my own child to worry over and I was a new Queen with a father-in-law about to pass away. It was over so quickly that there was no time to stand up for her or attempt to convince her to let Daryl go. Too bad though. Michael has always been a sickly man and never found a wife to bear him children. It would have been nice to see Clarisse come back and take up the throne after he passes," she sighed.

"You had an idea of who I was, didn't you?" I pointed out. Her question had been too direct, the story of my mother too heavy on her mind.

"Yes, the name had struck me as odd. Thankfully, however, Ogden hasn't put it together yet and Michael has been too ill for the past few days to attend the briefings by your Captain Corso. I wouldn't want to get his hopes up without just cause. But I think we need to see him now. Michael deserves to meet his niece and heir. Wait here." Vanessa was gone like the wind, throwing the library doors open with a wave of her hand and sending them crashing back together before the weight of her final words sunk in.

"Heir? Wait a minute!" I shouted after her, but the doors were too thick.

"I can't be his heir! I don't know anything about this place. I'm not from here and I'm not even an Earth element. I can't be his heir." I rounded on Theo who held his hands up in defense.

"I'm not sure what she meant by that either, but technically you can be his heir." He cleared his throat again and began scratching his head the way he did when he wasn't sure what to say. "You see, there is a kingdom for every Element. Suravia for Earth, Maravette for Air, Lotho for Water and Elevetia for Fire. The Ancient Kingdom never had a ruling Element because it's where all the other kingdoms derive from. But there isn't a kingdom for Life."

I blinked and sat down in a solitary chair, readying myself for whatever Theo was about to tell me.

"Life wielders were so essential to everyday common folk life that they decided to not create their own Kingdom, but instead assimilated into all five others and just be useful. Life Sorcerers, however, were granted the option of becoming rulers of kingdoms if they were born into a royal family and only if there were no other options for heirs to be had. That's how Heretia came into power in the Ancient Kingdom. She was her fathers' only child and a Life Sorcerer."

I sucked in a breath. I wasn't liking this explanation.

"So, you see, you very well could be the only option for the Fifth Throne once Michael passes on."

He took my hand, suddenly noticing that it was shaking.

"B-But I don't want that. I don't want to be a queen in a world I have no understanding of," I protested. "I don't even know if I plan on staying here once this is over."

"Mia, we don't have to discuss this tonight. We don't have to even think about it for a while. Yes, Michael is probably going to be the first of the Rulers to go, but not for a while yet. He's a spunky one, that Uncle of yours," Theo said soothingly.

"Won't he hate me? I am a reminder of my mother leaving him to be the High King. She was supposed to be Queen, not him. Won't meeting me just make him furious?" I asked.

Theo chuckled lightly to himself, as if my comment was some inside joke I wasn't privy to.

"You would just have to meet Michael to know that, leaving for love is never something he would hold against anyone. In fact, why don't we just pop down there and meet him now? I think we've got plenty of time before dinner," Theo replied through his laughter.

"What do you say, Mia? Ready to go meet your long-lost family?"

CHAPTER EIGHT

The walk was not a far one, but with every step I felt myself sweat more profusely.

"What if he doesn't like me?" I whispered and gripped Theo even tighter.

"He will love you as everyone does, Mia. Chin up, no worries. He is your family after all," he said.

We came to a stop in front of two ornate doors. A waiting footman stepped forward and knocked. Another footman answered and immediately bowed, then moved to the side.

I passed into a room that was alive with greenery. Bushes, plants, and trees grew from every corner and overtook bookshelves that lined the walls. It was like a fairy library deep in the forest with its rich colors and wonderful fragrances. I closed my eyes and breathed in deeply. It smelled like my mother.

I felt a smile cross my lips as I picked out certain scents among the herbs growing into the walls.

"Vanessa tells me I have an important visitor," I heard a sweet melodic voice call from a corner. I saw Vanessa standing in the middle of the room next to a chair that had it's back to me. She was finally smiling, a soft gesture that made her seem much more approachable than the woman who had dominated the room just minutes before down in the Library. She seemed almost motherly in the firelight.

"High King, may I present to you, your niece, Amelia Wardman," Theo announced and released my death grip to back away. Vanessa then moved to the side as well and another chair came into view.

I had to blink to see the tall thin figure sitting there in front of the bright fire, but when I did, my eyes filled at the corners. Michael looked just like my mother. It was the same comforting brown eyes, the same wiry build, identical soft lips, and the exact walnut colored hair, save for his was cropped close with a pointed Van Dyke beard flecked with silver streaks. Even his voice had the same lyrical cadence of my mother's. I forgot to bow and just stood there watching him stare back at me.

Suddenly, his mouth opened in a large smile and his arms flung wide open.

"All my life I have prayed to the Mother that She would one day bring my sister home to me. Instead, she has brought me an even more wonderful gift! Amelia! My sweet girl," he cried.

He rushed for me and in that moment, I had no words. I picked up my skirt and met him in the middle of the room, letting him catch me in an embrace. He smelled like my mother, and as I shed tears into his jacket, I felt him pat my head.

"Oh no, sweet child. No tears, for this is a happy moment! I have waited and hoped for so long that I might meet what remained of my family," he smiled.

I nodded, but the tears continued to come from me, shining as they fell from my face onto his double-breasted jacket. He pulled back and placed his thin hands on either side of my face.

"Let me see you! You look so much like her, it's astonishing!"

I gave a rasping laugh and grabbed his wrists.

"Amelia, I'm so glad your home. Don't you worry about Clarisse, we will take care of this and bring her home as well. I promise, we're going to find them. Then, we will all be here together and happy again for however long she wants to stay, which I hope will be a long time," he said happily.

I could see the utter joy in his soulful dark eyes.

"Oh, the stories you must have and all the things I want to tell you! We don't have enough time for a better reunion but know that I love you and I have waited for you to come home."

He embraced me again and I melted into it.

"Uncle Michael!" I cried.

We really must have been a scene, for there wasn't a dry eye in the room when we finally let go and turned to look at everyone.

"Oh, look at you all! Sobbing away like children. Dry up, Vanessa, you secret softie." Michael joked. I looked to see Vanessa staring at him confused, not a single tear on her face. But there was a definite softer tone to her smile, her voice, and a gentler kindness in her demeanor.

"Your uncle here has already ordered a Ball in your honor, Amelia. I've advised we put off the official meeting to discuss rescuing your parents until after. It gives you and Michael time to get to know each other, and our scouts one more day to hand in more reports on what's happening in the Ancient Kingdom."

I pulled back from my Uncle, confused. "You've already sent scouts out?" I asked and looked between the two Rulers.

"We sent them out the moment Captain Corso mentioned Michelo had kidnapped someone. That man doesn't move without Heretia's consent and anything she does that involves the Original World, can't be good news. So yes, we sent them out immediately and none have returned yet." Vanessa answered, the ice Queen creeping back into her voice.

"It's partly why we put off bringing you up here. We wanted our own intel first," Michael led me to the chairs and sat down next to me.

"Had I known who you were I would have gone running to you myself instead of waiting around with the others. But I haven't been feeling the best lately and been confined to my rooms and one single garden walk a day. It is curious however that Vanessa here had suspicions and didn't come to me with them. Seeing as how they concern my own sister and all."

Vanessa didn't budge, "I didn't want you upset if I was wrong. It has been twenty-three years Michael." No apology, not regrets. This woman was a force to be reckoned with. Theo's description of her being a waste of a thing physically and emotionally after the loss of her daughters didn't seem to add up to me. Where was the woman who let her son be bullied by his father, who never stepped in, who allowed it to get so bad that her only living child thought that running away was his only option?

I looked to Theo to see if he was confused by his mother's bold and confident actions surprised him, but his face gave nothing away, not even to me.

"No matter, I have a beautiful niece to dote upon and catch up with. Would you mind taking me for a walk around the grounds? I'm feeling much better and I want all the time I have with you." I nodded, flashing my uncle a thrilled grin.

Theo gave a small cough, "I'll go let the rest of the Guard know that the meeting will be put off until tomorrow." He turned and then smiled over his shoulder. "And inform Wynnie she needs to go shopping for the Ball tonight. Let me know when you're done with Mia, and I'll have Wynnie come collect her to get ready."

"You're really doing that? I thought it was a joke, you don't need to do tha.t" I urged my uncle to cancel such a waste of time, but he just laughed and waved me away.

"Nonsense, it's been a good while since we have had one and the nobles were bickering anyway. Besides, it will make finding Clarisse more important to the kingdom and to the people. No one can say no to a missing Princess." He winked mischievously.

"He's right, Ogden and Felicity will have a hard time refusing support and assistance when we've gone so public with who you are." Vanessa agreed. Theo audibly choked at her words. Everyone in the room turned to still see him standing by the door, his eyes wide in shock.

"Are you…purposefully, going against what Father wants?" Vanessa gave a small nod.

"You've been gone a while, my son. And even when you did stop by and say hello you never stuck around long. Things have changed around here."

Theo blinked twice.

"Don't get me wrong, I still love your father and we are still together. But I have seen the error in my ways that plagued your upbringing and I have actively worked to be better than that. Be the woman I once was. We don't fight, but I certainly do find my ways to put a foot down here and there. I see openings to make sure your father chooses the better decision."

So, this explained my confusion from earlier. At some point since Theo left the Stronghold, Vanessa had regrown a spine, seemingly a slightly sneaky one, but a spine, nonetheless. I wasn't sure how receptive Theo would be to this new mother of his, whether he would be thrilled or angry that it had taken her so long. Judging by how many mood swings I had seen, I didn't even want to hazard a guess at this point, but I wasn't going to have to.

"I-I need to let Will and the others know of the change of plans," he muttered quietly and left the room as quickly as possible. Vanessa sighed as she watched the door shut, obviously at a loss for how to talk to him.

"Let him be, Vanessa. He's a grown man. He'll realize you've changed, and he will come around." Michael counseled and held his hand out for Vanessa to take it. With a resigned smile she took it and gave him a gentle squeeze, "I know you're right Michael. I've just made so many mistakes. I just hope one day he can forgive me, and we can at least be friends."

With a nod in my direction, Vanessa left quietly, probably to get something organized for tonight.

"To the garden then? I have so many questions and I know you probably do too, dear." Michael reached for what I thought was an ornamental cane, but it seemed he did need a slight bit of help up from his chair. I steadied him as he got his legs under him and we made for the door.

For the next few hours, he and I walked slowly though the immaculate rows of hedges that took up the entire back lawn of the residence. We paused for spells on stone benches so he could rest and catch his breath. The entire time we did nothing but talk. I told him about mom and what she did for a living, about dad and how happy they were together. I told him about our house, the vacations we had taken, and my schooling. I told him I was a nurse and he nodded in agreement. "Seems to go well with your Element, it only makes sense," he affirmed.

He did seem confused however when I admitted that I, in the last few days, finally gained access to my magic. Trying to keep an air of happiness about the reunion between the two of us, we skipped over talking about moms kidnapping for a while and I allowed Michael to tell me about my mother as a child.

From her inability to stop collecting plants, and sometimes animals, to her horrid ability to get an entire dress dirty in thirty seconds flat. He laughed over stories of their mother chastising Clarisse for losing a pair of shoes in the mud and my mother's only response was, "I didn't lose them, I took them off because I couldn't hear the dirt talking to me."

I finally got the courage to ask how my parents met. The only story I knew was clearly a lie, and I wanted to truth.

"Oddly enough, your father came here to further his study. He was from Maravette and their Element is Air, so him being an Earth wielder studying there was no good. He came here to do some research at the public academy and that's where your mother saw him. She was working in the garden. She hadn't preformed the Rite yet, but we all knew she was an Earth Sorcerer. Your father had just turned eighteen and she was smitten with him. Of course, I don't think they even spoke for months. She was a Princess, and he was just a student. It wasn't until the night of her Rite when a large party was being held that she ran into him," Michael said. He looked up onto a balcony that loomed over our heads. "Right there, I believe," he pointed up and smiled longingly at it.

"Right there is where they talked, and their Pair bond was sealed. It was almost instantaneous. Clarisse never looked back," he explained.

I raised a curious eyebrow.

"Pair bond, what's that?"

Michael chuckled to himself.

"It's an ancient form of magic, a Blessing from the Mother herself. It's the person who is meant to be your other half, the other side of your soul and your magic. It's not common, in fact it usually only happens a handful of times across all Medeis every generation. Last time I heard of a true Pair bond, it was a Fire wielder and an Air Sorcerer both from Elevetia. But that was almost seven years ago now. Before that, Clarisse was the only Pair bonded witch I'd ever met," he explained.

I had never heard of this type of magic. My parents had never told me they were Pair bonded. I was getting used to realizing they hadn't told me much, but this didn't seem like something they should have kept from me.

Michael continued his story.

"They tried to hide it from our mother for a while, but not me. Clarisse couldn't keep a secret from me if she tried. I still remember the night she came to me, overjoyed and tears of happiness in her eyes. She was pregnant and she wanted me to help her tell mother so she and Daryl could get married. Mother didn't take the news well, but she had to accept it. Forcing a bonded Pair to separate is deadly for both and can destroy their magic. They were married shortly after, but Daryl refused to move into the Stronghold."

I could not see my father doing well in this type of lifestyle. He was a quiet academic, not meant for a life of royalty and balls. I couldn't really see my mother enjoying it either, but she was the type of person to keep doing what made others happy, even if it were to her own detriment.

"Then, one day, she just left. I had noticed her acting a little strange when she came for function, and meetings but I wasn't ready for her to just leave like that," he sighed.

My heart sank. She had been pregnant with me when they crossed over to the Original World, but why? What was so wrong with here that she refused to bring me up in Medeis?

"She left me a letter, your mother did. I found it a few hours after it was discovered that she and Daryl were gone. Everyone assumed they had run off to another kingdom, or the forests just to live in peace together," Michael continued.

I moved to face my uncle as he spoke of the letter. "What did it say? The letter, I mean. Did she explain why she had left?" Michael gave me a sad smile.

"For you, Mia." My heart sank, these are not the words I was expecting.

"Clarisse said she didn't feel you were safe here and she needed to take you away. She said that one day I may understand, but she hoped I never had to find out. Now that you're back, and it's been discovered what you are, I'm starting to think she may have been right. Heretia is a dangerous woman. There's no telling how obvious your magic would have been if you had grown up here, and she would have found you," he explained.

My hands began to shake. Was I in that much danger? Was I still in that much danger? Why would my parents have sent me here if this is the place they purposefully took me away from? They had spent their entire adult lives hiding me from people like Heretia and Michelo, only to throw me back in with no idea how to function here, no ability to control this magic I had been given, and no warning other than "Find the Prince."

148

"My father did tell me one thing before he shoved me through the portal. Something important he wanted me to do," I admitted with a shaky voice. My uncle leaned forward, intent on keeping his voice low.

"What was that love?" Michael asked.

I raised my gaze to meet his, hoping against hope that what I was about to say meant something to him. Maybe I had finally found who was meant to help me.

"Find the Prince. Dad said my heart would know his and his would know mine. Do you think he meant you?" I was reaching heavily, desperately trying to do what my parents told me. I had halted my search for this man for the last day, especially after Theo and I had argued over it back at the Safehouse. My uncle fit that description: he had been a prince when they had left. Maybe dad had meant my uncle.

"Your heart would know his, huh?" Michael leaned back and stroked his distinguished little beard that was manicured to perfection.

"That sounds to me like he was hinting at a Pair bond. I mean, don't get me wrong. I already love you immensely, but the intensity of his words suggests something more than familial affection. My question would be, why would your parents assume you have a Pair that could help you? You weren't even born when they left," he murmured.

I sighed heavily at another dead end to finding help.

"It's no matter. Don't stress over it. I'm going to be getting help from the Kingdom of Suravia and that's probably better than what this mysterious prince could offer anyway," I sighed.

My uncle shrugged his thin shoulders and looked up at the sun.

"Looks like we're going to be late to lunch, lets hurry up and we can eat in my rooms. I'm sure Theo's sweet little friend Wynnie will be ready to take you shopping by the time we're done. Ball starts at eight on the dot, so we can't be late. We are the guests of honor after all," he smiled.

149

My uncle's jolly bright smile offset his thin facial features and made him look younger.

I furrowed my brow and sat back, "Sweet friend Wynnie? Have you met her? The girl would eat you alive if given the chance," I said.

Michael's laugh was contagious and it sparkled into the air like a babbling brook.

"That's exactly why I think she's great! I like spunk, youth, and tenacity and Wyndetta Lily has all of that. The best part is, I can't stand her father. I've been rooting for her since the day she marched up to the Stronghold, not long after joining the Guard, and gave our Captain of Arms a dressing down over his knife throwing. Called him a one-eyed mule with his skill. The man threw knives for two months trying to get as accurate as Wynnie," he laughed.

I couldn't help but smile along with my uncle. I could totally imagine Wynnie flaunting her skills to try and prove herself. She certainly had showman qualities if provoked.

"Let's go then. I guess I need to be impressive if we want to convince the kingdom to help us find mom," I agreed.

Michael winked mischievously. "There's a politician in you yet, my dear. Let's go."

Chapter Nine

Wynnie and Ez were taken me shopping at the closest dressmaker to get ready. I could tell Ez was nervous about seeing me, but I calmed her fears as we walked out of the Stronghold together.

"I'm not mad at you, Ez. You did what you needed to. Were you worried your mother wasn't going to agree to help me, or were you trying to find a way to get me to stay?" I was curious as to why she met with her mother ahead of us.

"A little bit of both, actually. My mother is tough and would be someone to withhold help if she felt it didn't benefit her directly. After Tim settled me at home a wave of panic came over me that she would refuse to vote in your favor all because she didn't know who you were. I had to make sure she understood how important you were to the Life Community and to Medeis as a whole. I also, wanted to see if she could offer you a position as a Clinic Proctor." I was taken aback, Ez blushed slightly but continued.

"You had told me you were a healer in the Original World, so I thought if I could offer you a job as more than an assistant you might would want to stay. Not saying that you only care about a high-status position, I wouldn't assume you were that kind of self-serving person, but you could do good here and teach and heal and…." I stilled Ez's babbling words with a touch of my hand.

"Ez, you are too kind. That was so sweet of you and I'm so lucky to call you a friend." I told her, giving her a warm smile to ease her fears.

"You're not mad? I already talked to Theo and he still seems a little miffed at me, but you're not mad, are you?" I shook my head, brown hair flying in my face with the passing breeze.

"No, I'm not mad. You were doing what you thought was right. Theo will be fine. I think he jumped to a lot of conclusions about why you spoke to your mother, but he will come around."

Wynnie gave an exasperated huff from in front of us.

"For the Mother you two! Theo is fine, he gets moody at times when he thinks things aren't going the way they are supposed to. He's like that. He likes rules, order, and loyalty and when something goes against plan, he gets angsty about it. I promise you, he's already over it." Wynnie stopped dead in the street, hands on her hips to give us this lesson on Theo.

"Now, let's go shopping. I haven't been girlie in a while and I feel the need for something scandalous." I squeezed Ez's hand one last time and then quickly picked up my pace to race after a squealing Wynnie.

The next few hours flew by like a blur. A multitude of fabrics, colors, and styles were paraded in front of us. Somehow, the shop owner was already made aware of who I was and that the ball was being held by my uncle. A cup of tea was handed to me and then instantly replaced by a tall glass of wine once I was finished with it. Wynnie threw back three in quick succession, but a raised eyebrow from me suddenly slowed her down.

"Don't you want to be sober for the party?" I asked quietly. Her hand stilled as it hovered over a fourth glass and she slowly moved it back to her lap.

"I'm here." I whispered and grabbed her other free hand for a squeeze. Wynnie quickly recovered and was shoving me into a dressing room before too long, giggling like a schoolgirl.

"Try this one!" she tossed me a red concoction that didn't leave much to the busty imagination.

"Wynnie no!" I hollered and threw it back at her. "I'm just trying to get through the night, not attract unnecessary attention. This thing shows every ounce of skin I own." Ez chuckled and continued to strap herself into a dark green number that included a black corset around her waist.

"Well, then what do you want to wear? We've looked through almost everything and you haven't like one." Wynnie complained in her whiniest voice possible.

"That's not completely true, I like the green strapless one." I pointed to a dress that one of the attendants was still holding. It was all silk with an embroidered sweetheart neckline, the fabric gave a shimmering ombre look as I walked, and the silk sash was met in the middle with a large golden broach. The bodice was corseted in the front with three bones and fit me like a glove.

"It's too plain, you need something with a little more flare. The party is about you, not your uncle." Wynnie held the dress up to the light and I watched as the colors shifted from dark green to almost white as it moved.

"There is an extra piece that matches the dress," the shop owner offered, and my ears perked up.

"Can I see it?" I asked and motioned for Wynnie to bring me the dress back. She gave it over and I went to work stepping back in. Once it was securely fastened in the back, I stepped out and gasped at the piece the shop owner held in her hands.

It was a sash of sorts, but instead of draping across my shoulders it hung loose in the back and met up at a neck choker to hold it in place. The gold filigree design around the neck piece was astonishing and I marveled at how the thin fabric felt against my skin as they placed it on me.

"Oh, now that's flare." Wynnie whistled her compliments and I spun in place, staring myself down in the mirror.

"Some slippers and a set of emerald earrings will be just the thing." The owner ran off and produced two large teardrop emeralds for my earlobes.

"If you don't get that, Mia. I will." Ez warned from her chair that she had taken up residence in.

I smiled at my reflection. This is the most amazing I had ever looked in my life. Having never been to a prom in high school, or a formal in college, I felt like this was that moment where every girl thinks, "I look like a Princess."

"Box it up! That's the one." Wynnie clapped her hands and threw a sack of coins on the counter.

"Keep the change, we're taking these with us." My eyes widened at the sound the bag made.

"Where did you get all that money?" Wynnie waved away my concerns.

"When Will made me put my money away for safekeeping I took a chunk of it and bought some houses in each kingdom that I had turned into boarding homes. They keep the revenue coming in and I see them as a retirement policy for myself." Ez gave Wynnie a sly grin as the tiny blonde walked out nonchalantly.

"Once a Lily, always a Lily." Ez whispered to me from behind her hand, attempting to be sly. I tried to hold the stream of laughter back as we collected our boxes and headed back to the Stronghold to get ready.

Maids were waiting for us in one of the guest rooms and I paused at seeing them.

"What this?" I asked aloud and jumped when one of them came forward and took the boxes from my hands.

"His Majesty King Michael sent us to help you girls. Does anyone need a bath?" The eldest and most severe looking maid announced. Wynnie grimaced and then tried to secretly sniff herself, only to grimace deeper.

"Why not, might as well." Ez shrugged.

"We have a bath for each of you ready, Princess Esmeralda if you will follow Jalise here." A red headed maid curtsied and Ez smiled following her to a door to the left.

"Miss Lily, Georgaina will be helping you." Another red head, possibly Jalises' sister by the looks of her, curtsied and walked towards another door.

"Why did you even ask if we wanted one if you already had them drawn?" Wynnie snarked as she passed by the head maid.

"Princess Amelia, you will be with me." I nodded in understanding and followed her to the last door.

It led to a large room with a massive four poster King sized bed, plush couches, and chairs everywhere. A wall of books took up one whole side of the four-sided room.

"This will be your room for tonight, Your Highness. Rooms in King Michael's wings are being prepared for a more permanent place for you and should be ready tomorrow. I believe a room for Princess Clarisse and her husband are being readied as well for their return." I stumbled at this remark.

"He's planning on us staying?" I wondered aloud. Another person who thought that I wouldn't return to the Original World when this was over. I didn't want him to think helping me meant I would stay, because staying meant that I wanted to be his heir and I wasn't ready to make that decision.

"I do not presume to know what His Majesty is planning. I just know what is being done. Your bath, Your Highness." The severe looking woman motioned for a door to my right.

"I didn't catch your name." I mentioned as I passed by her.

"Rebekah, miss." I let a small laugh escape my lips.

"Is something the matter?" Rebekah raised a thin eyebrow at my amusement.

"My best friends name is Rebekah, maybe it means we will be friends." I mused and stepped into the bathroom. The water was steaming and rose petals littered the surface. I could smell lavender and cedarwood again, just like back at the Safehouse.

"I should hope not." Rebekah barked and then shut the door behind her as she left, leaving me alone to my bath.

I lost track of time after that. It felt like mere moments before Rebekah and another maid returned announcing my outfit was ready and my hair was too thick to soak any longer or it wouldn't get dry.

I was rushed into a robe and plopped down in front of a dresser mirror. I looked around and realized there was no plug for any type of hairdryer, so it must be done by magic.

"Hold still," the second smaller maid commanded. She began moving her hands around my head and mumbled a small enchantment. Air flowed through my hair quickly and precisely. Warm to the touch, but noiseless. This was better than any hairdryer I had ever used. I wasn't sure what Rebekah had meant by taking too long because the second maid was done in less than five minutes. I instantly missed the feel of the heated air and thought about asking her to come back.

Rebekah then took over and styled my hair high up on top of my head in a set of curls that suddenly had a shiny luster to them. She let two long curls drop right in front of my ears and swing onto my shoulders. Once that was finished and I stared slack jawed at the beauty of it, she began on my face.

Faster than lightning, she had a smokey green and black eye applied, my eyelashes darkened and thick, and my lips matted to a healthy natural color.

"See what you think." She turned my shoulders to double check her work.

"I look amazing." I reached to touch my hair, but she slapped it away instantly. I hissed and shook the now throbbing fingers out.

"Don't touch my work." Rebekah moved to hold up my dress and helped me into it, pulling the strings at the back just a bit too tight.

"You'll get used to it, just no fast dances and you'll be fine." She instructed like a schoolmarm readying her charges for a special outing.

"I don't see a tiara. Which one are you wearing?" Rebekah investigated the jewelry box that had come with the earrings that I was placing on as she spoke.

"Oh! Uh… didn't get one. I didn't think I needed one since I'm not really royalty." I stammered. Rebekah impatiently rolled her eyes at me.

"Well, it's too late now. You need to get going. The guests are already arriving, and His Majesty wanted to see you before the two of you went in." A slight sweat began on my forehead.

"How late is it?" I asked and looked around for a clock, but none was present.

"You, her Highness and Miss Lily were shopping much later than expected. No matter, we made do with the time and you are ready. If you would, follow me." Rebekah threw open my door and headed into the common area.

"Stop pulling at it! It's supposed to be that high!" I heard Wynnie shout from beyond the door and I rushed in to see what was going on.

Ez was shooing one of the red heads away from Wynnie who was busy readjusting the front of her high-low dress she had purchased. Blue really was her color and it made her eyes gleam brightly. The shoulders were cut out triangles and the large bell sleeves were lined with a thick ring of fur. There was even a hood to the dress that had a fur lining as well.

"I still think the fur is going to be too hot for you, Wynnie." Ez mentioned for the hundredth time since the shop.

"And I still think I look amazing anyway," she countered and stuck her tongue out in defiance.

Ez rolled her eyes and stopped when she saw me watching them.

"Oh Amelia!" she swooned and swooped down next to me.

"You look amazing." I nervously thanked her and then did a small spin.

"Let's get going, shall we? I'm starving." Wynnie grabbed both our hands and led us out the door.

"Wait, my uncle wanted to see me first. You two go on ahead and I'll see you there." Both girls waved me a goodbye and trotted off in the direction of music and laughter. I watched them giggle at some joke and then descend a set of stairs arm in arm. I looked down the hallway and suddenly remembered I had no idea where my uncle's rooms were in comparison to where I was.

"Excuse me?" I stopped a passing footman. He bowed his head and stood at attention, "Can you tell me how to get to King Michael's rooms? He is waiting for me."

The footman began to nod when a voice stopped him.

"I'll take her." The deep voice caused my heart to leap and do little flips in my chest. I stopped breathing for half a second but slowly turned to see Theo prowling his way over to where I stood.

His dark gaze took in every inch of me as I did him. The dark green double-breasted jacket was tailored perfectly to his sleek wolf-like form, the matching trousers immaculate. A golden sword hung at his waist and tapped perfectly in time to his lithe step. His hair was perfectly set as always, and his eyes blazed even greener as he neared me.

I had to catch my breath, hold my hands together to keep them from shaking, and take a small step back to steady myself. This man was stunning. It was more than a handsome face. His presence was the Earth personified. Steady as a rock, he held out his arm for me to take and without a word I did as offered. He smelled of oak and ember, felt like a warm fire, and when he spoke it sounded like a deep river flowing quickly and mightily through a forest.

"You look amazing, Amelia." His smile glowed and lit his face up, causing me to relax my nerves and smile in return.

"So, do you, Theo. I didn't know you could clean up this well." I attempted to joke to ease myself, but it wasn't working very well.

"Are you trying to say I'm not always clean?" his face fell into a serious scowl and I instantly started choking on my words, attempting to apologize.

"Relax, Mia. I'm joking with you. But thank you." He winked and I almost passed out from how fast my heart was beating in my chest.

We walked in silence around a corner before Theo spoke again.

"But really, you are stunning tonight. I hope you will save at least one dance for me." A thought suddenly struck me.

"Oh, I don't think I'll be dancing at all. I'm not sure if I know your dances here and the few I do know I'm not very good at."

I felt my cheeks heat up. Oh, please Mother, don't make me dance tonight. I pleaded in my head over and over.

"Well, then when something slow comes on, I'll come find you and I'll be the only one to dance with you. Better for me I guess." I blushed wildly at the thought of dancing with him, wrapped in his strong arms.

As these visions flashed through my mind, I felt that nagging feeling where Theo and I touched start acting up again, moving its way up my arm. I had half a mind to let it keep going, just to see what would happen when we came to stop in front of my uncle's rooms.

Theo seemed to act like he couldn't feel it himself, but I did notice he pulled his arm away quickly as we halted, and he knocked on the door.

"Thank you for getting me here. I appreciate the help." I moved to open the door when Theo called out to me.

"Mia wait!" I stopped moving and turned back to face him, anxious to hear what he had to say.

"You're missing something," he continued and stepped towards a large bush sitting in the hallway. With a wave of his hand, the branches began twisting and moving on their own. I watched with interest as they began to form a hard shape from the growth. Once it stopped moving, he plucked a crown from its branches and brought it over to me.

It was a thing of earthen beauty with its golden leaves at the base and blue flowers with pink seed pods towering up in three columns. Emeralds dotted around the hairline entangling with the golden leaves and it shone brightly as it were freshly made from metal and polished just for me.

"Every Princess should have a crown." Theo reached up and set the tiara in my hair, being careful not to move a strand out of place.

I touched it lightly and then looked up at him, stunned.

"Perfection." He winked and then with a low bow, left me there speechless.

CHAPTER TEN

Michael was in a fantastic mood and even had a bounce to his step as we walked down the hallway towards the ballroom.

"Did I mention how wonderful you look, love?" I rolled my eyes with a smile.

"Only five thousand times, Uncle Michael. And did I tell you how handsome you were in your black suit?" I motioned to his tailored dark design.

"It's slimming is it not?" he straightened one lapel and gave me a wink. I burst out laughing and held up my dress as we came down one last set of small steps.

"Alright, love. Are you ready to stun the masses with me? I haven't been this excited in a long while. I feel like I'm making a great debut as well." I swallowed a lump in my throat.

"Ready as I'll ever be." I whispered. Michael squeezed my hand lovingly.

"Your mother was always nervous too, not a fan of the limelight, but did she shine. Even without trying everyone was watching her. It'll be the same for you." He tweaked my nose playfully and I couldn't help but giggle. This man really did get me and the internal struggle of whether to go back to the Original World just got one notch harder.

"His Royal Majesty King Michael Robur of the Fifth Throne and Princess Amelia Wardman." I cocked my head to the side at the sound of Michael's last name.

"Something wrong?" he asked, seeing me disturbed.

"I just, I never knew my mother's maiden name." She had told me it was Smith my whole life. Why would she have lied about that?

"Oh well, if that's all." With a mighty step, Michael turned us around the corner and we came to the top of the steps that led down into the arena sized ballroom. My mouth dropped at the size of the room and the chandeliers that adorned its vaulted ceiling. They were monstrous and so lit up by candles and magic that looking at them too long began to hurt my eyes.

Rows of tables lined the walls, littered with hundreds of silverwares and sparkling clear glasses. Candelabras were spotted through the setting pieces, but not a single chair in the room. I gasped when I took in the amount of people present. It had to be well over five hundred guests in their absolute best, all standing still and looking up at us. At me. Feathers and fur, diamonds and rubies, silk and chiffon all waiting to watch me go crashing down these steps and land straight on my face. Or that's what was happening in my mind. I suddenly felt a cold panic settle over me as I realized how frail Michael had seemed to me today and I just prayed to the Mother he didn't trip and send us both flying. I frantically looked around for his walking stick, but it was nowhere to be seen. What was this man thinking?

With all the strength he could muster, my uncle gracefully led us down the steps. He never stumbled, never faltered, he didn't even hesitate to reach out for the rail. I beamed with pride at this new-found uncle of mine. He may be sick, he may be weak, but when it mattered, when I needed him most he came through. Even after only knowing him less than a day I could see my mother's love in him, her heart, and her determination. As we neared the final step, Michael gave my hand a squeeze.

"Bow at the bottom and then, if you would be so kind, take me to my throne, please." I squeezed his hand back in answer and did as asked. I figured the stairs would be a lot for him. We bowed low, and the crowd around us echoed the gesture. Everyone continued to watch in awe as I led him gently to his throne at the other end of the long room.

I was starting to wonder if some magic was making the space grow with every step but finally, we made it. This time I had to let Michael visibly lean on me to get up the last three steps to what seemed to be a makeshift dais. Gently, I stepped to the side as he turned himself and sat down as smoothly as he could. When he fully settled onto his plush throne, the music struck a faster chord and the party seemed to snap back to life.

I waited for a moment, confused as to what to do. No one was approaching me. I couldn't see any of my friends and the noise was just growing louder as guests laughed and danced to the sound of the wind and string band. I watched the musicians for a moment, trying to place where the instruments came from. I notice a lyre, a flute, even a drum-like object. I couldn't place the organ looking thing that made a high-pitched chiming noise instead of a deep wind blow.

I began to twiddle my thumbs together and I even caught myself chewing the edge of my mouth with nervous boredom. What now?

Finally, from the crowd I saw a hand wave furiously as if trying to grab my attention. I did a double take and strained my eyes only to breath a huge sigh of relief. It was Ez, with Tim in tow, running up the dais to me.

"Mia! What are you still doing up here? Let's have some fun, this party was for you anyway." She grabbed my hand. I took a step and then paused, wanting to check with my uncle first that he was okay here alone. He, however, was deep in conversation with another elderly man that had pulled a smaller chair up next to him. They were laughing like children at some joke that I had missed.

"I'm going with Ez." I whispered in his ear after I had touched his arm gently for attention.

"Go, dear girl. Go and dance and drink. Tonight, is about you and you alone." He waved me away with a flourish of his arms and I kissed the top of his head.

"My niece, Amelia. She's the absolute finest, Yusef, the absolute finest!" I heard him behind me talking to his friend as my own grabbed my hands and pulled me out to the party. Ez miraculously found flutes filled to the brim with a wine type drink and I took one heavy sip before handing it back to her.

"What? You don't like it?" she looked between me and the glass. I wiped my mouth from the taste of it.

"Not really, but what I am used to is a bit sweeter than that. Bitter and dry was never really my thing." Ez shrugged and downed both glasses herself. Tim immediately stepped in and took them away.

"Alright there! It's a party, not a competition," he chuckled, but I could hear the seriousness of his tone.

"Obviously, you forgot my sisters were here." Ez snarked but didn't reach for another glass. I began to search the room for something to do. I didn't know how to dance these dances. I watched for a moment and found them to be very rehearsed and put together, like the old minuets and quadrilles of the medieval era. In the multitude of documentaries my parents used to watch late into the night I had seen snippets of these steps but no one alive in the Original World still danced to them like it was common. Maybe the annual Renaissance fair that came to the state but nothing in everyday life.

I did find myself enjoying just watching the dancers and partiers step, clap, and twirl in synchronicity and even found myself slightly swaying to the music.

"Do you want to try?" Ez asked from behind me, giving me a slight startle as her question snapped me back into reality.

"Oh no, I have no idea what any of these are. I do prefer just to watch, it is pretty." I motioned to the floor and Ez nodded.

"I'm with you on that one, mom made us learn all of them and frankly I hated it."

Tim raised an eyebrow, "Does that mean if I ask you to dance you will tell me no?"

Ez just planted her hands on her hips and gave him a wry smile, "Well who knew that Mr. Tim Unda knew how to dance." She balked and then, with a toothy grin, grabbed his hand and hauled him onto the floor where they began laughing and twirling with the others. Something about what she said nagged at me again. I furrowed my brow as I found my way to the edge of the food table, I didn't want to be in anyone's way.

It was something about Tim's last name. It had struck me as odd two days ago when Will had mentioned it at dinner as well, but I had forgotten about it until just now when Ez said it again.

"Unda…" I mumbled out loud. "Unda…where have I heard that before." I thought back to before I came here. Someone in school with me? No, everyone had very typical last names in the Original World and Unda was certainly not typical. Where had I heard it?

I scanned my memory before it finally came to me, like a weight crashing down on my consciousness.

You were always a pathetic little boy, Michelo Unda.

My father had called the attacker Michelo Unda, I had forgotten the last name until just now, but I clearly remembered dad calling Michelo by the last name Unda.

I scanned the crowd till my gaze fell on Tim, but he was happily dancing and spinning with Ez, not realizing what I was thinking. Why had no one told me Tim was possibly related to Michelo? Frustration bubbled up inside of me. Was this more of the mistrust still bleeding through about who I really was? I jerked my eyes around before they finally fell on the tall red head that I was looking for.

He was in a group of older bearded men, all with swords strapped to their belts like he and Theo had. Theo was nowhere to be seen still and that did leave a little sting. I thought he would have been near me tonight, keeping me company, especially after giving me this beautiful headpiece. I shook the thought from my mind and continued my swim upstream through the crowd. Finally, I made it to the Guard Captain, and I gave him a sharp tap on his shoulder.

"Mia!" he cheered when he saw me, but I didn't match his happy mood.

"Can we have a moment?" I asked as politely as I could.

"Excuse me men, the Princess seems to want to talk to me." Will gave a mock bow to his friends. I didn't wait for him, I turned on my heel and led the way to a small, curtained alcove I had noticed.

"Are you okay?" Will asked the moment I pulled the curtain back and motioned him inside. Impatiently, I motioned again and he ducked his head to squeeze through the opening.

"Mia, what's going on? Is Theo okay?" he asked, concern in his voice.

"Why are you asking about Theo? I haven't seen him since the Ball started. Why would you think me coming to you have anything to do with Theo?" I asked, exasperated that he automatically assumed that any issue I had must be with Theo.

"Oh…well, I just assumed that you two would be close to each other tonight." Will scratched his head and looked anywhere but me.

"What? No! What in the world would make you think that?" I pressed again, but this was getting off topic.

"It's just that it's a party and I figured Theo would…." But I cut him off, trying to get back to the subject that was bothering me.

"When we you going to tell me that Tim was related to the man who kidnapped my parents?" I interrupted forcefully. I wasn't comfortable being this dominate in a conversation that could be seen as aggressive but I really didn't want to hear where Will was going with his other train of thought.

There was silence for a moment as my question sunk in with Will before finally, he scuffed a foot and shoved his hands in his pockets.

"Finally figured that one out, huh? I was wondering how long it would take." He gave a heavy sigh.

"Why didn't you tell me? Why all the secrecy?" I pressed even harder. For people who claimed they finally trusted me, it wasn't feeling like they did by withholding bits of information like this.

"Tim asked me not to. After I said it at dinner the first night you were here, he came to me and asked me to keep it quiet. He knew it was his brother that had kidnapped your parents and he worried that you would treat him as an enemy if you knew." Will admitted sheepishly.

"HIS BRO-" I stopped myself from screaming, "His brother?" I finished in a calmer tone. We may have been behind a curtain but that didn't mean someone passing by might not over-hear us.

"Yes, his brother. Michelo is his deceased sisters twin. I think with Tim being twenty-four that puts Michelo at just under forty. When his sister took the throne from their father at only twenty-four, Michelo was already gone. He had grown frustrated and left Lotho years before, swearing allegiance to Heretia as his Queen. No one speaks of his familial connection to Tim or Tom because honestly, there really has never been one."

"But why not just tell me, do I seem like the type of witch who would hold one person's actions against another?" My feelings were hurt, and I wanted to make sure Will understood that. I had noticed that even though he was an excellent tactician and leader, his ability to see when others were suffering was not that easy for him. You really had to spell out your position to him or Will could easily think you were already over it and move on.

"No, you don't. Tim asked me to say nothing. I didn't see the harm in it then, but I guess I can see where it might seem sneaky to you." Will's shoulder sagged.

"Sorry, Mia girl. Just do me a favor and blame this one on me, not Tim. He already has a lot of weight on his shoulders about his older brother, no good going off and making him feel worse about trying to keep it from you. It doesn't really make much difference if they are brothers or not. They haven't seen each other since Tim was five or six."

That made some sense, logically. Emotionally however, I was still slightly wounded.

"I appreciate the apology, Will. Just, stop keeping these types of secrets from me. I don't care how big or how little you think they are. I need to know," I said.

A sneaky grin suddenly broke out on Will's face and his beard widened.

"You want to know all the secrets running around?" he slid up next to me and grabbed me around the shoulders, pulling me in for a whisper.

"Well, I think I've got a big one that may just change your life." My eyes went wide with surprise.

"Really? What?" I whispered back.

"On second thought…it's really more of a rumor. A feeling really, so nothing's for sure. I guess I shouldn't say anything till I have proof." He snapped back up, his back straight, and hand running thoughtfully through his beard.

"Will! What is it? Tell me!" I gave a childish whine. Whatever he had to say seemed good and that little bit of nosey gossip side of me was itching to hear it.

"Come on, Will! Please!" I begged but Will just flashed me one more smile and vanished back into the party on the other side of the curtain.

I huffed and pouted for a moment, but he didn't come back so I just gave up and rejoined the party myself.

The music was still going strong and so were the dancers. I couldn't see anyone I knew right off the cuff so I found my way to a table and grabbed a non-alcoholic drink for myself. I felt a small tap on my shoulder, and I turned to find two younger girls, maybe around eighteen years old, grinning wildly and dipping into heavy curtsies.

They chimed in unison. "Your Highness."

"Oh!" was the only surprised response I seemed to blurt out. The two girls kept blinking at me, as if expecting me to do or say something.

"Uh," I floundered for something to say. "Can I...help you?" I finally asked, wondering what these girls could possibly be staring at me for. Their smiles were plastered but their giddiness was evident from the way they shifted back and forth on their toes like children.

"Princess Amelia?" The taller blonde one spoke at last.

"Y-Yes?" I prompted, the title catching me slightly off guard.

"Are you really from the Original World?" the brunette blurted and then slapped her hand over her mouth, shocked at her own outburst. The blonde gasped as well and they looked at each other wildly.

"Well, yes," I answered. I was increasingly more uncomfortable with this conversation.

Both girls instantly swooned at my simple answer and began jumping in place

"What's it like there?"

"Is it really so different?"

"How do the mortals get by with no magic?"

"Are you really on a mission to rescue your parents from Heretia?"

My head was spinning from all the questions these girls were throwing at me, one after the other in quick succession.

"I...I..." I stuttered unable to stop the flow of the never-ending Inquisition.

"I think that's enough ladies, the Princess doesn't necessarily want to discuss the Princess Clarisses' kidnapping."

I did another small jump as Theo floated to my side and rescued me from the excited girls. Both immediately bowed their heads in shame and stepped back.

"Your Highness," they muttered, chastised.

"I think that's enough bothering the guest of honor, don't you think?" he continued. Slowly, I felt his strong arm wrap around my waist and he pulled me close to his body. The heat was immense, but I had to wonder if that wasn't all in my head. I could feel the blush creeping up my neck and my heart gave a splutter from his nearness.

"Yes, Your Highness!" they squeaked and bowed. They both scampered off as quickly as they had shown up.

I breathed a massive sigh and relief and found myself relaxing against Theo's chest.

"Thank you, they were a little much," I said and turned to face him fully, his arm still wrapped around my waist.

"There are actually a few people that you probably do need to meet and make nice with if you want help. Do you mind if I pull you away from all this fun to do a little networking?" he asked.

I looked around at the steady stream of dancers and merrymakers. "I guess so. It's not like I was going to be joining any of the party, not really."

I dismissed the party around us and allowed Theo to guide me, still with his arm around my waist, to a group of men and women who looked very regal and very wealthy.

For the next hour, Theo did nothing but introduce me to nobility, wealthy merchants, and other important ministers and councilors to the Royal families. They would ask me questions about my mother, I would tell them what happened and how desperately I wanted to get her and my father back. Some asked about my profession, others my interests. By the end of each conversation, however, each one expressed how much they looked forward to supporting my search for my parents and their safe return. It was overwhelming, the feeling of care I received from these people. I did feel a little hesitation but when that happened, Theo usually stepped in and gently reminded the person of some favor they had received at the hand of Michael or of Vanessa recently. This gentle nudging seemed to be enough for them to verbally give me their support and they moved on.

Finally, I was exhausted enough that I found a moment to slip away. Theo and another gentleman were in a heady discussion over trade with the Ancient Kingdom and what it could provide all the kingdoms if the ports were only open. I found my way to the infamous balcony my parents had come together on and took a moment to breathe and be alone. I was taking in the cool breeze that danced on the brilliant night air when another figure joined me in my reverie.

"You're doing well for yourself tonight, Amelia."

I turned and brushed aside a strand of hair to see Vanessa coming to join me. She placed her hands on the railing and rocked back, seeming to breathe in the air as well.

"Theo is a big help," I mentioned, a feeble attempt to turn the attention away from me for once.

"Yes, he is that. His father trained him in diplomacy and politics very well," she said.

Vanessa cast a forlorn look in the direction of her son. He was laughing at whatever the gentlemen he was speaking with said.

"But it's more than that. You have a knack for this. Being a Princess, I mean. You have a way of speaking to people that makes them feel at ease. Much like Michael does, come to think of it."

I took that moment to look up to the dais and check on him, but he seemed fine. Now, he was in the company of an older sophisticated woman I had spoken with just a few minutes before.

"Well, I have a purpose for all the speaking. I want to get my parents back and I can't do it alone. It looks like I'm never going to find the prince my father spoke of so I need to get all the help I can elsewhere."

I shrugged and leaned forward, crossing my arms on top of the balcony railing.

"Prince? What prince?" Vanessa asked me, she turned to fully face me as I repositioned my bent angle to look up at her.

"It's the last thing dad said to me. Find the Prince, my heart would know him and his mine. No one seems to know who he would be. Dad didn't know many princes when he and mom were together here. They left so soon after meeting. Uncle Michael thinks it must be a Pair bond, but how would my dad have known about a Pair for me? I wasn't even born in Medeis."

Vanessa wasn't looking at me anymore, but over my head. She was thinking deeply about what I was telling her.

"He did know a Prince while he was here, and so did you," she admitted.

I stood up straight and took a step towards her, lowering my voice.

"Who? How?" I pressed her for answers.

"Your mother never had to announce that she was pregnant. Someone else did it for her, before she got the chance." Vanessa's cryptic words had me glued.

"It was Theo's third birthday party. It was a small affair since my father-in-law was dying, and we didn't want much attention at the time. Your mother showed up with your father in tow, and before she could say a word, my sweet, loving little boy ran up to her for a hug. Instead of hugging her, however, he rubbed her belly with both his hands and kissed it."

I sucked in a heavy breath. I wasn't ready to hear this. I had a feeling I knew what was coming, and my heart wasn't prepared for the blow. I took a step back, but Vanessa caught my hands, seeing my reluctance to finish the story.

"He kissed her belly and then turned to us. Announcing that his Princess was here and now the party could start."

My knees fell out from under me and I stumbled. Vanessa did her best to catch me but ended up just propping me up against the railing and then using her body to hide me from the windows where people could see.

I felt like I couldn't breathe. The edges of my eyes began to go black as I started to pass out from the excessive panting. This whole time. This entire time the answer was right in front of me and I was too stupid to see it. Of course, my father would have known Theo. Why didn't I force those edges of the puzzle together before? Theo wouldn't have remembered my father, but my father would have remembered how Theo reacted to my pregnant mother.

"Mia! Mia, listen to me," she snapped her manicured fingers in my face, and I blinked back the fear that was clouding my vision.

"I may not have always been the best mother when it came to Theo, but I do know my son, and I remember how he acted around Clarisse when she was pregnant with you. I had an inkling at the time, but now that I've seen it for myself, I can only think it true." She looked over her shoulder, my only guess was to see if Theo was close.

"You are a Pair bond and he needs to know. If the Mother Goddess has destined for you two to be together, then you must accept it. Your magic and his will only be stronger for it," she explained.

I began to shake my head, wishing this to go away. It was too much. I wanted to go home, I wanted my parents back and to go back to Missouri, my house, and my life. I didn't want job in a clinic in Medeis, or a throne, or a Pair.

"It will only destroy you the more you don't accept it, Mia. He needs to know!" Vanessa was beginning to raise her voice in irritation but I refused to listen. I had enough of this. Of this acting, of this playing around, of all the lies and mystery.

"NO!" I shouted and a burst of anger reeled up and lashed out, causing Vanessa to stumble away.

"No," I repeated, and without another thought, I ran.

CHAPTER ELEVEN

I ran through the garden as fast as my barely covered feet would allow me. The slippers I had chosen were becoming damp and since there was no padding at all I could feel every rock and twig as I raced over the walkways. I needed to get away, to think and to plan. This world was getting too much for me. At every turn, my hope and chances of going home were getting slimmer. First it was being a Life Sorcerer, a commodity rare and desperately needed. I wanted to help, but that meant never going home.

I began to slow my pace and I came to a slow walk, out of breath and far enough away from the Stronghold that the noise of the party was just a low rumble. I continued my thoughts on a clearer level.

Second, there was my Uncle. Such a sweet mean, but feeble and weak of body. The only two choices left for him was either my mother or I take up his throne when he passed, and my mother had already given it up once before. "For me." I muttered aloud into the night air.

So that left me, another thing that would keep me from going home.

And now, I sighed heavily and slumped onto a stone bench. My shawl snagged slightly, and I picked it away absentmindedly. Now there was a Pair bond with Theo. I didn't much understand how Pair bonds worked but from the small amount that Michael had told it to me, it sounded as if yet another choice was taken away. Would the Mother Goddess really punish me for rejecting it? Would she take away my magic over wanting to go home?

Tim's words kept floating back to me, *"So, tell me again why it's imperative you go back"* I knew he wasn't being mean with that statement, but they ate at me. What was there for me at home? I didn't have a job I only had one real friend who was leaving soon, and no love interest that would miss me. Really the only thing that would be there for me, was my parents and that was all based on if they wanted to go back once I found them.

I audibly moaned and shoved my face into my hands, this was impossible! What was I going to do? Suddenly, Will's suggestion that he had given not long after Tim's question popped into my head.

"I guess the only thing you can do is just keep going and keep doing what feels right until the decision just comes to you."

But what felt right? I stood and paced for a moment, lost in my thoughts when a shiver suddenly crept down my spine. I shook it away and kept walking but was interrupted by another one. This time, I perked up my ears and listened. Something was out there, watching me. I could feel it in my magic that something wasn't right and I tried to listen closely to discover what had caught my attention.

"Hello?" I called out. I was standing in a circle built into the side of the garden. A fountain lay silent in front of me, no water moving or spilling down. The hedges were tall and looming over my head. Where they felt like a haven of privacy only moments before, now they felt like a prison where something could be hiding behind every turn.

"Is someone there?" I called again. Nothing, but I knew something was there.

My adrenaline kicked in and my heart picked up speed. I felt in danger and my fight or flight senses were taking over. I slowly began to back away to where I had come from. It wasn't a maze, this garden. It was built more like avenues with rest spots in between to the immaculate flat lawn beyond it. All I had to do was go straight back and I would be safe, but from what?

I took a few more hesitant steps, my eyes darting all around me for any sign of danger when I heard the snap of a twig.

With a shout I turned to my left just as two dark figures emerged from the hedged alleyway to the next lined avenue.

"Who are you?" I asked loudly, hoping maybe someone from the party had just come out for air too. But these figures were wearing all black clothing that fit snug against their skin.

They were most definitely not guests of the party. Suddenly, two more figures materialized from my right and I picked up my pace.

"Leave me alone!" I cried and turned on my heel to run for it. However, I was no match for these intruders.

In a blur of darkness and wind, one of them was standing in front of me, blocking my path.

"Help!" I screamed at the top of my lungs, but the Stronghold was too far away for anyone to hear with the naked ear.

What could I do? I couldn't heal my way through this. I had no element to assist me and I knew so few spells for defense. I backed away, searching for any opening in the shrubbery to get away. In my panic I tripped over the shawl that hung down behind me. The movement not only tripped my feet up but snatched at my throat and caused me to fall, gasping for breath.

Now, down on my knees, I was helpless.

"Please!" I begged, trying to crawl away on my backside, but the gravel was biting into my palms.

"What do you want from me?" I gave one last attempt to get out of this, but all four figures remained silent. I felt more than heard the

177

singing of metal as the figure in front of me unsheathed his sword and slowly brought it over his head.

"No!" I cried out one last time, throwing my arm up and closing my eyes. I didn't even have time to shed tears, to pray to the Mother Goddess, to even let my life flash before me as the mortals said it did. I just closed my eyes tight and felt my heart fall as I waited for the blow.

A sickening thud rang out and the sound of pained gurgling escaped the assassins' throat. I opened my eyes and moved just in time as the sword from his hand came crashing down beside me. I looked up at the assassin, but he wasn't moving, just staring down at me. Only his eyes visible through the mask on his face. I blinked twice, "Wha-?" but then he fell to the side and I saw the reason for his halt in executing me.

There behind him, stood Theo, two blades drenched in blood and panting hard. He looked to me, a wild look in his eye and then turned his attention to the other three that remained alive. With a battle cry, he leapt over me and came crashing down on all three at once. I scrambled up to my feet and backed my body into the hedges. I didn't run from this, but stood there and watched as Theo eviscerated each one in turn.

I had hand it to the assassins, they didn't run from the fight. But they didn't win either. With clanging of steel and slashing of swords, I caught glimpses from the moonlight reflecting off their weapons. Theo dominated the trio with ease, striking down each one, blow after blow. He was brutal, he was swift, and he was ruthless. I stopped the queasiness in my stomach at the sight of the violence, for it wasn't the blood that bothered me, but the act of savagery he laid upon them.

I could feel his wrath coming off him in waves. It reached out and called to me, to help him, and to calm him down. But I waited, I didn't want to do anything that would distract him and get him hurt. Finally, the last assassin kneeled on the ground, wounded in the shoulder and leg. Theo stalked up to him, ready to finish him. I saw it in a moment, a last attempt at victory, a flicker of moonlight caught a hidden dagger as the final man desperately lashed out at Theo' gut.

"Theo!" I screamed and lunged for him, to save him. I couldn't see him hurt. It would eat me alive, I realized. But my warning wasn't needed in the least. Faster than I thought possible, Theo leapt and jumped over the dagger's path and in one sift movement, brought down his sword and cleanly removed the assassins head from his body. I gasped at the preciseness of it all, the feeling of it being rehearsed and perfectly choreographed. I knew now why Theo was so good at what he did, he certainly had to be the best fighter in all Medeis with instincts like that.

For a tense few moments, neither of us moved. Theo just looked down at the bodies and checked to make sure they were dead. Then finally, slowly, he looked up and our eyes locked. I felt it then, for what it really was. All those times my magic had been reaching for him, every time his had been making its way up my arm to reach me.

That's what it had been, the Pair bond trying to make its way to my heart, to seal it and make it real. I had been avoiding it, pulling away but now I couldn't. We couldn't hold back the feeling any longer and I saw, from just looking at him, Theo knew it too. He felt it as strongly as I did, always had. He had been pulling away from the Pair bond just as much and he was finally letting it in to his heart as well.

Slowly, agonizingly so, Theo made his way to me. His breath was still heavy, and his face had splatters of blood on it, but his hair was still perfectly intact. Not one strand was out of place.

"That must be some hair gel you've got there," I stammered out.

"What?" Theo asked, brows furrowing.

"Nothing. Forget it," I waved away my stupid comment and looked back up at him. His green eyes were clouded from battle, but they were beginning to clear as he looked me over, checking me for wounds.

"Thank you," I breathed, "For coming for me."

Theo blinked once and then very smoothly responded, "I told you, I feel you when you're in trouble. I have to get to you."

My heart sunk a little at that. I was a duty to him then, nothing more.

"I *want* to get to you Mia. I always want to protect you. Even if it means risking it all, I will always come for you."

This felt right. Without another thought, I reached up and kissed my Pair. I planted my lips firmly on his, wrapping my arms around his neck and pulling myself up to get closer. I didn't care anymore about the sensation I got when our skin touched, I welcomed it.

Gloriously, Theo responded. He wrapped both strong arms around me, as close to his body as he could without crushing every bone. He tangled his hand into the back of my hair and the other lifted me off my feet. My magic sang and so did his. Finally, I let it crawl all the way up my arms and like lightning, it pierced my heart. My whole body rang out with glee as his magic melded to mine and we become a Pair in the eyes of the Mother Goddess herself. We accepted the bond, and with a snap, I felt a piece of my magic break off and leave me, making its way down to his and mixing.

I pulled back from the kiss to see lights glowing, our skin like moon each with their own tint, his green and mine, as bright as the sun.

"Amelia, your eyes," Theo whispered and stared down at my face.

"What? What's wrong?" I asked quietly, not trying to spoil the moment of wonder as our magic danced around our heads, creating glorious colors and wisps of magic about us.

"They are yellow," he marveled.

I gasped and reached to touch my face.

"Yellow?"

Theo nodded, "It must be a Life Sorcerer thing."

He grinned and then reached back down to continue kissing me. I didn't stop him; I didn't care about eye color. All I cared about was him and how much I wanted to be with him. Now and forever. We lost ourselves in each other for a while longer. Eventually, however I pulled back and looked up at him, still wrapped in his arms.

"That was not what I was expecting when I got dressed this evening!" Theo flashed a sideways smile and I couldn't help but giggle at the sight. I was finally free to appreciate his features. His sharp jaw line that flexed against his temple when he clenched his teeth. The crinkles next to his eyes that showed up when he smiled. His dark eyebrows that shaded his even darker thick lashes. This man was too pretty for words, and he was all mine.

Attempting to distract myself from my now raging hormones, I looked down at his suit jacket and flicked away a fleck of drying blood.

"You still look good to me," I winked back at him.

What was happening right now? Who was I all the sudden?

"Do I? Well, maybe I should show you how good you look to me," he purred, leaning down to my ear.

His breath danced over the sensitive skin along my neck causing me to shiver and my body responded to the closeness.

I was leaning my head back, angling for another kiss and more, if Theo was willing, when the sound of feet pounding on the gravel met my ears. Instinctively, I moved to back away from Theo, but he tightened his grip on me pulling me even closer into his arms.

"Trying to deny me already, my love?" his face flashed with hurt and confusion.

"No! No, I wasn't thinking. I didn't know if you wanted people to know and it didn't cross my mind, honestly. I wasn't trying to hurt your feelings." I quickly apologized, feeling terrible and wanting to make it up to him.

Theo's face softened.

"Thank the Mother. I wasn't looking to be rejected so soon after being accepted. Not sure if my self-esteem could handle that."

I frowned.

"Self-esteem? You're a prince, an Elite Guardsman, possibly the most handsome man in both realms and you just saved me from four assassins in the middle of the night without a scratch on you. But me even hinting at maybe not wanting you and your self-esteem is hurt?" My eyebrows raised in surprise.

"Of course!" he brushed a strand of hair back from my eyes and looked down at me lovingly. "It would kill me to be rejected by the sweetest, kindest, and wonderfully giving woman I've ever met in my life. It's just a bonus that you are a princess and are stunningly gorgeous even at your worst."

I stopped breathing for a moment and my heart skipped ahead three beats. "That, and my father would actually never let me live it down. Possibly even hold it against me forever if my own Pair rejected me."

I had no time to respond to this before a large group of people finally came into view from the middle avenue.

"We saw the lights! What's going on out here?" Will called and then halted, staring at the carnage surrounding us.

The entire group behind him stopped dead in their tracks and watched Theo and me. We waited for someone to say something, but not one person moved or said a word about the scene before them.

"Wha-?" Wynnie started but Tim elbowed her into silence. Whatever she was going to say was probably not completely appropriate and Tim knew this was a moment that needed to be handled carefully, especially with even more people approaching.

Tim cleared his throat and gingerly picked his way through the ground and over the dead bodies.

"Is everyone okay?" he offered, attempting to be suave and skirt around the subject of Theo and I so close together. Our magic may not have been shining as brightly anymore but it still was dancing around us and Tim must have been a little wary to get too close.

"Yes, Tim. We're fine. Theo took care of the problem. It seems these people were not invited to the party and instead of asking nicely they decided to try and kill me over it." I was trying to joke, but Theo's face fell, causing me to clamp my lips shut from a smile.

"That's not funny, Mia. They could have killed you. We need to search the bodies and see if they left any evidence on who sent them." Will nodded in agreement, but still didn't move.

"First, before we do that. Can you turn off the swirlies that are blocking us from you right now. And possibly, let each other go?" Tim took a few more tentative steps and reached out to test what our magic would do. When nothing happened, Tim pulled back and Theo dropped his arms from around me.

"Well, this is…" Tim started but dropped his words when he couldn't find what to say.

"It's a Pair Bond."

Everyone turned to face Vanessa as she joined the group of concerned party goers. After my escape from her, she must have noticed Theo leave as well. Then when she saw what freaked everyone else out, she mut have realized what had happened out here in the garden.

"Theo and Mia are now a bonded Pair. The Mother has Blessed this, and their magic will forever be intertwined," she announced for us never taking her eyes from mine.

I nodded knowingly at her and she returned it with a nod of her own. It was a nod of thanks and understanding the decision I had just made. In a single moment, I had chosen Theo above all else. I had chosen magic, Medeis, and the throne if my mother didn't want it.

The decision was a heavy one but as I looked at Theo standing there, smiling back down at me with joy, I knew I had made the right one. There was no going back now, I had chosen what felt right. And I couldn't be more pleased. Will and the rest of the Guardsman stayed behind along with a few soldiers to pick over the corpses of my would-be assailants while Theo led me back to the Stronghold. The Ball was still going on full swing and no one present was the wiser for what had occurred out in the garden. It seemed like hours ago, but it couldn't have been more than thirty minutes since I had left to take a breath of air on the balcony.

No one was waiting to greet us, congratulate us or even see that we were being led around the outside of the Ballroom and out the doors. Vanessa cracked open the door and waved us through, trying hard not to catch anyone's attention. As Theo and I snuck through the opening, Vanessa reached out and took my hand. I paused and gave her my full attention, her face riddled with concern.

"Seal the Pair Bond tonight. Don't let anything stop you. Ogden can't go against you if you and Theo are Paired. You hold all the cards now, Mia. Don't waste this chance to get Clarisse and Daryl back home."

I was stunned at her words. Did she think I did this all for influence? That I allowed the Pair bond to take just to get my parents back? I was about to say something when she quickly shut the door in my face, and I stood rooted to the spot.

"Mia?" Theo's voice called to me.

I faced him. He was walking down the hallway to my rooms. I kept quiet, just thinking over what his mother had said to me. I stopped in front of my door and then paused, turning to face him. I took him in once more. Did he think the same thing about me? Was he just so happy to be accepted that he was willing to Pair with someone who was just using him? My mind reeled with questions, but there was only one way to find peace in my heart.

"Theo, I love you," I whispered.

The words rang out in the empty hallway like dead weight. With bated breath I waited for his reaction. Would he be stunned? Was he not ready to say it back? I was okay with the idea of him not feeling comfortable saying it to me, everyone got to that stage differently. I was an adult and I understood, but I just felt the need to make it crystal clear to him right there that I wasn't in this for influence or power, but for him and him alone.

Finally, Theo took a large step toward me and gathering me into his arms, soundly kissed me.

"I love you too, Mia," he answered and my heart soared with relief.

I returned his embrace and did my best to melt into his skin. Finally, he pulled back from me and I sucked in a breath noticing how dark his eyes had gone.

His deep green eyes were swirling with desire, and when outlined with his dark, thick lashes his beauty took my breath away. My heart hammered against my chest and his soul in my ribs strained to reach out and grab that piece of me that was within him. I began to pant as I frantically searched for the door handle behind me.

"I'm going to give you one minute to get in that bedroom and take that dress off properly before I come in and rip it off your body," he growled as I found the handle. With a yelp I fell through.

"Forty-five seconds!" he shouted as I slammed the door and began to tear at my dress.

"Oh! This stupid thing!" I cried to myself and began flinging my shoes off. I reached to grab the ribbons but could barely make it.

"Thirty seconds!"

He was at the door purring into the wood. I could hear him scratching at it. I felt like a sexually hunted rabbit and he was a wolf that could no longer restrain his carnal desire.

"Dear Mother!"

My entire body was hot as the same feelings that he was putting off caught me off guard. Finally, I was able to snatch at one ribbon and begin tearing them away.

"Fifteen seconds."

It was barely a whisper now.

I squeaked, why were there so many straps? I started to feel the dress loosen up when suddenly the door flew open and there he was. I turned in my half-undressed state to look at him. He was wearing only a black shirt unlaced halfway down the front, the tight green breeches hugged his well-defined thighs, hips and oh dear Mother! His manhood was already straining against the fabric. I blushed ferociously and kept scrambling for the ribbons at my back. With a snarl, he crossed the room and in what felt like one swift motion, spun me in place and shredded the dress from my body.

The lovely, now destroyed dress, fell to the floor and he lifted me from the puddle of useless fabric. He didn't care, and frankly neither did I. Theo carried me to the edge of the bed and sat me down on it, my legs over the edge. He knelt before me and began kissing my breasts, my stomach, and my thighs. I cupped the back of his head and moaned at the feeling of his warm breath on such sensitive skin that had not seen male contact in a long time.

I threw my arms out to move him to the side, and with the opposite leg, made him lose balance so that I was on top of him. He made a small noise of air leaving and then looked up at me, straddling his hips.

"Oh Mother, looking like that if you don't make a move quick this is going to be over already."

I looked down to glance at myself in the silk bra, garter, and panties I was wearing. The dark green stockings that the garters were holding up looked almost black in the darkness of the room.

"We need moonlight." I leaned forward and purred into his ear, using my other hand to stroke his manhood through his pants.

He shuddered and waved his hand, uttering a simple spell command. "Grow."

Two potted plants grew to grab the sides of the curtains and pull them back.

The moonlight was glorious as it streaked across the bedroom, lighting us up with a pale blue glow. I could really see him in that moment, and I shuddered in anticipation.

"This is in my way," I grunted. I grabbed the top of his shirt with both hands and ripped it in half to reveal his beautiful body beneath.

Every muscle was pulled taut against his olive skin and I took in a breath of awe.

"If you think this is amazing, you should see what's waiting for you down there," he pointed his finger to where I was sitting at his hips.

"We'll see about that," I giggled and scooted down to place myself between his thighs.

"You are a torturous witch," he groaned from behind closed eyes. Leaning over him I whispered breathily in his ear, "That's Sorcerer to you, little prince."

That was all he needed. With a snarl, he wrapped his arms around me a deftly flipped us over again. His entire body was able to block out the moon in that moment. His knee spread my legs apart and then the other joined him, his eyes never leaving mine.

"You're mine!" he stated and I nodded.

"Yes. I am!"

I felt the tip of his manhood teasing my feminine opening.

"Say it," he commanded and closed his eyes and moaned.

My hips arched every time he grazed that spot, longing for him to fill it.

"I am yours," I echoed to him, and he lost control.

I felt the entirety of him enter me and fill every inch of my womanhood. Once he had entirely seated himself, I felt him begin to move. It was slow at first, testing my rhythm out but once he realized I was ready as well he picked up pace. I closed my eyes and met him with every stroke.

"Theo!" I moaned, finding myself already close to release.

"Mia!" he whispered, slowing his movement. "Look at me, my love."

Slowly, I opened my eyes and gazed into the deep green depths of Theo's. The love I saw behind them pulled at piece of him inside of me even harder. It stretched and reached with an ever-growing tug on my spirit to rejoin his.

"You are glorious," he whispered in my ear and began moving again, this time at a deeper and more sensual pace.

I threw my arms around his neck and felt his soul reaching for mine this time, sending even more waves of pleasure through my body. His panting become more guttural with every moment until it was nothing but a growl escaping his throat.

"Mia. Mia," he moaned.

I reared back to let him enter even further. With a snap, I felt our magic slam into each other, mixing and entwining around us. My release came at that exact moment. Theo roared my name, rattling the walls.

I could feel the earth shake beneath us and the stars quake above in that moment. I clung to him tighter still as wave after wave of release surged through my body. Eventually, the surges subsided, and I slowly release my hold on his neck and back. Theo leaned down and kissed me soundly, continuing to rain my neck with kisses through his spent panting. I could feel our magic recede back, but those pieces of our soul were still intermingling around us and refused to be put back just yet. They yearned for interaction together, for peace in this moment a pure bliss of just being free of their bonds.

"Your beauty astounds me, your courage enchants me, and your love emboldens me," Theo recited.

I squirmed up next to him and wrapped one of my legs around his. His arm shot under me and pulled me even tighter. The warmth of his body ensconced me entirely and I breathed in his scent, letting it wash over me like a cooling balm.

"Was that what you wanted for our first time together?" I asked.

I looked up at his face and he looked down at mine, a smile twitching upward on his full swollen lips.

"It was more," he responded and kissed me sweetly. Theo swirled his arm in the air twice. I looked up to see where he was pointing and yellow rose petals rain from the ceiling as we laid there next to each other in silence.

"They're my favorite," I giggled and reached up to grab one, holding the delicate petals in the palm of my hand.

"Funny, they were always mine, too," Theo chuckled and flicked his wrist again, a single yellow rose appearing in it.

I smiled and took it, giving him another kiss.

"All that I am, I am yours," he whispered in my ear as I sniffed the rose.

"And I am yours," I responded, before resting my head on his chest and stroking his chest with my fingers.

"Oh, Amelia. You always feel so good when you touch me. It's like fire on my skin and your smell. You always smell like roses and the sun," he whispered.

I giggled at the thought of what he was saying, "How can someone smell like the sun?"

He turned in the bed to face me and pull me up against his still naked chest.

"Like warmth and trees and children laughing. That's what you feel and smell like. A summer day where everything is alive and well and nothing will ever touch that moment of perfection," he mused.

I closed my eyes and rested my head on his broad chest. "I think we need sleep. We've had an eventful night. Don't you think?" I yawned and I felt him settle me into the comfy oversized bed.

Theo pulled the covers up and over the both of us, tucking me into his side and wrapping both arms around me. I nuzzled the pit of his collarbone and breathed deeply.

"You smell like dark wood, moss, and twilight," I mused and buried my face deeper.

"How can someone smell like twilight?" he smiled. He was toying with me.

"It's like signing grasshoppers, fireflies, a warm fire, and blankets," I answered.

I heard him chuckle and wrap his legs around mine.

"Sleep now, my love. For tomorrow we dine with dragons," he whispered.

CHAPTER TWELVE

Morning came too soon for my tired body, but Theo's attentions were all that I needed to reinvigorate and get my mind ready for the day, even if it was in the gutter. Eventually, two maids gently rapped on the bedroom door and entered.

"Your Highnesses, breakfast will be at eight o'clock."

Theo moaned and rolled over to sit up. "Fine, just leave the clothes out and we will ready ourselves. I'll call you back in when the Princess is ready for you to dress her hair."

"As you wish," they bowed out silently.

"I guess that's our cue," I groaned and sat up. "Let's get this over with. I want to be on the road and finding my parents within the next day or two and not later. There's no way the entire group of High Kings and Queens will say no. Not after all the people you and I spoke to last night, even your father couldn't ignore them."

I heard Theo stumble just as a thought came to my mind.

"Speaking of that, where was your father last night? I never saw him, or no one pointed him out to me," I wondered.

I straightened to see Theo staring down at a pair of black pants the maids had left him.

"He wasn't there by the time you and Michael entered," Theo admitted darkly. "He came in, spouted off a few nasty sentiments about you and your Uncle, jabbed at me a few times, and then left. Mother went with him, but I saw her come back after a few moments, something about a headache. It was just an excuse, really. He knew what I would try to do to help you and he didn't want anyone walking up and to talk to him."

I nodded slowly, not sure what to say to help him with his frustration.

"Let's worry about it at the meeting. You don't know what he will say, and he may be trying to get to you. Get dressed and we will take this one step at a time," I counseled him and turned to finish slipping on the brown pants that had been brought for me.

"I'm not so sure about that, Mia. From what my mother explained to me yesterday, my father was livid when your mother left for the Original World. He and Michael have never gotten along, but he viewed your mother as more biddable. When he got stuck ruling with Michael instead, he grew resentful. Your uncle may be feeble of body, but feeble of mind he is not and has never been."

I nodded, agreeing with him. I had noticed as much for the little time I had known him.

"Ogden may use this as the way to break Michael into conforming to his every wish. Leverage, if you will. I also fear he thinks it will force you to bow down to him as well."

My back straightened and a small flame of fire burst in my heart.

"Well, he can think again. I may be my mother's daughter, but I can fight when need be. Albeit physically probably isn't going to happen, but I can make him think again about threatening me with my family."

The fire floated through my veins at the mere thought of someone using my parent's predicament against me, especially when it was for petty revenge. Theo finished zipping up his leather riding jacket and smiled.

"That's my girl. Hold on to that and throw it at him if he tries. You've got at least mom, Michael, and me on your side. The other two Queens are Felicity and Hester. Felicity sides with my father most of the time, but she's just a self-important narcissist at the end of the day. Hester, however, she's the oldest of all of them and the quietest. You probably didn't even see her at the Ball last night. The woman is ancient and wise, but even she makes decision that shock me occasionally. Her son is just as quiet as her. Bertrand isn't seen much outside the Academy, neither are his two children. All three pretty much checked out of the world when Bertie's wife died. I think he's hoping he dies before his mother and one of his two kids take the throne. I would guess Millie wants it. Her brother is much more concerned with leading the military forces he has been assigned. Millie, well she's funny and bright, but she is very shy until you get to know her. Father sees them all as weak, but they really just don't want to be bothered, Bertrand especially," he shrugged.

I nodded my head, taking in the useful information. Hester sounded like a Queen I wouldn't mind getting to know if I had time. Dad and Bertrand would very much get along if they ever got to meet, for sure. In the distance, I heard a low gong ring out.

"That would be breakfast. Let's not wait around." Theo held out his hand for me to take.

"Dining with dragons?" I repeated his romantic words from just the night before.

"Fire breathing dragons," he joked, interlacing his fingers with mine and placing a warm kiss on my hand.

Almost everyone had arrived in the Dining Room that seemed to be joining us. Vanessa sat up at the head of the table next to a supremely polished and severe looking man. I could only guess was the mysterious Ogden Varillian, High King of the First Throne, and Theo's father. As we walked through the doors, hand in hand, a silence fell over the crowd. All ages were seated at the table and all eyes were on me.

To break the silence, Vanessa quickly stood, her chair scraping on the ground.

"Good Morning! And congratulations on the Pairing, I trust you two slept well after such an eventful evening." Vanessa slowed down at the last two words and stared me down, her meaning evident.

I went slack jawed at her boldness. A blush crept up my neck and I began to open and close my mouth like a fish, unable to speak audible words in my horror.

"Very well mother. Thank you," Theo promptly answered for me.

Vanessa kept looking to me for an answer to the lingering question in her eyes but I was so floored that I couldn't even comprehend answering her. Theo placed me in a seat next to my Uncle, who was enjoying a single boiled egg and a slice of ham.

"Good morning, my dear. I hear you had an exciting night," he beamed, winking mischievously.

I spluttered the water I had been trying to drink back into the cup, which was extremely unladylike. Theo touched my shoulder to steady me and I tried to regain my composure as quickly as possible. With my hand on my chest to help slow the coughing, and my other on the table to steady myself, I took in a deep breath and looked towards my uncle.

I couldn't tell if he was sincerely confused at my reaction, or if he was playing games with me. Seeing how he liked to tease others incessantly, I didn't know which way to land on the question.

"Y-Yes, Uncle Michael. Theo and I accepted the Pair Bond last night in the garden. This was shortly after I was almost killed by intruders, but nonetheless, we realized what the Mother had planned for us and we are happy," I replied.

I reached for Theo's empty hand and squeezed it tight, he beamed back at me, green eyes twinkling in the morning light.

"Wonderful! I thought I saw something when he brought you to meet me, but I didn't want to say anything at the time. Well, this is great and I'm happy to hear it." He clapped his thin hands together and rubbed them vigorously. "I'm starving and I know you must be two after having sex all night so let's tuck in."

I almost fainted at his words and from the sound of everyone's gasping, I wasn't the only one.

"Mother bless my soul!" one woman wearing tons of jewelry uttered, her hand lightly fluttering to her chest.

"Oh, cool it Felicity, you've got four daughters. Like you don't know how that happened or something," Michael teased and cut his eyes in her direction.

I heard a quiet snickering from the old lady sitting next to my uncle. Her shoulders lightly bounced as she had to shut her eyes to keep from rolling them. This must be the infamous Hester; old and wise Theo had called her. Apparently, she had a sense of humor that Michael could trigger.

"See? Even Hester here finds me funny. The rest of you are just old stuffed shirts," he waved them off. Michael gave me another knowing wink. My face was ferociously red at this point and if those assassins hadn't all died last night, I wished they would come do it now and save me from this. In all my twenty-two years of life, never once had my parents asked me about my sex life. Nor did they ever mention theirs. I wasn't a virgin as of last night by any means, but it was a very private thing for me, and I had hoped to keep it that way.

I noticed that Theo's father had not said a word this entire time, just stared down the table at his son angrily. Never once wavering his gaze. Without any warning, Ogden jumped to his feet. With a loud voice, he announced, "I've had enough of this childishness. It's caused me to lose my appetite and I think we should get down to the business at hand. High Rulers, to the Throne Room. Heirs may join, and those in question." He glared with gritted teeth.

Theo stood as well, anger flashing across his face.

"Mia is an heir," he corrected.

His fists balled at his side and I could feel him readying for battle. Like a wired cat, all his muscles tensed, ready to spring if his father said so much as one wrong word.

"That's for the High Rulers to decide. All of us," he looked to Michael who stared him back down, displeasure clear. "Throne Room."

Felicity sprang to her feet, along with three of her four daughters. I looked around curiously for Ez, but didn't see her. Shouldn't she be here, too? I asked as much to Theo as he held his hand out to help me up.

195

"She probably went back home last night. She hasn't spent a night here since we left at eighteen, and I don't think anything in this world would entice her to ever do so again," Theo clarified.

Vanessa first watched her husband leave the room before rising and coming to join us. Footmen assisted both my uncle and Hester from their chairs, and I instinctively went to grab each of their hands.

"I've got you," I smiled patiently and made sure each one had a steady footing first.

A footman handed my uncle his cane and he was able to release me, but Hester was apparently a stubborn mule.

"I have no use for canes, girl. They just make my hand hurt worse," she muttered.

I nodded and continued to help her through the door. Suddenly, an older gentleman with graying temples jogged up to us, slightly out of breath.

"I was told heirs were asked to be at this meeting," he puffed.

Hester nodded and reached for him.

"Amelia, this is my only son Bertrand. Bertie, this is Mia, Clarisse's daughter," Hester introduced.

Bertie's face lit up and he nodded.

"The one she was pregnant with, or do you have an older sister?" he asked kindly.

I instantly felt a deep connection with Bertie and liked him immensely.

"No, I'm it. It was just us three growing up," I answered sweetly.

"Too right, too right. I am sorry to hear about Clarisse. I wouldn't worry about it. Ogden may be a sour puss, but I know him deep down and he will do the right thing. I know he's loud and authoritarian, but that's why we have five rulers and not one. Sometimes, our heads get big and we need others to talk us back down again."

Somehow, I couldn't imagine this gentleman and his fun older mother as bigheaded. He reminded me of some old country English gentleman who found fishing and shooting with his trusty dogs and hunting club more enjoyable than anything else in this world. He looked quiet and unassuming, but friendly and polite.

196

"That's what I'm hoping," I answered with a shrug and moved ahead to join Theo.

He led me down yet another long hallway to the front of the Stronghold where we faced the two double doors from last night.

"The Ballroom doubles as the Throne Room," he mumbled at my confusion.

He shoved open a door and I gasped; this was not the same room from last night. While it was still large, it was nowhere near the scale I had taken in the previous night. It was about half the size, but the dais was twice as big. No tables lined the walls and the curtains were gone. Only the one wall facing the balcony and garden led anywhere else.

"I'm guessing magic?" I marveled as we, yet again, descended the steps.

Theo's father was already waiting on his Throne, impatiently tapping his fingers. Vanessa joined him first and lovingly touched his hand. She leaned down and whispered something to him. Ogden, for a moment, lightened up his countenance and took her hand in his, gently kissing it.

"My parent's relationship is so strange," Theo pulled me aside as others began to file into the room behind us. "I never understood them or why they even married to begin with. I guess mother was once like him, but when my sisters died, she just wasted away. Father tried to nurse her back to health and he doted on her. He took his frustrations out on me, never her. I guess she's finally seeing what an ass he can be, but all the love he gave towards her makes her believe he's better than that and she stays for him."

I waited as Theo worked through his thoughts. I could feel that he wasn't really asking me anything, or for my opinion. He just wanted to come to his conclusion out loud to someone who would listen for a moment. He was having a hard time coming to terms with this new, slightly stronger mother, and his resentment and anger towards his father.

I gently just touched his arm and waited for him to finish. "Let's see what he has to say first. Then we can decide if we want to hate him together forever." I suggested. Theo gave me a slightly stunned look before grinning ear to ear.

"Man, you really get me." He winked and we took up the rear of the unofficial procession.

There were five large thrones sitting on the dais, with four smaller chairs in between them. Ogden was sitting in the middle, Vanessa in the throne to his right, and Hester in the throne to his left. Bertrand sat in between Ogden and Hester. On Hester's other side was an empty small chair and my uncle was being helped up the stairs to the last throne. A lump suddenly built in my throat.

"If I sit in that chair, won't everyone just think I'm an idiot for assuming I'm supposed to be here?" I asked quickly, a cold sweat breaking out on my forehead.

"This is your throne and no one else's. You have every right by blood, birth, and power to be in this seat. Michael is your family, and you are his heir right now, whether you like it or not. It seems you must play this card today, so play it well. Respond to no allegations, give them no indication that they are upsetting you. If you must speak, ask for Michael's permission first. Heirs have no standing in this room, they are only here to listen and learn," Theo whispered.

He quickly counselled me before he had to rush off to his own chair between his parents.

"Remember, you are powerful in your own way and you are this throne's heir. Nothing they say can touch you if you don't let them."

His face grew soft. He plucked my hand from the arm of the chair it was gripping with white knuckles. He gave them a gentle peck, then cupped the back of my head for a deeper kiss.

"I love you Amelia, with all my soul, body, mind, and heart."

"I love you too, Theo," I whispered back and nodded that I understood his directions.

I watched him go, longingly. Michael was suddenly there taking Theo's place in front of me. Everyone was settling into their seats, and I could tell this was about to start.

"Theo told you how this goes?" Michael asked.

I nodded weakly.

198

"Chin up, my sweet child. If you want to say something, just touch my hand and I will let you speak. Whatever it takes to get my sister back, we will do. And we will do it together."

His eyes sparkled with determination. I reached out and he grabbed my hands.

"You look so beautiful, just like Clarisse. She would be so proud of you. Let's not disappoint her, huh?" Michael winked and settled back.

King Ogden leaned forward and tapped his ring on the arm of his chair.

"The councilors and the Elite Guard may enter," he called out and the doors opened again, this time five robed men and women walked in silently. Will, Tim and Wynnie followed behind.

I breathed a quiet sigh of relief, more friends. Thank the Mother. As the eight new members approached, Vanessa waved and eight chairs appeared. They all took their seats with a bow.

"Now that everyone is here, let's get started. We have been hearing reports from both the Elite Guard and our own scouts that the exiled Princess Clarisse and her husband, Daryl Wardman, were kidnapped from the Original World a few days ago by Michelo Unda. We presume this is at the request of Heretia, Queen of the Ancient Kingdom, but we have no proof as of yet. During the attack, they sent their only daughter, Amelia Wardman, to our doorstep. Now, this seems to be a problem because of Clarisse's status as an outcast. It is written in our laws that anyone of the status outcast if beyond our reach and help from the moment the decree is signed and therefore, we are under no obligation to help her."

I stiffened in my chair, but Michael subtly raised his hand to soothe me. "Let him finish," he mouthed.

"It has also been ascertained that Amelia Wardman is a Life Sorcerer, proven in witness testimony by the unnamed Priestess who Rited her. This Priestess then did knowingly attack Amelia Wardman in an alleged attempt to protect herself and this kingdom from Queen

Heretia, who she feared would come looking for Amelia and, by extension, herself."

A few council members nodded. Apparently, they thought Heretia would do just that.

"It is written in our laws that such an attack with intent to do harm warrants death. However, the Priestess offered her full cooperation and apology and as such, was subsequently and magnanimously exiled to an unknown location instead."

My lasting resentment at the Priestess getting out of punishment for hurting me faded away. I hadn't known she was facing death. I never would have wanted that had I known earlier. Maybe Ogden wasn't really that bad of a guy then. He agreed to let her go, instead of taking her life. That had to mean something.

"Then, last night two things happened that the council may not be fully aware of," Ogden continued his long-winded rant of my life the past few days.

"One, Amelia Wardman was attacked by four unknown persons in the Stronghold gardens. We still do not now their identity, nor who controlled their actions. The Stronghold guards are trying to glean that information from their corpses."

Hester suddenly leaned to the side towards me.

"Sounds like a job for a Life Sorcerer," she muttered. I froze, sitting up straighter in my chair.

It had been mentioned that Life Sorcerer's could speak to the dead for a brief time. However, I had no idea how to do that and I had no one to teach me.

"Lastly, it is official that the Amelia Wardman in question is also a Pair Bond of Prince Theo's here. Have I missed anything?" he asked to the crowd, cutting off the last bit of news short and unimpressively.

I could feel Theo bristling in anger from where I sat. Ogden was dismissing his own son in front of everyone as a last and unimportant thought. By extension, he was dismissing me, a fact that didn't sit well with Theo.

"No, Your Majesty. That seems to be everything. The only thing to do now, is decide if Suravia is going to send troops or a small group on a mission to find and rescue Princess Clarisse and her husband," an older councilman stood. His bald head did nothing to hide the age behind his wrinkled eyes and sagging cheeks.

"A vote then. We can choose to send an entire army ready for war for the exile Clarisse," Ogden said.

My hand shook unwillingly at the way Ogden talked of my mother.

"We can choose to send the Elite Guard for reconnaissance, and if able, rescue. Or we can do nothing," he ticked off the three choices.

My guess was that this had been heavily discussed over the previous few days and Will had laid out the best options for them. All three choices sounded like something a Captain, not a King, would consider.

"Vanessa?" he looked to his wife, who smiled gratefully.

"Guard. I'm not keen on sending my son into the Ancient Kingdom, but I think an army will get us nowhere," she answered.

Ogden nodded, seemingly unsurprised. He looked to Felicity next.

"Nothing. Our laws state she is beyond our help and we owe her nothing. However, I am not against recognizing her daughter as the heir to the Fifth Throne. Amelia Wardman is not at fault for what took place twenty-three years ago," Felicity announced.

I was fuming at this self-important witch.

Ogden looked to Michael.

"Elite Guard," he announced in his firmest voice. "I want my sister home. She was a friend to each and every one of us growing up. I think some in this Court have forgotten that."

He gave Felicity a wicked side eye and then sat back out of her line of sight.

Ogden cleared his throat, "I say nothing. I agree with Felicity on this one. Clarisse chose to leave and go out twenty-three years ago. I do hold some reservations over this girl claiming to be her daughter, but now that she is Pair Bonded with Prince Theo, there is not much we can do about removing her from court. I do want a further discussion on removing her from the Heir's chair."

A loud clanging of wood on stone rang out. Theo was on his feet, towering over his father. "How dare you!" he hissed.

Vanessa sprang into action. "No, Theo. Not here," she pleaded, coming around to grab him by the shoulders and catch his attention.

Instead, he looked to me for direction and I shook my head. His mother was right, not here, not now. Not with one last vote to cast and so close to victory. Shaking in anger, he twisted his wrist, causing the chair to right itself. He sat back down heavily.

"That's right, Theo. Listen to the women," his father sneered at him.

I had to hold back from throttling Ogden myself.

"I believe it is my turn," Hester's surprisingly strong voice broke the tension.

"Yes, it is, Hester. What do you vote we do?" Ogden had a small sneaky smile playing across his lips.

Suddenly I wasn't as confident. If he was smiling, I should be worried.

"I vote," she paused for a moment. "Nothing."

She finished and I felt like I was punched in the gut. Nothing? This kind old lady was choosing to let my mother continue to rot in Mother only knows where.

"Well, that settles it," Ogden threw his hands in the air as Michael leaned forward.

"Hester!" he cried.

Vanessa looked just a shocked.

I happened to glance at Bertie, whose eyes were as wide as saucers.

"At least!" Hester pointed a gnarled leathery finger in the air, and everyone gave her their attention. "At least until we have proof that Heretia is behind this. I am not keen on entering other sovereigns' lands without due reason, and Michelo's actions do not prove it was Heretia who ordered it."

I suddenly understood why Hester had mentioned the dead guards to me. She wanted me to get proof. But how? No one practiced Life Sorcery anymore.

Ogden, pleased enough that he would get his way, sat up straight. "Well, that settles it, until we have proof of Heretia's guilt, Suravia will do nothing." He finalized his statement by rapping his ring twice again, ending the meeting.

Theo was straining to keep his temper in check. His breathing was uneven, and I could see the storm clouds in his eyes. He was by my side in a second, lifting me out of the chair, and attempting to whisk me away.

"Wait," I called, ignoring Theo's hand.

Bertie was helping Hester down the stairs. I hurried after them and moved to stand in front of her.

"I know what you're asking me to do. But, Your Majesty, I can't do it. I don't know how. I'm not trained, and I have no one to teach me," I pleaded.

She could not possibly mean for me to attempt something extremely dangerous so soon after getting my magic. Hester reached one hand out and touched my cheek.

"I sent Bertie away for a few years as a young man to train at a wonderful Academy in Lotho. It's run by their finest scholars and he came back with stories of the largest library he had ever seen, filled with knowledge that had been thought lost to the ages. What great time he had and all the friends he brought back with him. I certainly found what he learned helpful, too," she answered me.

With a nudge to her son, she continued down the stairs. Bertie gave me an apologetic smile and followed her. Theo walked up behind me, as did the rest of the Elite Guard.

"What did she say?" he asked me, thinking I had begged her to reconsider.

I watched as the wise old woman hobbled off, held up by her aging son. I had heard what she meant. Her years had taught her to give her meaning in other ways, including magically. In that touch, I had seen her meaning, felt her heart, and heard her thoughts. She couldn't outwardly commit to supporting entering other sovereign's lands. That would set a bad precedent in her eyes. But, she also believed Heretia had done this, so she wanted action. Instead of agreeing, she was disagreeing, but sending me away. Out of the reach of this Stronghold, with a group that wasn't under any one kingdom's control. To a place where I could learn everything I needed to find my parents myself.

"We're going to Lotho," I finally responded.

CHAPTER THIRTEEN

The boat Will had hired looked nothing short of a Viking longboat, complete with dragon heads and rows of oars sticking out from both sides.

"How long will this ride take?" I asked, as we started down the dock. My legs were still shaky from the almost two-day ride by horseback to the coast. I hadn't realized how far south the capital of Suravia was, having Teleported from the Northern Forest before. I had stopped to ask once why we didn't just Teleport again, after Tim had mentioned how long the trip would take.

"We have to take supplies with us. A single witch can teleport a few weapons on their own, but food, water, and all the weapons in our arsenal will be too much," Wynnie answered, showing me her multiple bags of knives, swords, and armor.

Will had instructed everyone to clean out or purchase anything they would need. Everything had to be kept secret. Theo was worried his father would try and stop us from leaving, or at least he could stop Theo and me. Ogden had no control over the other three since they weren't his subjects.

Immediately following the meeting, I had explained everything Hester had showed me with her mind and heart. Everyone in the Guard was completely for leaving, but it needed to be done quickly. I informed my uncle of our plans and he agreed as well, claiming he would be the distraction for us to slip out and get away. I wondered to myself what that distraction could possibly be as we continued down to the end of the wooden dock.

I could see sailors throwing crate after crate of goods into the hollow belly of the boat.

"Two days, if we leave just as the sun rises. Tomorrow night at the earliest," Theo answered my question and leaned down to grab the rest of his saddle bags.

He pointed with his other hand towards the East. My eyes followed the direction just as the sun began to break over the horizon. My magic reached out to greet the first rays that blinked their way through. It was if they were shaking hands, greeting each other with smiles and acceptance. I allowed the feeling to continue and the warmth of the rising sun crept over me. Starting at the top of my head and inching its way down my body.

Every ache and pain from the ride to the coast washed away as the sun tickled me alive again. I hummed sweetly and felt the warmth dive deeper. Opening my arms, I let another wave of my magic leap to the sun's embrace. They were singing together, skipping along the tops of the waves, my magic and the dawning sun playing as if children before me. It was a sweet game of tag back and forth glinting off the caps of the water.

"Amelia?" Tim called to me.

He stood beside me now, Theo having left to deposit his things below deck. I slowly opened my eyes, but refused to let the feeling go yet, smiling to myself and watching the sun rise higher and higher.

"Amelia, you're glowing," Tim whispered, so as not to startle me.

I looked down at my feet and sure enough, every inch was emitting light.

"I'm not glowing, Tim. I'm basking. I'm soaking up the energy of the sun and drawing it in to give me strength," I replied.

I wasn't sure how I knew this, but I did. Deep down, some instinct of mine cried for the sun and its power. I instinctively reached for it. I guess that's why I always loved my morning rituals with mom; they were healing me. It was the magic within me getting what it so desperately needed from the sun. Like a recharge of batteries, it refueled me.

Tim watched for another quiet moment and then nodded knowingly.

"I get that way when I swim. I feel the water flowing through my entire body. The sound of the waves in my ears is calming. It drowns out the rest of the world for a time," he mused.

I turned and reached for his hand. I wanted to try and share this feeling with him. He accepted it and I sent the warm tingle down my arm and he hissed in shock.

"This feels different than mine. This feels like electric fire. Mine always feels like a cool blanket being placed on top of a tired and sore body. This is humming with energy and excitement, while mine is relaxing and calming," he said in awe.

We stood there in silence for another moment enjoying the sun when our names were finally called, and we broke contact. As we walked up the gangplank, Tim touched my shoulder and waited.

"You're stronger than you think, Amelia. I can feel that. You've got more power in one hand than any of us do in our whole bodies. Whatever you've got inside of you is different than ours. Don't waste it," he whispered.

I was puzzled by his sudden warning, and barely knew what to say in response. "I'll try," was all I could reply.

I took Theo's hand to help me on the last step. Tim remained quiet but stayed near as we shoved off from the dock and headed Northwest, towards Lotho.

The deck came to life with men and women moving about, pulling sails, twisting ropes, and moving more barrels and crates. I had never been on a boat in the Original World, so being on a fully fledged ship in Medeis was a completely new experience for me. I didn't know what I was supposed to do, but I had heard going below deck and out of sight of the horizon could make a person even more seasick. So, I stayed up top and watched. No one asked me to help with anything, so I quietly stayed out of the way.

The Guard seemed to find some work to be done and were busy moving objects around. Tim was even helping the sailors at their tasks. I sighed and closed my eyes, taking in the sun's warmth. After a time, the rocking began to make me a little queasy, so I found myself staring at the horizon behind us, watching as the last speck of land vanished.

"The first time I watched Suravia disappear like that, a huge weight lifted off my chest," Theo whispered.

I turned to smile at him. "I can imagine. After meeting your father, I'm not sure I would have stuck around any longer than I had to either. He was a little much, even for passive aggressive little old me!" I joked, trying to lighten the situation. Theo only frowned.

"If you think you're passive aggressive, my dear, you need to think again. You're not anywhere near passive, but nor are you aggressive," he countered.

I raised a challenging eyebrow. "How so?" I had to hear this one. We may be Paired, but the man had only known me for seven days.

"My mother is passive aggressive. She finds ways to line up what she wants done while still acting like everything is fine. Sometimes it works, other times it doesn't," he began to explain.

"I don't think I like being compared to your mother. It's a little creepy," I scrunched up my nose in slight disgust.

"But I'm not. I'm saying that is what passive aggressive is and you are not that. You are something much more honest, yet much more volatile. I would classify you, if I were pressed, as a Protector," he explained.

The confusion on my face was evident.

"I see how you rise to the occasion, but you don't waste your energy on just anything. You try and calm things over and take the middle path when you can. But when you think someone needs you, there you are in whatever capacity is needed, even if it's just to listen. Like you did for Wynnie," he smiled. "Bet you didn't think I knew about that one."

I was stunned. Did Wynnie tell him what I said to her?

Theo smiled reassuringly, "It's a good thing, love. A compliment if you will. Wynnie seemed to appreciate it." He leaned down to kiss my forehead.

"Will is going to do some sparring on the deck with Tim and Wynnie in a moment if you'd like to join."

I spun in my seat to follow him. "You mean fight?" I asked as he skipped down the steps, seemingly at ease with the rocking of the boat.

"Why not? I don't see why you can't play with some swords. My mother can wield one, as can Felicity. And back in her day, Hester was known to be pretty impressive with a short sword," he shrugged.

He reached for a small blade from a rack that had been set up. Wynnie and Will were already sparring each other. I marveled at the dance they created. It was like lightning, but fluid and smooth. She would jab, he would dart and swing a leg. As I was watching in amazement, Wynnie even ran up Will's chest at one point to kick him in the jaw. Will rubbed his face, laughed, and punched out again.

"Are you going to teach me that?" I pointed.

Theo looked up from strapping a leather gauntlet to his wrist, squinted his eyes from the sun's brightness, and shook his head.

"No. Not today at least," he answered, tightening his coverings. "Wynnie has been fighting since she could walk, and so has Will for that matter."

"Are they better than you?" I teased.

Theo raised an eyebrow, tossing the silver blade onto his shoulder and widening his stance. "No one," he bragged, tucking an invisible stray hair back behind his ear, "is better than me."

I raised my sword. "Then show me," I challenged.

Before I could blink, Theo reached out and grabbed my wrist, twisting my hand down quickly but gently. He pulled me so close to him that his mouth was right next to my ear. My heart skipped as our cheeks touched and I felt the light sting of stubble on my face.

"Oh, I'll show you what I'm good at. But that will have to be in a more private location," he whispered.

For the Mother, this man was sexy. I about became a puddle of lovestruck witch goo on the deck of a ship in the middle of the ocean. Slowly, Theo backed away from me, letting his skin graze along mine as he did.

"But, before that, you need to learn how to hold a sword," he announced loudly.

Great, now everyone is going to see me impale myself. I blew some hair out of my eyes and followed behind Theo to an open spot away from all of Will's kicking and thrashing. Tim had joined in on Wynnie's side and they were both trying to take down their Captain together.

"You hit like a girl!" Will taunted Tim.

"I shoot and scout for a living, hand to hand isn't my forte!" Tim defended a right hook and jumped to the side.

"And I hit way harder than he does!" Wynnie chimed in and drop-kicked Will into a pile of netting.

Theo didn't even seem to notice his friends' banter as he began bouncing on his feet lightly to loosen up a bit.

"Okay, pay attention and do what I say," Theo instructed.

I reluctantly nodded and grasped the short sword with both hands.

"First off, switch hands," he said. He came around to my side and tapped my right wrist. "Dominant on top for power and direction. Left is there for support and balance."

I nodded and clumsily did as told.

"Next, keep your elbows up. Builds strength and keeps you ready for anything," he continued.

I lifted my elbows. I was thanking the Mother for all the heavy lifting of patients I had endured during nursing clinicals in school. I did have at least some muscle in my arms.

"Alright. Make sure that you never lose sight of your opponent. Watch your feet and keep them shoulder width apart from each other. If you move one, move the other as well," he said.

Slowly, Theo lifted his sword and brought it down easily. I twisted my wrist to block his blow. When they met, he advanced on me. Naturally, my front foot moved first and the adjusted itself.

"No, move the back foot first to avoid getting your feet tangled!" he instructed.

He brought his weapon down the other way which forced me to twist my wrists in another direction. The weight of the blade was already starting to create tension in my shoulders. We continued this small practice for a time before Theo moved into turning a circle instead of back and forth.

I listened to every instruction without a word, obeying his every command. As much as I hated fighting and violence, my run in with the assassins a few nights before had opened my eyes to my inability to defend myself. A lot of the problem came down to my magic and learning to wield it defensively, but being able to physically protect myself wouldn't be the worst idea. For the better part of an hour, we danced this little minuet we had created. Every now and then, Theo would get a bit faster to better my reactions, but he never pushed too far. As the sun began to rise higher into the sky, the heat became more apparent. I was sweating, not from exhaustion, but from the heavy weight of the sun bearing down on us.

"Can we take a small break?" I finally asked.

My arms were sore and my back ached. Most of all, I was thirsty. Will had long ago switched from hand combat to agility training. Wynnie was jumping up and down, swinging kicks, and leaping over barrels. Tim was impressively keeping up with her.

"I'm getting faster than you Wyndetta Lily!" he shouted over his shoulder.

Wynnie grunted in frustration. She kicked off from the top of a crate instead of jumping over it, squarely landing her feet in the middle of Tim's back. Tim fell with a thud and Wynnie continued her sprint around the obstacle course.

"No fair!" he called after her.

Wynnie stuck her tongue out and kept going. I chuckled at the fun this group had together. It was refreshing to see people who could be so serious at times, relax and just have fun. Theo handed me a wooden cup filled with water and took a swig from his own.

"Well, why you're nowhere near ready for a training yard, you take direction well. Maybe once we get on land, we can continue these trainings and get you to a point where I'm confident you can protect yourself in an emergency," he rattled off.

I nodded in agreement. I found myself enjoying the practice, both physically and mentally.

"I would like to. It's gotten my mind off my parents for a little while and makes me feel stronger. After what happened back in Suravia in the garden, I think I would like to even take it farther. Maybe even some hand-to-hand self-defense," I agreed.

I shivered at the thought of what could have happened in that garden had Theo not felt my fear and responded immediately.

"I don't ever want to feel that helpless again," I admitted, looking down into my water cup.

Theo reached out and pulled my chin up with a single crooked finger. "Neither do I, but we're going to fix that together. In Lotho, we will get stronger. You will get stronger. We will find you a teacher at their academy. Someone must have old books that the Life Sorcerer's used to study from. You're never going to be in that position again, whether I'm there or not. I promise you that."

I smiled and nuzzled into his embrace.

"Hey! Love birds! Let's eat an early lunch and then clean some weapons before dinner!" Will called.

"Clean weapons?" I looked up at Theo questioningly.

The only response I received was a sideways smirk and a tug on my hand.

CHAPTER FOURTEEN

I had fallen asleep early after dinner. Solstice wasn't far off, so the day was a long one, causing me to lay down while the sun was still up. I was abruptly woken by a scream and the sound of roaring and waves, which left me thoroughly discombobulated. I blinked through the darkness after jolting awake at the sudden noises. I looked around, attempting to place the noise, but was interrupted by a loud boom and the ship shuddering from a collision of some sort. I leapt out of bed just in time for Theo to come crashing through the berth door. He was panting, wet, and slippery.

"What in the Mother is going on out there?" I shouted above the noise of more screams and shouts.

"Remember when we killed the Nandina and I mentioned I had heard something was loose around Lotho?" he gasped for breath.

I nodded my head and had to follow Theo out the door to keep listening. He grabbed at a spear that was lying against the wall and ran up the stairs.

"Well, apparently I was right!" he shouted.

I raced to keep near him. The boat shifted suddenly, and I was thrown to the side of the steps. I cried out, but caught myself on the rope railing. Men and women shouted unintelligent commands at each other, cried out warnings, and scurried around the deck like frightened rats.

"Theo! What's happening?" I asked again.

Someone was running around and dousing torches, leaving the entire ship lit by moonlight and star glow. I didn't have time to glance around me before out of the depths of the ocean rose a monster the likes of which I had only heard of in fairy tales.

"Meet Cetus. Wild Beast of the Seas!" Theo shouted.

Cetus bellowed a roar so loud that my eardrums shook, and the bones of the ship rattled.

"Mother!" I began my curse, but it fell dead on my lips as the Wild Beast reared back and struck its massive, scaled head on the side of the ship.

Everyone standing found themselves flat on the ground from the impact. Again, the commands were called, and four sailors aimed and threw spears expertly at the Wild Beast's mid-section. Cetus screamed in anger, but the spears did nothing to its natural armor.

Theo shoved me behind him and brandished his own spear. I searched frantically for a weapon I could wield, but I quickly realized I was useless in this arena of battle. Cetus moved its massive neck and came to rest on the other side of the ship, rearing back to ram it again.

"Everyone get down!" Tim shouted from the top of the open steering deck.

As he did so, he raised his arms above his head and a pillar of water rose from the ocean. With a shoving motion, he slammed the water cannon into Cetus, knocking it back several yards. The pillar barely missed our heads as it came whizzing by, but the droplets still rained down, soaking everyone who wasn't already wet.

Wynnie, along with three other sailors, began making the same twirling motion with their hands. The air around our heads began to whip together in a circle, and a large tornado, larger than the ship itself, appeared. They gave a loud grunt and pushed the tornado toward Cetus. For a moment, Cetus was lifted into the air and flew away, but with a scream, it slashed the tornado in half with its tail, falling back down with a mighty splash. The boat rocked violently from the waves it created.

My mind raced for a solution. This was a creature of the sea and being such wouldn't be terribly affected by the elements having to do with the sea. What was the sea but Water and Air?

As if he was reading my mind, Will stepped forward with another tiny woman next to him. She gave him a knowing nod and together they planted both feet onto the deck with large stomps. In sync with one another, they bowed their heads over their fists and pulled their them apart. As they did, fire formed in the open space, growing larger and larger as their fists got further away. Cetus was already slithering its way back to the boat, this time at a ferocious speed. It screamed another hideous roar and reared back for another hit.

"Now!" Theo shouted, and in unison, Will and the female sailor stepped their right foot forward heavily and punched the flame in the direction of Cetus' massive head. With a boom, the two balls of fire raced to meet Cetus' head on before it could reach the boat. I sucked in a breath and grabbed Theo, steadying myself for the impact.

With a sickening crash, Cetus and the fire met over the water and Cetus was thrown back again, this time screeching in agony. I looked to Will and his fire partner who were both panting heavily, sweat coating their brow. The smoke hung thick in the air and we waited. Hoping the attack had finished Cetus, or at least made it decide to leave us alone.

I stood up straight from my protective crouch and looked around. Theo stayed down, too focused on searching the smoke for Cetus to see me move from around him. I took a hesitant step forward.

With a final enraged roar, Cetus surprised us all. It launched through the smoke and raced for the mast next to where I was standing. Instinctively, I threw out my hands and shrieked, shutting my eyes tight.

"Mia!" I heard Theo shout, but it was too late.

I could only stand there and take the blow that was coming. As my hands reached out, they came together and a like live wire they sparked. I felt my magic ignite like a firework and spear Cetus straight through the underside of its chin. In a split second, the bolt of light shot straight through the Wild Beast and impaled it. Roaring loudly at first, the sound then fell to a gurgle and Cetus crashed down into the sea and fell still. Two sailors near the front of the boat leaned over.

"It's sinking! It's dead!" they reported and a hush fell over the entire ship.

My heart was racing a mile a minute and the edges of my vison went blacker than the night sky above us. Just as my ears were going numb, I heard a cheer go up amongst the crew, but I didn't join. My knees gave out and I barely heard the thundering of Theo's steps, racing to catch me as I fell to the deck.

"Mia? Mia!" he caught my head and shoulders before they collided with the wood.

Theo called my name over and over, but my consciousness was slipping. I saw Wynnie's white hair tumble down over me, blocking out the moon. She lifted a dark object in her hands.

Cold water flooded my face and I sat up suddenly, spluttering. It took me a moment to catch my breath, but when I finally did, my vision had cleared and my ears weren't ringing anymore.

"Mia? Can you hear us?" Theo was beside me, trying to get my attention. I blinked and then nodded twice to let him know I was there. I coughed once more before finding my voice.

"W-What did I just do?" I stammered. My teeth began chattering from the adrenaline crash.

"Will? Can we get her a heated blanket?" Wynnie asked, looking above my head.

"Darla already ran to get one," Will answered. He wasn't even finished answering when the fire witch came into my field of vision and threw the warmed blanket over me.

216

"There ya go, sweetie. Breathe nice and even now. It's over," she soothed and tucked it around me.

Tim helped Theo shift me and then placed me into his arms. "Let's get her below," Tim suggested. He went before us to clear a path through the throng of cheering sailors.

"Thank you!"

"Good job!"

"Amazing!"

They lauded my praises, but I had no energy to even smile back. I wasn't even sure what I had done. All I wanted was sleep. Theo raced down the steps as gently as he could behind Tim, followed by our other two friends. I moaned at the final step and leaned my head back into Theo's shoulder.

"Almost there," Theo whispered.

He waited for Tim to open our berth door. The room was built to hold all five of us and our things, so once the door was shut, we were practically guaranteed privacy.

Theo laid me gently on the bed and Will leaned over, placing a hand on my blanket. Instantly the blanket rewarmed and I pulled it tighter.

"Okay, so let's all be very clear on what we saw. Mia just annihilated a Wild Beast with a light beam, right?" Wynnie blurted excitedly from the door after locking it behind her.

"Shhhh," I heard Theo chastise her.

"Sorry," she lowered her voice. "But really, we all saw that? I'm not dreaming up the most awesome dream ever?" Wynnie's voice hit a high note in her glee that I was positive even dogs couldn't hear.

"Yes, Wynnie. We all saw it. But what I want to know is how she did it," Tim said. I heard the creak of wood as Tim jumped and lofted himself into his upper bunk above were Will had staked his claim.

Theo arranged another pillow under my knees and then came back up to my head, wiping hair from my face. "Mia? Love? Can you talk or are you already out?" he asked me.

217

"I hear you," I whispered. Energy drained beyond belief. But like Tim, I too wanted answers, so I stayed awake.

"Do you know what happened just now?" Will prompted. He was trying to make sense of what he had seen and figure out how to explain it to the ship's captain.

"I just reacted. I didn't say or think anything," I explained slowly. "I'm not even sure what it was."

Theo continued to run his fingers along my head. "It's okay, love. You did great whatever it was."

"It was sunlight, that's what it looked like to me!" Tim spoke up from his perch. "Pure sunlight. You must have been unwittingly collecting it all day today and in your panic, released it on Cetus. It's a creature of the deep dark ocean where no light reaches. Air and Water did nothing but shove it around. Fire dazed it slightly, but its armor was too thick in the end. The only thing that can truly defeat something that has lived its life so far below the waves is light itself."

Everyone looked towards me for confirmation, but I just weakly shrugged my shoulders. "Beats me. You guys know more about magic than I do. If you say that's what happened, then I believe you."

Will sighed heavily and a knock sounded at the door. Theo sprang to his feet and blocked my line of vision. Wynnie turned to open it and a small wiry man with a grey beard stuck his head in.

"Captain Rawlings," Will greeted with a nod. Wynnie stepped aside to allow the ship's captain to pass through the door.

"If I had known we had a Life Sorcerer in our midst, I would have turned you away at the docks, no matter how much coin you handed me!" he scathed.

Will didn't move as the captain stared him down.

"I can't be held accountable if Heretia comes looking for the crew who transported her across the ocean to Lotho. So, from this moment forward, you must stay confined to your cabin. When we get to Lotho, I want you to depart immediately and never board my ship again. Forget this boat's name. I'll be changing it anyway after tomorrow," he whispered.

Wynnie made a noise as if to argue, but Will stayed her with a look.

"We understand. I am sorry for having to keep this information from you, but I do promise it is with good reason," Will apologized.

Rawlings bowed his head. He didn't raise his voice. This man wasn't angry at us, he was terrified of us.

"Her being the first Life Sorcerer in over twenty years is reason enough to keep it hidden. I and my crew will do our best to keep it that way as well, if not just for our safety, but yours," Will bowed in thanks.

Rawlings turned to leave. As his hand rested on the door, he stopped and turned to me. Theo stiffened at the pause, ready to defend at a moment's notice.

"However, I thank you, from the bottom of my heart. My crew is my family and this ship is my livelihood. Without them, I am a lost man. I wish safety for you and your friends. May the Mother Goddess bless you in whatever journey you are on. If the day ever comes that the threat to your life is over, you are more than welcome to look me up and we can have a proper feast to thank you for what you have done tonight. Until then, goodbye."

Silence fell over the cabin as the reality of what I had done sunk in.

"I'm sorry guys," I whispered.

Theo was instantly kneeling at my side. "Don't ever be sorry for doing the right thing. Whether it was intentional or not, you saved everyone's life on this ship tonight."

Will towered over Theo as he looked down on me. "You have to understand what your existence means to people. Some will be glad that you're near them, but others will see only danger. They are simply scared, and they have every right to be, not of you, but of what could happen if they associate with you. However, no matter what Rawlings or his crew says, I promise they will always remember this and be grateful for it. Fear is a powerful thing, but loyalty is stronger. You will forever have this ship's crew and its captain in your debt."

I nodded, Will's words easing my fears.

"Let's get some rest. We might as well enjoy this break for the next day, because once we get to Lotho, the wheels will get turning to bring your parents home. Tim has already sent word ahead by messenger to his nephew. The High Kings and Queens of Lotho will want to see us immediately when we arrive," Will explained.

Wynnie sauntered over to her single bed in the corner and grabbed an oversized shirt from her bag. "Thank Mother we have our own washroom for privacy. I love you guys, but I have made a point to never change in front of you and I don't want to break that streak now."

Her joke was met with halfhearted chuckles.

Theo settled down next to me in bed. "Rest, my love. It's over."

I fell asleep the moment my eyes closed.

We arrived in Lotho much faster than expected. When given questioning glances, both Tim and Wynnie shrugged it off.

"The Air and Water must be really in our favor. Who are we to interfere?" they replied.

Rawlings himself escorted us silently to the edge of the ship as it came to dock. When the gangplank landed safely on either side, he waited for us to disembark before any of his crew moved a muscle. I dared a look behind me as Theo herded me to shore. There on the deck, the fire witch Darla barely raised her hand and mouthed a noticeably clear, "Thank you." I felt her relief from where I stood. Everyone on the ship bowed in unison. I was moved by their small but significant gesture. Even with their captain's command to never acknowledge us again, they defied him to send me their wholehearted appreciation.

I sucked in a breath and continued to the waiting city of Lotho.

At the end of the dock, Wynnie handed Tim two of her bags and shouldered her last one. "I'll meet up with you guys later tonight after the meeting. I have to check up on something while I'm here," she said.

Her anxiety was evident, but she turned and stalked off before I could ask further. Before she was out of sight, Will called after her, "Stay clear headed!"

It was clearly a warning, but from what I couldn't tell. Wynnie didn't look back. She just gave a small hesitation in her step before disappearing into the crowd.

"What's that about?" I asked Theo who was readjusting his messenger bag.

"She has an aunt here that she hates. Apparently, the woman is worse than her mother when it comes to putting Wynnie down."

I stared at the crowd Wynnie had escaped into.

"Then why does she go?" I asked.

Theo sighed and bent to knock some sand of his boots, leaving them less shiny than he liked.

"The aunt has a daughter that Wynnie loves immensely and continues to remain close to. Every time we come into Lotho, she calls on her cousin for a visit. She is trying to help her gain the courage to leave the family like she did. But every visit just gets worse and Wynnie is having a hard time coping. So, she ends up drinking when she's here and Will is getting sick of it," Theo sighed.

I was about to ask why Will didn't help her with her drinking problem, but there was no time. A messenger ran up and bowed reverently to Tim and then handed him a piece of paper.

"Your presence is requested immediately at the High Castle, Your Highness. The High Rulers are waiting eagerly," the messenger recited.

"We're headed their now. Have someone prepare the Elite Guard Safehouse in the city with a maid. Please take our bags to the Safehouse and set them in the front room. We'll return there directly after the meeting," Tim instructed.

He looked up at the sun after dismissing the messenger and handing him his bags.

"It's just after noon, we got here much earlier than expected, so I guess the Rulers aren't going to let us rest first. Let's get moving," Will announced and tossed his multitude of bags into a cart, moving to throw Wynnie's in with them. Without another word, we took off up a dirt hill towards a busy market.

"The High Castle? Not Stronghold?" I looked around to take in the sight of this new place.

People of every color roamed around the docks. They were travelling between stalls, calling out to others, even hoisting large baskets full of goods they were either hoping to sell or had just purchased. It was busy, noisy, and it was alive. Everyone looked so peaceful and calm.

Lotho was the definition of a dance. If one were to stand on top of a building and look down the streets, the town would look alive with fluid movement. People swayed back and forth, stall to stall, greeting and talking, moving, and dodging. If someone stopped, people just went around them without a glance or thought. My attention was suddenly caught by one stall that had glass reflecting in every direction. I approached and reached my hand out, the chime twinkled in my fingers delicately.

"That is a fine piece! Enchanted to ward off little dark magics that might be cast for any ill reason over your home. It catches the magic and hurls it back into the air away from any harm or danger it might cause," a stooped old woman smiled.

She had a single twinkling, ocean blue eye. Her smile was large, and her hair was as grey as the moonlight reflecting on a river.

"It's lovely," I crooned.

I stared at it. Every color in our world was represented in the little glass talisman. It sang with the breeze. Theo came up behind me and nodded to the woman, who bowed her head low.

"Your Highness, your lady friend here seems to like the looks of my little trinkets. I would offer it to you for the low price of twenty-five coin if she wanted it," she smiled.

I smiled to myself, but Theo spoke before I could.

222

"My lady friend here would be the Princess Amelia of the Fifth Throne of Suravia," he said.

I wasn't sure exactly what I was expecting the woman's reaction to be, but she just gave me a knowing little smile and touched a crooked bony finger to her nose.

"I have no need of it, though it is stunning. I have no set place of residence yet to hang it outside of for protection. Maybe one day, but not today," I replied kindly.

The woman bowed her head in understanding. "Then, might I suggest a ring? Or some other form of jewelry to give the lady as a token of your Pairing?"

We both became rooted to the spot. How could she tell? I opened my mouth to ask, but she held that twisted finger back up with a tutting noise to silence me.

"Don't ask, it's obvious to anyone who knows how to look. I can see it in your aura. You are a mixture of yellow and black with a little tinge of green right next to your heart. His on the other hand is the deepest and richest green I have ever seen with a yellow beating mark right there over his heart," she explained.

She poked Theo in the chest and his face darkened. I could practically hear him growl deep in his throat. I sprang into action.

"Thank you for your time, but we really must be leaving. Do know that you have some of the loveliest art I have seen in a very long time," I smiled.

I hurriedly began to turn Theo in his place when a warm hand gently brushed my shoulder. The old woman had come out from around the stall and was looking up at me expectantly.

"I'm really sorry, but we must..." I started to say, but she halted my words.

"Do not fear it," she whispered.

I blinked, before leaning in close. "I'm sorry?" I asked.

She shook her head. "Don't fear it. There's nothing wrong with Death. In fact, it seems to need you as much as you need it," she whispered.

I blinked again and she had returned behind the stall as if she had never been speaking to me. A young woman had walked up, and she was attending her new client. I was an afterthought to her now.

"What did she say to you?" Theo asked with furrowed brow, he could tell that I was visibly upset.

"Nothing that I understand really. I'll tell you later, but it wasn't anything you should worry about," I waved him off and steered him down the street quickly. I was ruffled by her comment and I didn't want Theo to worry about me. We had bigger issues to attend to and an old woman's ramblings were not my main concern.

"You didn't get to tell me about how the High Castle worked. Is it different from Suravia?" I asked him, trying to get his mind off that strange encounter with the lady at the stall.

"A little. The people of Lotho are more open and freer with their thinking. The Kings and Queens of this kingdom turn to each other and the scholars from the Academy," he explained.

My ears perked up. "So, what does the academy teach?"

"Mostly about the makeup of magic. Water wielders have an ability to dissect spells and understand their underpinnings. They also teach a little healing here, nothing to the extent that Life Sorcerers' can do, but life wielders don't have their own Academy. So, this is the best place for it," he explained.

I looked up at the High Castle, blinking my eyes back from the bright sun. I could see blue banners billowing in the breeze from the ramparts.

"Do you think they could teach me anything here?" I could see Will up ahead, speaking to someone at the gate.

"Probably not, you said you were a trained healer back in your realm. The little that Water wielders can do already probably will pale in comparison to what you can do naturally."

This stunned me. "Why," I asked, "do the Life wielders not get together to share information. Being from an Earth Kingdom, Ez could probably teach them so much about plants and herbs. The scholars from Lotho could only add to that knowledge."

It seemed to me that the accumulation of all the different studies could only help the people of each country, instead of dividing them further.

"Because it's too dangerous. After Heretia began making Life Sorcerers disappear, everyone got tight lipped. They got scared and stopped communicating. We're going to have a hard time getting the ones that are left to come together for a possible war. They will want nothing to do with it at first. Creating a gathering of Life wielders will make them targets, and it's going to be a tough battle convincing them into it," he answered with a sigh.

"They're scared, Mia. We all are. We have been for a long time, but as long as she stayed in her own Kingdom, everyone just ignored her. With you here, that's all changed. Heretia gaining power, your parents being kidnapped, and then you being the first Life Sorcerer in so long, everyone is on edge. Everything is different now."

I went silent, not sure how to respond to this. This was all my fault. I never should have let Will and the Elite Guard talk me into the Rite. No one would have ever known I was a Life Sorcerer. I should have just kept pushing until Suravia found my parents and left none the wiser. My silence must have been deafening because Theo suddenly pulled me into an embrace.

"Don't start worrying about it. We're going to find help, that's why we are here. Lotho will help us, so will Maravette with Wynnie's insistence. Elevetia will be a different story, however, but we can deal with that when the time comes. We can do this, it's not your fault."

I pushed back from him and looked up into his emerald eyes, so steady and firm. Love oozed from every corner of his being and I sighed, nodding my head.

"I just wish I knew a way to end this now without anyone getting hurt. I also would love to know if my parents are okay," I whispered.

We didn't get to continue anymore of our conversation. Two armed men in radiant blue leather armor approached us.

"Your Highnesses, we are to escort you directly to the Throne Room to see the High Kings and Queens."

They bowed from the waist, something I was still not used to. Theo wrapped his strong hand around mine and led me inside. As we entered the towering castle, the bustling sound of the streets faded away.

Suravia, had been quiet, as if everyone were asleep and content. No one had been wandering the halls. It was very controlled. Lotho's castle was as alive inside as it was outside. Servants, butlers, and footmen floated around the hallways silently, as if they were walking on delicate lily pads. I could hear rushing water in every direction and saw many fountains hidden away in corners. Everything was coated in sapphires, glittering and gleaming from the flecks of liquid that sprayed from the fountains and basins they ran in to.

The Throne Room was a stark contrast to the sterility of Suravia. A huge reflective pool sat in the middle of the room with the five thrones encircling it at wide intervals. Smaller chairs were littered throughout the circle, creating a huge ring around the water. Vines hung from the rafters, the only pieces of architecture overhead since it seemed to be an enchanted open-air ceiling.

"It's lovely," I whispered in awe.

"Thank you," a deep voice answered.

I spun in place and found myself standing before an attractive young man. He couldn't be any older than Theo himself, yet he felt more playful. He had a constant smirk on his face, like he was enjoying a joke that only he could hear. Two sapphire eyes stared into me and I shivered from the heat of them. Shocking white hair bounced playfully, rocked by his hearty laughter.

"You must be Amelia. Tim has already told me about you. He seems to think highly of you and I can see why. Your beauty alone is enchanting," he smiled and bowed before me. Scooping up my hand and planting a light kiss upon it.

I blushed deeply and curtsied in return.

"I'm sorry, I don't know who you are. But you are right: I am Amelia Wardman," I responded.

Theo was on the other side of the pool, eyeing us warily, but caught in a conversation with Will. A door opened on the left and a small group of people began to file in.

"How rude of me! I am Thomas, one of the High Kings of Lotho," he announced.

I nodded my head again and pulled my hand away. I turned back to look up at the ceiling.

"I was just admiring how this room is constructed. It feels incredibly open, but at the same time, it's detailed and precise," I marveled. I waved my arms to some of the jewel encrusted motifs along the wall. "And the art is exquisite. How long have they been here?"

Thomas shook his head. "I have absolutely no idea. Since the construction of the High Castle, I suppose. I'm a much better diplomat than I am historian," he shrugged.

"Did you know that you were destined to become a High King? Were you okay with that, even though some saw you as illegitimate?" I asked.

Thomas caught why I was asking these questions. Apparently, he had heard my story. Instead of answering immediately, he led me over to the reflecting pool in the center of the room. I could feel Theo watching from far away, but Thomas' presence was so vast it seemed to block out everything else. His long blue robe shimmered with the life of the ocean as he placed me in front of him, looking down into the pool. With two strong hands on my shoulders, he looked down as well, face next to mine.

"In the element of water, there is both a turbulence and a peace to be found. As young wielders, we are taught that this is an element that can be tamed, but not forced by any means. Water is always in motion, always moving, like time itself. However, unlike time, water moves in many directions: past, present, and future. It is also an emotional and trusting element. It has always directed my life, and I believe that it will never lead me astray," he recited.

I looked down at my reflection. "You must trust in your path, Amelia. There are forces that the Mother directs, that we must learn to submit and give ourselves to. She would never give us anything we couldn't handle, and she always puts us right in the place we need be," he whispered.

I bent down and touched the cool water, watching tiny fish scatter away.

"In answer to your question, yes. I knew from the time my mother brought me here that I was to be High King one day. And yes, I was okay with having to learn this life, but like I said, I trust the Mother and I trust in my path to know that it can be conquered. I can overcome it," he smiled.

I stood back up and faced him. "I'm just not so sure of all this myself. I just wish my parents had prepared me a little more," I said.

I looked around longingly, wishing they were both there with me. Thomas gave a low chuckle.

"You, dear Princess, don't need anyone to prepare you. From what I've been told, you have everything you need right here," he poked my head with a strong finger.

I returned his kindness with a small smile. "I just wish that I believed that." I admitted.

Thomas gave a shrug as a bang of a gavel sounded throughout the room. An incredibly old looking man shuffled forward, and everyone started moving towards him.

I realized that it was time for the meeting to start and I moved to join Theo. As I approached, he relaxed.

"What was that about?" he asked, looking in the direction Thomas had wandered off to. I glanced over my shoulder and shrugged.

"Just friendly advice from one High King to another potential High Queen," I answered.

Theo threw one arm over my shoulders, steering me toward a pair of chairs set together near where Will was already seated. I looked over to see Tim seated to the right to his nephew who towered over him. Will had placed himself next to the old man who seemingly oversaw the running of this meeting. I casually looked around the room, taking everyone in.

"We seem to have some particularly important guests here with us today who have sent word ahead about some troubling news from the Ancient Kingdom. I suggest we let Captain Wilhelm brief us on all they know and what has been discovered before we discuss our actions," the oldest gentleman spoke.

He seemed gnarly and broken, but his voice was strong and clear. He radiated wisdom and it had a very calming effect. He turned and nodded to Will who bowed his head and began speaking.

Will told them everything he knew. From tracking the Nandina, to finding me after my parents' abduction, and discovering Heretia's possible involvement. He gave them every detail. I winced when he spoke about me being a future High Queen and had to ignore pitiful glances when my parents were mentioned, but overall, it was a precise summation.

When he finished speaking, he turned to relinquish the floor back to the elderly man.

"That was highly informative, Captain Wilhelm. I think the biggest question left for this Council is what do we do with this? For one, we must consider sending aid to retrieve the Princess Clarisse and her husband. Second, we must discuss preparations for war if Heretia does intend to proceed with the direction her actions seemed to be headed in. We have many skilled Life wielders in our kingdom, and it is our responsibility to protect them as much as anyone else," he said.

Every head in the room, save two, nodded. I focused in on the two who remained stoic. They were seated next to each other; a militaristic man with broad shoulders and a birdlike woman with a sharp nose.

"I see no problem with Suravia sending out envoys to discuss the ransoming of the Princess, but I'm not sure I see where that is Lothos' problem," the broad-shouldered man spoke in a low gruff voice.

The sharp woman beside him nodded.

"And who's to say Heretia isn't just peacocking? I don't understand where any good would come out of releasing Wild Beasts and going after a single Life Sorcerer," the woman chimed in.

Her voice was as shrill as her birdlike nose suggested. Theo tensed next to me, but I refused to retaliate. There was always one in every crowd, and apparently today was my lucky day to get two.

Thomas gave me a knowing smile and began to speak. "It's not just Suravia's kingdom that has been jeopardized, but our entire world. We all know what Heretia is capable of. Even though we have never been able to definitively prove she was the root of all the Life Sorcerer disappearances, we do know for certain that she murdered every other Queen in her own kingdom. With that little regard for life, I think it's safe to say she's not just peacocking as High Queen Lily puts it, but dead serious."

Everyone but the gruff looking High King and the High Queen Lily nodded in agreement. Another older and kinder looking woman with a head of gloriously silver hair raised her hand and began speaking.

"The biggest concern, however, would be estimating casualties and damages. We are small but mighty. From what we know of Heretia, she will keep every fight dead center inland. We must come into this with the understanding that we will be somewhat out of our element. What exactly are we looking at in her infantry size? I worry our people are vastly under equipped for land battles if it comes to that."

The oldest High King nodded. "I was concerned with the same thing, Ophelia, but before it comes to that, I suggest we look at the most pressing matter: the ransom and rescue of the Princess

Clarisse." Theo leaned over to me, motioning to come closer. I bowed my head to hear him better.

"That's King Vermir. I swear he's older than Hester, but the man has a firm grip on this council. Next to him is Ophelia. They are actually cousins, their mothers ruled together for many years and they now go hand in hand with most decisions. Ludwig is the loudmouth beast sitting next to that crone Lily. I've never been able to get along with either of them. Even when we would take trips here as a kid, those two and their children were always putting me down as best they could." Theo helpfully introduced me to the crowd of Rulers before me. I nodded in understanding and sat back up to listen just as Ludwig began to lose his temper over something Thomas had suggested.

"This is nonsense! I will not agree to wasting resources on some Princess who ran away from her own Kingdom and ignorantly got herself captured. Why is it that Heretia wants her? Maybe she did something to offend her and no one will tell us?"

My heart began racing and my face flushed in anger. Throughout all of this, the bad talking of my mother and her choices to protect me were eating at my nerves. These people didn't even know her, and they were judging her from the safety of their own thrones while she was kidnapped and hidden away suffering Mother only knows what.

"How dare you!" I seethed. My warning came as a hiss from between my teeth. Every head in the room turned to face me. My breath went shallow as the anger rose. This was the same anger from the first night I was in Medeis, the one that latched on to my magic and burst a fire.

"How dare you!" I shouted this time, unexpectedly.

"You sit there knowing nothing of my mother and throw false and baseless accusations about a woman you have never met."

My voice was getting very loud and I could feel my magic answer its call. It roiled in my veins, urging me to go further.

"Who are you to judge a woman for her choices, harmless as they are. You refuse to help her simply because you do not know her? My mother has never raised a finger to anyone in her life, let alone some nefarious Queen in another world. You know nothing about my mother, nor my father, nor me for that matter." My skin was struggling to hold back the power coursing through me when the High King responded. Darkness began to creep in around the corners of my vision. I pulled back quickly. No, this wasn't the place for this. I had to regain control.

I faltered slightly in my chair and reached for Theo. His hand met mine and the calming effect his magic had slowed my heart rate. I noticed a light sweat on my brow as my senses came back to me.

"Silly threats from some silly girl. I move we end this conversation now and remove her from our kingdom. How dare she throw about empty threats to me!" he argued.

High Queen Lily nodded in agreement and added her own nasty thoughts to the argument. "Why should we listen to this impertinent child? We know nothing of her or her mother. I agree with Ludwig, let us be done with this."

I could see Ophelia was chewing on her bottom lip, considering changing her mind. I did a light reach with my magic to feel her emotions. They opened like a flood gate to me. She was already nervous about an all-out war and their arguments weren't exactly unsound. Why should they trust me? Why should they help me?

I looked towards Ludwig and saw the nasty smile splayed across his lips. He had bested me, and he knew it. This stupid temper that kept showing up out of nowhere was ruining everything. I couldn't let him win. My inner turmoil was beginning to bubble forth, but I reached deep into Theo's magic and cooled my temper. However, I knew that for this meeting to proceed, I needed to excuse myself. I clearly was only going to become upset and cooler heads would do better. I fully trusted that Tim and Will had my back. I rose and addressed the room.

"I am going to graciously excuse myself for now. We came here to ask for help, but if all I'm going to hear is lies and accusations, then I am prepared to find help elsewhere. Just don't come crawling

232

to us when Heretia destroys you in her wake. We won't be there for you, just as you weren't there for us," I warned evenly. I didn't waste any time, I left before anyone could stop me. As the door began to close behind me, I heard an eruption of voices in the Throne Room.

"Why can't you shut your mouth!"

"See what I mean?"

"Have you no tact Ludwig?"

"Don't attack him over that girls' actions?"

"Apparently decorum is missing from this High Council today."

The arguments continued as I turned down the hallway and found a maid bustling by.

"Excuse me, is there somewhere private I can wait?" I asked her. The young woman smiled and led me to a library not far from where everyone else argued on.

"You can sit in here," she smiled and held the door open.

I thanked her for the space. As soon as she left, I pounced for the side washroom I had seen and splashed my face with cold water. I breathed in deeply, the last of the volatile emotions ebbing away. I looked up in the mirror and stared at the woman before me. What was wrong with me? I just hoped that I hadn't destroyed our chances of getting my parents back.

CHAPTER FIFTEEN

It wasn't long before Theo and Tim came looking for me, bringing me news and comfort.

"What's going on in there? Can you let them know I'm sorry? I don't want how I behaved to make anything worse," I word vomited all over them. In the silence of the library my anxiety had kicked in and I was growing terrified of what was being said without me there.

Tim held up his hands and sat down in a chair across from where Theo had settled near me.

"It's not going as badly as expected. Ludwig and Lily got a major verbal beat down from Thomas, Ophelia, and Vermir," he reported. "Once that was settled, it was decided that they would discuss the rescue and the war as separate entities under the impression that it actually is going to happen."

I urged him for more, but he just shook his curly head.

"Not much more has been decided. Thomas thinks we need to tread carefully, and I think I agree with my nephew on this. These are not a people equipped for all-out war. They are mostly merchants and traders. There is money, but not so much by way of an army. Just be patient, Mia. We will see this through, but be prepared for not everything to go your way."

"I'm ready for that and I'm okay with it. If they help in any little way, then I'll accept it," I nodded.

Tim gave me a reassuring pat and clapped hands with Theo before leaving again. I blew out a breath I didn't realize I was holding as the door to the library shut.

"I just hope I haven't made things impossible in there," I admitted.

Theo attempted to calm my nerves, but the only thing that did me any good was perusing the rows of old volumes. They ranged in categories from science, magic, literature, and art, to historical documents going back almost a thousand years.

"This library is amazing," I mused.

I glanced through a few more texts about the building of a grand tomb on the other side of the island. I read about enchanted dolphins that only allowed the most virtuous of magic wielders to cross and commune with the departed buried there.

"This is only the personal library of the High Rulers. The actual Library of Lotho is over at the Academy and it's five times this size and three times as tall. I'll take you there while we are here so you can run around to your heart's content," Theo smiled.

I grinned at his genuine offer and continued my searching of the wonderous texts. Time slipped casually away. Theo even began reading to me aloud from selections he found particularly interesting. I lounged in a chair, just listening to his words, beginning to nod off at the rhythmical cadence of his deep voice.

Suddenly the door swung open and Tim stuck his head in.

"It's done. They've made their decisions and they are ready for you now," he announced.

There was a pause as we refocused. I nodded and rose to follow Tim out of the library. With a glance over my shoulder, I took one last look at the grand room and wistfully hoped I would get to spend an entire day here soon. I was, after all, a nerd at heart.

The throne room was silent as we were led back in to retake our seats. I met Thomas' eyes and he nodded reassuringly, which was a good sign.

After we had settled and the doors shut behind us, Vermir began to speak.

"With many minds comes many ideas, insights, and emotions. This Council recognizes the grave declarations given by some of its members upon Princess Clarisse and is ready to apologize for the words exchanged negatively about her. Is the Princess Amelia accepting of this apology?" he asked.

I rose from my chair and stood there for a moment. Everyone waited for my response. As it would more than likely dictate the outcome of their decision to help me, I had to make it count. Everything depended on these people coming to my parents' rescue.

"Apologies from this council are accepted with an also apologetic heart. Please excuse my actions earlier. I am so sorry and hope it can be forgotten as we move forward in our joint endeavor," I announced. I heard Ludwig's chair scrape the hard floor but Vermir interjected first.

"Your heart was in the right place, and it is pure. As I said, many minds also come with many different emotions and we must be free to feel and think as we like. Always with respect. Your apology is accepted, and we may proceed."

He tapped his gavel down on the arm of his chair and I placed myself squarely back in my own seat. I gave a massive sigh of relief now that the first order of business was over.

I dared a glance at Lily and could just see the disgust written all over her beaky little face. She resembled a toddler that was just forbidden dessert for the evening. I resisted the urge to meet Ludwig's gaze and focused my attention on Vermir.

"This council has discussed at long length the actions we need to take regarding the grave situation Princess Clarisse and this kingdom are in at this moment. A Royal, no matter her history, has been kidnapped by a tyrant and that same tyrant has been kidnapping innocents from around our world, in effect, declaring war against us. Everyone in the room has family and loved ones residing in other kingdoms and we cannot let it pass without doing something about it. Our people are frightened, and we must give them something to calm their fears," Vermir stated.

I leaned forward in my chair.

"Lotho will not be sending their own spies and envoys into the Ancient Kingdom at this time. However, we are willing to support the Elite Guard in their mission to rescue the Princess. We will be sending physical aid by way of transport, supplies, and weapons to assist them under the agreement that they will also report any findings to us and give firsthand accounts of what they witness in the Ancient Kingdom," Vermir continued.

Will and Tim nodded in agreement. Theo and I gave each other a weary glance. Did that mean we were leaving?

"As far as war is concerned, we are fully committed in every way to fighting and defending our boarders and those of our neighbors from Heretia and her advancement. We cannot let her continue her reign of terror over us and we promise our investment into this war wholeheartedly. Preparations will have to be held off, however, until we have a deeper understanding of what we will be up against. High King Ludwig will hereby be awarded the command of War General and will oversee preparations and executions of all military advancements."

My jaw fell to the floor. They were giving this guy control of their army? The man who was the loudest protestor to it? This made no sense at all. Ludwig was up to something. He could potentially commit to everything, and then at the last minute pull his entire army out and leave us hanging there to die.

"That is all for today. Let us depart in peace. The Elite Guard will leave in two days' time for the Ancient Kingdom, once the supplies for their travel can be collected," Vermir finished grandly.

With another bang of his gavel, everyone rose to leave. I stood and crossed to Will who was already holding up his hands warning me to keep my cool.

"Let's go to our Safehouse here and I will explain more," he murmured, not wanting to be overheard.

I followed him out of the nearby door with Tim and Theo behind us. Tim sprang to the lead and showed us out of the castle onto the busy street. The town was still as active as before. No hint of war had reached them yet.

I wasn't surprised to find the Safehouse in Lotho was slightly different than the one in Suravia. It was only one story and made of a stucco like material. Will opened the door and we filed in, stopping when we came upon a scene of destruction and chaos in the front room.

There were bottles everywhere, glasses knocked over on almost every surface, knives sticking out of the walls and doorways, and a single tiny blonde woman passed out on a chair snoring loud enough to wake the dead.

"I think Wynnie found her way to the Safehouse alright," Tim whispered to Will.

Will grunted and stalked over. With one swoop of his arm, he snatched her up by the scruff.

"What the hell?" she shouted, coming out of her drunken daze.

Without a word, Will carried her one handed into the kitchen. The three of us ran behind to watch what he would do. Will raised her above a large tub of cold water and dunked her in it. She went down kicking and screaming, but the harder she fought, the longer he held her submerged.

"Will!" I called, but Theo held me back.

"This is his soldier right now, Mia. Not your friend. She was given an order," Theo warned, but I wasn't going to stand for this.

I gave one hard shove and escaped Theo's hold. As Will placed Wynnie back on her feet in front of him, I stepped in, arms out to block him.

"That's enough!" I shouted.

Will blinked twice in astonishment and then furrowed his bushy eyebrows at me.

"Move, Amelia. This isn't your place," Will warned, but I refused. Without breaking eye contact, I grabbed Wynnie's hand and marched her down the hallway behind us. I scratched her name on the chalkboard and opened the door. With a slam, that I made sure the boys heard, I shut the door. Wynnie winced and grabbed her head.

"I really screwed up, Mia," she moaned and slumped down on the bed.

"We all do Wynnie, we all do. When you're sober, I'll tell you about mine," I whispered.

Wynnie looked up at me apologetically.

"I'm sorry for doing this again. You're probably already sick of taking care of me. Everyone else is," she sighed.

I squared my hands on my hips and leaned over her. "Look at me Wynnie," I ordered.

She raised her watery eyes and my heart broke.

"Everyone has problems, everyone messes up. But as your friend, it's my job to help you instead of punishing you. I'm not going to sit by and let someone torture you over a problem you already torture yourself over. It does you no good," I explained.

I removed her boots and leaned her back against the bed.

"Yes, you need to get better. But what's been going on isn't helping and I'm about to go out there and change that right now. You rest for a moment and then join us for dinner if you feel better," I instructed.

Wynnie nodded and rolled over to her stomach. I waited until her breathing evened out and then I straightened up, ready for the fight waiting on me. If I was going down for this, I was going down swinging, metaphorically of course.

I passed Theo and Tim in the hallway who both looked dumbfounded. Theo moved in front of me, "You sure you want to go in there?" he asked.

"I'm not scared of him and neither is he of me. But I do want to talk to him," I straightened in defiance.

Theo glanced at Tim, who shrugged his shoulders. "Grown woman making a grown decision," he muttered.

Theo looked down at me once more with concern. "I will be just around the corner. Remember though, he may be my Captain, but you are my Pair. You say the word and I'm in there."

I nodded, the weight of the statement hanging heavy in that hallway. "It'll be fine," I soothed.

I gave Theo a kiss on the cheek and made my way down to the room Will paced irately. As soon as I entered, Will stopped moving. He crossed his arms and raised a furious brow in my direction.

"Give me one good reason I shouldn't send you back to Suravia right now. Wyndetta Lily is my soldier, Amelia. You had no right!" he began to raise his voice, but I wasn't having it. I straightened my back to its fullest height.

"But I am not. What I am, however, is a healer. In my world, mind and body are one, and when I see someone suffering, I will not stand by. Your continuous abusive treatment of her suffering doesn't help anyone, least of all Wynnie. I'm not saying she doesn't need to be punished for disobeying, that is absolutely your right. Punish her when she is sober and then get her the help she needs. Stop ignoring her trauma. She may be a soldier, but she is also a person," I hissed.

I steeled myself for the onslaught of excuses, accusations, and possibly even judgment, but I wasn't going to budge on this one. No one in this house was touching Wynnie again until she had sobered up.

"I'm not sure what happened to make her so destructive, but as her Captain, it is your job to train and lead your soldiers. I may not be a warrior in body, but I am in heart. So, I'm going to fight for

Wynnie. I am going to fight for her soul, her wellbeing, and her health," I continued.

Will relaxed his arms, his dumbfounded stare giving me the courage to continue.

"Throw whatever you want at me, but from this point onward, you will not torture her in that way again. Build her up Will, find her help, but don't put her in a place where she may never be able to return from. The girl is imploding from the inside and has been for a while. As long as she doesn't seek the attention she needs for it, it will only get worse," I explained.

I sucked in one final mighty breath and waited for his response. Nothing in the house moved, nothing breathed. The silence was deafening and I almost lost my nerve and backed down. Just as I was about to pull back from my conviction, Will stepped forward. I gathered my wits, refusing to budge from the position I had taken.

"There are few times in the life where I have admitted I was wrong, and today is going to be one. But I have to add that you are wrong, too," he sighed.

I blinked in surprise.

"How so?" I sniffed, waiting to hear what he had to belittle me on.

He raised his hand to settle on my shoulder gently. "You're not just a healer, Amelia. You're a leader, too. A much more astute one than I, it seems. I could possibly be so bold as to call you a Queen, but you would probably scoff at that."

I shook my head. "No Will, I wouldn't."

His eyes softened as I spoke.

"For my friends, I would take any role that would keep them safe. If you want to call it Queen, that's fine but to me, it's just being who I am. I may not always speak up or know the right thing to say in every situation, but I can't stand by while a young woman is hurting and no one is listening. I have seen things back during my studies in the Original World of people not being heard, and it never, and I mean never, ends well."

242

"I can imagine," Will nodded and sighed. "I'll let Wynnie rest, but she does have to suffer for disobeying."

I agreed and sat down.

"That's fine, but what I really want to talk about is the scouting mission to the Ancient Kingdom the High Rulers agreed," I changed the subject.

Will straightened and cleared his throat, shaking himself out of a mind fog.

"Sorry, you're right. I don't know how much more I can tell you, though. The Lotho High Rulers were reluctant to help you after you almost lost your temper with Ludwig, no matter how much he deserved it. Tim was the one to suggest sending out a team, but they didn't want that. They argued for something more concrete and us going was the only way to satisfy them. We hope to come back with your parents as well. We will only be gone for a short while, Amelia. A month, maybe six weeks at most. You won't miss us that much, I promise," he said.

"Miss you? What, I'm not going?" The idea sent my heart spiraling through the floor.

Will stared me straight in the eye and shook his head.

"It's too dangerous for you. You have no training and no skills in this kind of thing. You would be much better served here as an emissary of sorts," he explained.

I had almost stopped listening to him at this point, my mind racing with the idea that Theo was leaving for six weeks. Will apparently noticed my panic and came to kneel at my feet.

"We won't be gone as long as it seems," he soothed. "There is a war coming and you could act as a go between for Suravia and Lotho. You could always find work at a local health clinic and practice there for a bit. That was one of the main reasons we came here right? Like Hester suggested?"

With a silent shake of my head in defeat, I stood from the chair, replying, "You're right. I remember that I wanted to find a scholar to help me with my magic. I need to do that first before I do anything else and well before this war starts."

My thoughts raced with possibilities of what I could do in their absence, what I could learn here. The Academy here was said to be the best Medeis had to offer with only the brightest minds. Excitement began to well up inside of me as my brain raced with plans of action.

"If I'm to be of any help, it will only be if I really know how to use my Life magic against her!" I said fiercely.

Will held up his hands, stopping me in my thoughts. His demeanor drastically halting my mood.

"Whoa! Hold it there! Use it against Heretia? You don't think you're going to fight, do you?" he scoffed.

I stopped pacing and huffed.

"Well, not like mortally wound her with a sword, but use it to stop whatever she's trying to do or defend people instead. I'm certainly an asset in this, and if it means working on the front lines, I will do what I can," I clarified.

After my short single lesson with a sword only the day before, clearly fighting on a field of battle wasn't going to be my best use.

Will shook his head. "Over my dead body. You don't know the first thing about war, and you are not a soldier, as you so elegantly stated earlier. Besides, Theo would kill me if I ever allowed you near a battlefield. Where would you ever get the idea that you could stand up to Heretia in a battle of magic? She's had decades of practice and you've had a week. You think only six more weeks will prepare you to take her on? That woman would eat you for breakfast and then Theo for lunch cause his hot head would run in there alone after you," Will chastised.

I heard to door slide open and Wynnie walked in unannounced. "Let her fight," she said coldly and shut the door behind her again.

Will tensed, "You have no say in this, especially with the state you're in."

Wynnie crossed her arms. "If I had a coin for every man who told me that I would get eaten for breakfast if I ever trained to be a soldier, I would be richer than the High Rulers of all five kingdoms. No one was ever going to stop me from doing what I wanted to do, and Mother be cursed if I let you tell Amelia what she can and can't do. I've seen the power this woman wields, and if she can focus it right, there's no stopping her. She has more magic in one pinky than you or I could ever have, so who are you to tell her she can't do something?"

My jaw dropped to the floor. Wynnie was sticking her neck out far here. A week ago, she was thinking of ways to torture me, now she was staking her career on defending me. My heart swelled with pride at this young woman. Others might see her as rash, which she was, but she was also braver and more daring than any man.

"You don't exactly have any leverage here right now, Wyndetta. I suggest you leave this be," Will warned her off, but Wynnie planted her feet stubbornly.

"I will not leave it be. If Amelia decides she can take on Heretia, then she can. You nor I, and not even Theo, can stop her. In fact, I'll give her my own personal throwing knives to do so," Wynnie continued.

"Why are we giving Amelia knives?" Tim asked, opening the door.

"We aren't giving Amelia knives! Not for training, not for combat, and especially not to take on Heretia," Will answered.

"Take on Heretia?!" Theo parroted in surprise.

I rolled my eyes, disgusted with all of this male bluster.

"All of you just stop! No one said I was going to take her head on, and no one said I would be throwing knives." I stiffened my back and stared Will down, attempting to drive my point home.

"But if I did decide to battle with her on a field of magic, that would be my decision and mine alone," I countered.

Everyone went quiet, thinking of what that type of encounter would mean for this world. It was Theo that moved first. He stood before me and took my hand, kissing it lightly.

"If anyone can do it, it would be you, my love," Theo whispered.

No one else dared move or speak against his declaration. I squeezed his hand gently in thanks and then turned back to the waiting audience before us.

"Now, if you all don't mind, it is my turn to change clothes so we can all eat. We have a lot we need to talk about, mainly helping you guys get ready to leave. Which I'm still not thrilled about, by the way," I huffed.

Chapter Sixteen

After dinner that night, most of the group went out into the streets. I found Theo in a small enclosure at the back of the house. It wasn't necessarily a backyard, but there were a few trees with an unfamiliar fruit growing on them. I came up behind him and reached up over his shoulder to pluck one.

"Are they ripe to eat?" I asked into his ear and kissed it gently. He shivered at the feeling.

"You've never seen a moondate?" he asked. I lifted the greenish fruit up between us and shook my head.

"No, we don't have these in the Original World. What are they?" Theo grinned and took it from me. It was rough skinned, very round, and the green was like a lime.

"I guess you wouldn't have them in a place that didn't trust in magic. They're an ancient fruit that grow easily everywhere, so they're not exactly a hot commodity or hard to come by. Just about near everyone anywhere can grow them. But it's about what's inside of them that's important," he relayed. He cracked the moondate against the tree and it split right down the middle.

"Inside is a circle of seeds that hold magical qualities. They aren't magic in themselves, but for some reason, they are excellent additives to potions to help them last longer and taste better. If you have a concoction that needs a long shelf life, a few seeds of this will make it last. Life wielders love them," Theo explained. He showed me the inside of the fruit and I gasped. The meat was silvery white like the moon, and the seeds sparkled as if they shone with the twinkle of the stars.

"It's lovely!" I crooned and reached to cradle it in my hands.

"They are absolutely delicious, too!" Theo scooped a chunk of fruit meat out with his pinky and sucked it down.

I giggled and took a bite myself. He was right! Its texture was that of a banana with the juiciness of an orange, but it tasted like a combination of an apple and a grape.

"This is fantastic! I'm going to be eating these all the time now," I marveled.

Theo gave a throaty laugh. "Be careful with that, they are chock full of sugar and it'll get to your stomach after a while."

I smiled through eating the delicious slice of heaven on earth and looked up at the sky. The moon was waning, and a few thin clouds moved across its path slowly.

"It is nice tonight," I prodded, and Theo latched on to the hint.

"Would you like to go walk a bit in the market? There's no festival or anything going on that I know of, but this time of night it's still alive. It gets so hot in Lotho during the day and crowded by those in from out in the countryside, most townspeople wait until sunset to do their shopping," he said. I nodded with delight at the suggestion to go explore and relax for a while.

"Excellent! Let me grab some coins for a snack and we will head out. You might want to snatch up a shawl, it can sometimes get chilly if the breeze from the sea picks up," he added. I skipped to our room and plucked out a thin white wrap that I slung over my shoulders. After fluffing my hair and checking over my appearance one last time, I followed Theo into the night.

The air was balmy, and I instantly understood what Theo meant by wanting something to block out the evening breeze. I shivered slightly and pulled the shawl closer. Theo reached out and pulled me in, warming me with his size. I could hear the street market before I could see it. There were a lot of different noises: laughter, talking, and some wind instruments frolicking away. Hundreds of lanterns were strung along the walkways, shop fronts, and market stands in a multitude of colors.

I had to swerve from side to side to avoid the throngs of people dressed in their everyday wear. They carried boxes and bags of every shape. Small children ran in and out of customers legs, chasing each other, and giggling hysterically. A few women walked around carrying fruit and flowers, trying to shift their goods on the move.

Theo tapped my shoulder. I turned to see him pointing up to the rooftops where three young men were attempting to jump from one building to another in an amazing show of flips and spins. Twinkles of wind magic twisted through the air beneath them. I raised my eyebrow at the spectacle, but then switched my attention to the roar of the largest crowd watching. There, beneath the eaves, was a beautiful young woman red with embarrassment. Everyone was elbowing her and giving her side glances.

Theo chuckled, "What young men will do to show off." I huffed and elbowed him in the side.

"Let them have some fun, none of it hurts if they are careful. She's enjoying the attention. Every girl likes being fawned and flaunted over at least once," I winked. Theo made the space between us disappear as he hooked his arm around my waist, yanking me closer. I gasped and placed my hands on his hard chest, stopping my face from crashing into his.

"Really now? Every girl?" he asked. My insides purred as his eyebrow raised in mock questioning. I blushed wildly and shook my head.

"Young girls! Not grown women like me. We prefer to be told to our face. Which you did and look what it got you?" I laughed. I

249

tried to push away and continue our journey through the lights and sounds, but he just pulled harder.

"No, no. I think you meant every girl, no matter what age," he winked. I started shaking my head, my eyes going wide in terror. What was he going to do?

"Oh, Mother no! No, no, I didn't mean that at all," I started to protest vehemently, but he reached down, planted a hard kiss on my lips, and dashed off in a direction I couldn't see.

"Theo?" I called after him and waded my way through the crowd. I couldn't see him anywhere, when suddenly I felt a strong, large hand touch my shoulder.

"There you are you little jerk! Way to leave someone like that!" I howled. I spun in place, expecting to see Theo with some bouquet of flowers or something silly, but instead I came face to face with High King Thomas. I looked around, no one seemed to notice or care that one of their Rulers was among them casually in the street.

"Please tell me you are not out here alone with no one to enjoy such a beautiful evening?" he grinned. I gave him a smile in return and shook my head.

"No, not exactly. I was with Theo, but he just ran off on some hair brained idea a few seconds ago. I figured he would just show back up and I thought you were him. Sorry!"

Thomas shook his head and laughed. "I can only imagine what he is doing, but until he returns, do you mind if I keep you company?"

I looked around and nodded. I saw a cart that was baking an exceptionally fine smelling pie and loaves of bread.

"We could grab something to eat quickly while we wait for him," I shrugged and motioned to the cart. Thomas nodded and offered his arm. I took it and followed, a small happy spring to my step.

"Two raisin breads please, Mr. Whitney," Thomas smiled. He held up two fingers and then flipped a coin at the younger lad helping the baker.

"Absolutely Your Majesty. Is that all for tonight?" the man asked. Thomas nodded and took the breads from Mr. Whitney's hands.

"You keeping this boy on the straight and narrow still, Mr. Whitney?" Thomas asked the kindly looking old gentleman. The white-haired man narrowed his eyes in mock disgust at the pimply youth.

"This beggar? Yeah, every day I try, but his mother always spoils him. I'd never be able to get him into the Academy if it weren't for his work with me. If his mother had it her way, he would do nothing except sit around and fish. I swear to the Mother Goddess, Your Majesty, if it weren't for you and me staying on his case, he'd be useless," he smiled. Thomas winked at the young boy who grinned back wildly.

"Father is lying. I'm up every morning at dawn getting the shop ready, stoking the fires, and getting orders together for the early deliveries. I also study for at least three hours every day and then come out here and help dad with the cart. I've been serious about going and I promise I will. I want to be one of the Kingdom's top Fire Sorcerers and I'm going to be," he said. The young boy was beaming with absolute pride and Thomas let out a hearty laugh from his belly, making the other two laugh as well.

"I believe in you Marcus! I trust you'll make it and I trust you will do well. Your classes start in one month and I've told all the scholars about you. They won't make it easy, but they will make it worth your while and my money," he winked.

Mr. Whitney patted Marcus on the shoulder. "I know he's going to make us all proud, Your Majesty. Just you wait."

I was floored by the exchange. In Suravia, the Rulers were so inaccessible, even to each other. Here, however, Thomas seemed to be close with the people, taking interest in their daily lives and their future.

Thomas finished his talk with the baker and Marcus and led me away to a bench that overlooked a stage where three minstrels were strumming a tune I didn't recognize.

"You're paying for his education, I gather?" I munched on the delightful raisin bread. Thomas was halfway through his own and nodded, swallowing quickly.

"Yes, he's the first Fire Sorcerer in his family and right now we're a little low on them at the Academy. So, I decided to help young men and women like Marcus get the education they need. My reasons are nationally selfish, but he will be able to find good work if he masters the magic. It will help set his own family up for life," Thomas explained.

"I don't think it's selfish at all. You've given this boy an opportunity he wouldn't have otherwise. He will always be grateful to you for it. You should be proud of yourself for caring. There are some in Suravia who never would have done that." I was thinking of Theo's father, unless of course, it benefited him personally to do so.

"Yes, I know some of Theo's family and the other Rulers. Not the nicest characters, but they have been protected and they are doing well financially," he replied.

"Maybe you're right. I've also done some not nice stuff that I never really apologized for," I sighed. Images of my anger flew through my mind, but I wished them away. No point fretting over them now.

"I've never met Ogden, but if Ludwig is better, bless the Mother on your soul," he laughed.

Suddenly, I heard a violin give a beautiful note and I looked up to see Theo on the stage with the small minstrel band, violin in hand. I froze and my entire face went red.

"No," I whispered. Thomas stiffened beside me and looked between the two of us for a moment before falling off the bench with raucous laughter.

"It's not funny Thomas! Stop that!" I lightly punched his shoulder.

252

With a screech of the strings, Theo slid into a very solemn and romantic tune. The crowd quieted and turned to watch the handsome prince play the violin for his princess. I blushed wildly and looked down at the ground. It didn't take long for the crowd to realize who he was playing to. With wide grins, random people began to grab at me and pull me forward.

I tried to back away, but they kept at it, encouraged by their own High King who bodily lifted me with my arms pinned to my side. He planted me squarely on the stage. Theo smiled and continued his tune. I was so taken aback by this display, that tears began to sting my eyes.

No one had ever done anything like this before in my life. I stared dumbfounded and smiled at him. It wasn't a long tune, but it was certainly a lovely one. Theo finished with a flourish and bowed to me. The entire crowd exploded in applause. With a cheer, he handed the violin back and grabbed my arms, whisking me into a dance as the regular band began to play something I still didn't recognize. It was all very lively, and Theo's laughter was contagious as he spun me around. The lights from the lanterns warmed his features and softened them.

When it finally did end, I gasped and began to head back to the sideline, searching for a bench or chair to sit down on. Theo grabbed my hand and steered me down a lightly lit alley to get away from it all. I giggled and let him tug me into the shadows.

"You continue to find ways to impress me," I smiled and fell against his chest as he leaned on the side of the building.

"The violin is hardly impressive. What is impressive, however, is your blush. Therefore, I will continue to do things to shock and amaze you so that I can always see it," he smiled.

I faked insult and lightly punched his shoulder. "You're terrible...but I like it."

Theo smiled and pulled me into him for a kiss. I accepted it happily. When I finally decided to pull back, I looked deep into his eyes and saw all the warmth and love I felt from him. My heart was tugging and calling to be with him, but I just wanted to look at him for a moment in peace. I wanted to remember the way we were tonight. Before he left, before I started my work, and before the world rushed into battle.

"What are you thinking about?" Theo suddenly asked, giving me his most sultry stare.

I ran a finger along his jawline, highlighting the dark stubble that scratched at my fingertips.

"I wish this night wouldn't end so you won't have to leave," I admitted and then brushed my thumb over his lips.

He closed his eyes and leaned into my touch. "It won't be that long, I promise. We will be back soon, and you'll have me to yourself again," he crooned.

His voice was husky, and I could tell what he was thinking.

"Let's not waste this time then," I whispered, grabbing his hand, and heading back to the Safehouse.

No one was back yet, except maybe Wynnie who was probably still moaning and groaning off her hangover. Theo wasted no time, barely shutting the front door before he spun me in place and crushed me against his body. Our lips met in a fever of panting and pulling. I reached up to run my fingers through his still perfectly placed hair. And he began to tug at the ribbon at the back of my neck that tied my dress up.

"Bedroom." I barely broke the kiss to utter.

Deftly, my Pair swept his arm up under my leg and carried me to the bedroom. With a kick of his foot, the door snicked shut. My hands shook with anticipation as I began to unbuckle the straps that attached his quilted vest together and shoved it off him. He reached behind me to pry apart the wool dress and let it slither to the floor. I fumbled with the two buttons at the top of his pants and they finally came free.

As his breeches dropped to the floor, Theo lifted me up by my ribs and tossed me playfully onto the perfectly made bed. I squealed in surprise but sat up quickly to enjoy taking in the sight of him. He stood there for a moment at the foot of the bed, looking me over as I did him. His body was a work of art, chiseled from dark marble and made just for me. I propped myself up by my elbow and drank him in.

"When you look at me like that, Amelia. I want to fall to my knees before you and worship you like the Queen you are," he whispered.

I snickered, still uncomfortable.

"I'm barely a Princess," I corrected, but my words fell on deaf ears as Theo placed a knee on the bed and leaned over my naked form.

"I don't care what the world may call you, but to me you will always be my Queen. My heart, mind, body, and soul are yours, Mia," he breathed.

All the jokes escaped on his last breath before his lips lowered to caress my neck. I moaned in pleasure at the feeling of his skin on mine. The little part of his magic that always stayed with me wiggled to be released. My magic tugged at my heart and sang in my veins.

"I will always bow to you, never forget that!" Theo whispered one last time and I lost my mind in our lovemaking and enjoyment of each other. Tomorrow he was leaving, so I made the entire night count.

It was late into the middle of the night before we finally laid back, exhausted from the effort, but soaring from the exhilaration. I laid my head on his chest and stared up at the ceiling where our magic circled above us. It danced and played, twisted, and turned. I fell into a heavy sleep staring up at the swirls of color and light playing with each other.

Chapter Seventeen

"Amelia!"

It was the same whisper I had heard on the hilltop when I first arrived in Medeis. I sat up in bed abruptly and looked around. I glanced down at Theo who was fast asleep. I hadn't known him to talk in his sleep, so I doubted it was him saying my name.

"Hello?" I hissed searching the dark room that was barely lit by a half moon on a semi-cloudy night.

"Mia!"

I heard it again, this time from the hallway. I scooted to the side of the bed and grabbed a wrap that was laying across a chair in the corner of the room. Tying it on, I went to the door. Maybe someone needed me but didn't want to wake Theo with knocking on the door. Poking my head out I scanned the empty hallway.

"Is someone there?" I asked.

Oddly, I wasn't scared, but extremely curious. I walked into the hallway and padded softly to the front door. No one was moving, nothing made a noise.

"Mia!"

It called once more, louder. It was coming from the front room. Quickly, I came to stand in front of the large double window, overlooking the deserted street in front of the Safehouse.

"Who is calling me?" I asked one last time.

"Mia, we have waited a long time for you to come home. Even longer for you to become strong enough to speak to us."

The voice was low, ethereal, and right behind me.

I spun in place and gasped. While no living person stood before me, there was something there, but it wasn't human. I didn't run, however. Nor did I scream, I just froze.

A large column of black smoke floated in the space before me, not even an arm's length away. It fluttered slightly but didn't change shape.

"Who are you?" I asked.

I didn't want to spook whatever it was, but I needed to know what had been talking to me since I had arrived. This thing had been plaguing my dreams since even before Michelo kidnapped my parents.

"I am not a who, I am beyond a who." It replied cryptically. I scanned my mind, wondering if I was supposed to know what this thing was.

"What are you?" I finally gave up.

"We have chosen you to receive our power. Long ago, your mother asked for our Blessing upon your birth and we gladly gave it. We saw your power and agreed to hide ourselves within you and wait. We have waited so long," the voice floated in the air all around me, but that still didn't answer my question. It only gave me more.

"You didn't answer me." I pointed out calmly.

I wanted answers. Especially now that it had mentioned my parents and I was going to get them.

"Do not be afraid of us, in fact, you may even be in need of us."

I began to roll my eyes in exasperation from all the riddles, but something made me pause. I had heard those words recently. But where? I thought back through the last day and then gasped when I realized the answer. The woman at the shop when we first got to Lotho, she had said those words. No, not those exact words, she had said…

"Death?" I whispered and stared up at the black smoke that was now growing.

In fear, I stumbled back and fell into a chair.

"So, you did get our message? We knew you would remember something like that."

I bit back a scream, now I was afraid.

"What do you want?" I asked, my teeth chattering from fear.

"It's not what we want, but what you need. You need to get stronger. We have been with you since before your birth. Your mother asked for our help long ago and we have been there since. Death magic has always been a part of you, but now you can release it on the world. Stop holding back from who you are meant to be, accept your destiny."

It seemed to be growing in volume as well as size, the smoke getting denser, as if trying to take on shape.

"No! I don't want Death magic. I just want my parents back. Pick someone else!" I pleaded, but the smoke just grew darker.

"There are things in this world and the next, Amelia that are already in motion and beyond our control. Once you accept your destiny, then we can move to right the wrongs of the past."

The warning hung heavy. Right the wrongs of the past? I had no idea what this mysterious entity meant. I stared, dumbfounded, unable to speak the questions cluttering my thoughts.

"Release your power, Amelia."

It swelled again in size. With a scream, I jumped back, and tried to get way. I felt my head crash against the floor. Suddenly, I woke up from the dream.

"Mia!" I heard Theo shouting.

"Mia, wake up, love. It's just a dream!" Theo shook my shoulders as I thrashed around.

Finally, I was able to open my eyes. I blinked back the tears that were threatening to fall onto my face, and I reached up to grab my Pair. I wrapped my arms around his neck and pulled myself up. Theo gathered me up tightly and held me close.

"It's okay now, I've got you. I was just a dream," Theo chanted in my ear over and over.

I shook heavily from shock, unable to fully pull myself from the dream.

"Right the wrongs," I mumbled to myself, trying to make sense of what I had seen in my sleep.

"What?" Theo looked me over, confusion written in his brow.

"In my dream, Death came to me and told me that I had to right the wrongs of the past. That I had a destiny and I needed to release it," I relayed.

Theo pulled us up to the bed and settled me back.

"What are you talking about Mia? Death magic doesn't exist in witches. It's a folklore, no one has ever wielded it," Theo explained.

I just shook my head in response.

"I don't know what to tell you, Theo. In my dream Death told me that my mother had asked for help before I was born, and Death answered. It told me that I wielded Death magic and I needed to release it."

Theo looked unable to accept what I was telling him. "Mia, that's impossible. It was just a dream, don't read too much into it."

I grew frustrated and pounded my fist into the bed. "I can't explain it Theo, but this has been happening repeatedly."

I crawled over on my knees and sat down next to him. "The night before my parents were kidnapped, I had a dream of being told to come home. The night after my Rite I dreamed of a temple with a stained-glass window depicting three people. One was clearly the Mother Goddess, the other two were a man in black armor and a woman in white armor holding a sword. I heard something telling me to listen and learn. Now, I'm having a dream where Death itself informs me I have a destiny to fix the past."

Theo looked away from me, clearly at odds with what he was hearing and what he had been raised to know.

"I'm not sure what this all means, but it looks like my mother might have known I was special, and she asked for help in protecting me. Then, she left Medeis anyway just to keep me safe. I don't think I was ever supposed to come back here, but when Michelo arrived, they had no choice. Death said that things have been set in motion that we can't stop anymore, and I just need to accept my destiny. What if rescuing my parents is only the beginning? What if the Mother chose me to defeat Heretia? What if Death is helping me and I do really carry Death magic?"

Theo stood without a word and began furiously pacing the room, trying to process all this information. He ran his fingers through his hair, causing a single strand to fall out of place. His eyes were clouded with worry. I felt the anxiety that weighed on him, his fear that I might be right. I waited as he came to terms with what I was telling him. Once his mind had digested my words, he stopped pacing and faced me.

"Okay, so what you're saying is, you think you have Death magic?" he asked.

I nodded.

"And you think the Mother Goddess has chosen you to defeat Heretia and right the wrongs of the past?"

I nodded again.

"But what wrongs? Heretia's wrongs? Did Death say exactly what you will be fixing by getting rid of her? Because honestly the only problem is her right now. There were no issues before Heretia took the throne in the Ancient Kingdom. I'm not sure what wrongs you are righting."

I shrugged. "Death was vague on that part. It didn't clarify, but it was clear that I needed to learn to wield its magic before I could do anything."

Theo huffed heavily and looked out the window once more, the sky was beginning to show color as morning sun broke over the horizon. "I'm out of my depth here, Mia. I'm a warrior and a Prince, not a scholar of history or magic. In fact, there isn't anyone who knows anything about Death magic. As far as I know, Death has never blessed a single witch in existence with its power. There's a whole history behind that fact that I can't remember."

He flung his hand out in frustration. "I'm just going to have to trust you in this one. That what you're saying is real and that you do have Death magic. As terrifying as that thought is, I guess I must accept it. Here I am, about to leave you in a strange place, with people I don't fully trust as you begin your task as learning to wield Life and Death magic. Do you see how scary this is for me?"

I stood and padded my way to him, grabbing his shoulders for comfort.

"My job is to protect you, defend you and help you for our entire lives and just as you need me most, I'm abandoning you," he sighed. He hung his head in shame, the war within him evident.

"Theodeus Varillian, you listen to me. First, you are not abandoning me. You are going with the rest of the Elite Guard to look for my parents. That alone is a huge help, because I know if and when you find them, they will be in the best of hands getting back to me. Second, your job is not to protect me. I am a grown witch with my own magic, I can learn to protect myself. What I do need, however, is a Pair that supports and loves me no matter what I choose," I explained.

I kissed his cheek lovingly, the stubble scratching my lips. "I may even let you council me in decisions every now and then," I winked at him and he smiled forlornly.

"So stubborn," he muttered and pulled me in close.

Theo nuzzled his face into my hair and breathed in deeply, soaking in my scent. "Just promise me, that while I'm gone, you be extra careful not to do anything too dangerous. I want you strong but I also want you safe."

I squeezed him tighter, "I promise. And you must promise me that no matter what, you stay safe as well. I don't feel like going through this life without you, now that I've found you, would be fun."

As we stood there holding each other, a single knock came at the door. Tim popped his head in. "Will is ready for us to go. He wants us at the High Castle stables in fifteen minutes," he reported.

We both nodded and silently readied ourselves for the walk to the High Castle. The morning fog hadn't burnt away yet and only the fisherman and early shopkeepers were out. A few of the country folk had begun to trickle into town for their day of trade and bartering, but no one noticed us as we made our way up the street. Theo and I walked in silence holding hands and enjoying the feel of each other.

As we approached, I saw Wynnie and Will speaking with the elderly High King Vermir, his High Queen cousin Ophelia, and Thomas. They were reviewing a map and discussing other parts of the reconnaissance mission. Wynnie was explaining something when we walked up, and everyone fell silent.

"I think that's all we are going to need for now, Your Majesties. We must be off with the tide to get the best start possible. Daily reports will be sent back, and we should be reaching the Ancient Kingdom within four days. We leave our Princess in your care for the time being, but we know that she will be well treated and respected." Will finished, before whipping the map back up into a roll and stowing it away.

Thomas nodded to Will and then looked to Theo, nodding again in greeting.

Theo grasped my waist and pulled me away from the group. I was silent as he lifted my eyes to meet his. I tried to be brave and not seem silly in front of everyone. I knew he needed to go, but I still didn't understand how this world worked and he was the only thing that made sense this past week.

"Be brave, listen to your teachers, and don't stop thinking about me. You will be fine here and if anything were to happen..." he started to say, but I cut him off.

"Nothing is going to happen to you," I interrupted.

He shook his head to silence me. "If anything happens to me, go back to Suravia and your Uncle. They will know what to do about keeping you safe."

His instructions were brief and concise, like a soldier. I grimaced at the feel of his words on my heart but figured this was his way of protecting me the best he could. I nodded, reluctantly accepting his orders. Theo pulled back and stood there for a moment stroking my hair back behind my ears.

"I love you, Amelia. Mother knows I love you more than anything. Be safe and I will come back," he promised.

It was a simple promise, but one that I figured had a small chance of not happening. He clasped our hands and closed his eyes, muttering a spell under his breath.

"Mother protect and comfort," he whispered.

It was quick and my hands warmed under his. It was a straightforward protection spell. Every mother knew it and whispered over her children in the mornings. It was calming to know that he was looking out for me. I gave him one deep kiss and then nodded my head before going to stand by Thomas.

Theo looked to Thomas, "Make sure she is safe above all else."

He climbed onto his horse as Thomas put a hand on my shoulder, being careful to not make it look too comfortable there.

"I promise, Prince, she will be protected here. Heretia will not find her," Thomas swore.

Theo nodded gruffly and then kicked his horse into movement for the ship, with the rest of the Elite Guard beside him. I waved to Wynnie as she turned to smile at me. With a heavy sigh, I watched them go.

"Come on," Thomas directed from my side. "Tim made it clear that you were to stay in the safety of the High Castle while they were away in our family's wing."

I shook my head, "I couldn't possibly."

I started to protest, but Vermir raised his hand to silence my arguments.

"My dear, these are dangerous times. Being close to powerful Sorcerers and teachers is your only hope of mastering your magic and keeping her at bay." I guessed that was supposed to be the end of the discussion, because he began to walk off without another word.

Ophelia smiled at me and stepped forward, "Don't worry. We won't bother you. Wilhelm let us know that you were wishing to learn more about your magic while you were staying with us, so we summoned our best scholars to gather everything they had. Would you like to meet them? We've brought them to the library."

I nodded, especially at the idea of getting to spend more time in that glorious library the High Rulers had in the Castle. She smiled warmly and led me inside to the door. With a wave of her hand, it opened wide, and three men turned to watch us enter.

"Gentlemen! This is the Princess Amelia Wardman of the Fifth Throne of Suravia, Life Sorcerer," she introduced. The three men bowed low. I could see an entire table stacked as high as any man with books behind them.

"Princess, this is Reiko, Justice, and Dryan. They are our brightest and most knowledgeable scholars on Life magic in the entire Kingdom of Lotho. They have gathered as much as they could to help you learn your magic," she proclaimed.

The men stood and I took them in. Two were clearly on the older side, at least above fifty years of age but the third one was younger, maybe in his forties, with only just slightly greying temples. I bowed my head in return.

"I will leave you to get started," Ophelia swept out of the room and shut it with another flick of her wrist behind her. After watching her leave, I turned to the three men who had seated themselves and waited.

"I think we first need a demonstration of how far your basic magic skills are. We were led to believe that you were raised in the Original World and have little training," the younger man prompted. The other two nodded in agreement. I shifted on my feet, rubbing my hands together.

"Well, yes that's true. It is pretty dismal, but I never really showed any aptitude, so I warn you now that it's kind of disheartening," I admitted. "What would you like me to do?"

"Create a light orb," one of the older ones commanded.

A sweat broke out on my forehead. Great, one of the things that I was never able to do.

"Umm," I began, but they cut me off.

"Don't make excuses, just try. Focus your energy and say the words," he ordered.

I shifted my feet again but did as told. I cleared my throat and threw back my sleeves, widening my stance. Concentrating hard on a spot in the sky, I focused all my energy on it and spoke the words.

"Lux" I whispered.

Nothing happened.

I refocused and spoke a little bit louder

"Lux."

Still nothing. This was not very impressive. I decided to give it one last go. Somewhat deflated and embarrassed that now everyone was going to know how inept I was, I took a deep breath and very firmly quoted the Lighting Spell, "Lux."

Out of the corner of my eyes, I noticed the three scholars began to shift in their seats, lean forward, squint, and watch me closely. I looked around trying to see what they were staring at.

"Oh crap!" I shouted and stumbled back. My entire body was glowing heavily now, the same it always did when I attempted to perform a spell. I guess I hadn't really noticed it until now, but Theo was right. I wiped my hands on my dress, as if that would do any good.

"I-I," I stammered. I looked over myself as the light grew brighter and began to hum in my ears. My breathing had picked up.

"Fascinating," the youngest Scholar murmured and stood to look me over. "It seems as though your magic really has a mind of its own. You more channeled the energy into yourself instead of following normal magical formula of spells and incantations. Try to focus it away from you now that you've summoned it."

I nodded and held a hand in front of me.

"Lux," I tried to say calmly.

With a loud crack, light shot from my hand and hit a bookshelf, blasting everything into smithereens, and blowing a hole through the wood. The three men screamed as they all dove behind chairs and tables for cover.

When the dust settled, I looked to see them staring at me in amazement. The smell of charred wood and electricity filled the air as papers floated around us. I wiped my hand on my dress again to rub away the magic and stared at them in bewilderment. The men slowly came out from behind their hiding places with different looks on their faces.

The two elder men with horror and fear, but the younger one broke out in the largest smile I had ever seen.

"Oh this…" He nodded with a wide, excited grin. "This is going to be fun."

CHAPTER EIGHTEEN

After the godlike display of my inability to control magic, the two elder scholars decided that they were not qualified or willing to teach me anything.

"This craziness is more your forte Dryan. We want nothing to do with this," the oldest one shook his head violently. "My specialty is basic magic skills and Reiko has a knowledge of past Life Sorcerers and their powers, but this is beyond Life Sorcery and you know it. That's why you like it! Well, so be it, but we won't be a part of it."

The two men stormed out of the library with a slam of the door. I stared in disbelief.

"What was that about?" I asked once they left.

Dryan scoffed and then tugged at his Van Dyke mustache. "Cowardice, that's what that was. They're terrified of what they just saw because they don't understand it, but what you are is nothing to be afraid of. In fact, in all my life, I've only read about people like you."

I shook my head, "I'm not following. People like me? Life Sorcerers weren't terribly rare before Heretia and what I just did was a fluke. It probably won't happen again."

I waved in the direction of the meteor sized hole that now took up space on the bookshelf. Dryan shook his head, his long brown hair waving with the movement.

"I need to do more research, but from what I've just seen, I think you might be beyond a Life Sorcerer. But let's see what else happens when we try other things first," he smiled.

He began moving around hurriedly, opening texts, and closing them, searching for something specific. I stood to follow him and look over the books myself. They ranged from histories of magic and certain Sorcerers to Theories and Sciences of Magic. One arm load was specifically about Life magic and I picked one from the top of the stack and returned to my seat to look through it.

It took a while, but eventually Dryan came back around the table with arm full of old dusty books. His bright blue eyes twinkled with delight.

"Good, good! I should send those books with you to read when we're not together so you can get a better understanding of what Life Sorcery is supposed to look like. Then we know what to rule out," he said.

He quickly spread his books out on the floor and in a flurry began opening the covers, searching for just the right one.

"What other things have you done that don't exactly match up with normal Sorcery?" he asked, and then waved his hand for a parchment and quill to appear in midair. I raised a quizzical eyebrow. "It's just here to jot down notes because I think faster than I write."

He explained and then encouraged me to start.

"Uh, well, I'm not really sure what's considered normal or not. I glow when I perform strenuous magic as you saw. I've healed myself by just touching the part of my body that hurt. I also killed Cetus the Wild Beast with a beam of light on accident too," I shrugged.

Dryan's eyes almost popped out of his head at the last one.

"You really are amazing. But the question remains. What are you?" he wondered.

He looked over me with awe again and I huffed, slumping back in my seat.

"I'm a girl from the Original World who has no idea how to do anything and no clue what's happening to me. I want to find my parents and I want this world to be safe," I bit my lip, deciding whether or not to tell this man about the Death magic. Some part of my consciousness prodded me to reveal what I had been told in the dreams, that it was important for him to know. I decided to yet again, to do what felt right.

"There's something else I have to tell you, but it does not leave this room or our lessons. It's sensitive information that I don't understand yet and don't want everyone to know," I whispered.

Dryan straightened up and nodded, focusing his full attention on me.

"Based on your previous reaction, you might want to sit down for this," I instructed cautiously.

He warily sat down, readying himself. With a big breath to settle my nerves, I continued.

"It seems as though my mother asked for a Blessing when she was pregnant with me. A blessing of protection from Death. I don't know what she was going for, but what ended up happening was Death decided to grant me Death magic. So, not only am I a Life Sorcerer, but I'm also a Death wielder as well."

I held my breath, but Dryan didn't move. His eyes, already impossibly so, grew even wider as he sat there and stared at me. Finally, he stood and turned to face the window.

"Has Death has spoken to you?" he asked in a quiet tone.

I stood and nodded, "Yes, a few times, but it's all very cryptic."

In a whirl he turned and grabbed my shoulders.

"Mistress, you are not a Life Sorcerer," he whispered.

I stared dumbfounded, his grip tightening on my shoulders. I shook my head, unable to comprehend what he was trying to tell me.

271

He held up his hands and reached for a book that was on the floor. Dryan opened it to a page with a beautiful illumination of a figure cast in light and floating in the air. All five elemental colors surrounding the person depicted.

"It's hard to believe, but it's true. Your core element can present as Life, but in fact, you are not a Life Sorcerer. You are a Druid," he explained.

I stared silent at the picture and then turned to him, "What does that mean?"

"It means you are a living incarnation of the Mother Goddess. She must have picked you at your conception to be her conduit. Your mother must have known. She prayed for protection for you and Death decided to answer. Death and Mother Goddess are not exactly opposite, but they are not the same either. It's more of a partnership, with Mother ruling this world and Death assisting those in the Afterworld," he said.

Dryan stood and continued to take me in. "I can only imagine that she and your father begged for assistance in keeping you safe, knowing Heretia was out there. Death must have chosen to answer their plea."

I began to shake my head. This was too much to take in.

"That's why she hid you, Princess. That is why your parents ran away. To protect you until you were ready. We haven't had a Druid in over a thousand years. The last one heralded an era of peace that we have never seen since. She brought together all the kingdoms, and everyone lived in elemental harmony. You are a Druid, only one such as that can contain all the elements together and Death within one body without imploding. Normal witches scatter their brains if they so much as attempt to control an element that isn't their own. But you, you can wield all Five and Death," he continued but my thoughts were beginning to spin out of control. I heard a thump and looked to see Dryan kneeling before me.

"Mistress, I would be honored to teach you. It would be my life's joy to work by your side and bring your wisdom to the masses," he pledged. He took my hand and held it to his head in reverence. I waited a breath and then snatched it away.

"I have to go," I muttered.

Without another word, I dashed towards the door. I shoved the oaken monstrosity to the side and found a footman waiting on the other side of the door.

"My rooms please," I muttered and the man nodded, silently turned on his heel and walking away.

"Prince Timothy has said that everything in here is for your use as he cleaned it out of any real personal belongings long ago. Please feel free to make the room to your liking for your stay," he instructed.

I nodded, willing him to go and leave me in peace.

"If you need any immediate assistance, High King Thomas is at the end of the hall and you can summon us easily to your aid."

I gave another quick nod and waited until the door clicked behind him. I blew out a breath and headed for the window searching for peace. My view was breathtaking, overlooking the backside of the High Castle and down to a cliff that overlooked the vast ocean expanse. I took in the view for a moment and then had a thought.

Going back to the door, I opened it to peek out and saw the footman was still standing near it, waiting to help me.

"Excuse me," I asked quietly, as if anyone else around could hear.

The footman scurried over and stood ramrod straight in front of me.

"Is there a meditation spot here in the Castle?" I asked.

The footman gave a wide grin and nodded with a bow to his head.

"Yes, Your Highness, there absolutely is. We have a large meditation garden with a wading pool for the Royal Family members. As an esteemed guest, you are more than welcome to use it at any time. Would you like me to show you now?" he asked.

"I would like to change into something a little lighter and breathable. Where can I get that?" I was worried that I had no clothes other than the rough riding gear I had packed a few nights ago and had been depending on the Safehouses to provide everything else. The footman just bowed.

"Give me a few moments and I will have a maid bring up an assortment of traditional Lotho garments for you to choose from," he smiled and rushed off.

I continued to stand by my door, contemplating my next action, when Thomas' door opened and he came out with a lovely dark-skinned woman by his side laughing. I tried to duck back in without being seen, but it was too late.

"Princess Amelia!" came a booming voice.

I winced and reopened the door.

"Your Majesty! I was just returning to the rooms your uncle so kindly lent me for my stay and was about to head out again. I don't mean to bother you." I was trying to be polite, but also avoid any human interaction. My feelings were a jumbled mess and I needed some peace and quiet to sort through everything. The shock of Dryan's discovery hadn't completely made its way through me yet.

"Oh, you're no bother at all! You're our guest of honor. Come meet my betrothed, Alyssa Waterlily," he announced.

I stared at the breathtakingly lovely woman with brown eyes, perfectly tanned skin, and bright white teeth grasping Thomas' forearm lovingly.

"Yes! I have been so excited to meet you since Thomas told me of your arrival and your story!" she rushed forward, practically floating on air and took my hands, bringing them up to her chest in excitement.

"He has told me of what's happening and your heroic part in all of this. I just can't believe it all. You truly are a wonder and to land a catch such as Prince Theodeus and be his Pair, you are an amazing girl!"

I shivered at the mention of Theo and wished he were here to pull me into his chest, wrap me in his warmth, and block out all this other nonsense.

"It really is nothing. I've just been stumbling around and making a mess of everything," I laughed politely. I tried to pull my hands away, but she tightened her grip and gave me the most shocked face.

"Oh, but that's not true! Dear girl, you escaped Michelo, found yourself in a different world, escaped the Nandina, defeated Cetus, and then won an argument with Ludwig. All of this while your parents are being held hostage. You, sweet Amelia, are very brave," she cooed. My shoulders slumped. Hearing everything that had happened in such a short time made everything else that was being piled on feel even more exhausting. Thomas finally decided to step in and save me.

"My love, let's not remind the lady of all the tragedy that has happened to her. Why don't we leave her in some peace, and we will see her tonight for dinner in my rooms, just us three? Does that sound good Amelia? Nice and private and you don't have to face my less than enthusiastic counterparts for a while longer," he offered. This did sound nice and better than being a recluse, so I nodded.

"Yes, thank you."

Alyssa jumped up and down with glee.

"Good! What are you about to do? Thomas and I were headed to meet with my sister to do some wedding planning in town," she smiled.

She grabbed for Thomas' forearm and their happiness radiated, sinking my loneliness even further down. With everything going on and only getting worse by the day, would Theo and I ever get to be at peace like this?

"I was about to go and practice some meditation, but I'm waiting for a maid to bring me something more comfortable than this dress to wear." I pointed to the heavy woolen day dress that the Safehouse had provided for me. It wasn't ideal for sitting and moving around in in case I wanted to practice some yoga.

"Meditation! Oh, that will be wonderful for you right now. Your energies are very out of line and some yoga would do you good to put them right back into place," Alyssa fluttered her hands around my person and then tapped my forehead lightly, causing me to blink in surprise. Thomas let out a peel of laughter that took up the entire empty hallway.

"Don't look so stunned. Alyssa here is a Life wielder and her specialty is emotional and spiritual health. She is a very skilled Yoga and Meditation master here in Lotho. It's actually how we met," he smiled and looked down at his beautiful bride-to-be lovingly before continuing.

"After I took the Throne, I was all over the place mentally and Alyssa was called in to help me refocus. I think it took only one sitting to realize that we were mean to be, but I wanted to wait a time before we got married. Just to make sure my place was secure before I dragged her into this crazy life we have here," he explained.

I blinked again. I didn't know spiritual health was a thing for Life Elementals. Was that something I could learn? Alyssa nodded vigorously referring to Thomas' story.

"I took one look at his energy and mine leaped out and hugged his like they had known each other all their lives. It was a shock and I have to say our first session was a little rocky because I was so stunned," she giggled. Her giggle was infectious, and I couldn't help but to smile with her at that. That's how it felt with Theo, like a piece of me just left and went to him forever.

"That's so sweet. Well, I'm sure the maid will be here soon, and I don't want to hold you two lovebirds up. I guess I will see you for dinner?" I moved to head back into my rooms, but Alyssa caught my arm to stop me.

"Wedding planning can wait. You need real guidance to realign immediately. We will meditate together today and start the process. Thomas," the High King snapped to attention like a lovesick soldier, "Please send word to my sister that she can pick out any white flowers she wants. I didn't care anyway, and that I will see her tomorrow for my fitting. Amelia is much more in need of me and it's my job to help those who are spiritually suffering."

Thomas gave a quick nod of the head and started walking, only to give me a sly grin as he walked by.

"No, Alyssa, really. I don't want to keep you from planning your wedding. If you're doing all this, I'm sure it's soon and you have a lot to do," I interrupted. I tried to wave her off, but she just shook her head.

"No, I want to be friends with you, and this is what friends do. The wedding is two weeks away and I can always double check her decision. I doubt I'll hate it though. She is the florist and knows what I like," she smiled, whispering the last bit behind her hand as if it were a dirty little secret. Just then, a maid walked up with three more attendants behind her holding clothes of all colors and sizes.

"Your Highness? We were told you needed more comfortable clothes than the ones you came with, so we brought a wide variety to choose from," she bowed. I watched as they filed inside one by one and Alyssa followed, flowing into the room effortlessly. Once the maids had departed, Alyssa snatched up a light pink tunic dress with wide cut legs to allow more movement and handed it to me.

"You change into this. I'll rush to Thomas' room and throw on my Meditation gown I wore this morning, and we'll head out. Be quick now, we don't want to miss the midday sun. Its healing powers are the most effective for Life wielders and you need all you can get," she directed.

I caught the dress awkwardly and then heard her feet patter out as fast as a mouse. I stared dumbfounded for a moment and then quietly changed clothes in the bedroom. Not even two minutes later, there was a knock and Alyssa came gliding back into the room wearing a deep green meditation tunic shaped much the same as my own. The only difference was that she had a yellow sari dangling loosely around her neck. The finely stitched patterns caught the light as did the bead work on her long sleeve tunic. I marveled at how radiant she looked in those colors with her dark hair rippling down her back in a loose braid.

"Ready? Let's begin with a small meditative walking pose to guide us to the garden and begin to center," she directed.

She closed her eyes, breathed in deeply, and brought her hands together in a prayer position before turning and striding out of the room. Apparently, I was supposed to follow the same way. Not wanting to be rude and wanting any help I could get, I obliged. I breathed deeply and followed in her wake. I took this time to center my mind and try to calm the raging thoughts and emotions that were beating all around inside of me.

Luckily, no one was in the hallways as we passed in silence listening to the sounds of the water and breathing evenly. Eventually, we came to a door and Alyssa reached to open it. I instantly lost my concentration and stared at the room before me.

The Meditation garden was awe inspiringly beautiful. Bushes, flowers, trees, and an assortment of other plants lined every inch of the glass greenhouse. The smell from the flora was intoxicating, even though I didn't recognize half of them. I heard the quiet trickling of water at a peaceful cadence and the slight chirping of birds in the distance.

"Let's keep this pose and just walk for a bit longer. I can already feel you settling." Alyssa commanded. Her voice was now deeper, less feminine, and more comforting.

I did as directed and followed behind her. She remained silent for a moment, and I unconsciously matched her breath. We took a half turn around the path through the garden before stopping at a statue. It was a water fountain and placed onto its concrete backing was a yellow stone.

"I want you to reach out with your magic and touch this stone. It is the stone that represents Life and will help you focus your magic in a more harmonious direction."

My brow furrowed and I shook my head. "I can't do that. I don't have control over my magic and I'm not sure what will happen if I try. It does weird things when I try to control it."

I felt a warm palm cover my forehead and her fingers situate on top of my head.

"I am aware of the control you have of your magic and it's fine. You don't need to perform an incantation. Just feel around with it gently and slowly. You need to trust yourself and your magic. Fear and anxiety have no place in your future. Magic is ours to wield," She soothed.

I nodded once and felt her take her hand away, the cool air taking over the spot her warm hand had reassured me. It was if my third eye was opening for the first time. I took a breath and then found the spot in my chest where I usually felt my magic come from and slowly, very slowly, sent out tiny tendrils to touch around the ground to find the stone in the fountain. One tendril snapped out quickly and I gasped. I tried to reign it back in quickly and began to hyperventilate in fear.

"Shh, no. Don't let fear stop you. You control the magic. If you're not happy with what it does, then just make it behave. It is yours to command, so make it go slower and be gentler," Alyssa's voice stayed calm and collected.

It took a moment for me to regain control of my breathing. Eventually, I started to reach out again, and this time willed the magic to go slower. Much to my shock, it obeyed and touched around softly, searching for the fountain and the stone it held.

"Excellent! Now, call it back in slowly. Don't let it just snap back. Place the energy your magic collected from the stones back into your sacrum and then slowly feel your way back up your spine and open your eyes," she coached.

I felt the magic receded slowly back as her hand rested on my shoulder.

"When were you going to tell me that you were a Druid?" her voice was alarmingly quiet, but calm.

My eyes flew open in fear and I froze.

"H-How do you know?" my voice wavered, but she gave a small knowing smile.

"Look at the stone," she smiled, and I followed her gaze.

"Oh no!" I cried out, reaching for the stone that was no longer yellow. It was now broken into a color wheel of white, green, blue, red, yellow, and black.

"Seems that you hold all the elements, dear," she smiled. Her voice was even and untroubled. She didn't seem afraid of me at all.

"How many of the elements glowed at your Rite?" she asked.

I gulped, thinking back to that whole ordeal with the Priestess.

"All of them, but Life is the one that glowed the brightest and even shattered when I held it," I admitted.

Alyssa whistled, "Phew. That's powerful. No wonder they just assumed you were a Life Sorcerer. I would have thought a Priestess would think twice and test you this way to see if you were a Druid, but from what I heard, she wasn't giving you much of a chance for anything."

I shook my head in agreement. The Priestess' fear halted everything when she was trying to kill me.

"What else is going on in there that wants to come out? I see another force fighting within you for release. It doesn't really want to take you over, but it certainly does want to be known," she prodded.

She was staring at the space around my body. I clasped my hands together, suddenly nervous to tell her the truth. I was mulling over the consequences of too many people knowing about the Death magic when Alyssa reached out and touched my hands with her own. I felt a calming energy sweep over me and slow my breath.

"It's okay. You don't need to tell me if you're not ready, but I do need you to know that like it or not, one day it will become known. It's better to have people around you who understand than no one at all," she said. I blinked back tears and nodded. Her kindness was overwhelming.

"Death," I whispered, trying to form the words on my tongue. "I have the magic of Death as well."

I felt a weight lift from my chest as I admitted it to Alyssa. She didn't respond verbally, but placed her hand on her chin thoughtfully.

"Do you think Heretia knows?" she asked.

I shook my head in answer. "I don't know."

"There now, doesn't that feel better to say it out loud? To get it off your spirit and release it to the world? It doesn't change a lot, but at least it makes it easier to deal with to give some of the knowledge away," she smiled softly.

"I think we can stop here for today, but I suggest we work on acceptance and control every day until you've really gotten a handle on who you are and what this all means. Are you seeing anyone else about understanding your power?" she asked.

I nodded again. "Yes, I have been given a teacher who seems to want to help me, he was the first to realize I might be a Druid and was excited to work with me. However, I did blow a hole in one of the libraries bookshelves in the process."

Alyssa had to slap a hand over her mouth to keep from busting out laughing. "Oh, I'm sorry, it's just, well, that is a little funny don't you think?"

She shrugged with her dainty little shoulders and I cracked a smile. She was right. Better to laugh it off as a funny accident than to take it to heart and blame myself.

"Let's get you back to rest. After today, you will need a relaxing bath to wash away the tension and then we can meet for dinner with Thomas. I'm sure he is going to want to know that you're feeling better. He really cares too much," she beamed, thinking about her future husband bringing her joy. Her entire essence began to glow, and she seemed so happy and content. I could only hope I looked like that when I thought about or spoke of Theo.

"So, when did you know that you and the Prince were Paired?" she suddenly asked me, and I jumped. Could she read my mind?

"Oh, uh, not long actually. Not even three whole days. We had been feeling something since we met, but we didn't trust each other so we ignored it. But then I was attacked, and we couldn't deny it anymore. It happened so suddenly we didn't have time to talk or discuss it, we just, Paired," I said with a shrug, but I felt my heart flutter reliving that moment.

"Since then, every time he's close, I feel that part of him reaching out to get even closer. Now that he's gone, that piece is quiet. For the first time since coming here, I feel lost. He was there almost from the moment I got here, and without him, I'm not sure how to act or what to do with myself. It sounds silly because he hasn't even been gone a full day, but already I'm missing the feel of him being near."

I hugged myself with my arms. I didn't mean to keep going on about Theo, but once I started, I couldn't stop. Alyssa's warm hand touched my arm in reassurance. Her smile told me she understood what I was feeling.

"He will come back, and soon, too. He knows what he's doing, and he is good at it. Have you ever seen him work?" she asked.

I paused and then gave a small nod. "Briefly, in the garden. He showed up and killed them all before I could even blink. It was so casual for him and it didn't bother him at all. I'm not a fan of violence, but he was impressive, I'll admit."

"He will be back soon, don't worry. He loves you and will come home," she reassured again. I nodded and followed her out of the Meditation Garden.

Back in Timothy's rooms, I found a maid busily cleaning and removing some articles of decoration that could possibly be considered too masculine for a Princess. When I opened the door, she immediately stopped and bowed low to me.

"Your Highness, would you like to me leave?" she asked.

I shook my head.

"No, can you please run me a bath and then get me something appropriate for a private dinner with High King Thomas and Alyssa tonight?" I asked.

She gave me a brief nod and swiftly exited.

I took a moment to look around the room again and smiled. It was very whimsical, and the décor seemed that of more belonging to an aspiring author than a warrior. Books lined two walls and there were empty desks everywhere. I ran my fingers over one dusty spine and noticed that the title sounded very daring and heroic: *The Adventures of Hiddleman and the Five Mountains*. I took it from the shelf and decided that it would be a good read while I was here.

Cracking it open to the cover, I saw an inscription made in the tiniest little shaky scrawl, "This book belongs to Prince Timothy of Lotho. Take it and suffer."

I grinned at a vision of a tiny version of the man I knew today with his crazy curly hair writing this with all intention of keeping the promise. I sat down to begin the first few pages and was beginning to really get into the story when the maid came back to let me know that my bath was ready.

CHAPTER NINETEEN

I had decided to take a short nap before dinner, the days' events having drained me further than a bath could take care of. As my mind fell into an abyss of thoughtlessness, I felt a presence nagging at my senses to pay attention. Trying to ignore it, I squeezed my eyes shut tighter and rolled over. The crunch of leaves as I moved startled me and I sat up in surprise.

"What the....?" I asked aloud but stopped as the sound of my voice echoing caught me off guard.

Stunned, I looked and found myself back in the temple. The stained-glass window was still there, and I could see it clearly lit from the sun behind it.

"What now?" I called out frustrated to be having yet another dream like this so soon after the last one.

"Are you listening yet?" came the voice of Death and I shot up to my feet.

"You mean listening to the part where you didn't mention I might be a Druid? When were you planning on telling me that one? Would have been nice to know at the start of this whole ordeal. Like a warning the night before Michelo kidnapped my parents. Instead of telling me to come home, you could have explained what was going on," I shouted, frustrated.

The temple hummed with an energy that wasn't present last time I had dreamt about it.

"If you undo the binds on your magic, everything will come to the light. Listen and learn."

I was so sick of the riddles and half answers.

"No! Enough is enough. My parents are missing and more than likely in danger and the one thing that seems to have the answers won't even begin to help me. All you do is drop bombs on me with no explanation. I need answers," I demanded into the air.

My complaint went nowhere as the voice of Death seemed to have vanished. I sighed in defeat and looked back at the window that depicted the three figures.

"Who are you?" I asked them aloud.

As I stared my eyes shut once more in exhaustion and I turned once more on my pillow.

I finally found rest before the maid woke me up for dinner with Thomas and Alyssa.

"How long until I'm expected?" I asked rubbing my eyes clear of the sleep.

"A little over an hour," she replied.

I stared thoughtfully at the floor, thinking over what Death had told me about learning.

"Can someone bring me Dryan from the Academy? I need to speak with him urgently," I requested.

The maid assented and left the room swiftly. I climbed out of the bed and waited in the living area for him. My mind raced with what he might tell me, what I would ask him. When the door handle twisted, I stiffened my back, the stress was getting to me and making me jumpy.

Dryan was ushered in by the maid. He looked a little more bedraggled than when I had left him earlier in the library. He bowed low, almost stumbling from the number of books in his arms.

"Your Highness, I have been doing research in all the libraries the capital has to offer and I have collected a vast amount of information on the last Druid, her power, and how she was instructed as a young child. I think I may have found a good way to keep you safe while you learn more about it," he said quickly, having hoped this is what I called him in for.

I could feel his excitement leap around like a child on its first day of school.

"I do appreciate all your hard work and I'm glad you brought everything. I had another dream about Death since I left you earlier and I think it's time I get to work on understanding this whole Druid business," I responded.

Uneasiness set in as I turned back to him.

"Even though, I am not completely sure if you're correct in thinking I'm more than just a Life Sorcerer, I am going to commit myself to learning about being a Druid. In case you are right, it may be our only hope against Heretia right now," I continued.

"I completely agree, Your Highness. Do you want to see what I have brought for you?" he asked.

I looked at the clock on the wall and saw I had some time before dinner, so I nodded.

We sat down at a large oaken desk that had been cleared earlier of Tim's belongings. I settled in for whatever was about to be thrown at me. Dryan pulled two old volumes from the stack and brought them over, flipping the brown one to the first few pages.

"Here we have a life account of the last Druid, Meloni. She was born on a harvest moon to a lot of celebration. She was only the second Druid ever born, after the great Augustina that was sent to help usher all witches away to Medeis when it was first created," he began.

He pointed to a drawn portrait of a very solemn and kind looking older woman.

"This is Meloni here. You can see her mother in the background of the drawing. Her mother was pretty important as the bearer of a Druid."

"How did her mother know Meloni was a Druid before she was born?" I asked and bent over the text, trying to decipher some of the old language.

"It seems as though when a woman is carrying a Druid, the mother can sometimes take on the powers of the Druid while still in the womb. Meloni's mother was a Fire Sorceress living in what was is now the Ancient Kingdom. Our separate kingdoms didn't come into existence until after her death, but lands were still lightly divided by Elemental powers," he explained.

"So, my mother did know," I muttered.

I leaned back with a thud into the chair. The breath was knocked from me as the realization that my parents had hidden all of this from me for so long. Not once had they ever hinted that I was special or different from other witches. I guess just being different from normal mortal children was enough for them.

"Yes, I do believe that she did know and that is why she begged the Mother Goddess for help. Heretia was only beginning during that time, and my guess is that she was afraid for you. Death answering with a bargain seems to be a little odd to me. Maybe Princess Clarisse asked for you to have the strength to be the greatest Druid this world had ever known? I don't see why she would have accepted a deal that would have guaranteed you facing off with Heretia if she didn't want you to handle it."

"No," I admitted, "that doesn't sound like my mother."

I shook my head and continued glancing through the pages. I absentmindedly flipped through another and came to the biography of her early years.

"So, this is the story of how she came to control her power? All her teachers and lessons?" I asked. Dryan nodded and pointed to a certain part.

"It's pretty cut and dry in this book. However, this other one I found is the actual journal kept by her youngest tutor of what she learned and when. It appears they brought in Sorcerers from every element to teach her their highest forms of magic. She also was brought tutors on politics, government, geography, and more. It's as if they expected her to be the High Queen of all Medeis. At some point though, there is a break in the journal, and it doesn't pick back up for some years. It correlates to a time in her biography where she wandered off, looks as though around age seventeen. Apparently, Meloni decided to go live amongst the Magical Beasts and nature for a time. When she returns, that is when real peace begins."

His synopsis was brief, but I could understand why she might have left. I was barely twenty-two and had only been living in this realm for a little over a week. At seventeen I can only imagine the strain of expectations that had been placed on her for her entire life. I was only just learning about this and the heaviness weighed down on me like a boulder. I could only imagine what seventeen years of preparations, lessons, watching, and probably being told everyday she was different could do to a kid.

"Poor thing. Is there ever a moment after that time of wandering where she took off again?" I asked, trying to connect to the human that was Meloni.

Dryan shook his head. "Seems not, but she once she established peace, she did it quickly. Meloni set up a government to do the main ruling while she became more of a benevolent Priestess and protector. There was only one battle during her lifetime, and once she was brought in, the entire war ended quickly and fiercely. In fact, she came back from her wandering because of that war."

Dryan flipped the page and an image flashing with color flared before my eyes, taking up two entire pages. I squinted to take it in, and then gasped. It was the blonde woman from the stained-glass window in my dream. She was just as young and beautiful here, standing in the exact same outfit and wielding the same weapon. However, the hand drawn illumination was much more detailed and her beauty clearly evident.

"It's horrible," I whispered and leaned in closer.

There was the beautiful Meloni, decked out in white lightweight armor with her two hands lifted above her head. A ring of yellow encircled her entire being. She was standing on top of a brown hill. Below her was a field of carnage. I'm not sure how the artist was able to bring it to a single illustration, but it looked as though thousands upon thousands of men, women, horses, cattle, and even Magical Beasts lay dead on the field. It wasn't an easy death; no one just laid there with their eyes closed. In the picture, the people and creatures were suffering. Entire people were being ripped apart by invisible hands and blood spilled from the stumps of horses' necks. Every face was marred by screams of agony as the bloodshed ripped through the memory.

But that wasn't even the most frightening part. The worst part was Meloni's eyes. She wasn't happy, she wasn't sad, she wasn't even the unfeeling murderer. As she stood there with her hands raised and her body shining from the tint of gold paint, she looked angry. She was consumed in wrath. As if she believed these people deserved every agony, she laid upon them. I sucked in a breath as her yellow gaze bore into to me and I had to turn the page away from it. They were the same color my own had been since the night of mine and Theo's Pairing.

"What was the war over? Why was it that bloody?" I asked quietly, unable to read the script myself.

Dryan cleared his throat.

"There was a large group of dissenters called the Uprising who were moving towards the ways of the old pantheon of gods. Part of their rituals involved sacrifice and partaking of the sacrificial body. They thought it was what made them stronger, able to see the future, perform higher magic and even, defeat entire armies. We know now,

290

after careful research, there was a certain potion they fed the sacrifice that would seep into the body of the followers and poison their blood. It was making them insane and it was permanent. Any child born of these people would also be insane with the blood poison, but that really didn't matter for too long for the child."

I turned my head, "Why not? Did Meloni murder all the children too?"

I was shocked, but Dryan just shook his head.

"No, because there were no children left. You see, the sacrifice wasn't cattle or lamb as normally would be. The Uprising used their own children," he explained.

I paled and felt the bile rise in my throat.

"There were no poisoned children left to get rid of after the final battle because…because the followers had eaten every last one of them the night before in preparation."

I went from shocked to horrified. I slowly flipped the page back to the illustration of Meloni wiping out an entire people for the monstrosities they had committed, and instead of being worried at her angry glare, I felt it grow inside of me.

"That's absolutely disgusting," I muttered and moved to shut the book. "That an entire people could poison, murder, and then eat their own babies is beyond anything I've ever heard. No wonder she didn't just defeat them, she wiped them out completely."

Dryan nodded, "She had to. The blood was poisoned and so was their livestock, just by interacting with their excrement and sharing water with them. She was forced to not only exterminate every last breathing thing on that battlefield, but she had to boil their blood, destroy the soil of the earth around them for miles, and had to purify the water from every river and stream touching their dwelling sites. It took months to completely cleanse the land of the poison, and even then, she didn't let anyone live there."

Dryan opened the second book and turned to a certain page. "There have been some settlements there in the past few hundred years, but it is still tradition to not go too far into it. So much so that when the Ancient kingdom built their capital city, they built it on the edge and were gate-keepers for a time over it." He pointed to an early map of Medeis.

I furrowed my brow, looking it over. "The capital of the Ancient Kingdom's name is Purge?" that seemed a little ominous and frankly ridiculous to me.

Dryan shrugged and put the book away.

"Well, they wanted to remind everyone what the land beyond had been and what had happened there. I guess at the time it made some sense."

I looked up at a beautiful desk clock that Timothy had left behind and sighed.

"We need to end our lessons here for the day. If you want me to keep the books safe, I can in the desk, and we can resume tomorrow." I waved my hand to point to the drawer I was talking about. Without warning, it opened, and I gasped. Dryan seemed to startle slightly as well.

"Was that me?" I asked.

Dryan stood and walked over, looking at the drawer and putting his hand up underneath it. I rose from the chair to study it as well. I placed my hand on my mouth, still staring in dumbstruck wonder at what I had just done.

Was this really me? The girl who couldn't even make fire one month ago for her father's birthday candles. Could never encourage a simple daisy to sprout in her mother's garden. Had the hardest time even boiling water for pasta in her first apartment. I shook the thoughts away from my head. My anxiety must have been evident, even to Dryan who gave me an understanding smile.

"You need to believe in yourself, Princess. I know for a fact Fire Sorcerers put a great deal of stock in just willing themselves to be able to perform better magic and they think it will make you stronger. Belief in yourself and your magic is key for them."

Dryan gently deposited the two books into the drawer and closed it himself. I was grateful for that. For all I knew, if I tried that again, I would blast the drawer right back out the other side of the desk and into the wall behind it. I walked to the edge of the window again and looked out, as if some answer would be there waiting on me. Dryan sighed heavily and came to stand with me.

"Princess, I do not have the answers for you. Only the Mother will know what you are to do with your gifts. If she sent you here, and let Death become a part of you as well, she certainly seems to think the situation dire enough. The Mother will show you the way. She will be your guide. In the meantime, I am gathering all our top Sorcerers from every element that we have at the Academy to begin lessons with you. You will need to study every day," he said. It all sounded exhausting, but if it was what it took to get stronger then I had no choice.

"I guess you're right, but what if all of this still doesn't make me good enough. Theo and the Elite Guard will be back in about six weeks and then we go from there. What if six weeks isn't enough?" Dryan just chuckled and placed a hand on my shoulder.

"Princess, every day is enough. Every day you try is another day you've gotten stronger and better. Don't give up! We've barely begun, and I for one haven't had a student fail me yet," he exclaimed in a jolly and upbeat tone.

"Yeah, but none have ever been me," I muttered under my breath.

"No, but," he grinned again with that wicked smile promising fun, "I enjoy a challenge. Until tomorrow morning! Library at nine o'clock. Don't be late!"

He waltzed off right out of my room. As he shut the door quietly, I couldn't help but smile inwardly at the crazy little man with twinkling eyes.

CHAPTER TWENTY

Dinner with Thomas and Alyssa was blissful. I continuously complimented the food. We had an in-depth conversation on how different food preparation was in the Original World compared to Medeis and how food was experienced in the two worlds. The idea of drive thru windows was mind shattering for them and they insisted I never mention it to the food vendors in the city.

"Next thing you know, we'd have all these 'McDonalds' and 'Burger Kings' popping up and I just really don't see how you can keep quality food made on that level. Nope, I'd rather keep it the way we have it and enjoy every morsel of this expertly prepared cuisine," Thomas chuckled.

He patted his full belly and Alyssa chittered a pretty laugh, stroking his arm.

"I don't think we have any worries dear. Our people are extremely attached to the old ways and don't really like change that much," she said.

I cringed slightly at that statement. What if they didn't like me? What if I was too much of a change for them?

Alyssa caught my look and lowered her hand, "Oh, I'm sorry Amelia. I didn't mean it that way." She began to apologize, but stopped herself, slanting her eyes towards Thomas. She guessed that I hadn't told that many people of what I had been learning in my dreams.

"Why are you sorry? I don't think you said anything wrong," Thomas said. Alyssa gave me another apologetic smile and I sighed.

"No, it's okay, Alyssa. He probably needs to know. It's only a matter of time anyway," I sighed. I wiped away some wrinkles on the skirt of the grey dress I had donned for the evening and took in a breath.

"It seems as though there are going to be a lot of changes coming soon. Dryan, the scholar I've been working with, has discovered something about me that I was not aware of." I began.

Thomas sat forward and gave me his full attention. Worry etched across his brow.

"I am not just a Life Sorcerer, Thomas. Apparently, I am a Druid," I admitted.

I waited in the silent pause. No one breathed, no one moved. I watched as Thomas' entire body went rigid, muscles feathering in his jaw line, eyes widening. Alyssa watched him, careful to make a no movement so as not to spook him. I just stared him back down, defiance written on my face. I wasn't going to be afraid of this any longer and if Thomas wasn't going to understand, then to hell with everyone. An entire minute ticked by before I finally broke the standoff myself.

"Well?" I prompted. I silently begged Thomas to say something, anything, to let me know I hadn't melted his brain. In a flash, which made Alyssa and I both jump, Thomas was up off his feet and pacing behind the chair which he had just occupied.

"Druid? That's not possible. We would have known. Your mother would have known," he whispered.

I was beginning to see the tell-tale signs of a full-blown freak out coming. Alyssa did as well, and she turned in her seat to reach out a hand for him.

"Thomas, love. Please come sit down and we will discuss this rationally. There is no need to panic," she crooned, attempting to settle his nerves.

Thomas halted his pacing and looked at Alyssa in shock. "You knew? You knew about this and didn't tell me?"

Alyssa nodded her head. "I figured it out earlier today during our meditation with the fountain stone. Remember how yours were always blue? A Druid will turn them different colors. It also wasn't my story to tell. I knew Amelia would pick the right time to let you know, but she was still processing everything and needed peace while she came to her reality," she said in a soothing tone. Alyssa reached out to me and took my hand gently.

"That was very brave of you, Amelia. You did a great job and I am so proud of you for facing your fears," she smiled. Her smile was so gentle and sweet that I couldn't help but grip her hand in return it with a grateful smirk.

"Thank you, Alyssa, but I'm going to need a lot more of you starting tomorrow. Dryan wants to start my Druid training in every magic available," I explained.

Alyssa just nodded her head.

"Don't you worry about that. I will, however, need one day off to get married in two weeks," she winked.

I nodded my head and giggled. "I'm pretty sure I can call off all lessons that day to attend."

"Hello? While you two are over there being all nice and calm, I have only just learned about this and am still losing my mind over the thought that we are in the presence of a Druid!" Thomas shrieked. He started waving his arms around like a screaming monkey to get our attention. Alyssa waved him away.

"You'll be fine dear. Druids are people, too. They aren't gods to be treated like broken glass. Presence of a Druid? Really Thomas, she is still the same woman from yesterday," Alyssa chastised.

Thomas seemed slightly reprimanded by her scolding and sat back down in his chair. He puffed out his cheeks and ran his large tan hands through his thick fluffy hair. I couldn't help but feel sorry for him.

"I know it's a shock, and I should have told you earlier, but as Alyssa said, I needed to figure it out for myself first," I explained.

His eyes darted to mine. "And have you?" he asked.

I blinked, "Have I what?"

"Figured it out? I mean, if you are a Druid, then everyone is going to depend on you to end this fight with Heretia before it even starts. Everyone is going to expect some awe-inspiring death blow and for this all to be over in one fell swoop," he exclaimed. I lowered my eyes and went pale.

"No, no I haven't figured it out, but I'm trying to. Dryan is gathering everything he can, and we will begin training tomorrow morning," I answered.

Thomas didn't move for a moment, but finally decided to nod approval at this plan.

"Have you written to Theo yet? I think this is definitely something your Pair needs to know," he said.

I shook my head. "No, this is not what he needs right now. He is in an extremely dangerous position and worrying about me even more than he already does is going to get him hurt. Or worse, he'll rush back here, and the rest of the Guard will be left exposed. They need him right now more than I do. I've got Dryan and his scholars, I've got Alyssa, and if you're willing, I have you. I need you all as my friends and teachers in this. I have to learn a lot really fast to be of any use."

The information weighed down on the young High King. With a final nod from him, Alyssa grinned and stroked his muscular arm.

"It'll be alright dear. Amelia will be fine, and we will, too. Just let her decide to tell the rest of the world when she's ready. I don't think blabbing to everyone that will listen is the safest option at this point," she said.

Thomas turned to his bride-to-be and smiled warmly, reached for her hand, and kissed it. "You're right, my love. You always are."

298

With a sigh of relief, we ended the meal and parted ways for the evening. Alyssa promised to come to me once my lessons were over with the scholars in the afternoon and we could keep working on balancing my elements. I had consciously made the decision not to mention Death speaking to me in my dreams, or even possibly wielding Death magic. The poor man had enough of a shock for one night.

Dryan was waiting on me the next morning, but not in the library as he stated. After I finished breakfast, a footman retrieved me and led me outside to what looked like a practice arena for horses.

"Princess!" Dryan waved me over towards him.

I walked over to the small group of men and women waiting for me.

"Good morning, I hope you slept well and ate a good meal because today we are going to be pushing you limits to get a good base reading on where you are with every Element," he said excitedly.

I deflated.

"Let me answer that: low. As in, five-year-old low. Pretty much treat me like a pre-pubescent witch with anger issues. That's basically what I am anyway," I shrugged.

A few people in the crowd chuckled.

"I'm not joking," I said, but no one seemed to care that I was serious in my personal assessment of my abilities. Dryan walked over and clapped both hands on my shoulders.

"Don't worry about that. Everyone here is aware of exactly who and what you are. Every one of them is ready and capable of handling anything you throw at us, figuratively or literally," he winked.

"That's not funny," I frowned.

"Nonsense! Let's get started. I say we go with Life first since that's what you presented as your strongest and then we'll go from there. Our finest Life Wielder at the Academy has been studying the ways of the Life Sorcerer and she can instruct you through what you need to know, even if she can't demonstrate it," he explained.

I nodded and faced the middle-aged plump woman with the sparkling blue eyes and short, curly blonde hair.

"My name is Regina. Why don't you go ahead and just try a Relaxing incantation?" she directed.

I breathed in slowly and recited the spell in my head. I was stunned to find that I found myself settling down and my muscles relaxing from their tense state. The worry ebbed away and all that was left was determination and peace.

"Did I do it? I felt like I did it," I smiled. I was giddy with excitement.

"I believe you did, Princess. Now, heal a wound," she said, turning to face two newcomers to our group.

"He was brought in just the morning by his mother. Apparently, this young man decided to run ahead and didn't listen. He got knocked over by a cart and we think he has a broken wrist." She waved her hand, and a small boy came forward sniffling with tears streaking down his face. My breath caught as the little boy's mother walked forward, holding onto his shoulders with a white-knuckle grip.

"The pain has already been numbed for him and kept on ice with strict instructions not to move it. I was going to just bandage it tightly and stick him on bedrest, but this was a much better opportunity for you since it's more realistic."

I felt my heart leap as the mother stopped the boy before me. All my nursing instincts kicked in and I knelt quickly before him, reaching for his wrist. I checked his temperature with my hand, felt his pulse, and gave him a good once over for any other injuries.

"Don't use your eyes, Princess. Use your magic," Regina instructed.

"I don't know how," I said. "He needs help now and I can't do it."

The boy whimpered again, and his mother let out a sob.

"Please," she whispered. "Please, he wants to be a musician and play the fiddle. If he can't use his wrist right, he will never get to do that."

I looked into her eyes and saw how scared she was. My heart broke into a million pieces and images of Theo playing for me only a few nights ago in the town center flew through my mind. I looked back at the boy and he grimaced. That was it! That was all I needed. I reached down into my magic and let it move my arms and limbs for me. Instinctively, I placed one hand on the side of his head, sending commands to numb and contain the pain that I was about to cause. I commanded his nerves to block out all signals while my other hand went to his wrist. My magic pulsed on contact and it recognized the injury.

"Coligo, apio, oblinito," I whispered. "Connect, bind, seal."

I ordered his muscles, bones, sinews, and tendons to reform. I showed his body how to fix itself. Without me blocking out the pain, it would have been excruciating.

The break had been nasty, and deep. I had to command my magic to pick out a few fragments of bone that had chipped off and push them through the wound, up and out of his body. I commanded the bone to regenerate new growth in their place. Once I knew the inside was complete, I focused on the tissue of the skin and broken blood vessels.

All in all, it took me about five minutes, but to me it felt like forever. I had to focus on every reconnection and repair. Finally, I checked it over one more time with my magic and then once with my eyes, turning his wrist in different directions to make sure it was straight. When I took my hand off his temple, he gasped and clutched at his wrist.

"There might be some slight soreness there for a few days. I did my best to correct some swelling, but everything in your body reacts when it's been healed, so I would suggest ice and heat rotating every few hours for a day or two. Be slow to pick the fiddle back up. Ask your instructor for strengthening exercises. I had to completely create some pieces of your body from nothing, so they don't have muscle memory yet," I instructed.

I took his wrist again and moved it around asking if it hurt. He shook his head. His mother was beaming by the time I stood up.

"Thank you!" she shouted and flew at me, wrapping her thin arms around my neck.

"Oh! Thank you, Princess! We haven't had a Life Sorcerer in so long. I was so worried because I knew the best the wielders and healers could do was set it and send home spices and herbs for pain, but you were able to completely heal him in minutes! This is a miracle! Thank you!"

I accepted her hug and then held out my arms for the little boy to join us, and he did so happily. After they were escorted away, an applause broke out from those watching, I had forgotten they were there. Regina stepped forward and grinned.

"You are much more adept than you let on. That's magic that only the most advanced of Life Sorcerers were able to do," she smiled.

"Don't look too deep into it. In the Original World I was a healer. They don't have magic there, so knowledge of the human anatomy from the start is an absolute necessity. Can't really play around with it, or you can hurt someone without magic to fix your mistake," I shrugged. Regina nodded, acting like she understood.

"There is not much I can teach her, other than some practice working in our clinics and Sick and Injured Rooms. I don't see that she needs basic handling of Life magic lessons from me. I will take her every morning to the wards to handle cases that come in and oversee her growth," Regina announced.

Everyone began clapping, but I didn't feel too terribly victorious. Life was only one element and I still had four to go. I already felt tired. If my caution at using my magic was voiced, no one in this arena seemed to care. Next was Earth. Dryan explained he wanted to try this next since my parents were Earth wielders and my Pair was an

Earth Sorcerer. The core basics of Earth were Revitalize, Grow, Move, and Calling to fauna in the area around me.

"You are excellent at Revitalize, which is no surprise because Life qualities transplant to renewing dead earth and life. You are good at that. Calling is not so difficult for you either it seems, but I take it you cannot understand them," the austere young man who towered over me said.

"However, you need lessons in Grow and Move. We will meet after your Life lesson every day in the forests behind the wards for work on those qualities so you can learn to hear the animals speak. Being able to Communicate with them is vital if we are to go to war. Animals, especially birds, are critical messengers."

Dryan agreed and then turned to me so that I could face him to begin my examination for Water. I shrank from the glare the Earth Sorcerer sent my direction. I wasn't pleased to be spending time with him on anything.

Thankfully, Water was nowhere near as difficult. Hydrate, Rain, Redirect and Scrying were not terribly difficult, but I could only manage them in small amounts.

"I would suggest meeting in the Meditation Garden at the end of every day until you've mastered these qualities," Dryan declared.

I breathed a sigh of relief. Thank the Mother.

Air was a little tricky. Calling a breeze was quite different from Calling an animal. Breath I found simple since I had seemed to have already mastered it during my many meditations. Lastly, was Storm.

"This part of Air is hard to master for most and is the base of almost every weather spell we cast. It is also the most dangerous, I won't even test you on it today with too many people around. You may accidentally hurt someone."

I felt defeated, then turned to face my final Scholar, Fire. I waited patiently as a large, battle-hardened woman stalked in my direction, sizing me up and finding me wanting.

She scoffed at me and sneered. "This is useless. Fire is too dangerous for playtime. I'm going to go ahead and assume you are worthless in all Fire qualities and just go ahead and say it's a waste of time."

Dryan coughed and stepped forward to speak, I was too stunned to even look at him.

"Now, now, Jersica. She is the Druid and will be able to master fire easily if she has the right teacher. You are, without a doubt, the finest Fire Sorcerer in Lotho and the most qualified to teach her safely. If you could please just examine her and then make your assessment," he pressed.

Jersica sneered at me again. I could already tell that this wasn't going to end well.

"Start a fire," she commanded.

She pointed to a wood pile she had created at the other end of the arena, far away from everyone. The entire crowd quickly scooted behind me and then further back behind Jersica as well. I shot Dryan an accusatory look and he shrugged.

"It is the most volatile of elements," he apologized.

"You're a water sorcerer," I fired back.

He winced and shrugged again.

"Enough chatter! Light the fire!" Jersica shouted.

I gulped hard and tried to remember what Dryan had mentioned to me the day before about Fire magic. Believing you can do it is important. I straightened my back and concentrated on the pile of wood. I narrowed my eyes, praying to the Mother that everyone was far away from danger. I flung out my hands with the simple audible command of, "Ignis."

Everyone held deathly still. No one breathed, no one blinked as we waited to see what would happen. A few moments passed and I was about to give up and try again when suddenly a crack rang out. In the middle of the pile of wood, small little sparks flashed around and the sizzle of wood catching flame spread throughout the arena. In another moment, the entire pile was safely set ablaze and didn't spread beyond it.

Without thinking, I whooped for joy, punching both fists into the air, and jumped as high as I could.

"Ha! Did you see that? I did it! Dryan, did you see me?" I shouted, my heart and spirit full to bursting with pride.

I spun in place and smiled brightly as Dryan ran forward to hug me.

"That was amazing, Princess! You did it in one try!" he exclaimed.

I squealed again and looked back to see the fire blazing warmly in its place, and then to Jersica, who was the only one looking pissed at my accomplishment.

"That's all fine and well, Princess," she hissed the title as if it made her sick to speak it. "But that's only the beginning. Fire is more than just lighting wood or boiling water. It is battle! It is war. You will meet with me every day before your last lesson for fitness training and combat lessons."

"Jersica, I'm not fighting like that if there is to be a war," I countered.

Jersica scoffed again. "Why? You can't break a nail? One o'clock, this arena, eat beforehand, and wear something more suitable for exercise instead of those pretty dresses you seem to adore."

I looked down at my skirts and huffed. Clearly, she was going to be worse than the Earth Sorcerer. Jersica stalked off without another word and the rest of the instructors followed. Only Dryan stayed.

"I am most impressed by you, Princess! I will write up a schedule for you to follow every day, starting with Life in the morning and ending with some meditation with Alyssa in the late afternoon."

I nodded but halted with a thought. "Except Alyssa and Thomas' wedding day. We're taking it off completely. No lessons, no training, no meditation. For her or for me," I instructed.

Dryan seemed to have forgotten about the High King's wedding altogether and he nodded in understanding.

"Tomorrow then, nine o'clock in the Medical Ward," he said.

We said our goodbyes and I asked a guardsman for the time.

"It's just after lunch, Princess."

I sighed. This was going to be a long six weeks.

CHAPTER TWENTY-ONE

If I thought I was going to find a moment of peace outside of my Meditation time with Alyssa, I was dead wrong. From sunrise to almost sunset, I was running from one lesson to another every hour on the hour. I started with Life at nine in the morning, which went very well. I had always loved helping others, and this was just another extension of who I truly was deep down. I was a healer at heart and bringing comfort to those in need was my life calling. I hated seeing others in pain and being able to ease it, or fix it all together, made me feel alive again.

Life was followed by Earth, which progressed quickly. I was communicating with birds and moving objects as big as a house by the end of the first week. However, the scholar in charge of me, Rufio, still seemed to hate my guts. Every little thing I did wrong was instantly pointed out and sneered at, but when I was getting better, I got nothing more than a nod. If it weren't for Alyssa and Dryan encouraging me outside of lessons, I would have stormed off long ago. To hell with his nasty pointed nose and pointy eyebrows. He reminded me so much of Ogden it was overwhelming. Nothing was ever good enough.

I then moved on Air, which we stayed out in the woods for. I didn't struggle as hard as I thought with the magic. I was quickly mastering storm calling, and my favorite exercise was sending small breezes up under a bird's wing to watch it soar higher into the sky.

"Don't get in the way too much of the Mother's plans. There might be a mouse that bird was tracking for its only meal that day and you interrupted the flight," Handel, the Air Sorcerer, would remind me. This had me paying more attention to what my actions might create. I stepped in less often until I was asked in the Clinic, becoming more aware of when my talents were needed, and when they weren't.

After Air, I would head to the garden for a mix of Meditation with Alyssa and Water with Dryan. Together, with those two teaching and encouraging me, Water quickly became my second easiest element. By the time of Alyssa's wedding, I was creating little animal figurines and had walking them around the room. I was successfully rerouting streams and pulling water from the air to create rain with barely a thought.

Last, after a quick light lunch and clothing change, was Fire. I dreaded this every day, mostly because Jersica was a nightmare. The first day was nothing but pushups and running in circles. She enjoyed being my taskmaster. I'm not going to lie, day three almost broke me. After the third plank and jump, I wanted to heave my lunch up all over the dirt floor.

"You're weak! How are you ever going to fight in this war if you can't even stay standing more than ten minutes!" she roared after I almost tripped over my own feet during a leap over a rope she was circling on the ground for me to avoid.

It didn't help that every time I stopped, Jersica sent a bolt of fire towards my feet or my head to make me either duck or dodge.

"I'm not sure if you heard me the first day or not," I panted, ducking from another bolt of fire. "But I'm not going to fight like that."

Jersica stopped. Clearly, she had thought I wasn't serious the first time. "And why not?" she recoiled the rope back into her hand.

I refused to sit or kneel in her presence, but my legs were starting to shake, and my knees were practically knocking together from exhaustion.

"It would distract Theo too much. He has to fight, if it comes to it, and me being out there would only keep him from focusing on staying alive. Besides, Meloni never entered the battlefield when she destroyed the Uprising. She stood on a hill and wiped them out. I just need to focus on growing my magic," I explained.

I was starting to regain my breath and stood straighter to face the warrior glaring down at me. She didn't respond for a moment and when I went to open my mouth again to speak, I had to duck. With a roar, Jersica launched a massive fireball at my head.

"Why would you ever do that to yourself?" she shouted and picked me up by the front of my tunic shirt. My feet came off the floor and I had to scramble to regain my footing.

"Put me down!" I insisted. I started kicking and slapping her hands.

"Why should I? If you prefer to be handled by others, then how is this any different?" she growled and then tossed me back. I lost my footing and fell directly on my butt, pain searing up my spine. I was stunned for only a second before I fired back.

"I do not prefer to be handled!" the argument only seemed to incite her further.

"Really? So that's why you're letting your little lover boy tell you what you can and can't do? You're going to sit on the sidelines and watch hundreds, if not thousands, die while you figure out how to control your magic?" she sneered.

"Meloni didn't sit on the sidelines and strike thousands down with a single spell. Whoever told you that was dead wrong. Meloni was a warrior and fought alongside her men and women on the field, drenching herself in the enemy's blood. She knew her magic wasn't strong enough to take out the numbers that were there, so she had to fight tooth and nail first to help whittle it down until she could finally defeat them."

Jersica loomed over me, her face dark with hatred. "But here you are, pretending you're going to save all of us with a flick of your wrist if given enough time. Well, let me be clear Princess, you haven't got time to be that strong, Meloni wasn't even that strong and she had seventeen years on you. Meloni knew where she belonged, and she never let anyone tell her otherwise. It's probably a good thing she never found her Pair because she might have destroyed him if he ever insinuated that she wasn't strong enough."

I stood with a leap and got right in Jersica's breastplate. She was head and shoulder taller than me, but my anger was mightier than my logic.

"Theo would never think I'm not strong enough! How dare you! You know nothing about him. He just wants me safe." I retorted. Jersica forced me back with a deliberate step. I stumbled into the stone wall, my hands flying behind me for balance.

"Then why do you let him already control what you can and can't do? If you were strong enough to fight on a field of battle and stay alive, he wouldn't have to worry, would he? And last, Princess, but certainly not least, why would you be letting someone else call the shots in war and not yourself? If you are the Druid, you are the Commander!" she hissed.

My breath hitched at her closeness and I winced away from the words.

"No one tells you what you can and can't do. Learn to protect your Pair by becoming the stronger of the two in all ways and learn to be a leader. Right now, I see nothing but a sniveling Princess," she scoffed. "We're done for the day. Don't show up tomorrow if you're going to be a useless weakling. I don't have time to be training someone who isn't going to help."

Tears puddled in the corner of my eyes and she stalked off. Thousands of thoughts raced through my mind, crowding every inch of me. They told me I wasn't good enough and that I was useless. I was never going to be strong enough to do any of it. They told me the Mother made a mistake, my parents and Theo were going to die for nothing. I was going to be killed because I was too stupid and weak to do anything right. The thoughts kept coming and raging inside me, boiling to a breaking point when finally, I screamed.

"AHHHH!!"

I ran for Jersica who hadn't left the arena yet and jumped to reach her head. With all my anger and might, I willed a spear made of fire into my hand to pierce her chest with and launched it straight at her heart. I was sure it wouldn't hit the intended target. But, without much of a glance, she dropped and rolled to the side. She regained her footing in one swift movement and watched as the spear blasted into the stone wall, creating a large crater hole the size of my torso.

I rose from my kneeling position and stared her down, heat rising from my neck and running down my palms. Without looking, I could feel flames flickering along my fingertips and I clasped my hands tight. Jersica looked to me, the wall, and then back to me, but I never stopped staring at her. After a moment, she let out a snort and then grinned at me wickedly.

"It's a start!"

She turned and walked away from me, unscathed.

Life continued this way until the day of Alyssa and Thomas' wedding. Jersica and Rufio continued to be the bane of my existence. I still wasn't learning any real fire magic, but I was finding myself a little stronger and faster on my toes. Jersica had even begun teaching me some defensive maneuvers to protect myself if I was ever attacked again.

The morning of their wedding, Alyssa woke me with giggles and feathers. She tickled my nose until I finally sat up, pushing her away.

"Come on silly! I want you to be a part of this. I can't talk to Thomas all day!" she moaned the last two words like a petulant child and then gave me a very fake sad face. "I need someone to keep me company."

I rubbed the sleep from my eyes, "What about your family? What about your sisters?"

"They are all busy helping set up. I'm practically alone! Come be with me today. Let's get ready!"

Alone to Alyssa must have not included the fifteen maids and dressers waiting for her. They bustled around with important jobs to do, the bridal suite alive with people. The entire day was like that. At every second, there was something to do. There were dresses to wear, flowers to arrange in her hair, drinks to drink, and rituals to adhere to. Before the wedding, Alyssa had to go to the temple and be cleansed by the Priestess, making her ready to be a bride, and make an offering of happiness to the Mother Goddess.

I stood silent for that entire proceeding and just watched, taking in everything, and cataloging it. This would be me and Theo one day, and I smiled at the thought. Alyssa wore a stunning gown of effervescent white to this ritual. The maids and I did everything in our power to keep the gorgeous piece pristine.

"We can't ruin your wedding dress," I muttered once into her ear while walking back.

Alyssa giggled in response.

"Silly, this isn't my wedding dress. It's just the Blessing dress. I have another one for the formal family lunch, an actual wedding dress, one for the Feast afterwards, and one more for Thomas to see me in after the door is locked and everyone goes away."

My jaw fell at the amount of clothing she was to wear just today. No wonder there were so many maids running around! It was a carousel of clothing and I was just a pony stuck to the floor along for the ride.

I had no idea what I was in for, but I kept paddling down the stream of madness and held my head above water. Before I knew it, Alyssa and Thomas were married. They had ridden through the streets of Lotho to a grand procession, and we were all drinking and dining until the wee hours of the morning. I slumped back in the chair next to the Bride and Groom and breathed deeply. I hardly remembered everything from the day.

It was most certainly busy, but seeing the happy couple made me smile. The love they had radiated from their lips, bodies, and souls as they sat there curled up together on the plush couch where they were being served dish after dish. I looked around the hall and noticed everyone else was just as thrilled at the union as they were. Needing a break, I looked to the left and right, finally noticing a double window door leading to a balcony. Fresh air!

Without thinking, I grabbed my goblet of wine and headed out, yearning to breathe in the sea and fill my lungs with its salty goodness. No one even cared that I was walking away as the laughter and chatter continued behind me, fading as I shut the glass doors to the noise. The crashing of the waves was endless and soothing. I breathed in deeply as I came to the edge of the balcony, my swishing skirts the only other noise.

The dress Alyssa had lent me was stunning. The gown had been meticulously crafted to show off an hourglass figure, with a red bodice laced in the front and gold scrolling stitching outlining the panel bodice. White satin graced my backside and the skirt opened to two pleated panels with matching red silk peeking out. It had a red hood that was merely decorative but gave it a sort of heaviness that helped keep you upright with all the weight from the front. I played with the sheer trumpet sleeves of white satin for a moment before looking back out at the ocean.

As I had done every night for two weeks in the privacy of my borrowed rooms, I talked to Theo out loud as if he were there.

"You should see this, my love. They are stunning together and this whole place is gorgeous. I can't wait for you to come back and do this for ourselves," I whispered. "I love you, come home safe."

My heart sank with sadness at the lonely feeling talking to myself brought. I blew a kiss into the wind and turned to rejoin the lively wedding party behind me.

The day after the wedding, everyone was back on schedule. Even Alyssa showed up for our Meditation, though I insisted she go away with Thomas and enjoy their alone time.

"Nonsense!" she waved me away. "We leave after this for a little cottage along the beach where no one will bother us for at least a week, but I will be travelling in every day to continue your lessons. You are more important the spending every second of every day running naked throughout a house like a couple of wild children."

I blushed a deep scarlet at the thought, but Alyssa laughed wildly and instructed me to sit so we could continue our work. I threw myself back into my studies and found I was mastering qualities left and right. Regina began to demand that I start learning to Summon and sent me home with tome after tome on the subject.

"We will start attempting to Summon at the end of the week, so read every bit and don't skip a word," she directed. I wasn't thrilled, but I knew she was right. I had mastered everything else in Life except Summoning the Dead.

Rufio even started to give me little compliments sprinkled throughout the lesson. Water and Air were advancing in leaps and bounds, but Fire was only just starting to heat up. Jersica had decided to start showing me how to wield the element instead of just running my body through Herculean workouts. Every day I grew a little faster and every day I grew a little stronger.

It wasn't until a week after the wedding that I found myself being called into the High Throne Room for a conference. I hadn't been expecting it, so I was a little dumbfounded they wanted me. Thomas and Alyssa were officially back and had resumed duties. I hadn't necessarily had a meeting with the other High Kings and Queens yet since the Elite Guards departure. I hadn't even seen them around much and just assumed that they wanted an update on my lessons.

I hadn't formally announced that I was a Druid to them either. But they must have guessed at this point that something was up if I was taking lessons from all these different Elemental Sorcerers. No one met me outside the door when I came at my summoned time and I waited patiently. Finally, a small woman opened the door and beckoned me in. Everyone was silent as I walked in. Chairs were placed evenly around the pool and vines still hung from the ceiling. I let the attendant lead me to a seat between Thomas and Ludwig, who gave me a nasty side eye glare as I took my place.

Vermir cleared his throat and the silence grew even more deafening once I was settled.

"Princess Amelia, we have brought you here today because some news has come to us that we feel you need to be aware of immediately," he began.

I cocked my head to the side. Had they heard from Theo?

"Oh?" I encouraged him to go on.

"As you are aware it has been some days since we have received word of the progress of the scouting party that accompanied the Elite Guard into the Ancient Kingdom in search of your parents."

I nodded.

"This afternoon, not two hours ago, we received a distress call from one of the parties," he continued. I felt my stomach drop and my hands went clammy.

"D-Distress call?" I stammered and looked to Thomas. He refused to meet my eyes. Instead, he stared down into the reflection pool with utter sadness.

"We don't want you to worry, but it seems something has happened. The entire party has been split up. No one knows where the Elite Guard has gone. It seems they got into the city of Purge, but they were spotted, and an alert went out to Heretia. To still find your parents, but also remain anonymous, the party split. The Elite Guard went further into the city and the accompanying scouting party circled back to ready a ship to moor off the edge of the coast. They were going to attempt a mad dash with your parents once they retrieved them," Vermir explained. My ears were beginning to go numb.

"That was two days ago. No one from the scout team has heard or seen them since and they are beginning to worry. There has been talk that Heretia has captured some spies and is holding them in the

Royal Palace in Purge. We think they have the Elite Guard," he finished. The air left the room as he concluded his report.

All the blood in my body went cold as ice. My face and knees went numb.

"No," I whispered, the tremors started in my fingers and began to work up my arms. The feeling of ants running up and down my veins enveloped me. I felt myself grow dark in panic, the uncontrollable emotions that had plagued me since coming here were reaching out for control and I didn't have the presence of mind to hold them back anymore.

"Amelia? Mia! Listen to me!" Thomas cried, reading my distress.

"Mia! I've sent for Alyssa and Dryan. We need to get you to calm down. Mia? Can you hear me? Alyssa is coming, hold on!"

He was shouting and smacking my arm, but the feelings just kept crawling up my body. I couldn't move, couldn't breathe, couldn't even think as a cloud descended over my consciousness. I lost my vision, and everything went black. My entire consciousness, my soul, my magic, everything went inward. Trying to escape the feelings of pain and suffering, I retreated within myself. I blocked out the world of light, water, and twinkling chimes and reached down, down, down into my depths. I scraped and tore at my soul looking for that piece of Theo. I could find him! I could get him to answer me. I could get him back if only I could speak to him. But that flutter was silent. I reached for it, cradled it gently, but it didn't exist anymore. No flutter, no spark, nothing. It was grey and empty.

Agony tore through my insides as I fell deeper into the darkness of my soul, tumbling head over heels reaching for something, anything to save me. Finally, I felt a tug, a pull from somewhere deep within my consciousness and a lilting voice hissed in my head.

"Yes, Princess?"

It was Death. I was screaming for help and nothing answered, except Death. Death listened to my plea for help, my plea to find Theo and to bring him and my friends and family home. I cried, and I thrashed, and I yelled, and I bawled, and Death listened.

Finally, Death spoke again.

"Then rise, Princess. It is time."

I felt it happen. Like a snap of a branch, the tether holding me to this world torn asunder, and Death was released from its meager holdings. Magic swarmed me, filled every inch of my soul, my body, and my mind. I began to rise.

"Stand back! Get everyone out of here! Thomas, get the rest of the High Rulers out of this room and don't come back in until I say so! GO, GO, GO!" I faintly heard Alyssa shouting at the top of her lungs in the far distant background.

"Princess!" Dryan's voice rang in my ear. "Princess! What's happening?"

Their voices were becoming clearer than they had been before the news of Theo's disappearance. I was becoming more acutely aware of my surroundings. My hearing heightened, smells were stronger, and the light was brighter.

"Embrace me, Princess," Death whispered one last time in my ear before I brought myself back to complete consciousness.

Alyssa was the first thing I heard. "Amelia! Amelia, stop!" she cried.

I blinked twice and looked down from where my body hung in the air. Black swirls of mist licked at my feet and my fingers. Save for my head, they were the only parts of my body not completely ensconced int the darkness. They were waiting for my command. I'm not sure how I knew they were waiting, but I did. Somewhere inside of me, I had fully unleashed Death into my magic and there was no putting that genie back in a bottle. I blinked again and saw Alyssa and Dryan standing there beneath me, ready to catch should I plummet to the ground.

"Amelia? Please! I know this isn't easy, but you must control yourself. You have to come down and we need to think this through," Alyssa cried again.

She was so worried, but I wasn't sure why anymore. I was stronger now, and certainly more in control of my feelings now that

Death was whispering a plan in my ear to get my loved ones back. I nodded at Death but let Alyssa and Dryan think I was agreeing with them.

The look of relief on their face was comforting and I commanded the mist to deposit me back on my feet gently. Alyssa ran for me, wrapping her arms around my waist as I slumped slightly from the gravity taking back over. Dryan took my other arm and began to wrap it around his head to hoist me up, but I waved them away.

"I'm fine. Really, I am. I'm sorry to scare everyone like that but..." I trailed off.

Death still whispered in my ear.

Alyssa shook her head and crooned, "No, it's alright. We didn't know what would happen, so we removed everyone but Dryan and I. We will take you back to your room now to rest. Thomas and the others are working on trying to reconnect with the scouting party and will update you the instant they know anything."

I nodded and let them me lead me back to my rooms, but Death was still whispering. Neither one of my friends wanted to leave my side, but I feigned exhaustion and got them to go check on the others. The halls and rooms around me remained silent, on order of the High Rulers to not disturb me at all in any way. I was grateful for their generosity which made my next move even more upsetting.

Hours later, after being checked on two more times by Alyssa and insisting I was fine, I slipped out of the High Castle and tiptoed into the city for the Safehouse. There were no guards that would even think to look for a slight disturbance in the clear night as I cast a new spell of Cover over myself. Thanks to Death, I now could become invisible to anyone not looking for the shimmer of someone walking along the street by moonlight.

The Safehouse was completely empty and I bolted for the first room. Quickly, I wrote my name on the chalkboard and stepped inside. I smiled at the genius of this magic as I stepped into a tiny closet sized room, teaming with black fighting armor. The lightweight leather felt delicate in my hands, but I would be able to move quickly and sneak around in the night. I grabbed a complete set and then two riding outfits.

Stuffing them away quickly, I ran to the kitchen and grabbed every loaf of bread and flask I could find, filling them to the brim with water. With a final glance, I raced back toward the High Castle, stopping to turn a slight left to the practice arena. I was going to need weapons, lots of them.

No one was around, which did surprise me as I made my way to the armory. I wasn't sure how to wield anything here, but a boot knife and a sword would come in handy. I was at least quick enough to stab and run at this point. Silent as a temple mouse, I reached for the rack of knives on the wall for the smallest one. An orb of light suddenly flared behind my head and I gasped, turning in place, and searching for something large to duck behind.

"No point hiding, Princess. Come on out. You clang around like a blind pig searching for a truffle in the desert," Jersica sneered.

I straightened my spine before standing and walking around the barrel I had so uselessly tried to utilize. Jersica and I stood there in silence as she appraised me repeatedly.

"Fool's mission, huh? You really think you're ready for that?" she asked.

I knew her question was a trap and I firmed my mouth against her.

"I have to be, I don't have a choice anymore. If Theo and my friends are captured, then the time for training must be done. No one else can do it. No one else has..." I paused, rethinking my next words.

"No one else has Death on their side," she finished for me. I couldn't stop the shock of her knowing my secret from reaching my face.

"Oh, don't worry, I still don't even think the High Kings and Queens, aside from Thomas, realize what happened today. But I guessed it, and apparently, I guessed right. You've unleashed Death and now you think you can take on Heretia yourself? You must be crazy."

My pulse quickened at her mocking tone. "I might be, but I'm the only hope they have and I'm not wasting anymore time. I figured, you, of all people would understand that. Aren't you the one always pushing me to be more assertive? Well, here I am, and you will not get in my way."

Jersica silently thought for a moment or two, and then grunted, nodding her head in approval.

"Then you're going to need this," she said and revealed a silver dagger from her hip, holding it out to me. "This is my favorite blade, gifted to me by my father on the day of my Rite. He was the most accomplished silversmith in Medeis and made this for me. I have never been defeated in battle while wielding it and I assume you won't disgrace it by being beaten either."

I paused, not moving to take the blade.

"Quit being so cynical and just take it already. Take it and go. Don't come back without them," she ordered.

I waited a moment before stepping forward to take the cold blade in my hand. I nodded my appreciation, sheathing it in my belt.

"You're also going to need this," she pointed to a double-edged curved blade sitting on a sword rack. "You may not be able to wield it well, but if you pay attention and don't be stupid, you'll be able to do some damage to get away before they get you."

I nodded my thanks again and took it, heading for the door and to the boat waiting on me.

"And Amelia?"

I halted, her using my given name was certainly cause for pause. I turned to face Jersica one last time.

"Give her hell," she whispered.

I turned away from the Fire Sorcerer and left the room, padding my way to the dock and to battle.

Epilogue

Theo breathed a large sigh of relief as his feet touched Lotho soil. The journey had been rough, and very disappointing, but they had made it back in one piece. Even with the change of plans, everyone but one scout had returned. Discussion was thrown around about going back for him, but time was too short. Everyone assumed he would go to a waiting spot that had been assigned and hold tight.

"Go ahead of us to the High Castle and report what happened," Will grunted from behind him, hauling the last of the bags on the dock.

Theo realized that Will was just trying to get rid of him and all his anxiety of how Mia was doing since they had left.

Theo nodded and ran to the gates of the High Castle. As he flung the doors open everything in the Castle halted and everyone within sight stared.

"We need to see the High Kings and Queens immediately. Where is the Princess Amelia? Make sure she knows I'm back," he ordered.

No one moved, but Theo didn't even notice. He stormed into the Throne Room and threw back the doors. All five High Rulers were sitting their shock evident on their faces.

"Prince Theodeus!" They all shouted in unison, with two rising from their Thrones.

Theo made his way to the center of the room and stood next to Thomas.

"We made it back, but we have bad news. We ran into problems just outside of Purge," he announced. "Seems someone recognized us and alerted Heretia. She cast a spell to dampen our magic and we knew we had to get out. In our race to get to the coast, we lost one of your scouts, but with no time to go back, we had to leave him. Everyone had instructions to make it back to Elevetia and make contact from there if they were separated, so I wouldn't worry too much. He seemed like a smart lad."

No one was moving, so he continued, "We know where Clarisse and Daryl are being held, however. We are ready to reload and move back out as soon as Wynnie gathers more intel and finds another way in."

He clapped his hands together and smiled. "So, there's the report. Where is my Pair? Has she been good for you or are you ready to throw her out on the streets for all the trouble she may have caused?" His joke fell on deaf ears.

"What's the matter? You guys look as if you've seen a ghost?" Theo laughed.

He made his way around to the other side of the Thrones, looking out the main door and straining to hear the racing of Amelia's feet after she heard the news of his return. Vermir cleared his throat and leaned back.

"Prince Theo, Princess Amelia is not here anymore," he admitted.

Theo stopped walking and slowly turned to stare at the King.

"Excuse me?" he asked in barely a whisper.

"We received word two days ago that you had been captured. We were practically readying for war. Amelia had a mental breakdown of sorts and we set her up in her room while we figured everything out."

Theo's blood rushed to his ears.

"Where is she?" he asked as calmly as possible. Thomas stood and held his hands out to Theo in a soothing gesture.

"Now, Theo. We need you to remain calm right now. Everything is upside down now that we know you're not captured. We have a lot of questions that need answering and you panicking for your Pair isn't going to help."

"WHERE IS SHE!?" Theo roared and the entire room shuddered at the power in his command.

"She's gone," a small voice interjected. "She went to go get you, your friends, and her parents back."

The voice was smaller than Amelia's. Theo whirled with a vengeance but found Thomas' hand holding him back from lunging at the small woman standing in the doorway.

"Alyssa, this may not be the time," Thomas warned her gently, but the woman approached anyway. She was lovely, and Theo had to blink away his anger to see clearly.

"She left that night, Theo. Jersica saw her and helped her get ready," Alyssa whispered.

Theo sank to the ground, his knees giving out completely. The woman kneeled before him and placed her hands over his.

"After you left Lotho, we found out Amelia was a Druid. She's been in training since you left. We were also working on tapping into her Death magic. When she heard you were missing, I think she broke through the mental barrier and Death gave her the strength to leave. I'm so sorry, Theo!" Alyssa pulled Theo's eyes up to meet hers, pity etched into every inch of her pretty face.

"Amelia went to face down Heretia and get you back."

ABOUT THE AUTHOR

Stephanie Welch is a writer, business owner, dog fancier, wife, and devoted mother to two amazing girls. She has called many cities home in her native state of Georgia and was briefly transplanted to South Carolina where she studied history and education at Newberry College. Stephanie has been writing short and full-length stories from an early age, never dreaming that one day her words would lead to the greatest adventure of all.

Dear Reader,

I hope you enjoyed reading *Stones of Destiny* as much as I loved writing it. Mia and Theo's journey will continue in two more books that hold even more magic, adventure, and trials. Feedback on my work is always welcome, as are positive reviews on Amazon.com and Goodreads.com. For more information and conversation on Mia's continued journey, as well as other books that are in the works, please take a moment to visit me on Facebook at www.facebook.com/AuthorStephanieWelch or on Twitter @AuthurWelch.

Again, thank you for reading along with me, and be on the lookout for the next book in this series: *Into the Darkness*.

Kindest Regards,

Stephanie

The complete works of the

INTO THE DARKNESS SERIES

by

STEPHANIE WELCH

STONES OF DESTINY

CHAINS OF DARKNESS

ASHES ARISING

www.ingramcontent.com/pod-product-compliance
Lightning Source LLC
Chambersburg PA
CBHW060358260626
47160CB00006B/2352